FRIENDS
GREED & MURDER

Simone

Enjoy the read

FRIENDS

GREED & MURDER

STEVEN WINER

To order additional copies of this book, contact:
Xlibris
844-714-8691
www.Xlibris.com
Orders@Xlibris.com
836303

CONTENTS

CHAPTER 1

Isiah Daniels, a 45 year old black man, was nervously sitting at the defendants table in Court Room 607 in the Lee County Circuit Court of Florida. He was flanked by his experienced Fort Lauderdale criminal attorney, Todd Hawkins. The 12 person jury was entering the Courtroom from the jury room and being seated in the jury box to announce their verdict on two counts of first degree murder. One of those counts was for hiring someone to murder his wife, Sophie Taylor Daniels. Judge Tanner Andrews, a white, highly experienced Judge, who normally presided on the Palm Beach County Circuit Court, located on the opposite side of the State, looked exhausted after the three week trial. The Judge was prepared to ask the foreman of the jury, a 41year old black woman, if the jury had reached their verdict. The jury was a mix of 6 women and 6 men. Three of the men were black. One of the male jurors was a Latino. The other two men were white. Five of the six women were jurors. The other juror was a woman, the foreman, who worked as a receptionist for a Fort Myers real estate company. The jury was a mix of white collar and blue collar workers, retired persons and home makers. Several were married, some single and several had been divorced.

Isiah, prior to his trial, was the Chief Executive Officer and President of Jetta International, Inc., a publically held computer design and manufacturing company of hardware and software parts for resale to many well-known computer companies around the world. The Company had over 6,000 employees in 12 plants all located in eastern states up the Atlantic coast. Isiah worked out of the main administrative office located in Fort Lauderdale. His office was 30 miles south of The Boca Raton Country Club community where he and his wife, Sophie, lived. Isiah had worked for the Company for 20 years. He started on the assembly line in the plant located in Jupiter, Florida. That job was chosen by Isiah when he was hired. He wanted to learn the workings of the Company from the bottom up. He quickly worked his way up the ladder to his current position in just four years. An unheard of fast track for any employee, especially a black man. Of the 6000 employees, less than 5 percent were black when Isiah became CEO. However, Isiah was an educated hard worker who made smart decisions. He was also related by marriage to the founder of the Company.

Isiah had received his MBA from the University of Miami Business School. During his last year in graduate school, Isiah was awarded a part time internship for Jetta at its main administrative office. He graduated third in his class when he received his MBA degree. Isiah had received a fully funded athletic scholarship for four of the five years he attended the University of Miami. His Bachelor degree was in Business Administration. Isiah's first year in college was in a local junior college. His final year in graduate school, after his athletic scholarship had lapsed, was fully paid for by Jetta International. His employer expected great things from Isiah. And he came through for the Company. Isiah was the first black executive to work for Jetta International. There were other black employees working at different plants, but most of them had only a high school, or GED, education and were working in low paying blue collar jobs. However, there were several other blacks with MBA's working for the Company. Most of them graduated from black Universities or non-prestigious public Universities. They all worked exclusively in non-Management administration positions at several of the plants.

Donovan Taylor, the President and CEO of Jetta when Isiah was still in college, never promoted black employees. Isiah was the exception. Several of the black MBA's believed they should have also been able to be promoted more quickly. Donovan Taylor, however, thought differently about them. Many of the higher level employees, both black and white, were incredibly jealous of Isiah as he received promotion after promotion over all the black MBA's as well as the white Ivy League MBA's. All of whom had more seniority than Isiah. Jetta was a publicly held company with its stock traded on the S & P Fortune 500 stock exchange. A large minority of the company's outstanding stock was owned by twelve very wealthy entrepreneurs, which included Donovan Taylor. Two of the twelve shareholders were on the Board of Directors with several of the full time executives, including Isiah. Isiah was the only black member on the Board.

Isiah had been married to Sophie Taylor, the 44 year old beautiful white daughter of Donovan Taylor. Donovan, at the time of Isiah's trial, was the Speaker of the House of Representatives for the State of Florida. He was the leading candidate for the nomination, by the Republican Party, for the next Governorship of the State. Donovan was a large minority owner of Jetta International owning just less than 12% of all the outstanding shares of stock. Donovan had sold a large block of his stock one year after the Company went public and became extremely wealthy.

Isiah met Sophie Taylor at the University of Miami while working on his Bachelor's degree. Sophie's intention was to attend an Ivy League law school, however, after much prodding by her father, Sophie agreed to attend law school at the University of Miami. Isiah and Sophie had been married for almost 15 years and had no children. That was a choice made by both after being seriously persuaded by Donovan and his other daughter, Anya. Shelia stayed quit on the subject. When Isiah decided to marry Sophie, he also married the entire Taylor family.

Isiah's family, Otis and Clover Daniels, felt much differently. They wanted grandchildren. However, they said nothing to their son or their daughter-in-law. It was a subject that seldom came up with Isiah's parents. The Taylor's and the Daniel's seldom socialized unless it was necessary. Sophie, at the time of her death, was a partner in one of the largest downtown Miami law firms. She had major connections, through her family, for procuring large corporate clients from all over the Country. She produced millions of dollars in fees for the firm. Her salary was in the low seven figures, slightly more than Isiah made as CEO at Jetta.

"Madam Foreperson, has the jury reached a unanimous verdict on both counts of first degree murder?" asked Judge Andrews.

"We have Your Honor," replied the 41 year old black Foreperson."

"Will the defendant please stand," said Judge Andrews as both Isiah and Todd Hawkins stood up. "Madam Foreperson, what is your verdict as to the two counts of murder for hire and murder in the first degree?"

⟶ ⟶ ●◄ ⟵

The Taylor family had sat in the first row of spectators in the Courtroom since the beginning of the trial. Donovan and Isiah had originally started out with a good relationship. Or, at least as good as it could have been, since Isiah was black. The lone reason Donovan reluctantly agreed to his daughter's marriage to Isiah was because it fit perfectly into Donovan's business and political ambitions. That's as cold as Donavan Taylor was. Sophia's mother, however, admired Isiah and had a decent relationship with him, considering her husband's attitude about blacks. After their initial reluctance for their daughter to become involved with a black man, Donovan grew to accept it and, at times, was even kind to Isiah. Donovan also, in private, admired and respected Isiah as a man and especially as a businessman. Isiah was a smart, hardworking, good looking, personable, articulate, and athletic black man. He was always a good husband to his wife. He treated her with love and respect, yet never showing any feelings of being belittled by her success. Even though she was white and made more money than he did as a black CEO of a large billion dollar publically traded corporation.

Both Isiah and Sophie accepted that having children was something that Sophia's father didn't want. They all understood the potential problems those children would incur growing up in the world at that time. More significant, both had high powered jobs that kept them working 60 to 70 hours a week. It was quite a shock, on the part of Isiah's parents, that their son could have been charged with the horrible crime of murdering his wife. Even though Donovan Taylor loathed most blacks, he too was somewhat surprised that Isiah would be charged with such a crime. He knew, within, that his daughter loved and respected Isiah. But in his heart, he believed that Isiah was guilty.

Isiah's parents, Otis and Clover Daniels, sat towards the rear of the Courtroom, with most of the black spectators. They never believed, from the time Sophie was found bludgeoned and dying on her neighbor's door step, that their son was capable of such a crime.

The venue of the trial had been changed from Palm Beach County to Lee County, on the West coast of the State. This was due to the massive press coverage of the entire event. It was a press circus from the time Sophie's body was found by the police. After all, Sophie, the high powered lawyer, was the daughter of one of the most powerful men in the State, and possibly, the next Governor of the State. Yet she was attacked in her home, in the kitchen, in the early hours of the morning. She was drinking a cup of coffee, before getting ready for work, and was left for dead by an intruder. Sophie had no idea who the intruder was, and he had no idea who she was. Isiah was out of town on business visiting several of the Company's plants at the time of the murder. Nothing was taken from the home, so robbery was quickly ruled out. The police examined the manner of her death and quickly concluded that it had to be done by an amateur. It was far from any type of professional job. At first the police believed the killer was someone Sophie knew, or that her family knew. Maybe even a political or business rival of her father's. There was no evidence of a break in. She must have let him in.

Sophie was not only smart and beautiful, but was also a strong woman. She had her blue belt in Taekwondo and was working her way on being awarded her black belt. She fought back hard against her attacker. The killer came into the home with an old Smith & Wesson, model 617, which was fully loaded with ten 9 millimeter rounds. After the intruder got through the security gate where Isiah and Sophie lived, he opened the side door of their home with a key and was prepared to punch in the home security code but he didn't hear any beeps. The security system was off. Sophie didn't even know an intruder had entered her home. He then looked for Sophie with the intent to immediately shoot her.

His first attempt was futile. When Sophie saw the intruder with a gun in his hand she immediately leaped towards him and kicked the gun out of his hand. It fell to the floor and a small piece of the wooden handle broke off the weapon. Then for the next 15 minutes of horror, the intruder attempted to beat Sophie with small kitchen appliances and a frying pan. She was still alive but had little strength left. He then dragged her to one of the main floor bathrooms. Sophie continued to try to fight for her life. However, the intruder then attempted to drown her in the bathtub. This was before Sophie had slashed him several times with a steak knife that she grabbed in the kitchen during the attack. Sophie, who was badly beaten and exhausted, finally blacked out while in the tub. The amateur intruder believed she was finally dead. He was exhausted and his arms were bleeding and he had a small cut on his face. Then he looked at Sophie and she seemed to be familiar, but he couldn't remembered her.

He knew he had to clean up the scene. However, he couldn't tell the difference between his blood and Sophie's. There was just so much blood everywhere. He knew the police would eventually find his DNA, even though he wore medical gloves. His DNA was in the Florida system. He had spent some time in the Florida Lake Correctional Institution. A maximum security facility, for three years, convicted of armed robbery. He had also been accused of various other minor offenses over the last 10 years and spent some time in the Broward County detention facility. The intruder went back to the kitchen to retrieve his gun, not knowing that a piece of the handle had broken off. He knew he had botched the job badly. The person who hired the killer neglected to disclose to him about Sophie's background in self-defense. In retrospect, he also never even asked any relevant questions about his victim when he contracted to murder her. All he wanted was the money.

Due to the condition of Sophie's home after the intruder left, he was certain the police would be able to quickly identify him and immediately start tracking him. The intruder left just as he came in, through the side door. He put the key to the side door back under a small flower pot where he was told it would be. The killer's clothing was covered in blood, leaving a blood trail from the side door across the front lawn to where he had parked his old 1984 Chevrolet Vega. In hindsight, he should have rented a car under a fake identification. However, the original plan seemed too easy. Sneak in with the key and codes, shoot Sophie, steal some expensive jewelry and a few other items and be gone in a few minutes. What a big mistake. It was just starting to get light outside. Luckily, he had put sheets on the front seat of his car anticipating some blood, but not the amount he had on him from Sophie or his wounds. He did, however, bring a change of clothes in case of a problem with blood.

He immediately changed his clothes, in his car, and wrapped his bloody clothes in a plastic bag he brought with him. He then drove out the back entrance of the development to the nearest gas station, a couple blocks away. Luckily, it had a self-serve car wash. He washed his car on the outside to get any blood off the door and handles. He did his best to clean and wipe down the inside. He dropped the plastic bag with his bloody clothes and the sheets in the trash at the gas station. He went to the mens room. He washed his hands and his wounds on his arms. No one was in the wash room at the time. He saw a container with some cloths used to dry the cars at the car wash. He grabbed several cloths and wrapped his wounds. It was still early in the day and he was hopeful that no one had seen him do any of those tasks. The intruder was surely not one of the shrewdest criminals.

Sophie gained consciousness while still soaking in about 10 inches of water. She fought her way out her front door. She crawled across the street to her good friend's front door. She was only dressed in her night gown and robe and cried for help. Her friend and neighbor, when she heard someone trying to yell at her door, went to investigate. She saw a woman lying on her front step. She didn't even recognize Sophie since she had been beaten so badly. Her face was covered completely with blood. Sophie tried to tell her neighbor about the intruder, but she immediately became unconscious. The neighbor, Diane Saunders, called 911. It took less than 5 minutes for the local EMT's to arrive with three police cars and a fire engine. Sophie lived in a very upscale neighborhood. Sophie was taken to the Boca Raton Hospital and brought immediately into an operating room where three emergency surgeons, led by head surgeon, Dr. Dominick Hamilton, worked on Sophie's wounds for over an hour. Donovan and Sheila were in the operating waiting room in less than an hour after being notified by the hospital. Isiah couldn't be reached. Her parents were waiting for news from the surgeon. After two hours of waiting, her parents were notified that Sophie died on the operating table. She never uttered a word.

―――――――――――

Isiah's early years were spent in Overtown, Florida. It was one of the poorest cities in the Miami area. Otis and Clover Daniels had four children, two boys and two girls. Isiah was the youngest of the four. Evy was the oldest, Dakala came next then Kimbel. Their parents knew that the only way their children would be able to get out of Overtown, and its poverty, was through education. Even with both of Isiah's parents working, once Evy was old enough to help take care of the other three children, it was impossible for their parents to help them with their school work and take care of the house work. They were too busy working just to put food on the table. Evy dropped out of school after the eighth grade in order to help around the house. She also got a minimum wage job to help bring in a few more dollars. Dakala was then able to graduate high school. However, she immediately had to go to work since her grades were not good enough to get into any college with any financial help. And the family needed the money.

Kimbel got involved with a gang his senior year in high school and was shot and killed while attempting to sell drugs to several undercover police. Isiah saw everything that was happening at his home and knew he had to work hard in school to get the grades necessary to attempt to be able to go to college. Isiah did everything he could to stay out of trouble. He was very athletic. He played football and basketball in high school and was the only real survivor of the four children. He saw what had happened to his siblings and he vowed that was not going to happen to him. He was the perfect son, student and athlete. Gangs attempted to lure him in, but he did what was necessary to stay straight. It was hard, but with the help of his coaches, it worked. He received nearly all "A's".

Evy got pregnant at 18 which only added one more mouth to feed. She didn't even know who the father was. Life in the Daniels' home was difficult. Isiah was their parent's only hope for success, and he knew it. His principal vision was to get his parents out of Overtown and help his two sisters and nephew have a decent life.

Isiah graduated high school with a 3.9 grade point average. He was an All City point guard for the basketball team and an All City running back for the football team. He was offered a number of scholarships to several community colleges in the area. The best offer was from Broward Community College in Pembroke Pines, Florida. It was one of the best scholastic Community Colleges on the East Coast of Florida. He played only basketball since the school had no football team. In addition, he took a full load of university classes. He lived in a dormitory room with 12 other athletes and received two meals a day with his scholarship. His parents and two sisters were proud. His parents and Dakala came to almost every game. Evy stayed home to watch her young son. Isiah only played a few minutes in each of the first 5 games his freshman year. But after each game the coaching staff saw his potential. By the last few games he was the starting point guard for the team. Isiah also kept his grades up and never missed a class. He saw an opportunity that could finally give him an opening to get out of Overtown. Isiah was a hard worker and very ambitious.

There were always several scouts, from different large Division one Universities, at every game Broward played. When Broward made the playoffs, Isiah's first year, several scouts approached him. His grades were good, his attendance at his classes was perfect and he was a smart basketball player. He was always a gentleman and never would speak to a scout unless his father, Otis, was with him. The scouts saw his natural ability as an athlete as well as his knack to not steal the spot light from other players. There were still Overtown gangs continually trying unsuccessfully to recruit Isiah. That was the last thing Isiah needed, He was embarrassed when any gang members showed up at the college or at his basketball games. He made that fact known to his coaches on the team. The college security force took care of that problem. It worked.

As the point guard for the Broward team, he would pass the ball to any player he thought had an open shot to score. He was not the kind of player who attempted to make every shot himself, even if he possibly had an opening to score. Several large, division one universities were very interested. Florida, Indiana, Florida State and Miami all were willing to discuss a scholarship, which would include room, board and all tuition. Isiah told all three schools that he would discuss it with his father and make a decision after the playoffs. His mother and father were so proud of him. They both hoped he would take the Miami offer since it would keep him close to home allowing his parents to be able to see him play often. Isiah was aware of that fact. So after the playoffs, Isiah knew that no matter the offers, Miami was number one in his mind. He also wanted to be close to his parents and siblings in order to help them as best he could. More than anything, he wanted to play big time basketball, and graduate from a good university, so that someday he might be able to help his family have an opportunity to leave their current living conditions.

After the playoffs, Isiah was chosen as the Most Valuable Player for the tournament. All four schools, plus South Florida University, were all rushing him for a decision. All of the schools only had a certain number of scholarships and they needed to fill them with the best players available before other schools grabbed them.

Isiah and his parents discussed the pros and cons for all of the scholarships offered, but each of them knew that Isiah would accept Miami's offer. Two days after the end of the playoffs, Isiah contacted the coach of the University of Miami basketball team and told him he wanted to accept their offer. Within three hours the coach was at Isiah's home with the contract for him to sign. It was three weeks before the end of Isiah's second semester of his first college year. It all happened so quickly. His father wanted Isiah to wait to sign the contract with some more discussion and thought. But Isiah knew what he wanted.

"Isiah, don't worry about contacting Broward college or the University to let them know you are transferring to Miami," said

Mickey Conrad, the Miami coach, "it's all been taken care of. I will get one of my assistant coaches to meet you at the student union at Broward and you can sign all of the documents for the transfer at that time. I have taken care of signing you up for all your classes for your first semester at Miami. You'll be a sophomore with four years of eligibility left to play ball. I noticed when I reviewed your transcript that you were taking some business courses, so I have placed you in the required English and History classes as well as an economics and an accounting class. Your grades are high enough for you to qualify to go directly into those classes. You will also be in a physical education class that I teach. You'll be in one of my classes each semester as long as you're playing basketball for Miami. Your grades for all of my classes will be "A's". All of the transfer costs have been taken care of. My assistant will also take you to your new dorm room in the athlete's dormitory where you'll be sharing a room with another basketball player. Trust me, you will like the room, your roommate and especially the dining facilities. There will be plenty of good food. There is also a weight room you'll need to use at least an hour a day and a full basketball court for you to practice whenever you're able. You'll also get a schedule for basketball practice. Discipline is important. I don't tolerate being late."

Isiah was a little overwhelmed and Otis and Clover couldn't quite keep up with the enthusiasm of the coach.

"This a great opportunity for me coach. My family and I really appreciate it," said Isiah.

"Wait, there's more," said Coach Conrad, "the school will be moving your parents and your sisters and your nephew into a three bedroom apartment just off campus."

"Wait," said Otis, "Where did this come from? My wife and I need to see the apartment to determine if we like it and, most important, to determine if we can afford it."

"Don't worry about the rent, one of the schools boosters owns the building and you'll be paying the same rent as you're current rent for your home. My assistant coach will make all the arrangements for your move including taking care of your current lease with your landlord. This way you can walk to the basketball building to watch Isiah practice or play anytime. There will be two tickets at the will call window for your family for each game," said Coach Conrad as he took the signed contract and hustled back in his car before anyone could ask any more questions, or worse of all, back out. Isiah and his family were in disbelief.

"Mama," said Isiah, "I told you I would get you out of this filthy neighborhood someday. I just didn't know it would be so soon. I really wish Kimbel could have been here for this."

With that remark, Clover started to cry.

"I am so sorry if I upset you Mama," said Isiah.

"Your right, Isiah," Clover replied, "I too wish Kimbel were here. But I am just so proud of you. A mother couldn't ask any more of her son."

CHAPTER 2

The first semester of Isiah's sophomore year was a great deal different than Broward Community College. There were many more students, faculty and administrative people on campus. Even though the University of Miami was a private school with a much smaller student population than most public universities, to Isiah it was still like a small city. Each of his classes were in different buildings. His dormitory was blocks from the main student union. He had three hours of classes on Monday, Wednesday and Friday with an hour or two in between those classes. There were two hours of classes on Tuesday and Thursday with an hour in between those classes. Those down hours between classes gave Isiah some time to study. However, his coach expected, at least, an hour a day, seven days a week in the weight room plus time each day on the basketball practice floor.

Basketball practice started in the middle of the fall semester, while football, which was the largest sport on campus, was in high gear. Basketball practice was several hours a day six days a week. How was Isiah going to fit everything in each day? The first game started on November 8, just two months after school started, while football was still just in the middle of its season. The basketball season was comprised of 30 games and progressed through the beginning of March the next year. The school expected their team to finish with a winning record in the Atlantic Coast Conference, or ACC, as it was known, so as to be seeded high for the ACC tournament. That determined the true ACC champion for that year. About 20 of their games were away games. The team either flew or took a bus to those games. The basketball budget could only afford for the team to stay in moderately priced motels when they were out of town. Usually athletes were looked up to, but if you were not a national star, and you're black, people had no interest in them. Isiah found that out quickly. The 17 man team was composed of over half being black. Isiah was used to playing with nearly all black players in high school and junior college. This was a new experience for Isiah.

The goal every year was to be invited to the national tournament called March Madness. That tournament determined college basketball's National Championship. That was the goal of every college and university in the Country that had a basketball team. A total of 322 universities and colleges competed for that title. The Miami Football team had played in 41 bowl games over the years. They won 5 National Championships in 1983, 1987, 1989, 1991 and 2001. In contrast, the basketball program had yet to win a National Championship. They played in a total of 10 March Madness tournaments, but had failed to win enough games to advance to the final 16 teams. The University had a combined record in March Madness of 6 wins and 10 losses over the last 25 years. But each year there was always hope. The entire basketball team, all of the basketball boosters and the entire coaching staff hated the fact that the entire Country looked at the University of Miami only as a football school. The pressure on each basketball player was sometimes overwhelming to win games and be invited to March Madness.

Isiah felt that pressure a couple of days after he moved into his dorm room. Clayton Reed, a junior forward on the basketball team, was Isiah's roommate. Clayton was a starter and would usually play 35 minutes out of every 40 minute basketball game. Mickey Conrad, the coach of the team, thought that Isiah and Clayton would get along well. Both came from adjoining poor neighborhoods in the Miami area. Isiah even remembered playing a game against a rival high school team that Clayton played on. They lost badly. Clayton didn't even remember Isiah. He was two years older and the star on his team. The coach felt that maybe Clayton could help Isiah adjust. Clayton was the star player for his high school team which won the Florida state title in its class. He was the Homecoming King, won the 110 meter hurdles State championship in high school two years in a row, was on the University of Miami track team and was very confident and outspoken. Everyone thought that Clayton was going places and would do well after college. The coach hoped that Clayton could help Isiah by giving him more confidence in himself and make him a better player. However, Clayton thought of himself as 'the man'. He was better than everyone else. However, his grades were so bad that he had to have a tutor almost every day. He barely could make the 1.8 grade point average needed to stay on the team. His only hope, in life, was being drafted by a professional basketball team and make millions of dollars someday. That day would never come for Clayton.

Isiah felt somewhat discouraged around Clayton and thought of himself as just a one dimensional person when Clayton was around. All Clayton talked about was basketball and women. He skipped classes and missed tests all the time. How he was still on the team was a mystery to Isiah. But Isiah said nothing. No matter how Clayton treated Isiah, his ambitions were important to him and Isiah kept himself disciplined to achieve them. Clayton did, from time to time, treat Isiah well, even like a kid brother. He did introduce him to some people on campus. Some of those people didn't even go to school at the University. They just hung out there. Isiah never knew there were basketball groupies.

Every so often a few of the boosters would show up for practice and talk to the players and coaches. During one of the late practices, in October, several boosters showed up. They wanted to meet the new players who were just recruited. The most important and usually the best of the recruits were the ones who came from community colleges. They were usually stars on their community college team and had good grades. They had to be high performers in order for the University to spend so much money on scholarships and make a spot for them on the 17 man roster. It was not like the football team that had an 88 man roster.

One of the boosters who came that day was Donovan Taylor, the majority owner of Jetta International, Inc. Isiah had no idea what Jetta

International, Inc. was or what they did. All he knew was that Donovan
Taylor was rich and gave lots of money to the school and expected the
basketball team to win. If Donovan didn't like you, he would somehow
convince Coach Conrad that maybe someone else should have your spot
on the roster. Clayton gave Isiah the low down on Donavan and told
him how to answer the questions he was probably going to be asked.
Isiah thought that he could answer for himself. However, Isiah was
aware that it was not only his spot on the Miami roster at stake, but
also his whole family's future.

Donovan Taylor had two daughters, Anya, who was a junior at St.
Andrews High School in Boca Raton. That was a private Episcopalian
school, very exclusive with only 500 students. And Sophie, who
was a senior at Amherst College, one of the top 5 private colleges in
Massachusetts. Its tuition was $65,000.00 per year. In order to be
accepted to Amherst, one needed to secure between 1330 and 1550 on
their SAT scores and have no less than a 3.95 grade point average in a
highly rated high school. Isiah got a 1220 on his SAT and he thought
that was good. After all, he went to Overtown High School. A rundown
drug running school for thugs. His 3.9 grade point average probably
would barely be a 2.5 at St. Andrews High School. But Isiah was
smart. He just needed the opportunity to show that fact to the world.
No matter how bright Isiah may have been, he still worried as to what
he and Mr. Taylor were going to talk about? He hadn't had a lot of
interaction with white people, especially rich and successful white men.

After Donavan spoke to two of the freshman on the team, one from
Birmingham, Alabama and one from Sarasota, Florida, he made his
way over to Isiah.

"So you are Isiah Daniels, the transfer from Broward Community
College. I heard you won your conference title last year. And you were
the MVP of that tournament."

"Yes sir."

"Well," said Donavan, "I know you can play basketball, I saw you
a couple of times last year. So tell me about yourself and your family."

"I'm from the Miami area," started Isiah, "I played basketball and
football in high school. I have two sisters and a brother. I had two

brothers, but one of them died a few years ago. I also have a nephew. And I am really blessed to be playing ball for Miami."

"Two things you should know," said Donovan. "One, I know everything that goes on with the Miami basketball program, including everyone's background and school records. Second, I know that Clayton Reed, the hotshot on this team, told you to say exactly that. Am I correct?"

"Yes sir."

"Can't you speak for yourself? I heard you're a pretty smart kid and a damn good basketball player."

"Thank you sir," said Isiah, "and I can speak for myself. In fact I prefer it that way. I just wanted to make sure I didn't say the wrong thing. I understand that you are one of the largest contributors to the school's athletic department and a huge Miami basketball enthusiast."

"Isiah, the only time you can say something wrong is when someone else tells you to say it. You need to be your own person. You're probably the smartest person on this team. Now remember that," said Donavan. "I know about your family and their history. I know what your father and mother do for a living. I know all about you and your history. Your family is living in one of my buildings and paying very little rent because you're going to take this team to March Madness. You're also going to graduate with a very high GPA, with honors, and maybe even come and work for my company someday. So how do you feel about those thoughts?"

"I think you give me too much credit Mr. Taylor. I had no idea it was your building where my family is living. That I really appreciate, more than you can know," answered Isiah.

"I don't think I give you too much credit," said Donovan. "You will be a star and you will be an honor student. I know people. No matter where you may think you came from, that has no bearing on where you are going to go in life or what you are going to make of yourself. In fact, every once in a while I have one of the up and coming team members come to my home for dinner. I like them to meet my family. I have two wonderful, smart and beautiful daughters. One of them will be going to law school here at Miami next year. When she graduates she will go to work for the Miami law firm that represents my company. I'm sure you two will have many political and social issues to discuss, or should I say argue about. I'll get back with you in a few weeks about the arrangements," Donavan said with authority. "Now don't listen to any of those other players, especially Clayton Reed, concerning what to say or how to live your life. Clayton will just end up being a looser. You do it your way and I know you'll be a much better person for it."

"I appreciate your confidence in me and I look forward to meeting your family. I'll remember what you just told me. Thank you sir."

Then Donavan moved on to talk with Coach Conrad. Isiah was shocked. He had no idea any boosters invited players, like himself, to dinner at their home. Isiah didn't even have a suit. Just one more stress in his life. He needed to talk to his mother and father about what he just heard. They would help him. Little did Isiah know that he didn't need any help from anyone. His future was already set. Also, little did he know that Donovan Taylor had big ambitions politically? Donovan needed smart black men and women to endorse him and help him politically. Donovan would do anything to achieve his ambition of someday becoming Florida's Governor. More important, little did Isiah know how much Donovan actually detested blacks. He looked at them as all lazy and drug machines. Donovan was always on the lookout for those limited few exceptions. Maybe Isiah could be one of them. That's why he and his family were being treated the way they were. Little did Isiah know how Donovan Taylor would change his, and his family's future.

———⟫●⟪———

Sophie and Anya Taylor grew up with a privileged life. Both their father and mother wanted the best for them. Their father Donovan, was a self-made man who came from a relatively lower middle class family. His father worked for Ikea in Sunrise Florida, one of Ikea's first stores in Florida. He worked his way up to manager and made a decent living. Donovan went to public school. Got good grades, and got accepted to Florida Atlantic University just after it was established in 1964. He majored in business administration and was very ambitious. He wanted the best for himself and eventually a family. He vowed to someday own a home in the most expensive area of Boca Raton. Florida Atlantic University was located in that community.

Donovan liked good things. He graduated, with honors, and, with the help of his father, also got that first job with Ikea. He was a hard worker and quickly became manager of the Sunrise store. Becoming the manager of the store was not exactly what Donovan had in mind for the rest of his life. He pushed the owners of Ikea to promote him to regional manager for the area comprising several states. He passed over his father quickly. With Donovan running several stores, Ikea did very well. Since Ikea was a private company, several of the owners noticed him and his management style. Donovan helped increase sales in all of the stores in his region. From there he was eventually asked if he wanted to buy into Ikea and become a minority shareholder. That was nearly unheard of. He didn't have the sufficient funds for the buy-in as a 5% owner. So he borrowed money from his family, his high school and college friends and anyone else he knew who would lend him money at a high interest rate. Donavan, and his lenders, were confident they would make a large profit. They all believed in Donovan. He was certain he would be able to pay everyone back relatively quickly.

Between dividends from his Ikea stock and the bonuses he earned as regional manager, Donovan paid everyone back, with interest, in less than a year. He was promoted to national manager and helped open a dozen stores over the next several years. He was making good money and received another 5% ownership interest for the high return that the major owners were receiving due to his hard work. He was, at that time, the only owner actually working full time for Ikea. All the other owners were retired and only served on the Ikea Board of Directors.

After working for just six years he had saved up enough money to open up a small business producing computer hardware and software parts for small computer companies and a few other businesses in the Miami area. He started the business with several good friends he graduated with from business school. Ikea was not happy to see Donovan leave. They offered him a large compensation package to stay, but Donavon was savvy enough to know that eventually he would make more money in a company where he was the majority owner and his own boss. So, with the funds he received from the sale of his Ikea stock, Jetta International, Inc. was born.

It was started in Donavan's garage in the outskirts of Sunrise, Florida, when Donovan was only 28 years old. Donavan ran the business, and his two partners, who were a little older, were just investors. They believed that Donovan would eventually make them a fortune. They were right. Donovan was smart, cunning, a terrific salesman and a generous person to his partners. Jetta opened its first plant in Sunrise, Florida, and moved its corporate office to a small office space in downtown Fort Lauderdale. By then Jetta had 75 employees and was growing faster than Donovan envisioned. It was becoming difficult to deliver product timely with its ever increased sales. A good problem to have. Donovan hired several recent MBA graduates from the University of Miami and University of Florida. The computer business was evolving so quickly, Jetta had a hard time redesigning their products to meet the ever changing demand. So Donovan had to hire several additional engineers. The company took off. Donavan made millions after the first 8 years. He bought out his two partners, who happily, made a large profit on their investment. The rest was history.

Donovan was so busy working 10 to 12 hours a day, 6 to 7 days a week that he didn't have time to date. However, after hiring a regional manager and had a management team in place he would open a new plant nearly every 12 months. Finally, after several more years, Donovan decided to live a little on the money he had made. He enjoyed watching basketball and was much more impressed with private schools verses public universities.

So he started attending the University of Miami basketball games. He eventually, for business purposes, purchased a private box and invited his largest customers and local managers to all of the games. He thoroughly enjoyed the good life. The liquor flowed and there was always an abundance of food. His business was growing so rapidly that he finally purchased a group box that held 50 people. There were only two group boxes at the Miami stadium. The other one was exclusively for University VIP's. The President of the University and other officials would stop by Donovan's box, from time to time, and he got to know many of the administrators and professors working and teaching at the business school. He eventually was designated a school athletic booster due to the amount of money he donated to the athletic department. Donovan made sure that the majority of the money he donated went to the basketball program and to scholarships for basketball players. The football program had more money than it could use.

The University always attempted to direct most athletic contributions to the football program. The cost to hire good coaches for the football program was expensive. After all, Miami was a football school. It was Donovan Taylor's desire to change that image. The basketball coaches were impressed with Donovan's thinking and honored his requests for his contributions. Donovan even purchased several apartment buildings in and around the University to help out the basketball players families. No one had ever done that before. He became an icon for the University's basketball program. Whatever Donovan wanted, or whomever Donovan thought should get a scholarship always seemed to happen. Donovan's goal became the schools goal of eventually winning a basketball national championship. That never happened. However, it wasn't for lack of trying.

During one of the basketball games, a beautiful young lady, named Shelia Skeffington, came into Donovan's box. He saw her immediately.

"Welcome to my corporate box, Ms......." stuttered Donovan.

"Shelia, Shelia Skeffington," as she helped Donavan out. "This is my first basketball game at the University. I am a math professor and was invited to come and see all of the excitement that had been going on at our basketball games the last few years. The Chairman of my department invited me."

"Well, how do you like it so far?" asked Donovan. "Oh, by the way, my name is Donovan Taylor. This is kind of my box. Please feel free to stick around. Our food is much better than the University's box. Don't tell them, but I have the Rascal House Delicatessen on Miami Beach deliver some really good food. I need to work on the University's food menus for next season. People pay a lot for these boxes."

"I am really enjoying the atmosphere of the whole experience," replied Shelia, "and I do know who you are. You have really made yourself a name around here. I think I may stay for a while. The Rascal House does make a mean corned beef sandwich. And your secret is safe with me."

"I'd like that," said Donovan, "come down to my seats. They are in midcourt."

"Oh, you're busy entertaining all of your guests. I will just get a sandwich and enjoy the rest of the game," said Sheila.

"No, I think I have talked enough about computers today," replied Donovan, "it's time to have some more interesting conversations that doesn't include spread sheets. I would rather talk about algorithms."

Sheila laughed and the two of them went to the seats overlooking the middle of the court. It was the last 5 minutes of the game and Miami was beating Florida State 69 to 56. Miami was going to win a game. More interesting was the fact that Donavan may have finally found someone that he would consider asking out on an actual date. Something he hadn't done for years. However, as aggressive of a person he was, he didn't quite know how to start that conversation.

Finally after finishing her corned beef sandwich and Miami winning the game, Shelia said to Donovan, "Are you busy next Wednesday evening? I have two tickets to Phantom of the Opera and the person I was going with had to leave town for some emergency. Would you like to join me?"

"Not only would I like that, I think we should have dinner before the performance. I know several good restaurants close to the amphitheater. How about if we meet at The Roof Top on West Las Olas Boulevard at 5:30. You can leave your car there and I'll bring you back after the performance."

"Perfect, it's a date," said Shelia, "or is it just a get together?"

"It's a date," said Donovan even though he had seen Phantom twice before. He did enjoy the show both times, but he knew he would enjoy it even more this time.

CHAPTER 3

Donovan and Shelia's first date went well. They had much to talk about at dinner. Donovan finally told Sheila, after a couple of drinks, that he had already seen Phantom. He even had two additional tickets that he couldn't refuse from one of his regional managers. He originally thought he would go with another friend, but when the opportunity came from Sheila, he couldn't refuse. She was flattered at his interest in her and somewhat intrigued with him. Donovan had a great laugh, but not too loud, when she admitted that she had also seen it before. Donovan immediately turned to the next table. There was a young couple almost finished with their dinner. Donovan asked if they would like to see Phantom that night. They were thrilled. They asked to pay for the tickets, but Sheila refused. They immediately paid their bill, thanked Donovan again and hurried off to catch the first act.

Donovan and Shelia both felt somewhat relieved and just ordered another drink. At the end of a wonderful couple hours together, Donovan told Sheila that he worked in downtown Fort Lauderdale, a couple days a week. He spent the other 3 to 4 days each week traveling to his plants or to locations where he was considering opening new plants. He was always on the go. He told Shelia if she, or a couple of her friends, ever wanted to go to a basketball game, she should call him at his office. He always had plenty of tickets. It was a big box. He gave her his card with his contact information. If he wasn't there, he said to ask for his assistant, Karin, and she would get her the tickets. Shelia kind of thought that may have been some sort of a brush off. He could have asked her to a game himself. Maybe he just thought that the night was fun, but it was time for him to move on. However, she enjoyed his company and had some interesting conversation.

As the two of them got up to go to their separate cars, Donovan asked if he could have Shelia's number.

"I really had a good time tonight," said Donovan, "the food was good the wine and drinks were terrific, but the company was better. I would really like to do this again sometime soon."

Shelia was very relieved to hear that and quickly gave him her number, both at her apartment and her cell phone.

"Oh, do you live with someone at your apartment or do you live alone?" Donovan felt embarrassed after he asked her that question.

"If you're asking if I am seeing someone, the answer is no," replied Sheila, "I haven't been in a relationship for some time. I spend my time working at the University teaching several beginner math classes and also several calculus classes. I am also involved with several advanced woman's math clubs trying to convince more women to get involved with math and science."

"Oh," said Donovan, "kind of a feminist thing to advance women in the sciences."

"Well, something like that, but it's also social. It's been difficult to find good friends, men and women, especially when they find out you're a math geek."

"Well, I like math geeks," said Donavan, "I am always looking for good engineers, computer wizzes and math geeks to help out in my business. It's not easy to find good qualified people."

"Really?" said Shelia, "I could always help you with that. I see that you own your own business, Jetta International, Inc. but I have no idea what you do?"

"How about we save that discussion for another evening?" Said Donovan, "I'll call you soon and we can get together."

Shelia was a little taken back by that response, but agreed to get together again. She was very much up for that. She actually wondered if she would ever see Donovan again as they both walked to their cars. Donovan, always the gentleman, walked Shelia to her car and then gave her a kiss on the cheek. She then reciprocated by a passionate kiss on the month. After which she really felt embarrassed. Donovan was shocked. He never thought that Shelia could be such an aggressive woman, but he liked it.

"I definitely will call you soon," said Donavon who really found her attractive. She was his kind of woman. After all, he hadn't had much time to date since he started his company. A little companionship would be a good change.

"By the way, which apartment do you live in?" asked Donovan.

"It's the one just off campus called the Franklin Arms, apartment 316."

"Great," said Donovan, "I know just where it is. I own it."

"So you have been the person raising my rent every year. Maybe we shouldn't see each other. You may raise my rent again if you turn out to find me a bore?" laughed Shelia.

"I don't know anything about that. I have a management company that handles all that. Also to be fully transparent, I do charge a little over market on some of my apartments in that building. I set up some of the athletes parents in some of the smaller apartments at a reduced rate. It helps the young athletes to be near their parents. They do much better on the athletic field and in class," confessed Donovan, "maybe I can do something about your rent?"

"'Don't get the wrong impression. I think what you do is a good thing. If I have to pay a few dollars more for that reason, I'm on your side."

Donovan thought, what a compassionate comment to make. He made sure she got in her car and he closed the door and she drove off. Donavan walked to his car thinking that he really had met a warm, intriguing and smart lady. Maybe even a future relationship. Smart, pretty and a kind heart. What else could he ask for? He thought about her all night, and then called her the next morning. They started seeing each other when both of their crazy schedules allowed. Donovan's life had just changed.

Isiah's first year at the University of Miami was hectic and strenuous. Between his classes, studying, weight room, basketball practice and traveling for the away games, Isiah was enjoying life but was exhausted. He had no problem keeping his grades up and doing well scholastically, but he was somewhat frustrated on the basketball court. His roommate was averaging 19 points a game and playing an average of 36 minutes of the 40 minute game. Isiah was averaging less than 4 minutes a game and just 3 points. He understood that he was just a sophomore with 3 more years of eligibility, but he wanted to play more. It was hard, for someone who was always successful, to have to sit and watch other people do what he thought he could do just as well, or better. All that practice time, team meetings and travel was tough. Mickey, the coach could see his frustration. He wanted to play more. But so did all of the other players sitting on the bench. Miami was having a mediocre season and unless they could get into the ACC championship series final, they probably would not be invited to March Madness. So Mickey had little to lose by changing some things around. The starting point guard, Martell Dixon, who was playing an average of 30 minutes was benched in a conference game against Wake Forest. Their record was worse than Miami's and they were in last place in the ACC. Mickey decided to start Isiah and let him play 30 to 35 minutes. To the shock of the coach, most of the other players, the boosters, Martell Dixon and especially Donovan Taylor, Isiah scored 16 points and had 12 assists. That accounted for nearly one quarter of Miami's points and they won by 16 points. But that was Wake Forest. The next game was against the number one team in the ACC who were ranked number 2 in the nation, Duke University. The game was at Duke and Miami was a 14 point underdog. Duke had won 5 National championships. They were in 11 Final Four appearances at March Madness. Over the last 20 years, 11 Duke Players had been chosen National Player of the year. And 71 Duke Players had been drafted to play in the professional National Basketball League.

Mickey had to decide whether or not to let Isiah start the game or go back to Martell Dixon as the starter. Again, what did Mickey have to lose? So, Isiah started the game, to the surprise of most Miami fans.

Up to that point in his life, he had never had an experience like he did that day. 16,000 Duke Fans went wild when Miami beat Duke 79 to 75. Isiah had 24 points and 19 assists. Miami had found a new starting point guard. Martell Dixon was not happy, but Mickey had a long talk with Martell after the game, and as a senior, Martell understood the importance of winning. Mickey made it very clear that Martell was going to be playing in every game, but he needed to keep Isiah as his starter as long as he kept playing the way he played the last two games. That day changed Isiah's attitude and emotions. National broadcasters were interviewing him after the game. He was now someone, not just another player on the bench.

Donovan Taylor and his daughter Sophie were at that game. Donovan asked Isiah to fly back to Miami with him in a plane he had rented to come to the game. He also invited Isiah to come to dinner, at his home, the next evening. Isiah cordially refused the plane ride and told Donovan he needed to fly back with the team. However, he said he would take him up on dinner. Donovan told Isiah that a limo would pick him up at his dorm at 6:00 PM. He would be brought back to the dorm by 10:00 PM, which was curfew. Sophie was impressed with this man. He was smart, polite, a great basketball player and good looking, even though he was black. She knew how her father and sister, Anya, felt about blacks. So she didn't actually socialize with many. Only the blacks that came to dinner at their home and the few in her classes at Amherst. However, lately she wasn't at most of those dinners since she was attending college in Massachusetts. Her best friends, and all of her sorority sisters always put down black men. So did her father, unless they were playing basketball. According to her father, they were lazy, had no ambition, always wanted to date white woman and normally ended up in jail. But Sophie couldn't wait to have a conversation with Isiah the next night at dinner. He seemed different than other blacks she had socialized with at her home. All though Sophie never really had any meaningful discussions with any of those black athletes or even any other black men.

On the trip back to Miami, the team watched the national sporting news on CNN and all the sport media commented on was Miami's upset of Duke, the number 2 team in the nation. But the real chatter of the sporting world was the play of their sophomore point guard, Isiah Daniels. Isiah felt somewhat embarrassed about all of the hype on television, but the next morning a large portion of the Miami Herald's sporting page was focused on Miami's new point guard. Where had he been most of the season? People on campus stopped him and congratulated him. Even two of his professors acknowledged him in class. How life can change on a dime, Isiah thought. But could he keep up his last two performances? What happened to that confidence his roommate, Clayton, had attempted to instill in him. Even his parents called him and wanted him to come to their apartment for dinner that night. Isiah wanted very much to do that, but he had given his word to Donovan Taylor that he would go to dinner at his house. His mother understood that it was important to keep promises and not to disappoint people who can help him move up in life. He could always come another night. But Otis, his father, was not very happy about it. He hoped all this publicity would not go to Isiah's head. His father had heard that Donovan Taylor used people, mostly blacks, then spit them out. Donovan was a man not to be trusted. But Otis kept his mouth closed. Isiah needed to grow up and learn the real ways of the world. There were still 10 games left before the ACC tournament so only time would tell if all this big time talk would last. Isiah's father just didn't want his son to be disappointed. Yet in the same vein, he didn't want it to go to his head either. Isiah had no idea how his parents thought of his new notoriety. All he knew was that his parents wanted him to get out of Overtown and its poverty and make something of himself.

The next evening at exactly 6:00 PM a very long limo showed up at Isiah's dorm. On his way to the limo Isiah was being harassed by all of the other athletes in the dorm, especially the football players. Isiah just smiled and knew that most of them were just jealous they weren't invited. The ride from South Miami to Boca Raton took about 35 minutes. There was water, liquor, snacks, newspapers and videos for Isiah's pleasure. Isiah didn't touch anything. He was too nervous. He had his best white shirt and a pair of black pants. His mother had saved for 6 weeks, as part of each of her paychecks, so he would have something to wear if anything like this happen to come up. Isiah thought about his mother and felt that he was dressed properly. However, Isiah was still a black man. He was nervous how he should act. He had never spent time in a rich white man's home with his privileged family.

When Isiah arrived at the Taylor's home, the limo driver came around the limo and opened the door for him. Isiah didn't know if he was supposed to tip him or something like that. But he just said thank you. The driver was black also. Neither spoke a word to each other on that 35 minute ride. Isiah didn't have any idea what to say. He was still embarrassed that he was chosen to break bread with this rich white family. He was certain the limo driver had never even been invited in their home. He walked up to the double door entrance and rang the bell. Another black woman, dressed as a maid, opened the door and welcomed him. Isiah felt awkward. She escorted him to the library and told him that Mr. Taylor would be down in a few minutes. She told him dinner was at 7:00. Before Donovan came to meet Isiah, Anya Taylor, Donovan's youngest daughter, came into the library dressed in a short red top, a pair of white capris and sandals.

"So you're the new big shot black man on the basketball team," said Anya. "Daddy loves to entertain the players that do something special during some of the games. Especially the black ones. You must have really done something special. Usually daddy invites two or three players at a time. Can't wait to hear what you did," as Anya got up and left as fast as she came in. Isiah didn't get to say a word, especially about the 'black' comments. He could feel that Anya was not too keen on blacks. He wondered, after seeing Anya, if he may have been a little too anxious to accept the invitation for this dinner. He also had no idea what he would be talking about during dinner. Especially with Anya. He hoped the rest of the Taylor family took the lead. Luckily he had to be back by 10:00. Where was Mr. Taylor? Isiah had been waiting about 15 minutes, but it felt like an hour.

CHAPTER 4

The maid finally came into the library and showed Isiah to the dining room. The dining table was big enough to seat 16 people very comfortably. However, there were only settings for five people. Anya was the first to come into the dining room still dressed the way Isiah saw her just a few minutes ago. She sat at the side of the table where there were three place settings. Isiah was still standing near a corner of the end of the dining table where there were no place settings.

"What's your name?"

"Isiah, Isiah Daniels."

"Why don't you sit down," said Anya, "you can sit on the side next to where my daddy sits, at the head of the table."

"I think I'll just wait until your father comes in," said Isiah. "That would be the polite thing to do."

"Polite," laughed Anya, "that's the last thing we are in this house. Just sit down. No one is going to bite you. Blacks are treated well in this house."

Just as Isiah started to walk to the place setting Anya mentioned and he was going to say something about Anya's comments on him being black, Sophie Daniels came into the room, dressed with just a pair of slacks and a white blouse, and sat down next to her sister. "I hope Anya hasn't been harassing you too much. She likes to scare the players daddy invites here for dinner. I hope she didn't offend you too much. Please sit down. My father and mother will be here very soon. They like to make their grand entrance. My name is Sophie, what's yours?" Sophie thought that Isiah was very handsome for a black man. He didn't have the characteristic large lips and large curly black hair.

"His name is Isiah Daniels," uttered Anya, "and he plays basketball. Daddy must really like Isiah since he invited him by himself. He must be really good."

"Anya, let the man speak for himself," remarked Sophie. "Sometimes she likes to talk a little too much. So Mr. Daniels, what year are you at my father's favorite school, and what are you studying?"

Isiah finally got a word in, "I'm a sophomore. I transferred from Broward Community College. I play point guard and I am studying business administration and finance."

"Well, a smart one," said Sophie, "not many of those on the basketball or football team these days. I like that. All Miami really cares about is how well you can play football. But you're playing basketball. My father's favorite sport. I've been told that the average grade point of a Miami football player is 1.98. Just enough to stay in school and still play football. Every one of the starting football team believes they will be drafted into the NFL and make millions of dollars. It's a shame the school doesn't take more of an interest in their academics verses their ability to run with a ball. 95% of those men are always very disappointed each year. Not only do they not get drafted, they don't even graduate. Now, I understand that the basketball players, starters or bench sitters, all believe they will be drafted into the NBA and receive a multi-million dollar contract. After all, basketball is where the real money is. Their average grade point is at least around 2.0, but most don't get drafted and only a handful graduate. So what's your plan? And what's your grade point?"

"My goodness, Ms. Taylor, you do like to talk and you do get right to the point. And please call me Isiah," said Isiah with a slight attitude.

"And you can call me Sophie. So answer my question." Said Sophie also with a slight attitude thinking that this black man also speaks well since she can understand every word he says. Very unusual.

Just as Isiah was about to answer Sophie, Donovan Taylor and his wife, Shelia, walked into the room. Both were dressed casual, which put Isiah more at ease. "I hope I'm not interrupting your conversation

Isiah," said Donovan, "my girls like to talk. Sometimes they're a little too direct."

"No sir," said Isiah with a bit of sarcasm, and afraid of what Donovan may think when he was about to finish his sentence, "your daughter, Sophie, was just asking me about what I may do after I fail out of school."

"Now daddy you know I wouldn't ask that to a guest of yours," remarked Sophie a little embarrassed. However, she was really impressed that one of the athletes would actually say that to her father. Especially a black one. She thought that this black man may be special.

"Now Sophie, a little less cynicism in this house is the way we act. Don't be so heartless to our guest."

"I was just kidding sir," admitted Isiah, "Sophie was just asking me about my future ambitions."

"Good, I like a little buffeting around the dinner table," as both Donovan and Shelia sat down at their designated places. "So go ahead and finish your thought Isiah. I would like to hear your answer myself."

"Alright," said Isiah. "I don't plan to be drafted into the NBA. I enjoy playing basketball and football, but my scholarship is for basketball so that's what I'll play so long as it pays for my school. My parents can't afford for me to go to school let alone a private university like Miami. They have three other children plus a grandchild to take care of. Basketball is my way of getting out of Overtown and getting a respectable job, and hopefully help my parents, my siblings and my nephew. My GPA is currently 4.0 and I plan to keep it that way until I graduate. I'll be one of those athletes that actually does graduate, Sophie. I also plan to go on to get my MBA. Somehow I'll find a way to do that. I have 4 years of eligibility to play basketball, so my first year of graduate school will be paid for with my scholarship. I'll find a way to finish that last year so I can get that MBA, even if I have to work."

"Great answer Isiah," said Donovan. "And if I have anything to do with it, I'll make sure that happens. Ladies, it's been a long time, if ever, that I have invited such a bright, articulate and talented athlete to dine with us. And he is also quite handsome girls. So, tonight enjoy this man's company."

"That's quite an observation coming from my husband," remarked Shelia.

The rest of the evening Anya and Sophie didn't say much. Their maid brought in the salads and about a half hour later, the main course. She seemed to give Donovan a look each time she brought something into the dining room. Isiah wondered how the Taylor's actually treated their black help. All the while Donovan gave Isiah a summary of his business history and how he started his company, Jetta International. He also rambled on about his upbringing and obstacles he had to overcome to make it. He did, however, give a lot of credit to Shelia, his wife. He then praised Anya for her initiative as a scholar and athlete at St. Andrews school. But Isiah could tell that he was most proud of Sophie. She graduated first in her class in high school and was in the top 1% of her class at Amherst. He boasted that he had already spoken to the Dean of the University of Miami's law school where Sophie had already been pre-approved for next year's first year admissions. He bragged about the fact that she would make a fine attorney. She liked to talk a lot and ask probing questions. Isiah had already found that out. Her biggest client would be Donovan's company. That, and her high grades and law review experience, would get her employed at the large downtown Miami law firm that represented Jetta International, Fischer & Logan. They have 12 offices, with 600 attorneys, all over the Country including an office in London. Douglass Fischer and Donovan went way back. James Logan seemed to be a good lawyer, but Donovan didn't know much about him. It may be in Donovan's mind, but every time he goes to the firm, Logan seems to avoid him. Donovan thought that strange. Especially since Mr. Logan handled most of Jetta's legal work.

Shelia hardly got a word in that evening. Sophie listened, but Isiah could tell that her father was planning out her life, including her law school, her grades and class rank. Isiah could tell that was not what she really wanted to hear. She seemed the type that wanted to go to an Ivy League law school like Harvard or Columbia. But she was polite and smiled every time Donovan gave her that proud glance. If Donovan wanted her close to him at the University of Miami, that was where she was going to be. Isiah was sure that Donovan seemed to always get his way. Isiah could observe that Anya was not vey enthralled at all the attention Sophie received. Isiah thought that there may be a problem there.

The last part of the evening, when the maid brought in the dessert, Donovan proudly admitted that he was the person who found Isiah and that Isiah was going to become the player that finally took Miami into the national championship tournament before his career as a basketball player was over. Sophie looked at Isiah and could tell that he also wasn't thrilled with Donovan's hopes and dreams being pushed on him. Their eyes seemed to talk to each other, and they both felt that one day they may even become friends. Her friends may not be enthralled with that, and she knew that her father really wouldn't be happy about that, but Sophie didn't seem to care.

Even though Isiah and everyone else said very little that night, as Donovan monopolized the conversation, Isiah did enjoy himself and felt fairly comfortable even though it was an all-white rich family. The time went by fast before the maid knocked on the dining room door to tell Isiah it was time to get back to the dorm before curfew. Isiah then shook each of the Taylor's hands before he left. But he felt something connect when he and Sophie said good night. He thanked Donovan and Shelia for the fine dinner and conversation. He told Donovan that he hoped he could live up to his expectations. Donovan had no problem letting Isiah know that it wasn't whether or not he could, but that Isiah was going to live up to those expectations. That frightened Isiah somewhat. Now he sensed what Sophie probably felt about her father's expectations for her. The next few years would be interesting. But Isiah was confident about what his ambitions were and no one was going to interfere with them, not even Donovan Taylor.

The courtship of Donavan and Sheila seemed both long, but yet, at the same time very short. Donavan's schedule only allowed him and Sheila to get together once or twice a month. However, those get togethers were always something that Sheila remembered. After several months and a couple of dinner dates at high priced restaurants, Donovan decided to rent a plane so that he and Sheila could fly to Nassau in the Bahamas for a romantic fine dining experience at the Atlantis Resort. Then they could do some gambling after dinner. Donavan "loaned" Sheila $300.00 and told her to play either black jack or the slots. Her mathematical mind was best suited for black jack. This was her first time she had playing black jack, and she was good at it. She watched others playing the game and she caught on immediately. She won money and repaid Donovan, and still walked away with several hundred dollars. Donovan was shocked. Donovan, a skilled gambler, lost a couple thousand dollars at the crap table that night. The biggest surprise for Sheila was that the short trip didn't actually end until the next morning. Donavan had reserved a suite, just in case he could convince her to stay. Sheila, after some deep thought, decided that she didn't have any problem with that. It probably was time. It was quite an exciting experience for her. They stopped by the small sundry store, in the hotel, to buy a tooth brush and other sundries that they would need for the night. That night their relationship changed.

Sheila thoroughly enjoyed every date that Donovan arranged for them over the year since they met in Donovan's box at a basketball game. Donovan knew that he and Sheila would make the perfect couple. She understood his need to work many hours to continue to expand his company as well as volunteer to help the Universities basketball program. That gave Sheila as much time as she wanted to enjoy her teaching at the University and working with talented students. Just over a year after they met, Donovan arranged a weekend in Las Vegas at the MGM Grand Hotel. Unbeknownst to Sheila, Donovan made arrangements for the last night to have an Elvis impersonator marry them at a mall, in a small marriage kiosk. He did have the courtesy of telling his parents what he was planning and hoping that Sheila would agree. They were thrilled that he finally met someone he could settle down with. They had met her several times and felt she was a fine woman and would make a great wife and mother. If she agreed, he promised his parents that he would have a reception somewhere in Miami after the newlyweds returned.

Then Donovan called Shelia's parents. They had never met, but they had heard all about Donavan from Shelia, including the very unusual dates he had planned for her. They had also heard of Donovan's company and his rise to notoriety in his field. They saw his picture in the paper, from time to time, concerning his gifts to the University of Miami, but Sheila never brought him over for them to meet. Donovan, being very out of character, actually asked for their permission to marry their daughter. Both of Sheila's parents where on the phone and talked for some time. They knew that Sheila enjoyed Donovan's company very much and was always enthusiastic to go out with him since she never knew where they would end up on each date. It was the first time her parents ever saw their daughter so happy dating any man. After 40 minutes of discussions, and without ever meeting him, they approved Donovan's request. Donavan promised them that their daughter would never have to worry about her life. She would be able to keep her job as long as she wanted and most of all, Donovan wanted a family. Grandchildren was the best surprise during that phone call. They couldn't wait to meet Donovan. They hoped the reception would be soon after they returned. Donovan didn't disappoint them. Donovan promised a dinner with his parents and the Skeffington's as soon as they returned to Miami. He begged the Skeffington's not to tell Sheila. He wanted to surprise her. It never even crossed his mind that she may say no. And she didn't. Donovan explained that he had spoken to her parents and received their blessing. Sheila couldn't believe that, but, in fact, that was the type of person Donovan was when he wanted to be. And Sheila loved him for it.

When Mr. and Mrs. Donovan Taylor returned from Las Vegas, both their families got together for a wonderful dinner at Chef Allen's in Aventura, Florida. A very high end, expensive and cozy restaurant. Everyone got along well. Each of the newlyweds were their parent's only child. Both sets of parents believed that each of their children couldn't have chosen a better mate. Everyone got along much better than either

Sheila or Donovan thought they would, and it was a night each of them would always remember.

A week later, the wedding reception was held at Joe's Stone Crab restaurant in Miami's South Beach. The restaurant was closed to customers since 400 people were invited. There were people present from the mathematics department, the school's administration, including the President of the University, the entire Basketball team, and many of the Miami Boosters. Most of the management team from Jetta International, Inc. were in attendance along with both sets of parents and their immediate families. Donovan paid the entire tab. Life was going well for Donovan and Sheila. Who would ever believe that anything bad could ever happen to such a lucky and loving couple? But life makes strange turns. The Taylors would find out in due time how their life could also change 'on a dime'.

CHAPTER 5

Isiah's sophomore year was going by very quickly. With everything he had on his daily schedule, he barely had many chances to see his family. They only lived several blocks from campus, but Isiah's academic work load, basketball practices and games, both home and away, made time scarce. But he always tried to make time to have dinner with his family at least twice a month. Donovan invited Isiah to his home for dinner several more times during that year. Those times he was not alone. Other athletes were also asked, including some football players that had been selected as All Americans. Quite the distinction. Those players would be drafted by the NFL and make a lot of money. Miami won the ACC conference in football and also won the Sugar Bowl, on New Years Day against Nebraska 42-14. They ended up number 5 in the final all coaches' poll which ranked all 123 division one football teams in the Country. Another successful year for the football team.

Basketball was still in the middle of the season with two months more to go until the 64 teams would be invited to March Madness. The Miami basketball team was only mediocre that year, as in most of the recent years. Their hopes of being one of the 64 teams chosen was fading as their record had more losses than wins. Isiah, on the other hand was playing well but other than the Wake Forest and Duke games, he was only starting in just a couple more games. The coach started Martell Dixon as the point guard in most of the games. He was a senior with much more experience than Isiah, but Isiah had the talent. However, Isiah did play nearly half of each game. Isiah's time would come. Donovan knew that, but it still bothered him. Coach Conrad gave Isiah enough playing time for appropriate experience for the next year. This year just wasn't going to be Miami's anyway. And this was Martell's last year.

Isiah never missed any classes, even with his full academic schedule. He was still getting straight A's in every class. Donovan was delighted. Even after working five or six 12 hour days at Jetta, Donovan was on the road, unofficially, scouting for new players to enhance the basketball team for next season. After one of the home games, Donovan came down from his box and went into the locker room and approached Isiah. He asked Isiah whether or not he had spoken to his daughter Sophie other than when he had his first dinner at his home.

"Mr. Taylor, I barely have time for my classes, studying, basketball practice, games, weight room training, and still have time for dinner with my family a couple of times a month," said Isiah. "I didn't know that Sophie even wanted to speak to me. I only met her at your house for a few hours that one night. I thought she was at school in Massachusetts."

"She was impressed with you the first time she met you," replied Donovan. "She has spoken to me often about you and asked how you were doing. She doesn't do that for just any players. I think she has a slight crush on you."

"How can that be? We only met for a few hours and hardly spoke to each other. She knows where I came from. Most of all I'm black," said Isiah. "That's not the formula for any kind of relationship. You must know that, sir."

"It's a new world Isiah," said the politically minded hypocrite, Donovan. "White and black couples are everywhere today. I guess you and I have to try to keep up with the times."

"Not poor black men and rich white women," said Isiah, "that just doesn't happen. I am surprised you even mentioned it to me. If I said that to my father, he would give me a tongue lashing. Black boys stay away from the rich white girls. That's just the way it is."

"Sophie is different. She is smart, loves intelligent interesting people, white or black. She is much more progressive than I am. But she is becoming her own woman," replied Donovan.

"So you believe that your daughter wants to go out with me on a date?" surprisingly said Isiah.

"Maybe. I can't believe I am saying this but why don't you ask her? She'll be in town for a couple more days before she goes back to finish her senior year. Then she is coming to Miami for law school. You two will be at the same school for a few years."

"Does your wife feel the same way as you do?" asked Isiah. "It would be the talk of the campus, especially with your notoriety, and probably not good gossip. People on campus don't think highly of me now, since I don't seem to have time to make a lot of friends. They think that since I'm an athlete, I believe I am better than most of the other students."

"You are better Isiah. You're a special black man, don't you know that?" You are reading most people wrong. Give her a call. You know my number and here is her cell phone number. She has a car, so she can meet you somewhere around campus. I'm sure you know some good places to eat around campus."

"The only good food off campus is my mother's cooking." Said Isiah.

"Well, bring her there. She can probably charm your parents," replied Donovan.

"I don't think so," said Isiah. "Not sure my parents would even approve, no matter how smart or rich she is. They don't trust any white people, except maybe you. You saved their world by renting them that apartment so close to campus. But dating your daughter? That probably is not a good idea."

Donovan was thinking the same thing, but said it anyway, "Your choice, but trust me, you will be missing something that someday you may regret. Say hello to your parents. They are good hard working black people."

Donovan walked away and started shaking hands with everyone he went by. How in the Hell does this man believe I should ask his daughter on a date, thought Isiah as he watched Donavan get into his limo. He doesn't even like black people. However, that night Isiah thought about what Donovan said. He thought a lot about it. Maybe he would just call her and chat and see what happens. That would be the way to find out what Donovan really thinks about a black man dating his daughter. After all, they will be at the same University for the next several years.

Isiah wasn't going to tell his parents about his conversation with Donovan until after he spoke with Sophie to see if her father was just making conversation or he was serious. The last thing Isiah wanted to do was embarrass himself. But Donovan wouldn't have said what he said unless there was some truth to it. Although, Donovan always has a plan. Politics always came first with Donovan. Maybe Donovan has changed his mind about black people. Isiah had heard some talk about Donovan actually going into politics. He would need the black vote and all other minority votes if he wanted to win some state office. So, Isiah decided he would call her the morning after the Wake Forest game before his first class. He wouldn't be back to his dorm room until midnight after the game. And the next night he had basketball practice until 7:00 PM.

Sophie probably wouldn't drive from Boca Raton to campus that late for anyone. Also, Isiah had to get up for classes early the next day. But Isiah thought, why not give it a try. Maybe he needed a diversion. How would he ever know that the call to Sophie the next day would change everyone's life forever?

⟫●⟪

The morning after the Wake Forest game, Isiah got up at 6:00 AM from a rough sleep. He had aches and pains from the game the night before. They lost by 22 points. He was elbowed several times in his ribs and back without a referee calling any fouls. Sometimes the officials just let the players play and look away when there's a flagrant foul. It's just part of the game. Donovan didn't even ask Isiah about the rough play when they spoke after the game. Isiah knew what he was getting into when he agreed to play big time college basketball.

He immediately woke up his roommate Clayton like he did almost every morning so they could both go to the weight room. Clayton, a senior, really was getting fed up with having the perfect roommate. It seems like the tables had turned. Clayton wanted to change roommates but didn't say anything. He knew how much the coach and Mr. Taylor liked Isiah. They needed to be in the weight room by 6:30 or they lost some privileges. An hour workout was required before the entire basketball team had their team breakfast in the athlete's cafeteria. Clayton would have slept hours more if Isiah didn't wake him. Clayton hated it. Originally, Coach Conrad wanted Clayton to be the right influence for Isiah, but it was Isiah who turned out to be the influence for Clayton. Isiah started to actually like Clayton, but just didn't understand why such a talented athlete was so lazy.

After the team breakfast was over, Coach Conrad would give a 15 minute critique of the past night's game. However, due to how badly Miami lost, the coach just got up and went into his office. The players knew what that meant. It was going to be extra workouts before the next game.

Isiah went back to his room, took a shower and got ready for his first class at 10:00 AM. He picked up the phone several times and looked at it and wondered, should he or shouldn't he? He finally called Sophie's cell phone. The call went to voice mail. He thought she may still be sleeping since there was just a couple days left before her break was over. But then he tried her home phone number.

"Hello," said an unfamiliar voice.

"Is Sophie there?"

"She's outside doing her laps in the pool. Who may I say called," said Anya. "Oh, let me guess. It's Isiah Daniels, the big time black point guard for the Miami Hurricanes."

"Yes it is," replied Isiah who thought it was uncalled for what she had said. "How did you know?"

"You have a distinctive voice. A non-black voice," said Anya.

"What does that mean?" questioned Isiah, thinking that he talks like most black men.

"You just have a distinctive voice. I remember it from the times you were here for dinner."

Isiah didn't believe a word she said. "Would you please tell Sophie I called. My number is 555-2324. I'm leaving in 20 minutes for class. Otherwise I'll be back in my dorm room at 3:00 this afternoon."

"Any message Mr. big black guy?" sarcastically said Anya.

"No," and Isiah hung up. He was upset. He thought that even though she was still in high school that didn't give her the right to be so snooty and bigoted. Isiah didn't think he had a chip on his shoulder when it came to the white/black thing, but he was a little embarrassed how he just hung up on her. What would Mr. Taylor think? Maybe she really didn't mean anything about him being black. Although, she was Donovan's daughter. He hoped this wasn't going to be one of those bad days. He waited 20 minutes, but there was no return call. So Isiah went off to class.

Isiah got back from classes just after 3:00. There were no messages on his phone. He needed to study before he had basketball practice between 5:30 and 7:00. Maybe Donovan was wrong and Sophie didn't want to speak with him. Maybe Donovan was playing with Isiah to see if a black man would actually call his daughter. So Isiah decided not to call again. Either she called him back or he would just forget about it. Twenty minutes into working on his English class paper, the phone rang. Isiah let it ring three times. After four rings voice mail picks up. He really needed to finish that paper. But he decided to pick it up just before the fourth ring.

"Isiah, I heard you called me this morning," said Sophie. "I wish my annoying sister would have told me you were on the phone. I try to do laps each morning when I'm home. But it's not that important. She could have brought me the phone. She said you were a little annoyed with her."

"I don't know how she got that idea?" said Isiah knowing that he really was a little annoyed.

"She can be a bitch sometimes, especially with black athletes. Or maybe she's just jealous. Whatever. How are you? I haven't heard from you since dinner at my house several months ago. I had a feeling you would call me sometime."

Shocked by that remark, Isiah answered, "I have really been busy with all my classes, practice and games, it's been a little overwhelming sometimes," as he was uncomfortable with that response.

"I have been keeping up with your statistics," said Sophie, "even though the team isn't doing very well this season. For being your first year, averaging 8 points and 12 assists a game is really good. Daddy says that next year Miami will be going to March Madness with you as their starting point guard. I'm impressed."

"I didn't know you followed basketball. Thanks, but I do wish we could win a few more games," said the shocked Isiah. "I was just wondering if you were busy tonight. I thought it would be nice to get together before you go back up North."

"I was just thinking about going out tonight. What time is your practice over? Or, can you get out of practice tonight. Give Coach Mickey some excuse about your family."

"No, I can't miss practice. It's over at 7:00. Then I can take a quick shower."

"Well, then we'll just start a little later. I'll pick you up at 7:30 outside the gym. I'll be in a red BMW convertible. It will be a late dinner at Bird & Bone at the beach and then we can dance and have a couple of drinks at the club LIV. Travis Scott, DJ Khaled and Kayne West are performing tonight. My treat. Are you up for it?"

There was a short silent moment. Isiah didn't know what to say. He had heard of those places and knew they were really crowded and expensive. Everything at South Beach was expensive and everything started late and went into the wee hours of the morning. He couldn't let her pay for all that. But he didn't have much money. Spending money was not part of his scholarship.

"Are you sure about those places? I heard they're quite high class and expensive," Isiah said being a bit embarrassed, "and I have to be in the weight room at 6:30 sharp tomorrow morning."

"No problem," said Sophie, "I'll drop you at the weight facility before 6:30. You won't be late, I promise you. See you at 7:30 tonight. And dress casual," as Sophie hung up.

Isiah didn't know what just hit him. He never missed a night of sleep. Even when he was cramming for finals he always went to bed early so he felt good when he was taking his tests. What was he getting into? Either this was going to be one of the greatest nights of his life or it would be the downfall of his college career. He had classes most of the day after the weight room. His last class, the next day, he needed to turn in his English class paper. He wasn't even half way through with it. He couldn't imagine what life would be after a night with Sophie. But he was going to find out.

CHAPTER 6

At just after 7:30 PM, Sophie arrived at the gym on campus driving a red BMW convertible. The top was down. Sophie was wearing a short red print sundress, red heels and at least twelve bracelets on her left hand. Her hair was brown, naturally curly, and down to her shoulders with blond highlights. Isiah had no idea she was wearing extensions in her hair. He wouldn't even know what they were, or even that such things existed. She was quite the site for Isiah. He thought this was not a girl who would be going clubbing with a poor black man wearing black pants, old brown loafers and a long sleeve white shirt.

"I know you just got done with practice, Izzie, but where did you get those clothes?" said Sophie wondering if this was really what he was going to wear.

"My name is Isiah, not Izzie," said Isiah calmly. "I'm sorry that my wardrobe doesn't meet your standards. This is the best I have. We can call this off if you want. I'm just sorry you had to drive all the way from Boca to go out with a black bum."

"Slow down Izzie," replied Sophie, "and don't be so judgmental. This black/white thing is not your thing. It definitely isn't mine. That's my father's and sister's thing. You should know that by now. We're just going to South Beach and it's time for me to help you come into the 'new Miami age'. As to your name, everyone calls you Isiah. I'm not everyone. You can give me a pet name if you want. I'd be flattered. Now get in the car, we're going back to your dorm room and get you some different clothes."

"I told you I don't have any different clothes."

"Then get in the car, let's get this first date on the road."

Isiah had no idea what he had just got himself into. He was already embarrassed due to the way he was dressed, but more than that he implied that Sophie was a racist. How could he have done that? It was going to be a late night so he had to quickly change his attitude or the night may end much sooner than both of them wanted it to. But it was hard for Isiah to do that.

"Where are you going?" asked Isiah. "This isn't the way to South Beach."

"One quick stop and we'll be on our way Izzie."

About a mile from campus was a large mall, The Shops at Sunset Place.

"What are we doing here?" asked Isiah in a dubious manner.

"Just follow me."

They walked to the middle of the mall where there was a twin set of curved steps which led to the second floor. Sophie took Isiah's hand and dragged him up the steps. At the top they took a quick left and walked about 100 feet to a Tommy Bahama store. Isiah was shocked and didn't know if he should be nice about this little side trip or whether he should be mad. As they walked into the store a young blond haired man, in his late twenties, walked up to them and said, "Hello Ms. Taylor, what a nice surprise. And who is this handsome gentleman with you?"

"Don't touch him, John, he is with me," said Sophie loudly. "He swings my way, not yours. And he plays basketball for Miami. He is hot, isn't he?"

"Damn it! All the good ones are straight these days. I didn't know the 'U' even had a basketball team. I thought they only had a football team." As if Isiah wasn't already a little upset. That comment really started getting him mad. "So what can I do for you two tonight?"

"We are going to the club Liv tonight and I want you to dress Izzie."

"What?" angrily said Isiah.

"Don't worry, Izzie," said John. "Sophie's father and the owner are good friends. He helped the owner start five Tommy Bahama stores and a restaurant. Any friend of Donovan Taylor's always gets one set of free clothes."

"Now you see why I brought you here Izzie. It's free. Pick out what you want."

"Sophie," said John, "let me do it. Are you sure you play basketball. I thought basketball players were all 7 feet tall?" Again Isiah was getting upset. "Anyway, don't worry. You'll love what I have for you."

John quickly went and got a pair of pleaded khaki pants with cuffs. A green and brown flowered shirt and a pair of brown slip on loafers with tassels. John could tell just by looking at Isiah what his sizes were. "Try these on. You'll look like a million bucks! Oh, I love that word 'buck'," exclaimed John.

Begrudgingly, Isiah went to the dressing room and put on the clothes and came out. "Perfect," said John, "what do you think Sophie?"

"Love it. We'll take them."

"Just let me steam out the creases for you and you can walk into the club Liv and every man will be looking at you Izzie," claimed John.

Isiah didn't know what to say. He knew it was going to be a unique evening, but what a humiliating and embarrassing start. He began to feel like a kept man. But then they quickly left the store and were on their way to South Beach.

When Sophie drove up to Bird & Bone restaurant, the valet said hello to Sophie and welcomed her back. He even said he would call ahead and make sure their table was ready. Isiah didn't know what to think about all of this. It was happening so fast and everything was so out of character for him.

The art deco restaurant was nothing like Isiah had ever seen before. It was loud, crowded with unique drinks flowing everywhere. When he looked at the menu there were no prices on it. He made a comment about that to Sophie. She just shrugged her shoulders and said if you can't afford it you just don't come. But Isiah wanted to know how he was going to pay. Sophie just said that the bill, including a 25% tip automatically went on her father's tab. So she said just order what you want, but first she wanted a drink.

Isiah drank a beer, from time to time, but wasn't really a drinker. So Sophie ordered him some exotic drink that he had never heard of. When it came to the table the waiter opened his lighter and flicked on a flame. There were sparklers flickering and some type of flower coming out of the tall glass with yellow liquid in it. He sipped on it for the whole meal. It was terrible. Sophie had several drinks. When the meal that Sophie had ordered for Isiah came to the table, the portion was so small it reminded Isiah of the portions he use to eat at his parents when he was a kid. But that was because they were poor. He mentioned that to Sophie and said that the portion was so small he hoped it was the cheapest entre on the menu.

"Take a guess at what that meal cost," asked Sophie with a grin.

"$50.00?" said Isiah believing he was guessing high.

Sophie laughed and said she had no idea how much it cost, but she knew that nothing on the menu was less than $100.00.

Isiah was astounded. Was this how the rich and famous lived. He wasn't quite sure that this was his kind of life.

"For that amount, does it come with potatoes or a side of something?

"Izzie, you are funny. I like you. It's fun watching you tonight. Get used to it if you want to go out again."

Isiah wasn't so sure he wanted to answer that comment so he took his three bites and finished the meal. He couldn't wait to get back to the athletes cafeteria and eat a real meal.

Club Liv was even more out of Isiah's comfort zone. It didn't even open until midnight. It was so crowded and loud he hardly heard a word Sophie was saying to him or any of her other acquaintances she spoke to that evening. He knew they had a table in the club somewhere, but they seemed to sit at different tables during each of the very short brakes that the bands took. There were three different bands. They were all recording artists, but Isiah never heard of any of them. Sophie introduced most of them to him, but he could hardly hear their name let alone even remember them. He danced and sipped a coke for four hours until Sophie finally said it was time to get him back before his first class that morning. Isiah was truly exhausted. Sophie was in heaven and enjoyed watching Izzie in his new world.

On the ride back to campus Sophie said, "Should we do this again tomorrow night, but at a different restaurant and club? It's my last night before I have to go back to school."

"I would really like to, but I have a full scrimmage tomorrow night against the junior varsity team," lied Isiah. That was just not his type of life.

When Sophia dropped Isiah off at his dorm, she got out of the car, walked around and opened his door. She gave him a long sexy kiss. "I had a blast. But most of this was just to let me blow off some steam. I really am not one of those trust fund babies that likes to live that way. I like it once in a long while. I'd really rather just have a burger at Chili's. I'm glad you said no about tomorrow night. But how about dinner at a burger joint on campus. You must have one here. You can even pay. Daddy won't mind. I know you were lying about your scrimmage."

"It's a date," said Isiah as he quickly changed his attitude about Sophie. "Meet me at my dorm at 7:00. I'll wear jeans. And please don't call me Izzie anymore"

"Okay. Sounds great," admitted Sophie. "I can't wait."

———————⟫●⟪———————

The morning after Sophie Taylor Daniels was murdered, at her Boca Raton home, both detectives, Morgan Blackburn and Darby Lynch, knew that there may not be sufficient evidence at the scene of the crime to immediately determine who may have committed her murder. And this was before they even saw the crime scene. This case was different from most of their murder cases. In this case, the victim was not at the scene of the crime. She was on an operating table in a hospital at the time the Boca Raton police arrived at the scene. In most cases, pictures of the victim would have been taken. The scene would have been cleared of any unauthorized persons. No one would be allowed to touch the body or disturb anything pending the arrival of the medical examiner, identification personnel and the detectives handling the case. None of that happened. So the two detectives lost much of their necessary tools in their tool box to start their investigation.

With that in mind, the detectives went to the scene of the crime to determine what the first responders did uncover. That would include the EMS personnel that transported the victim to the hospital. The difficulty was that there was more than just one scene for this incident. First there was the victims home, including the kitchen, hallway, main floor bathroom, side door, front yard, the street in front of the victim's home, the front entrance area of the Saunders's home, across the street, and any other areas of the Saunders's home that the victim may have been.

The seasoned detectives wondered how diligent the Boca Raton police were concerning blocking off all those areas with crime tape? Did they check every person they found at the scene for blood, DNA or items they may have picked up? Were unauthorized persons cleared from all those scenes? Did they make sure that no one touched anything, especially the body? Or did anyone disturb anything pending the arrival of the EMS personnel? Did they obtain the name and addresses of persons who may have been present or seen something? Did they take any statements from anyone present or even from Mr. or Mrs. Saunders? Did they keep witnesses separate from each other so they couldn't discuss what they saw? Did they prevent destruction of fragile evidence such as footprints, tire tracks, blood trails, etc.? Did they note their time of arrival or the weather conditions, especially at the outside crime areas? Did they photograph all of the scenes, including inside the victim's home, outside the victim's home and the crime areas of the Saunders's home? There was so much for the detectives to determine. The autopsy report and the observation of the victim and her wounds could wait until later. However, the detectives were not aware that the family of the victim were in the process of contacting a Board Certified Pathologist to perform a private autopsy for a more fully independent examination of the cause and manner of death after the County pathologist finished his autopsy. Had they known that, they would have gone to the Medical Examiner's office first. They thought that the body would be there for some time. All of these tasks would make the investigation that much more difficult to determine.

With all of that in mind, the detectives were off to the Daniels's home in the Boca Raton Country Club. When they arrived at the scene of the crime, there was crime scene tape around the home of the victim, but no tape anywhere else. They observed two blood trails but no markers were put on the ground to indicate each spot of blood. There were two patrol officers from the Boca Raton police force present supposedly to guard the scene until the detectives arrived.

"Officers, who handled the forensics for this incident?" asked Darby.

"The Chief called our Forensic Service Manager to come and take care of the scene," replied one of the officers.

"What about the Chief, did he come also?" again asked Darby.

"I think so," said the other officer, "at least he was here for a while."

"Were there pictures taken of anything to do with the crime? How about an inventory taken of anything involved with the incident in the victim's home?" asked Morgan.

"You need to speak to the Chief and the Forensic Services Manager," said one of the officers.

"Why are all those people going in the Saunders's home?" asked Darby.

"They probably are asking them what happened to Mrs. Daniels," answered the officer.

"How many murders have you been involved with officers?" asked Morgan.

"We don't get too many homicides in Boca and actually this is our first," replied one of the officers.

Morgan was astonished. He was just about to go to discuss this mess with his partner when Darby came over and said that he wouldn't believe what just happened.

"Oh yes I will," said Morgan, "this whole crime scene is compromised. I'm not sure what we will definitely be able to determine what happened here even with a full investigation. I think we may need to call our own forensic team and have them start over."

"That is bad news. Here is some more," responded Darby, "I just got off the phone with the Medical Examiner and after he is finished with his autopsy, a private forensic pathologist, hired by Isiah Daniels, is coming to pick up the body and transport her to Tampa for a private autopsy. The Medical Examiner said his report will be complete in a day or so and the toxicology report and DNA results from the matter he found under the victim's fingernails and the blood at the scene will be complete soon."

After that news, Morgan Blackburn called the West Palm Beach Sheriff and also the States Attorney's office for the County to let them know the status of the current investigation. Both were furious and knew that Donovan Taylor would be looking for scapegoats concerning the botching of his daughter's murder investigation. Heads were going to roll. Both detectives immediately called the Chief of police for Boca Raton. He wasn't available. What a mess. Both Morgan and Darby knew that they were soon going to receive a call from the Governor. Hopefully, at the end of the day, they still had their jobs. The only silver lining was the fact that Donovan Taylor and the Governor were not members of the same political party and the Governor knew that Donovan wanted his job. Murder and politics. This was going to turn into a media circus. Just as the detectives were going to go in the Daniel's home and wait for their forensic team, the local and national press showed up. And where was Isiah Daniels? One would think that he would be in touch with the detectives handling his wife's case as soon as he could. But there had been no communications with the victim's husband. Very strange. The circus was just beginning.

CHAPTER 7

Sophie Taylor Daniels corpse was laying on the Palm Beach County Medical Examiner's table. Her body had just been brought to the Medical Examiner's office, by a private ambulance service, one hour after Dr. Hamilton pronounced the time of death. Her parents were at the Medical Examiner's office to identify the body at the request of the Sheriff of Palm Beach County. The detectives assigned to the case, Morgan Blackburn and Darby Lynch hadn't yet arrived. Both detectives had been with the Palm Beach County Sheriff's office for over 12 years. They had handled many of the high profile murders and suicides that had occurred in that County. That didn't satisfy Donovan Taylor.

"When can I see my daughter," said Shelia Taylor to one of the intern medical examiners, as she was crying and being consoled by her husband.

"Mrs. Taylor, the Medical Examiner is in the process of cleaning her and preparing her for viewing," answered the intern. "I know you would not want to see her in her current condition. You need to remember her as your beautiful daughter."

"It will take some time," said the other intern, "the attack on your daughter was extremely brutal," being very insensitive. Just then the two investigating detectives arrived.

"Morgan," said Darby to her partner as she took him aside, "these people are important people and also in deep mourning. Mr. Taylor is the Speaker of the House of Representative for this State. He may even be our next Governor. Remember, a little compassion would be appropriate."

"Since when has the standing of any person involved in an unsolved murder made you so compassionate," angrily said Morgan. "Just because they are the victim's parents, and he has such an important position doesn't mean we treat them any different than anyone else. How many times have you told me that?"

"But this is different. Sometimes discretion is the better part of valor. This is one of those times," replied Darby. "By the way, have you found out where the victim's husband is? Shouldn't he be here?"

"He was somewhere in North Carolina at one of his plants dealing with work matters," said Morgan. "He was just notified about his wife a few hours ago and he is on his way here."

"How about we get our act together. We have worked together for a lot of years. We can't disagree on anything in front of possible suspects, who are also the victim's parents. Let's go in and see when the Medical Examiner will be ready for the Speaker and his wife to identify the body. CSI is probably finished with the scene of the attack and there are at least two dozen police canvasing the Daniels neighborhood to see if anyone saw or heard anything. After all, this act was done early in the day. Very unusual. It couldn't have just been a random event."

"All right," admitted Darby, "you're right. I'll tell the parents that as soon as we find out the status of the victim from the Medical Examiner, we can give them a more informed status of the possible events leading up to their daughter's death.

It took another hour to clean the victim enough to make her presentable for her parents to identify. Both detectives explained to the Taylor's that the Medical Examiner would come out and tell them when they could identify the body. Donavan was livid, but both detectives assured them that it would be better for them to view their daughter for the last time once she is at least presentable. Donovan understood and comforted Sheila, but that last hour of waiting felt like an eternity. It was almost 10:00 PM the night of the attack before Sophie's parents were able to view and identify her as their daughter. It was the worst day of their lives. Even cleaned up she hardly looked like the Sophie they loved. Donovan wanted to know why Isiah hadn't shown up at the Medical Examiners' office yet. He had a private plane and there was an airport in Palm Beach just a few miles from the Medical Examiner's office. What could be more important than being there when they identified his wife's body?

Isiah had his business trip planned to his North Carolina plant for over a month. He always attempted to visit all of Jetta International's plants at least once a year. Isiah had improved, diversified and expanded Jetta's business and its profits since Donovan Taylor resigned from the company and ran for a seat in the State House of Representatives. However, recently Isiah had found some discrepancies in several accounts at the Durham plant. He wanted to audit that account himself, even though the plant manager was a reliable black employee that Isiah had promoted to that position himself. When Isiah was notified about the events at his home and what had happened to his wife, he immediately contacted the company's pilots to get his plane ready for a flight to the West Palm Beach airport. Isiah wasn't able to start his own audit of those questionable accounts.

Palm Beach County is Florida's third most populous County, with almost 7% of Florida's population. Its airport is also one of the busiest in the State. Getting a flight plan ready and approved for landing at that airport wasn't instantaneous. It took time. The detectives understood that. Sophie's parents couldn't understand the fact that Isiah wasn't there with them, no matter who attempted to explain the issue. It wasn't until 10:30 PM that evening when Isiah's plane landed at the airport. He had his driver meet him at the airport and drive him directly to the Medical Examiner's office. Isiah arrived just after his in-laws were able to view the body. Both of Sophie's parents were in shock. When Isiah arrived he attempted to communicate with Donovan, but it was as if Isiah didn't exist. That brought back memories as to how Isiah was treated when he was a young black man. Isiah's mind quickly reverted to years past.

"Where have you been God Damit?" said Donovan. "Your wife is dead and her body has been disfigured. How in the Hell did this happen?"

"Donovan, I have no idea," replied Isiah. "I have been in Durham for the last couple days. I attempted to call Sophie several times but there was no answer. Her cell phone went to voice mail. What do the police say happened? Was it a botched robbery? Did Sophie know the person and let them in? Was there a break in? I have so many questions. How can my Sophie be gone?" as Isiah started to cry. He had no one there that wanted to comfort him. Shelia was forced by her husband to ignore him and Donovan gave him looks that Isiah remembered as a young black man. It was as if this was all his fault. Isiah didn't understand any of that. He knew how important Sophie was to her parents, and how devastating this turn of events must have hurt them. But she was his wife too.

Isiah and Sophie had been married, very happily for 15 years. In all that time, Isiah, for the most part, had only been treated that way, off and on, and then only by Donovan. Isiah was aware of Donovan's feelings towards blacks. However, Isiah thought he was the exception. Isiah had never been treated as badly as he was being treated that evening by both his in-laws. Maybe without Sophie, Isiah was now just another black man, no matter how much Isiah had accomplished for Donovan's company and his pocketbook.

"The Medical Examiner is going to do an autopsy in the morning," said Donovan. "He has agreed to put Sophie first in line as a courtesy to me. I want you, Isiah, to arrange for a private autopsy immediately after Sophie's body can be removed from this office. I don't trust the government. I want an independent doctor to give me their statement as to her cause of death and how it may have happened. And I want you to communicate to me the name and address of the private pathologist's contact information the minute after you contact him. Most of all, I don't want any law enforcement personnel, including the detectives assigned to this case, to examine Sophie's body until the second autopsy is complete. Do you understand?"

Isiah understood and was glad that the family didn't have to stand in line to wait for the results of an autopsy. The Palm Beach County Medical Examiner's office normally has over 2,800 autopsies a year. There is always a backup. Mistakes are probably made, from time to time, due to the overwhelming number of bodies. Isiah understood Donovan's concerns about Sophie's autopsy by an overworked Medical Examiner's office. However, Isiah was a little confused as to Donovan's distrust of the government and the detectives. He was basically in charge of the State of Florida's government behind only the Governor. And it was Donovan's intention to run for Governor as soon as the current Governor's term was up. But Isiah knew to never question Donovan when it involved his family. When it came to family, Isiah was still just an outsider black man.

"Donovan, please don't be concerned, I am here and I will monitor the direction of the investigation and work directly with the authorities. I'll make sure that there is a complete and independent examination of the cause and manner of our Sophie's death. I will find the best pathologist in the State. We will find out who did this, their motive and make sure they pay dearly for it."

"You better make sure that happens, and happens quickly boy! I am putting you in charge of this terrible tragedy and you better make sure that no one drops the ball," barked Donovan as he took his wife out to their limo where their driver had been waiting for most of the day. In the 15 years Isiah had been married to Sophie, and all of the time at the University of Miami, never did Donovan call Isiah 'boy'. Isiah wondered where that was coming from. Did his father-in-law believe that he had something to do with his daughter's death? Is his hatred of the black community resurfacing? Isiah had seen a slight change in Donovan's demeanor and personality ever since he announced his intention to run for Governor, but he didn't think much of it. The stress of running for State wide office is very difficult. Or could it be something else?

When the Taylor's arrived home there were dozens of phone messages from every friend and State Representative, including the Governor and the Lieutenant Governor. There were dozens of arrangements of flowers, every kind of food possible and their maid was just sitting in the kitchen crying. Their personal physician had the local pharmacy deliver a prescription for sedatives. Their maid also told them that two detectives had called and wanted to come by the next morning to speak with them. They had mentioned that they had briefly spoken with them at the Medical Examiner's office late that day. Donovan told the maid to call them first thing in the morning. He would call them in a day or two. He told her to tell the detectives that Sophie's husband would deal with them. Then they both took a sedative and went to bed.

Isiah went to his home in the Boca Raton Country Club only to find that the home was designated a crime scene with crime tape surrounding it. Most of the block was also closed off. Only residents with proper identification were allowed through. None of the officers or CSI personnel noticed Isiah sitting in the back seat of his black town car. It was about a half a block from the street barriers. So no one, including dozen of the members of the press who were still there, approached him for purposes of asking questions. Isiah didn't want any publicity, which he knew would probably be contradictory and even racial since there were multiple news agencies attempting to take pictures. Why the police allowed reporters to photograph the blood trail from the Daniels home to the home of their neighbor and to take statements from other neighbors was perplexing to Isiah. At the time, Isiah didn't know that Diane Saunders, and her husband, had already retained an attorney to speak to the press on their behalf. They had no idea what to say or do and were scared at ramifications against them. This was going to be a high priority case.

So Isiah asked his driver to take him to the Ritz Carlton in West Palm Beach where he would check in until he could get back in his home. He had his suit case with him and the Ritz had a large sundry selection for anything that he may need. He was well known at that hotel since he and his company had many events there and used the facilities for the company's clients and employees to stay while they were at Jetta's home office. He and Sophie had also stayed at that hotel dozens of times themselves.

Isiah decided he would speak to the detectives first thing in the morning. He thought that not calling the detectives immediately may cause problems, but he was too exhausted, emotional and overwhelmed to be able to be completely coherent with the authorities at that very late time of a very long day. A mistake? Probably.

Donovan had given Isiah the contact information for detectives Morgan Blackburn and Darby Lynch and instructed Isiah to call them as soon as possible. Those instructions sounded like Donovan was still Isiah's boss. Why was Donovan on the war path against Isiah? He had no idea. But Isiah still wasn't going to speak to the detectives that evening. Isiah still couldn't believe that this was happening to him. Isiah was sharp and knew that the first person, on any suspect list, when a wife is murdered is always the spouse, especially when that spouse was black.

⎯⎯⎯⎯⎯⎯⎯⎯⎯⎯⎯⎯⎯⎯⎯⎯⎯⎯⎯⎯⎯⎯⎯⎯

Isiah was certain that the authorities would speak with Sophie's law partners at their Miami office. Isiah would soon be shocked to find out that Sophie was in the process of possibly firing Jetta International as one of her firm's clients. This was being done even though the CEO of the company was Sophie's husband. Also, Jetta was one of the firm's largest clients. Jetta had paid over $5.5 million a year in attorney fees to the firm. Usually it is the client that fires their lawyer when they believe that the attorneys are not representing them properly. But this was just the opposite.

Sophie's partners were furious when she said she was in the process of firing Jetta, but she assured her partners that it was necessary due to circumstances that she was unable to disclose until she had a long conversation with the Bar Ethical committee, her husband, her father and the local police authorities. Certain investigations needed to be completed for a determination whether or not criminal activity was occurring within Jetta which were being aided or covered up by her law firm. Sophie didn't want the firm involved in any criminal investigation for any of their clients. Under the current environment, lawyers are always dragged into many investigations of their client's possible criminal activity. The last thing Sophie wanted was any member of her firm to be subject to any possible indictments for conspiracy or withholding evidence concerning any possible criminal matters. Client privilege only went so far. If the authorities determined that the law firm was a co-conspirator in any criminal enterprise, client privilege no longer existed. That was Sophie's main motive to find out the true facts before she acted on firing any client.

Sophie had, in the last few days, just become aware of possible inappropriate matters that had been happening within Jetta International for some time. She needed to confirm all the facts before letting her firm handle any more of Jetta's legal work. Her partners just didn't understand Sophie's motive. But Sophie remained silent on the issue.

Sophie contacted a local attorney who she went to law school with and requested that all of Jetta's current legal work be transferred to her firm. Dustina Washington, a black lawyer in a large downtown law firm, who was a good friends of Sophie's, and graduated law school with her, agreed to accept the legal matters pending written approval by Jetta. Both Dustina and her husband, Jayden Robinson, were good friends with both Sophie and Isiah. Jayden was executive vice president of Xavier Corporation, an import/export company based out of New York. He was in charge of the Miami office. Both were black and grew up in Miami. Sophie promised the written authority for transferring the legal matters in a day or two. She needed to speak with Isiah as soon as possible. She knew he would be back from his North Carolina trip in a day or two. However, she had indicated to her friend Dustina, that there may be a reason that she wouldn't be able to handle Jetta's work either. But Sophie didn't elaborate on the issue. She needed to speak with Isiah first. Everyone was quite confused.

The whole Miami office of Fischer & Logan knew that Sophie was Isiah Daniels' wife. He was President and CEO of Jetta International, Inc. Also her father, the current Speaker of the House of Representatives for the State of Florida was the founder of that Company. There had to be a huge reason, along with a very difficult decision, on the part of Sophie to let Jetta go as a client. However, her partners respected her judgment even though they would be losing a large amount of attorney fees.

Sophie wouldn't explain, to any of her partners or Dustina, her knowledge of the reasons she wanted to let Jetta go. However, they respected her decision and her reasons for waiting for a full disclosure concerning that decision. They knew that in due time, they would find out all of the facts. Most of her partners wanted to know whether or not the firing involved her husband or father? Sophia just asked her firm for their indulgence for the time being. Two days later, Sophia Taylor Danials was dead.

⟶➤●◄⟵

At midnight on the day Sophia Daniels was murdered, Detective Lynch attempted to call Isiah on his cell phone, however every time she tried it went to voice mail. They knew he had arrived at the Medical Examiner's office just after they left at about 10:45 PM. He wouldn't be able to go to his home since it was designated a crime scene. She and her partner couldn't understand why he hadn't attempted to call them. They even called Isiah's parent's, who were aware of the events of the day since they had heard it on the news. They had no idea where their son was. Isiah had purchased his parents, a new home in Plantation, Florida, a few years after he graduated. Donovan had agreed to let the Daniels stay in his apartment until Isiah could afford to move them somewhere off campus. However, Donovan raised their rent to market value. He knew Isiah could pay the increase in their rent. Detective Lynch accused Otis Daniels of lying and covering up for his son, who the detectives thought may have been hiding at his parents' home. Otis thought that the detective would never have accused a white parent of that act. Otis hung up on detective Lynch. Both detectives felt that Otis was hiding something from them. It didn't even occur to them that Isiah was in mourning in some hotel. Was that because of his race? They were both seasoned detectives. Even before they were going to interview Sophie's law partners, Isiah was placed first on their list as a suspect. They needed to know who he may have hired to murder his wife. They needed a time line on Isiah's movements prior to his wife's murder. Since it was very late, they finally decided to continue their search for Isiah the next day.

Everything they were going to do in this investigation would be put under a microscope by the press, the Taylor family and their immediate supervisors. So they decided to get some sleep, instead of visiting Otis and Clover's home late that night. Instead, they would put together their agenda early the next morning. Both were not happy that they had caught this case. Their lives would never be the same by the time the person or persons, who committed this horrible crime were behind bars.

CHAPTER 8

Anya Taylor received a phone call from her father the day after her sister was murdered. She could hardly talk she was so hysterical. All her father could understand during the conversation was that Anya knew that the black husband of her sister hurt her and she was coming home that day. Donovan tried to persuade her to wait until the next morning, but Anya refused. She wanted to know the details as to how Sophie died. Her father refused to discuss that over the phone.

"Was it that nigger Isiah?" cried Anya.

"We don't know Anya. This just happened yesterday," replied Donovan. "We'll know more after the investigation and an autopsy."

Donovan was still attempting to get her to wait until she calmed down before she drove over Alligator Alley by herself, but Anya just hung up. It was her only sibling and the person she looked up to most even though she hated what she did for a living. Sophie always made sure Anya stood up for herself, made sure she dated good men and would do whatever was necessary to make sure she kept her out of trouble. Anya was a rebel in High School. So Sophie's influences didn't always work, but Anya ended up turning out fine. Her father wasn't enthusiastic about her choices for college, her vocation or most of the men she dated even though she never dated athletes and always stayed away from black men. They actually scared her, but no one would ever know that fact since she hid it well. After all, her brother-in-law was black, and a successful one. Anya was not happy that her sister had married one of them. Anya was never thrilled about that fact, even though she actually thought of Isiah as one of the good ones. She just thought of most black people as being so inferior. They were crude, impolite and so different from whites. They even spoke differently. Even though Anya was a bigot, she did associate with a few black men. In her world it was hard to avoid them. Her father had many over for dinner, but she never really knew many black women. All she knew about them was what she saw on television, and that never left Anya with a good feeling. She did go to college with many black individuals, but she never socialized with them.

Anya didn't want to follow in the footsteps of her sister. She needed to be her own person. She refused to go to college on the East Coast of Florida or to any of the Ivy League schools her parents insisted she attend. Her parents were disappointed but they finally supported their daughter's decisions begrudgingly. They loved both their daughters. Anya turned out to be an enthusiastic environmentalist. Something no one would have ever imagined. And not just any ordinary one, but one who spent most of her wakening hours trying to save the world from its destruction through the discharge of greenhouse gases and other toxic materials. Where and when Anya changed her life to that direction, trying to save the world, was unknown to anyone who knew her. Maybe she just wanted to be as different as possible from her family. She was always looked upon as a rebel and not the type of person who would organize large protests against corporations or small entrepreneurs who used or discharged chemicals in their businesses that damaged the environment.

After graduating from high school, near the top of her class at St. Andrews, Anya had her pick of universities to attend. However, she decided on a relatively unknown university in Estero, Florida, a suburb of Fort Myers. It was called Florida Gulf Coast University. It was a relatively new and small University with just 8,000 students, at the time, but known for its emphasis on environmental issues. Climate change was incorporated into almost every class synopsis. Those issues were also intertwined into every major at the University. Anya wanted to major in environmental engineering and FGCU was one of few universities that offered that major. It also even had an MBA and Ph.D. program for it. Due to her good grades in high school, she received a full four year scholarship for tuition with additional funds to allow her to live at off campus student housing. FGCU didn't have the usual university dormitories. All student housing were apartment style living. A new concept that came about when the University began in the early 1990's. At the time, it was the first new University to be built from scratch in over 50 years. The land for the University was donated by wealthy land owners and environmentally conscience corporations. Anya chose a one bedroom apartment at the Estero Oaks Luxury Living apartments which was just two miles from campus. Anya didn't want any roommates. She had found her passion and didn't want anyone interrupting her school life and new passion. However, she met some very charming and warmhearted people who lived in the complex. She even became good friends with several of them. At the time of her sister's murder, Anya had received her PH.D. Degree years before in Environmental Engineering. She took a job at FGCU as a professor and was working her way towards full tenure. Anya liked men and dated a few. However, she never embraced the institution of marriage. Her sister was a large part of her thought process on that subject.

Her family was somewhat surprised and disappointed about her thinking on marriage. But again, still proud of their rebel child ending up as a professor. Anya also had several consulting contracts with local corporations to advise them on their environmental issue. As a professor, she stayed close to student housing and rented a home in the Reserve at Estero. That was only just a mile further from the University. She enjoyed mingling with the students whether at the outdoor student's pool on campus, the gathering room in the off campus student housing complexes or at the student union on campus. She dated several men periodically, all of whom were either graduate students or instructors at FGCU. None of those relationships were serious. Anya never was able to make firm commitments when it came to men. She just wasn't the kind of person who wanted a lifetime relationship. Children were not an important factor in her life. Her work was too important to her. She saw her sister's marriage as a merger of two entrepreneurs, one white and one black. Sophie and Isiah only saw each other a few times each week. They associated with black friends. That was not the way Anya wanted her life to turn out.

⟹➤●◄⟸

Despite her thoughts on marriage, Anya and Sophie were always close. Anya was four years younger than Sophie so they never attended the same school at the same time. When Sophie graduated high school, Anya started high school. So they didn't have any of the same friends. But she loved her sister and was very proud of everything she accomplished, other than her marriage and her clients. It gave Anya the incentive to follow in her sister's footsteps only in the academic sense. But Anya didn't want to have anything to do with the law. She hated it and looked at lawyers as people who always found ways to represent the people and companies who did bad things in the world. Some of Sophie's clients changed the world, and not in a good way.

She was happy for Sophie when she graduated law school and hoped she would spend a substantial amount of her time helping indigent people with their legal issues and not just representing rich clients for the sake of making money. That never happened. It upset Anya who voiced her opinion, in a civil manner, to her sister more than several times. But her sister always told her to grow up. Sophie was going to let her sister save the world. Sophie liked the life of working in a large law firm. Representing large clients and making big money. Some of Sophie's largest clients, other than Jetta International, were some of the largest polluters in the world. She had represented Saudi Aramco, the largest polluter of greenhouse gas pollution in the world. Other companies she represented were Chevron Corporation, 3M and National Iranian Oil Co. All large polluters. It made Anya sick.

Anya was also perplexed why her father ever hired Isiah Daniels and let him be promoted over many of the white employees who had worked for her father for years. When Isiah became President and CEO of his company, Anya was disappointed in her father and felt sorry for all the white MBA's who had worked hard for years at Jetta and were passed over by a black man. She often wondered if it was all political. Isiah was smart and, for the most part, a very nice guy, but she never pictured her father as a closet progressive liberal person. So why Isiah? Anya knew Isiah was capable, but she was extraordinarily surprised when Sophie married him. A black man. Anya's worse nightmare. Sophie did date a few black men, from time to time, when she was in college. Probably, Anya thought, that since a lot of them came to their home for dinner her father would approve of having some black men as friends. But marry one? Anya just never understood.

Anya knew her father was in politics and a black son-in-law was a good optic. But Sophie marrying a black man? But she still loved her sister dearly. Anya was very glad that her sister and Isiah decided not to have children. There were too many bi-racial children in the world, at least in Anya's mind. She was devastated when Sophie was murdered. Who would do such a thing and why? It had to be because she was married to a black man? Or was it a black man? Or was it even Isiah? Or was it someone from Sophie's work? After all she represented dozens of large corporations, some of which were the largest polluters in the world. She was very vocal about those facts. That made many people wonder about Anya. Even the detectives investigating the case had Anya on their suspect list. If they only knew the deep feelings Anya had for her sister. If there was anyone Anya would even consider killing, it would only have been Isiah.

Anya was so distraught over the events surrounding her sister's death, she finally realized she couldn't drive alone. She went to see one of her oldest friends who lived in one of the University's apartment complex at the same time she did, Deena Hawkins. She told her the situation and Deena agreed to drive Anya to her parent's home. Deena had received her MBA in business administration. She would take a couple of sick days from her regular job and as a teaching assistant, so she had a couple of days to help her good friend. Anya cried nearly the full two hours it took to drive to her parent's house. Shelia Taylor welcomed Deena to stay with them even though their home was the center of chaos. It took several minutes for both of them to get through the crushing news press outside the Taylor home. Deena felt very out of place knowing who Anya's father was, but she kept herself out of the way in slept in Sophie's old room.

Anya confronted her father, "How did this happen? Where did it happen? Do the police have a possible suspect?"

"Anya go lie down. We'll explain everything as soon as we find out," answered her father.

It was very late by the time Anya and Deena arrived in Boca Raton. They were both exhausted.

"Trust me, I have spoken to the highest police authorities in the State and they confirmed that the current detectives working the case are some of the best in the State. They will find out who and why some pervert did this to your sister."

"Was Isiah involved?

"Why would you think that?" asked her mother. "What a strange thing to say. Isiah and Sophie had a wonderful relationship." But Donavon heard that and he thought about it for a while and wondered the same thing. Was Isiah involved? He just couldn't ignore the thought.

Anya turned to her father. "Isiah is black. People in the Taylor world didn't have inter-racial marriages. You know that. You even promoted him to run your company. Don't you think some of your long time white employees would have been upset?" asked Anya, as she wouldn't leave the subject alone.

"Stop that kind of talk right now," interrupted her mother. "Your father doesn't work for Jetta anymore. Even if he did, why would Isiah murder Sophie? Please just go to sleep."

But Donovan couldn't get that thought out of his head. He knew that Isiah had been hiring many new black employees. Some of them were business majors or even MBA's from mediocre schools. He was promoting them over the white Ivy League MBA's that Donovan had hired years ago. What was happening at Jetta? He had carefully reviewed all of the financials of the business that he received as a minority shareholder. Recently several plants were having some unproductive quarters while the rest of the business was booming. Did Isiah understand that? What was he doing about it? Was that why he was in Durham when Sophie was murdered? Or was it an alibi? Was

Isiah embezzling money? Was he having an affair? Did Sophie find out about it? Donovan was having some bad thoughts.

Anya still couldn't leave the issue alone. She thought about it for hours. Where was Isiah? She didn't see him in the house at all. Why was he not with the family? He must be involved? She thought about that for a long time before she finally fell asleep. Deena also couldn't sleep. She didn't know what she had just gotten herself into. She just agreed to drive Anya home and all Hell was breaking loose inside and outside the Taylor home. Anya's sister was brutally murdered. Why was she there? Several hours later she finally fell asleep. The next morning was not going to be pleasant. Deena wanted to leave the home as soon as she could. Little did she know that the chaos would also be thrust on her?

⟹▶●◀⟸

Isiah woke up early. He knew he had to speak to the detectives who had left several messages for him on his phone. He also needed to contact a private pathologist to perform an autopsy on Sophie and then call Donovan with their contact information. Donavan was a difficult man who always covered all his bases. If Isiah hired the wrong pathologist, he knew he would hear about it for some time. He also promised Donovan that he would handle the investigation for the family. He realized that morning that would be a problem. Donovan would never agree with the manner Isiah handled that task.

First things first. Isiah called Morgan Blackburn. It was 8:30 that morning.

"Where have you been Mr. Daniels?" said Morgan very sternly. "Didn't you know your wife was murdered yesterday? We have been trying to find you all night. Where in the Hell are you?"

"Give me a break," said Isiah mockingly, "you knew damn well that I was in North Carolina when I heard about the event. I can't just magically show up at your whim. I got back here as fast as I could. I went to the Medical Examiner's office, but you had already left. My home was a murder scene so I went to a hotel for the night. It was very late. My wife was murdered. I was distraught."

"You talk as if the murder of your wife was an event? Said Morgan. "It was a brutal murder. We want to speak with you as soon as possible."

"You attitude is ridiculous! I know my wife was murdered and your ignorant comments are not appreciated," said Isiah. "I'll meet you wherever and whenever you want. Just tell me where and when. And I would appreciate it if you would speak to me in a respectful manner. Also, when you have uncovered any clues in solving this murder I am the person you deal with. I am the person who is handling the investigation for the family, not my father-in-law. Do you understand?"

Morgan wasn't quite sure if he could believe Isiah. From the short conversation he and his partner had with Donavan Taylor at the morgue the evening before, he was sure that Donavan Taylor was in charge. He would just see how things unfolded. Both detectives hoped that there wouldn't be any family arguments about the investigation. Since, the real truth was that Morgan and his partner were in charge of the investigation. And wherever the facts took them would be the final decision as to whom was going to be charged.

"Please come to the Boca Raton police department at 2:00 PM this afternoon and ask for either Morgan Blackburn or Darby Lynch. Will that be convenient for you Mr. Daniels?" said Morgan in a more civil manner.

"I'll be there," and Isiah hung up.

Morgan and Darby had made an appointment to speak with several of Sophia's law partners that morning. They weren't sure where that may lead. However, there was always an irate client or two as well as partners who were jealous of the victim's success due to her father's position. Or maybe someone in the firm didn't like a woman as their boss. Stranger things have happened. They were about to find out.

CHAPTER 9

The two detectives met with the two senior partners of Fischer & Logan P.A. in downtown Miami. Both Douglass Fischer and James Logan, the two original lawyers who started the firm 35 years ago met with both detectives in the main conference room on the 40th floor of the Miami Towers Building located on Brickell Avenue. There was a beautiful view from their main conference room to South Beach and the Atlantic Ocean.

"Can I get either of you some coffee or water or something to eat?" asked Fischer.

"No thanks, we're fine," said Morgan." As you probably know by now, we're here to speak with you about one of your partners, Sophie Daniels."

"What a shame," said Fischer. "A beautiful woman and brilliant legal mind lost forever."

"We are sorry for your loss. Ms. Daniels was brutally murdered recently at her home in Boca Raton," said Darby. "What can either of you tell us about Sophie? Did she have any enemies, clients or employees that complained about her or her work?"

"Not Sophie," replied Fischer, "she was very much liked by the entire staff, attorneys, administrative employees and especially her clients. She treated everyone well."

"Tell us about her clients?" said Darby. "We know she represented high profile clients and brought in a lot of fees for the firm? Any of them upset with her?"

"She did a fine job representing all of her clients and she did bring in a lot of fees," again replied Fischer. "She did, however, mention to the firm's Management Committee, that she may be in the process of dismissing one of her clients. All of us on the Committee found that a little unusual since it's usually the client that fires a firm."

"Oh, really," remarked Darby, "and which client was that?"

Both Fischer and Logan looked at each other and were a little embarrassed when Fischer finally said, "Jetta International."

"Wasn't that her father's Company?" asked Morgan.

"Well, technically it was his Company," answered Fischer. "He is still a minority owner of the Company. When he took the Company public he sold a lot of his stock after the required waiting period. As you know, Donovan Taylor retired from Jetta and ran for the State Legislature. He is currently Speaker of the House for the State. His son-in-law, Isiah Daniels, is presently the President and CEO of the Company."

"Well, that's a strange coincidence? Donovan Taylor leaves the Company and his son-in-law takes over running a publically owned company," remarked Darby as she turned to look at James Logan. "By the way, you haven't said a word Mr. Logan. Do you have any idea why Ms. Daniels would want to fire her own husband's Company? They must have been a very good client. I understand they are a large publically held company. They must have provided a ton of fees for the firm."

Logan looked at his partner as if to say to him that he should answer the detective's question.

Fischer, after a few long seconds, finally answered the detective's question. "A couple of days ago, we had a Management Committee meeting and Sophie, who was a member, was present. She told the Committee that she may be in the process of possibly firing Jetta International. We were all quite surprised. We all knew her relationship with the Company and it was one of the firm's largest clients for production of fees. Several of the Committee members pressed her on why she would fire them? All she would say was that she would give the Management Committee a formal response after she confirmed several matters and had a discussion with her husband. She insisted on speaking with her husband before she told the Committee her reasoning. It was quite strange, especially since that Company's fees were a large part of Sophie's compensation."

"So, as of today, neither of you have any idea why Jetta International was maybe going to be fired?" asked Darby. "How about you Mr. Logan, again, you haven't uttered a word."

"That's because I have nothing to add."

"You don't know anything more or you don't want to tell us anything more?" questioned Morgan.

"I think we have told you everything we know," said Fisher, taking Logan off the hook. "If there is anything further you may need from us feel free to call me direct. Here is my direct number," as Douglass Fischer handed Morgan his business card. "We need to contact all of Sophie's clients and assign them to new attorneys and try to keep as many as possible with our firm. That includes Jetta International since they haven't officially been fired."

"Are you sure that there isn't something you may want to tell us now Mr. Logan?" asked Darby. "Now would be the time. If you know something about the firing of Jetta International or Donovan Taylor or Isiah Daniels that may affect Sophie Daniels murder it would be much easier on you, and the firm, if you told us now. Then we would be able to help you," said Morgan very convincingly.

"We don't know any more than you do detectives," said Fischer very harshly, as he showed the detectives to the exit.

As the two detectives were in the elevator on the way to their car in the parking ramp, Morgan and Darby were both certain that James Logan knew something, but wasn't willing to share it.

"I think I'll talk to someone at our office before we meet Isiah to look into James Logan and give us a report on his background," said Darby, "I feel sure he knows something about all this. Maybe he knows something concerning Sophie's reasoning concerning Jetta. We need to find out."

"I agree, I also could tell that something was bothering him," said Morgan.

———— ⟫●⟪ ————

Before going to the detective's office early that afternoon, Isiah called a private pathologist. He did some quick research on who was considered the best pathologist in the State of Florida. His sources all told him that The Autopsy Doctor Company out of Tampa Florida was considered the State's best. Isiah contacted them and told their office manager the circumstances of his wife's death and who his father-in-law was. Dr. Benedict Hawkler was then recommended to do the autopsy. The office manager recommended that Isiah make arrangements to have his wife's body transported to The Autopsy Doctor's lab for the autopsy and all toxicology tests. Isiah told the manager that he would call them back as soon as the Palm Beach County coroner's office had completed their autopsy and tests.

Isiah then called his father-in-law to discuss the autopsy and told him the name of the pathology firm he had retained to do the private autopsy along with the doctor's name. They also discussed the final arrangements for his wife.

After the two finished those subjects of their conversation, Donovan said bitterly in a loud voice, "Where in the Hell are you boy? Shouldn't you be here, at my home, handling the investigation?"

"I am at the Ritz Carlton, Donovan," replied Isiah in a calm voice, "I couldn't go home last night after I saw you and Shelia at the morgue. My home is a crime scene. I was exhausted and it was too late to call anyone to take care of anything. So I went to the hotel and went to bed. I was Sophie's husband and also devastated by her death. I needed to be alone for a while. Your home is crowded and the press is everywhere. I have already been in touch with the detective's handling the investigation and I am meeting them in a few hours. As I just told you, I have arranged for a very highly recommended private pathologist to handle the private autopsy as soon as the body is ready to be moved from the County's morgue. I will be calling Gardens of Boca Raton Memorial Park to make arrangements for a small family service and burial in the Taylor plot. A public service is out of the question Donavan. I will not have hundreds of people, and the press, at my wife's funeral. Is there anything else you want to say to me?"

"I want a copy of the County's autopsy report plus the results of every toxicology test that was performed. I want to know the cause of death and where the Hell the police are in apprehending the perpetrator or perpetrators," replied Donavan. "Then get over to my home immediately after you talk to the detectives. I want a full update. Do you understand me boy?"

Isiah paused for a few seconds and then replied, "I'll be there when I can get there. Sophia was my wife and I will do what I believe is necessary. Do you understand that sir?"

Donavon immediately hung up. Isiah was furious. What had changed Donovan's attitude towards Isiah? He didn't even ask about the office or anything to do with the business. Isiah then thought about how very difficult it was for a parent to lose a child. He remembered when his brother Kimbel died and how difficult it was for both his parents. Maybe Isiah should give Donovan some time and a little bit of room? But he was going to tell him to stop calling him boy. He had earned Donovan's respect over the years, even if he was black. No one was going to call him boy anymore. However, in the back of Isiah's mind, he believed that Donovan may have thought that he had something to do with Sophie's death. He needed to get the detectives working to find the bastard that murdered his wife. Until then, he and Donovan may not have the relationship they had in the past, even if that relationship was mediocre at times.

Isiah then called the funeral home. He spoke with Darrin Cole, the owner and funeral director for Gardens at Boca Raton Memorial Park. Mr. Cole and Donovan Taylor knew each other well. Donovan had purchased family plots in the most exclusive area in the Park for his family and their spouses and children. He had also been the largest donor for the Park and sponsored a fund raiser for the Park every year. Isiah had met Mr. Cole at several of the fund raisers and

Mr. Cole remembered Isiah who also contributed funds to the Park each year. Isiah knew that Darrin Cole knew a lot of people, mostly as acquaintances, due to his position at the funeral park. He was sure Mr. Cole remembered him only because he was the only black person at all of the fund raisers each year.

Mr. Cole gave his condolences to Isiah and made a comment that it was unfortunate that they needed to speak under the current circumstances. Isiah thanked him and explained how he would like the funeral to be conducted. Grave side with only family and maybe a few friends, but no more than 30 people. He asked Mr. Cole to say a few words and also to contact the Taylor family reverend, at their church, to conduct the service. Mr. Cole understood and said he would take care of everything. He would arrange for their best coffin and all of the embellishments. Any flowers that may be sent to the funeral park would be forwarded to Donovan's home. Isiah asked Mr. Cole to order six dozen yellow roses to be placed strategically at the grave site for the funeral. They were Sophie's favorite.

Lastly, Isiah told Mr. Cole about the private autopsy. Isiah wasn't certain when that would be completed in order to set the funeral date. Isiah told Mr. Cole that he would call him when he had a date certain and then the flowers should be ordered. An obituary was being drawn up by the funeral home. All of the necessary general information had been given to Mr. Cole some time ago with all family member's information. The funeral home would email the preliminary draft to Isiah at his personal email address for Isiah to add any additional information or make any corrections. He was going to email a copy to Donovan since he believed that would be an important issue to him, however, he didn't mention that fact to Isiah. It was a pleasant talk and Isiah instructed Mr. Cole to either call Isiah or email him directly if he had any questions. Isiah made it clear that he alone was to finalize everything. If Donovan, or anyone else, were to call the director about Sophie's funeral, Isiah told Mr. Cole to direct them to Isiah. Mr. Cole understood the instructions. However, Mr. Cole would never turn down any request that Donovan would make. Again, he didn't mention that to Isiah.

"I appreciate your cooperation concerning this funeral, Mr. Cole. Be sure to send the entire bill to my office address. My home is still a crime scene and may be for some time," said Isiah.

"No problem sir," said Mr. Cole, "however, I just want you to know that Mr. Taylor had contacted me a few hours ago."

"What did he want?"

"He wanted to come and see me about the funeral arrangements in a few days," replied Mr. Cole.

"You do understand that it is my wife that I am burying. And I am paying for this. You can be cordial to Mr. Taylor, but, as I said, refer him to me about any of the funeral matters."

"I understand, but Mr. Taylor can be quite demanding."

"You can be a convincing man yourself, Mr. Cole. I'm sure you can handle the situation," replied Isiah and he then hung up.

After those conversations it was time for Isiah to meet with the detectives. He got in his car and started toward the Boca Raton police station. He wondered if the detectives had identified the killer and found out the motive. He would soon find out a lot more than that.

CHAPTER 10

Several days after Sophie's death, the Miami police received a call from Amy Sutherland, a tenant in a rundown apartment on the 1700 block of NW 1st Court in Overtown concerning an unusual smell coming from the adjacent apartment. Sutherland had knocked on the door several times that day but no one answered.

"Are you certain that the tenant hasn't just left town for a few days and left some food out that may have rotted?" asked the desk Sergeant at the police station.

"It's not that kind of smell," said Sutherland. "I tried to call the management company but they said that they couldn't get here for several days. It's typical for management to show up on time to get their rent, but it's impossible to get them to do anything else around here."

"Well what is it exactly you want us to do Ms. Sutherland?" asked the Sergeant.

"I can't live this way anymore. And I'm afraid the tenant may be badly hurt or even, God forbid, deceased."

"Do you know this person or have this person's telephone number?" asked the Sergeant.

"I believe his name is Clayton Reed. He is a tall black man who, I believe, used to play basketball years ago. He plays all the time at the playground next door. I don't believe he has a job. He usually has people coming and going from his place all the time. I haven't seen anyone around for several days. He may have a cell phone, but I have no idea. Please come and check it out. Please," begged the tenant.

"Give me your name, address and telephone number and I'll call you back in a few minutes," replied the Sergeant.

Amy Sutherland gave the Sergeant all of her information he asked for. As soon as he hung up he went into his desk computer and checked out Clayton Reed. Mr. Reed had a long list of misdemeanors and several felonies allegations. Mostly dealing with the distribution or use of various narcotics and several minor assaults. He was a 47 year old black man. He must have had a good lawyer. He spent very little time in the local Miami holding cells. He was always bailed out within 24 hours. The person who bailed Reed out each time was Isiah Daniels. Reed was never tried on any of the crimes and was always released with the charges dropped. His lawyer was Sophie Daniels of the Fisher & Logan Law Firm.

The Sergeant thought that all of that was a little strange but something about it vaguely came to his mind. Then he remembered an All City basketball and football player named Isiah Daniels from his high school days. In fact, the Sergeant thought he may have played football against him once or twice. He was a hard man to tackle. The Sergeant called several officers over to the precinct desk and asked them about this Isiah Daniels. Some of them remembered him. He played point guard for the University of Miami. Clayton Reed also played for Miami. A coincidence? Both were great ball players but their teams just didn't have enough talent to make it to the 'Big Dance'. Several even remembered his coach, Mickey Conrad, who eventually got fired allegedly for never making March Madness. Daniels never turned pro but instead went to work for some big company, but none of the officers knew its name.

"Do any of you know a lawyer named Sophie Daniels?" asked the Sergeant.

"I'll check my computer base to see what I can find out about her?" said the IT employee for the department. "Why do you need to know Sergeant?"

"Not sure yet, but there is something a little out of the ordinary going on with this guy Clayton Reed. Now do I have two volunteers to go see a little old lady on the 1700 block of NW 1rst Court in Overtown about some strange odor coming from Clayton Reed's apartment?"

No one volunteered.

"How about you two, Edwards and Schmidt. You don't look like you're doing much. I'll call the lady and tell her your coming. Here is her information."

"Shit, why do we always get the bottom of the barrel assignments Serge?" asked Abbey Schmidt.

"Just shut up and go. Mrs. Sutherland is waiting for us."

Isiah arrived at the Boca police department just after 2:00 that afternoon. He asked to see detectives Blackburn and Lynch. He said he had an appointment. The desk Sergeant called Morgan Blackburn's office to tell him that there was someone at the desk to see him and detective Lynch. Isiah was then escorted to an interrogation room.

"Glad to meet you Isiah," said Darby, "you're a hard person to find. You don't mind if we turn on the camera. It's just police policy."

"Why? Am I in an interrogation room? Is that a two way mirror? And why are you recording this?" asked Isiah. "Am I a suspect?"

"Well, let's just say you're a person of interest," answered Darby.

"Why would you think that I murdered my wife? We have been happily married for nearly 15 years. We both had our professions, a wonderful marriage and everything was going perfect until some deranged man broke into my home and brutally murdered my wife early in the morning yesterday. Where do I fit into that scenario?" questioned Isiah.

"We just want to talk to you," said Morgan. "We just want to eliminate suspects. As you know the spouse is always a suspect. That's all we're saying."

"Okay, I understand that. Especially if he's black right? But why the interrogation room and why are you recording this?"

"Just police procedure," said Morgan, "you can understand that, can't you?"

"So what is it you want to know from me? I thought this was a burglary gone badly? Do you know who the person is that murdered my wife? How did he get into the development? And how did he get into my home? Did he break in?"

"Let's take it one step at a time," said Darby. "First, where were you the night of your wife's murder?"

"I was in Durham, North Carolina at my company's plant meeting with all of the management personnel for the plant. That meeting had been set weeks ago. I was to be there for three days, but a phone call from my office about my wife changed that schedule. You already know that. I went to see my in-laws at the County morgue that night. I arrived late. It took me some time to get from Durham to the Palm Beach airport. Neither of you two were at the morgue when I arrived. You had already left. I had a difficult discussion with my father-in-law and agreed to take over monitoring this investigation. Then, stupidly I drove home. It was late. I was confused. My wife had just been murdered. I didn't even think about the fact that my home was a crime scene. After I saw the police tape I drove to the Ritz Carlton and booked a room until I could return home. So who murdered my wife?"

"Why the Ritz?" asked Morgan. "There are dozens of good hotels closer to your house?"

"My company uses that hotel for gatherings and meetings. We put up our clients and employees at the hotel. My wife and I go there for weekends to get away. Everyone knows me there. Why is that important?"

"The person who murdered your wife worked at the Ritz for a short period. That was just last year after he was released from the Broward County holding facility for shoplifting. He was a bus boy during breakfast in the all-day restaurant. Here is a picture of him, do you know him?" asked Darby.

"So you do know who murdered my wife. No, I do not know this man. I do not remember ever seeing him at the Ritz. Who is he and how did he get in my house? Why my wife?" questioned Isiah as he almost started to cry.

"The man that murdered your wife is a career criminal and not a very smart one. He has committed a half a dozen small crimes, spent some time in prison, but never did anything like this before," said Morgan. "In fact you and he have a mutual friend. And by the way, he didn't break into your home. He knew exactly where your extra key was hidden under the flower pot at the side door."

"What exactly are you saying? Hardly anyone knows about that key. And who is the person we know in common. I can't believe that can be possible."

"Your wife's killer has several names," said Darby as she looked Isiah straight in the eyes. "But you know him as 'Dusty' Francis. Does that ring a bell? His real name is Mason Francis. He is 39 years old and from a neighborhood adjacent to Overtown, the same place you grew up. In fact he only lived about a mile or so from you when you grew up. You may have even gone to high school together."

"Now I know you're playing games with me," uttered Isiah, "I don't know any Dusty or Mason Francis. He is younger than I am. I never saw him at my elementary or high school. If he didn't live in Overtown he wouldn't have gone to school there. Explain to me what is going on? Is this some type of interrogation to try to trick me into confessing to have hired this Dusty, or whatever his name is, to kill my wife? If it is, it's not working. Why would I kill my wife? Do you actually have this Dusty in custody? If so, I want to see him."

"Why would a smart guy like you, who has everything in the world going for you, hire a 39 year old white friend from an area around your old neighborhood to kill your wife? Did you really think you would get away with it?" calmly said Morgan. "Was it because your father-in-law was having a difficult time getting sufficient resources to run for Governor? Did he blame you because people who give large sums of money to politicians don't back a candidate whose daughter married a black man?"

"That is all ridiculous," shouted Isiah, "enough with the games. And what does me being black have to do with anything? Why would I kill my wife if my father-in-law was having trouble raising money? I didn't even know that. Both of you, and especially my father-in-law and me, know that none of this is true. This interview stops here. I know my rights. My wife was a lawyer for crying out loud. Either arrest me or I am leaving. And the first place I am going is to see Donovan Taylor and straighten this out," as Isiah got up from the interrogation table and started to walk to the exit.

Just before Isiah walked out of the room, Darby said to Isiah, "Do you know Clayton Reed?"

Isiah stopped in his tracks. "What did you just say?"

"Clayton Reed, do you know him?

"This must be a dream. I haven't seen or talked to Clayton in some time."

"But you know him, right?" again asked Darby.

"Of course I know him. When I was an undergraduate at the University of Miami, a long time ago, he was my roommate. We played basketball together. I haven't seen or heard from him for some time. I have no idea where he even lives. And what does Clayton Reed have to do with anything? This is getting stranger by the minute. If you want to talk to me again, call my lawyer. I'm going to see Donovan." And Isiah left the building.

When Isiah got in his car he immediately called his mother. She answered the phone after two rings.

"Mom, I have to ask you a question."

"Isiah, where have you been? And how are you doing? I still can't believe what I am hearing about Sophie. It's all over the TV."

"This is no joke mom."

"I know and I'm so sorry about Sophie. I just couldn't believe it when the police came to see me and told me about it. But you can still be civil when you speak to your mother."

"Mom, did the police talk to you about someone named Mason Francis?"

"Why yes. Your father and I knew Mr. and Mrs. Francis years ago. They were a very nice white family. Both passed some time ago. Misses died of cancer and Mister died of an infected leg injury at work. Why do you ask?"

"Did they have a son Mason? And did he go to high school with me?"

"That is exactly what the police asked us. I told them that they did have a son Mason, but you and he weren't friends. I never heard you speak of him and he was never at our house. I knew everyone you brought to our house. You all played basketball and football in the street for hours."

"Did the police ask you anything else?"

"Not really, just if any of your brothers or sisters were friends with Mason. I told them that I wasn't really sure, since I never met the boy and don't recall any of my children mentioning his name."

"Thanks Mom. I appreciate it. I'll let you know the date and time for Sophia's funeral. I want both you and Dad, Evy, Nicki and Dakala there," said Isiah and he hung up.

Clover thought that was a very strange phone call. She still didn't understand. She just felt so bad for her son. How could someone kill that beautiful woman and take her from her son.

Isiah drove directly to Donovan's home. He just could not understand how Clayton Reed and someone from the neighborhood next to his could have been involved in the murder of his wife. And how did the murderer know about his spare key? Maybe he heard something when he worked at the Ritz when Sophie and Isiah were eating? So many questions. Donovan would know which lawyer Isiah should call for advice. Isiah kept telling himself that the police obviously were just trying to make sure Isiah had nothing to do with the murder. But they were surely going about it in a strange way. However, they never did tell Isiah that he was eliminated as a suspect. They probably wouldn't have said that even if it was true. Isiah knew he had to cover all bases. He was a smart man. He needed to retain a lawyer and somehow get the police off his back. They needed to be able to find the real killer or killers of his wife.

CHAPTER 11

Abbey Schmidt and Morton Edwards drove to the 1700 block of 1ʳˢᵗ Court in Overtown to meet with Amy Sutherland. When they arrived at Sutherland's apartment they found an elderly woman, 76 years old, well-groomed with an apartment that was decorated 30 years ago. Even though she had few possessions, everything was clean and in its place. She was very accommodating from the time she answered the door. It didn't take the officers very long to smell some odor coming from the next apartment. Overtown was one of the poorest neighborhoods in Miami-Dade County. However, years before, it was a high middle class location. Some of the original occupants from those older days, before the 'wrong' element started to move in, were still living in Overtown. Amy Sutherland was one of those people. She never wanted to move. Even when crime started to escalate in the area and drugs were being sold on nearly every corner, Ms. Sutherland looked the other way and kept to herself.

"Can you smell that odor coming from my neighbor's apartment? That is not food cooking. It has to be something else. I hope it's not very bad. Maybe someone is making drugs to sell. Would you please check it out? I can't stand it anymore."

"Do you know the name of your next door neighbor?" asked Abby. "Are you friendly with him?"

"His name is Clayton Reed. He's black you know. Not that I care. They all seem to be moving into this neighborhood these days. He has never bothered me since he moved in, but he always has people coming

86

and going all the time. Both black and white people. They aren't ever loud so it never really bothered me. I have spoken with Mr. Reed several times and he seemed to be very nice. He sure is tall."

The officers had not been on the job for a long period of time, but they had been patrolman for several years and had smelled the odor of dead bodies several times. They thought that may be the case in the next apartment. They didn't have a warrant to go into Clayton' Reed's apartment, but the possible odor of a corpse was an extenuating circumstance that would allow them to break in to see what was causing the smell, even without a warrant. Morton Edwards, however, decided to call his desk Sergeant and confirm their right to check out the apartment without a warrant. They were told to do it immediately.

The officers asked Ms. Sutherland to stay in her apartment. The two patrol officers then went to break in to the apartment when they noticed that the door was unlocked. Lucky break. Abby Schmidt took out some vanilla extract she had in her pocket and put it under her nose and gave some to her partner to eliminate breathing in the obnoxious odor. Officer Edwards thought they were supposed to use Vicks vapor rub, but no one had any. However, the vanilla extract worked fine. When the officers open the door, the entire apartment was a mess. The stench was bad. They found Clayton Reed dead lying with the upper part of his body lying on his dining room table. He had been dead for some time. He was shot, execution style, with a single bullet to the back of his head.

Officer Edwards immediately called Miami CSI to come to the apartment to examine the scene for any evidence as to how and who may have killed Clayton Reed. The officers knew not to touch anything. They immediately put up crime scene tape across the front door. That was the only way in or out of the apartment. Officer Schmidt did notice a shell casing on the floor next to the stove. Obviously the killer was not a professional. She took a pencil and picked it up and placed it in an evidence bag. It looked like a 9 millimeter shell casing. CSI would be able to check the type of gun used and determine if there were any prints on the casing.

In 15 minutes CSI showed up and started their examination of the body and apartment. The coroner also arrived and waited for CSI to finish their tasks. The coroner was getting ready to take the body to the County morgue for an autopsy. One of the CSI officers indicated that Clayton had been dead for at least a full day or maybe longer. The autopsy would confirm that. The two police officers then started to canvas the building to see if anyone saw anyone enter the apartment or hear a gunshot in the last few days. They had no luck. Most of the people they spoke with were black and knew Clayton. They were all very surprised. They played basketball together just down the street.

After a short while, a CSI officer found, under the dining room table $21,400.00 mostly in $50.00 bills all with nonconsecutive numbers. They would check the bills for fingerprints. They also found a piece of paper with the name and number of Dusty Francis. Also written on the paper were the words '$1,500.00 for the job, meet at 10:30 McDonalds on Moapa Boulevard in Overtown'. CSI would also check for fingerprints on the note. Several CSI personnel went out to canvass the area for a possible murder weapon. They checked garbage bins and street water drains. That search was successful. A 9 millimeter Glock 26 with one round fired was found in a sewer drain a block away. The patrol man knew that he had probably found the murder weapon. No one else would toss a perfectly good weapon in a sewer, at least not in that neighborhood.

It didn't take long for Officer Edwards to check his computer in his car concerning this case. He was a little surprise to see an all point bulletin for a Mason "Dusty" Francis from the Boca Raton police. What did that have to do with Clayton Reed? Edwards called the Boca police and was directed to detective Darby Lynch. She was informed about Clayton Reed, the note as well as the cash that were found in his apartment. Darby was confused at first, but told officer Edwards not to touch a thing and a she and her partner would be in Overtown as soon as possible. She also wanted Clayton's body for her pathologist to do the autopsy, but Edwards didn't have that authority. She was told to call the Miami-Dade County morgue.

It only took Isiah 20 minutes to get to Donovan's home. When he arrived, there were masses of press yelling questions at him. Only Donovan, his wife, Anya and Deena were in the home. Donovan had four private security vehicles with two private security agents in each car outside the home. It took Isiah nearly 10 minutes to get approved to get in the home. Donovan, always the politician, wanted to keep the press and even his political friends and especially his political enemies away from his home until after the funeral. However, every news agency in Florida and even several of the National cable and network news agencies were reporting on the murder of the Florida Speaker of the House's daughter.

There was speculation by many on the cable networks that it may have been a family member who may have hired Mason 'Dusty' Francis to murder Sophie Daniels. Where they got that name or information none of the reporters were saying. However, every interview by a reporter with any police authority indicated a 'no comment' or said that the investigation was ongoing. Donovan was furious with the Boca police as well as his son-in-law who was to take care of keeping the press away and to silently be responsible to find out the real facts of the murder. The one bizarre fact was that Dusty Francis wasn't even in custody yet. How did the press know about him?

"How in the world did this circus start concerning my daughter's murder?" Donovan was screaming at Isiah. "How are we ever going to find out the true facts of this horrible event now that the press is speculating about everything? And who in the Hell is this Dusty Francis and how did the press know about him?"

Isiah looked at Donovan and tried as hard as he could to stay calm and said, "They think I did this Donovan. How and why would they think that? I need to hire a savvy criminal lawyer. Someone who can straighten this mess out and help me find the real killers."

"Don't come to me for help you lazy, good for nothing nigger!" again shouted Donovan.

"Stop that kind of talk Donovan," said Shelia. "You have no right to say those things to your son-in-law. You have worked with him and admired him for what he has done for this family and business for the last 16 years. And when did you all of a sudden become this much of a bigot? You have hated blacks for a long time, but this time you have gone over the top."

"He may be right Mom," interjected Anya who was listening to the conversation. "Black men are inherently vicious and mean. Present company excluded maybe."

"You too Anya? Where is all this coming from? I seem to be in a home where I really don't know who most of you are. Maybe I have always been in the wrong house."

"Nonsense Isiah," said Shelia, "you are one of the best things that happen to Sophie and everyone in her family knows that. Everyone is just a little upset right now."

"Thank you Shelia. I'm not really sure about the rest of you. I don't know what I may have done to disgrace you, but this cold shoulder is really uncalled for. All of you know that I would never hurt Sophie."

Deena was listening to all of this in horror. She couldn't understand why this kind of conversation was happening when all that was supposed to be happening was a family mourning the loss of a wife, a daughter and a sister. They were all supposed to work with the authorities to find out how and why Sophie was murdered. After all Deena just gave Anya a ride home and now she has been asked by Anya to stay to help her through the funeral. Deena was not ready for this kind of conflict and bigotry among Anya's family members.

Deena went over to Isiah and introduced herself to him as a good friend of Anya. But what she had just heard from Anya, and her family, infuriated her. She asked Isiah if she could get her things and leave with him. He could take her to the Greyhound bus station so she could go back to Fort Myers. She no longer wanted to stay in that home.

Deena had heard enough and wanted to stay out of the family matters. Isiah was in shock and mystified. Who is the woman talking to me? Why does she want to leave with me? But Isiah was furious with Donovan and Anya. He wanted out. So he told Deena to get her things and he would take her where ever she wanted to go.

As Isiah was waiting for Deena, he looked at Donovan and said, "Where did you get the name Dusty Francis? And how did the press get that name? I just heard that name for the first time during my so called interview, which was in fact an interrogation, with the Boca detectives."

"I know everything that goes on. That stupid Dusty Francis left his DNA and fingerprints all over your house. He had a note that must have fallen out of his pocket during the encounter with Sophie. It had your name and Sophie's name and your address on it. It also had the date of her murder and the time 7:30 AM with an amount of $1,500.00 written on it. Is that all your wife was worth to you? The Boca detectives told me about the note. How much insurance have you got on her life? How much insurance does her law firm have on her life?" asked Donovan. "So tell me what your motive was? Why did you kill my little girl?" as Donavon broke down and started to cry.

Deena had just come back with her suitcase. Isiah wouldn't even answer his father-in-law. He just gave him a dirty look and said, "You really are an asshole. I defended you for years. I know a lot more about you than you would ever want the public to know. I also wouldn't put anything by you including even killing your own daughter. You're just a narrow-minded broken down old man who only wants power. You really hate blacks, but talk a good game if you can use them to your benefit. You can't even raise the necessary funds to run for Governor. Your friends won't even talk to you anymore unless they need a favor. They probably wouldn't even give you any money for your campaign when you asked. You have no feelings for anyone. I'm so sorry Sheila. But you know I had nothing to do with this. How dare your husband speak to me like that?"

Isiah picked up Deena's suitcase. They walked out the door, right through a large group of press yelling questions at them, and drove away.

—————»●«—————

It only took 1 hour for detectives Blackburn and Lynch to arrive at the Reed apartment in Overtown. They spoke with the CSI personnel who showed the detectives the money they found as well as the note by the telephone. There were dozens of fingerprints in the apartment which they would work on. There was also a 9 millimeter shell casing on the floor by the bed. There was a partial print on it. They also showed the detectives the Glock that was found a block away. Both Darby and Morgan knew that Sophie owned a 9 millimeter Glock 26. They needed to find out if it was the murder weapon and if it was Sophie's gun. Officer Edwards told both detectives they would let them know what they found out.

One of the CSI officers asked the detectives if this murder was connected to the murder of the Speaker of the House's daughter.

"It must be since we have determined that Dusty Francis was the guy who murdered the woman," said Morgan. "He was not what one would call a sophisticated criminal. He was just a small time punk near Isiah Daniels' old neighborhood, who got over his head when he worked his way up to a contract killing. And all for just $1,500.00! He left the crime scene in really bad condition. He was such a rookie. Whoever hired him had no sense at all. There were several persons who saw several cars leave the scene before the victim crawled over to her neighbor's home. One of those cars must have been Dusty's."

Dusty thought he could just sneak into the house since someone had told him that there was a spare key under a flower pot at the side door. So whoever hired Dusty knew the family. Dusty thought he would just go into the house, find Sophie and shoot her. What a stupid man. He did no research and had no idea that Sophie was into self-defense. She somehow must have gotten the gun out of his hand and it fell to the hard wood floor during a struggle. A piece of the handle broke off. Imagine using an antique wooden handled gun for a hit. Really stupid. His blood was all over the house. His car had to be full of blood. The local police will canvas all the gas stations around the victim's home where there was a washroom and car wash. It took them only two hours to find his bloody clothes along with the gun he threw in a garbage bin at the gas station. His blood was still in the sink in the wash room. It was a Smith & Wesson model 617 and a piece of wood was broken off the gun. The piece found at the victim's home fit the broken handle perfectly. What a stupid man. There is an all-points bulletin out for his car and for Dusty. He won't get far."

"So how does Clayton Reed fit into all this?" asked the CSI officer?

"We'll figure it out," said Morgan. "From just what you told me today someone probably paid Reed somewhere in the neighborhood of $25,000.00 to murder Sophie Daniels. Reed couldn't or didn't want to kill her, so he hired a stupid and cheap small time crook who lived near Isiah Daniel's neighborhood to do the deed for just $1,500.00. Then Reed kept the rest. But then someone murdered Reed. Was it Dusty? Or did some third person tell Reed to hire someone from the husband's old neighborhood to do the deed in order to push the police in the wrong direction? Either way, someone killed Reed and he is involved in this case somehow. After all, he was a pusher, mostly broke and a bad guy. He was always panhandling for money. He actually thought, a long time ago, that he would be drafted by an NBA team. Not even close. His life went downhill after playing big time college basketball. He picked up jobs where ever he could and even sold a little dope on the side, but not enough to get pinched by the police. Obviously, the person who murdered Reed didn't want him talking. We'll figure it out," said Darby.

"We'll call you directly Detective Lynch as soon as we have the results of the autopsy and all our reports on the scene of Reed's murder," said one of the CSI officers.

"Great, but the cause of death seems fairly obvious. A bullet to the back of his head. We're still working the case, so keep us informed of anything that may come up, especially if it's unusual. We have a couple of suspects and several more people to interview. Thanks for all your help."

"Oh, by the way there is one other matter that may help, said Officer Schmidt. "We checked Reed's criminal sheet. He had been arrested several times on various minor matters. Each time he was bailed out by Isiah Daniels. He never was convicted of any of those charges. His attorney was Sophie Daniels, your homicide victim, I presume."

"Really? Now that's more than a coincidence. Thanks. Send me a copy of Reed's sheet."

That last comment really put both detectives' antennas up. Isiah had been adamant that he had nothing to do with his wife's murder. He seemed to be pushing the police in all different directions. He had to be close with Clayton Reed to bail him out and have his wife represent him. Isiah had to be the prime suspect. Both detectives agreed. Now all they had to do was prove it.

CHAPTER 12

Isiah and Deena were on their way to the Greyhound bus station for Deena to go back to Fort Myers. While driving there, Deena was a little afraid to say something to Isiah, but she finally did.

"I understand that you may be looking for a local criminal lawyer. I didn't mean to over hear your conversations with your family, but my brother is supposed to be a very good criminal lawyer and has his office in downtown Fort Lauderdale. He has handled all kinds of criminal matters including dozens of murder cases. Again, I don't mean to be presumptuous, since you may have another lawyer in mind, and I don't mean to intrude, but if you want to just speak to him I am sure I can arrange it."

"I know I'll need a criminal lawyer sooner or later. The Boca detectives were quite fixed on me as one of their main suspects," said Isiah. "I really appreciate your suggestion. At least that would be a place to start. Would you call him for me and set up a meeting tomorrow or the next day? I really mean that and I appreciate your help."

"Of course. Maybe I'll give him a call now and tell him I am in town. Then I could even have a chance to see him, his wife and kids. It's been a while," said Deena. "Maybe he can pick me up at the Greyhound station. I'll give him a call right now."

"Why are you doing this for me? You don't even know me," asked Isiah.

"I know Anya. And she is being an ass about all this and was treating you like a low life. I can tell that's not the case," replied Deena.

"Anya has told me about you running her father's business and how you've grown it. I didn't have any clue she was such a bigot. I really thought I knew her."

Just as Deena started dialing her phone, Isiah saw red flashing lights in his rear view mirror. Then several burst of a siren sounded out. Isiah was being pulled over by the Boca police. Isiah thought, not again.

Isiah pulled over to the side of the road and the police car parked right behind him. One of the two police officers walked up to Isiah's car and knocked on the side window and told Isiah to roll down the window.

"Drivers license and registration, sir."

As Isiah was retrieving those items he asked the officer, "Why am I being pulled over officer? You know who I am. We have met several times before. I live near this neighborhood."

The officer ignored what Isiah had just said. "There have been some burglaries in the neighborhood and you seem to match the description of one of the perps. What are you doing in this neighborhood driving such an expensive car?" questioned the officer.

"You have to be kidding. I live here officer, you know that. You stopped me before and we have chatted. Why are you doing this?" asked Isiah, "You know I own this car. You may have heard, my wife, Sophie Daniels, was the woman who was just murdered several days ago," as Isiah gave him his license and registration.

"Who's the white woman with you?"

Isiah then explained that he was just at Donovan Taylor's home. He is the current Speaker of Florida's House of Representatives, and Isiah's dead wife's father. He explained that Deena was a good friend of Mr. Taylor's younger daughter. Isiah was just taking her to the Greyhound station so she could take a bus back to Fort Myers. The officer looked carefully at Isiah's driver's license and then turned his flashlight in Isiah's face, and then in Deena's face.

"Please get out of your car Mr. Daniels," stated the officer, as the second officer got out of the police car and moved to the passenger door.

"What is this all about officer? Did someone put you up to this?" said Isiah as he was very confused. "My license and registration tells you that everything I said is true."

"As I indicated, there have been some burglaries in the area. I just need to find out if you are who your identification says you are," answered the officer. "This car may have been stolen along with the registration and driver's license."

"Have you received a report of a stolen Lexus?" asked Isiah.

"Don't be a wise ass. Just answer our questions."

The second officer said to Deena to also get out of the car. He asked her for her identification. She told him that her purse and Identification were in her suit case. Then both Isiah and Deena were handcuffed and put in the back of the police car.

"Are you doing this because I'm black and driving with a white girl in a rich neighborhood?" asked Isiah.

"Shut up boy, we'll check this out," as the officer started to type on his computer.

"Officer, call detective Morgan Blackburn or Darby Lynch. They can vouch for me," said Isiah.

Both officers laughed and found it humorous that a black man would know the names of two Boca detectives. They both thought that he must have been interrogated by them at some time.

"Does this happen often, Mr. Daniels?" asked Deena.

"Unfortunately it happens too many times," said Isiah, "These two officers know me well and will be apologizing to us in just a few minutes."

Deena then said to the officers, "Please uncuff me so I can call my brother. His name is Todd Hawkins, a criminal lawyer here in the area.

"Sure he is," said one of the officers, "and my brother is F. Lee Bailey!"

"Just leave it be Deena," said Isiah, "we'll be out of here in a few minutes."

Just then the officer on the computer indicated that he had confirmed the license and registration for Isiah who was correct about his wife who was murdered a few days ago. The officer told his partner to uncuff Deena and the officer on the computer uncuffed Isiah.

"We are sorry Mr. Daniels for the intrusion," said the officer, "it was just a mistake. We were just doing our jobs."

"As a black man that lives in this town, I am embarrassed for its police force. You both damn well knew me. Who asked you to stop any black men driving a fancy car tonight? Was it Donovan Taylor? Or was it one of your detectives who wanted me to believe that I am a criminal and looking for trouble. Whomever it was, I will find out."

Without even blinking, one of the officers said, "Again we're sorry sir, it won't happen again."

"Sure," said Isiah, "you white folk sure do dislike black people. I just don't understand. It must just make you feel superior in some crazy way."

"Well," said the first officer, "maybe your right. Maybe someone may be trying to send you a message?"

"And what would that be?" asked Isiah.

"I'm just a patrol cop. That's way above my pay grade," laughed the officer as he drove away.

Deena was scared the entire time. After Isiah thought about what the officer had just said to him, he drove off, and he calmed Deena down and indicated that things like that happen sometimes in Boca. However, Isiah was still trying to comprehend the statement the officer had just made to him. Deena was totally surprised a cop would speak to Mr. Daniels that way. She thought that in such a small town, most police would know the Taylors and the Daniels. She was naïve. She then called her brother and told him about Isiah and his wife as well as the incident she just went through.

Todd Hawkins was upset about the police stop and said he would look into it. But he was also enthused to be able to possibly represent Isiah. Sophie Daniels murder was national news. So they agreed to meet at Hawkins' office the next morning at 10:00 AM. Isiah told Hawkins he would take Deena to the Ritz and get her room for the night. He would then bring her with him the next morning to his office. Todd was very appreciative of Isiah doing something like that. Todd had heard good things about Isiah and his Company. He knew about his wife since she worked at one of the best known law firms in Florida. She was a star there. The murder had also been on the news constantly.

Deena had quite the day and more of a unique experience than she was up for. She had a quick late dinner with Isiah at the Ritz and then she went to her room. They agreed to meet for breakfast at 8:30 the next morning.

━━━►●◄━━━

Isiah went to his room and made some calls. First he called the manager of the Durham, North Carolina plant, Dijon Jackson. Isiah had explained why he had left so quickly and didn't finish the audit with him. The manager understood. He told Isiah that he had heard about Sophie through the Jetta gossip line and also on the news. He didn't seem very surprised, but gave Isiah his condolences and told him he would take care of everything until Isiah was ready to come back to work. Isiah appreciated that. He trusted his manager. Isiah was the person who promoted Dijon to his present position. He told him to continue to audit the books on those several strange accounts that they had talked about at the plant. Isiah wanted to go over them with him as soon as Sophie's funeral was over. Isiah was concerned that something may be wrong with those accounts, but wasn't quite sure what. He asked his manager to check if any of those particular accounts were also in any of the Company's other plants. He also wanted to know if any other new accounts had been opened at any of the other plants about the same time and with the same types of orders. The orders were quite large and very unusual. Dijon told Isiah that he would have a report ready for him in a few days. He told Isiah not to worry about it, he would handle things until Isiah was ready to discuss business. He knew Isiah had too many other matters on his mind at that particular time.

The manager Isiah was speaking with was a black man who Isiah had promoted over several white candidates for the job. The manager could tell by their conversation that Isiah may have been a suspect in his wife's murder. However, he didn't mention that to Isiah. He understood the plight black men have in large business situations and as CEO's of large companies. Plus it gave the manager some time to take care of the accounts that Isiah was concerned about. Since Dijon had control of those reports he could manipulate them in a manner that would make Isiah feel comfortable.

Next Isiah called the West Palm Beach County morgue to find out the status of Sophie's autopsy and if the body was ready to be released. He finally got the pathologist who performed the autopsy on the phone.

"Where have you been Mr. Daniels?" said the pathologist, "your wife's autopsy was completed sometime ago. You know it had been expedited. I am just writing up my reports. The toxicology report and the report on any DNA on the body and under your wife's fingernails have also been determined and sent to the detectives. I understand the detectives already know the name of the person who killed your wife. I have been told that every officer in the State is looking for him."

"Why didn't someone tell me this?" angularly said Isiah.

"Your father-in-law has all that information. I thought he would have told you," answered the pathologist.

"So when can I have the body picked up?" questioned Isiah.

"You really don't know what's going on do you?" sarcastically said the pathologist.

"What the Hell does that mean?" Isiah said harshly.

"The body has been picked up by The Autopsy Doctor, a private forensic pathology group so that Dr. Benedict Hawker could perform a private autopsy. You must know them. They told me you hired them," said the pathologist.

"What is going on? I don't understand."

"Ask your father-in-law, he consented to everything."

Isiah was furious.

"Please email me all of your reports with copies to Dr. Hawker as soon as they are complete," asked Isiah. "I need to get to the bottom of this," as Isiah hung up. He didn't even ask what the cause of death was or if she had been violated in some fashion. He was just mad. Someone was setting him up. But who? And Why? Was it Donovan?

Next Isiah called the funeral director, Darrin Cole, at the Gardens of Boca Raton Memorial Park.

"Mr. Cole, I should be able to let you know the date for my wife's funeral. The private autopsy is currently being performed."

"No need Mr. Daniels. Your father-in-law has already set the funeral for 11:00 AM two days from today," said Cole, "but he told me to have the funeral exactly the way you and I spoke of it."

"I thought that you were to deal with only me Mr. Cole?" asked Isiah.

"Well, dealing with you and dealing with Donovan Taylor are really about the same thing. I didn't feel right not speaking with him. After all, it was his daughter and he is the Speaker of the House," said Cole.

"Damn it Cole it's me and only me you were to deal with. I'm the one paying you. Do you understand? And what about the obituary?"

"Mr. Taylor reviewed it and made some changes. However, I haven't sent it to the newspapers yet."

"Don't do anything more with it until I review it. Understood?"

"Yes sir. I'm so sorry if I may have misunderstood anyone," admitted Cole as Isiah hung up.

After those two calls Isiah wasn't really in the mood to contact the detectives, but he wanted to make sure that they believed that he was cooperating in the investigation.

So Isiah picked up the phone and dialed the Boca police department. When the desk Sergeant answered, Isiah said, "May I speak with Darby Lynch or Morgan Blackburn, please, Isiah Daniels is calling?"

"Neither of them are here right know. May I leave a message?"

"Please tell them that I called and have them call me tomorrow afternoon so we can set up a meeting with my lawyer and me. And, by the way, thank them for having me detained tonight. Tell them that their tactics aren't going to work on me."

The Sergeant had no idea what that meant.

"I'll tell them as soon as I speak with one of them," said the confused Sergeant.

Isiah hung up. His head was twirling after his calls to the County pathologist and the funeral director. What was Donovan doing taking charge of the funeral? Donovan specifically told Isiah to do that. Who called the Boca police to make sure he was stopped that night and detained? That had not happened in a long time. All the police, in that area, knew Isiah and his wife and knew they lived in the neighborhood.

Something was going on. But what? And by whom? Isiah took a small bottle of Crown Royal out of the mini bar and had a drink. He hoped that Deena's brother was an experienced criminal lawyer with good credentials and that they could work well together. Then Isiah laid down and finally fell asleep about 20 minutes later. The next day would be a challenging day.

CHAPTER 13

At 8:30 the next morning Deena and Isiah met in the coffee shop at the Ritz for breakfast. Deena had not seen her brother, Todd, for quite some time. She was anxious to see and talk with him again and to renew her relationship with his wife, Kellie and her niece Donna who was 14 years old. After all they were her only family. Her father had a heart attack 7 years ago and her mother died of lung cancer soon thereafter. Those were bad days. Her and her brother seemed to drift away after their parent's death. Deena had not seen Kellie or Donna for nearly 3 years. She felt bad, but her life as a business woman was very important to her. And the few classes Deena could teach kept her very busy. That could only happen at FGCU and in growing Fort Myers.

Deena thought of excuses why she hadn't driven the 2 hours to come and see her family once in a while, but that seemed like a waste of time for her. The highway does go both ways. Anya understood that Deena and her only brother and his family had just, sort of, grown apart. That happens to families. Especially these days with families spread all over the Country. Sometimes a few hundred miles will just make it the right excuse not to see family. Both her and her brother had put their lives into their work. But after her incident with the police, Deena determined that time is more valuable. So this time she really wanted to have a good time and not dwell on the past. Seeing her family would be pleasant for her and she recognized that. Anya wasn't sure she felt quite the same.

Isiah was thinking about much different matters. His beautiful, loving wife was brutally murdered and the police believed he had something to do with it. How outrageous. He knew people always thought of him as a kind and gentle person. How could people think he was capable of something like that? If his father-in-law was turning on him, Isiah knew that it would be difficult to convince the detectives he was not involved. Donovan was one of the most powerful and ruthless men in Florida. Isiah again hoped that Todd Hawkins was the right lawyer. There were so many better law firms in the Miami/Fort Lauderdale area who had excellent criminal lawyers. However, so many of those firms had other lawyers that had represented Jetta International in different matters, or were on the opposite side, from time to time. It was very important that even the appearance of a conflict of interest should not be an issue in Isiah's defense. There were also other boutique criminal law firms, or sole practitioner criminal lawyers, in the area, but Isiah knew nothing about any of them. Some advertised on television for DUI representation, others for various other misdemeanors. Those were not the type of lawyers Isiah needed.

Isiah knew he would be receiving a call from one of the two detectives soon, so he kept his phone on. He didn't want any appearance that he was trying to avoid them. Even if he was with his lawyer when they called, he would at least have a valid excuse to set a time for all of them to meet.

Deena had called Kellie, who graciously agreed to pick Deena up at her husband's office and take her back to their home. It was only a few miles away. Kellie was very excited to have some time with her sister-in-law. Donna would be in school, but would be home by 3:00 and Kellie had planned to have Deena stay at their home for a few days. In that way Deena and Donna would also have substantial time together. So Deena called her employer and FGCU and told her supervisors that she would be out of town for a few more days on a personal matter. There wasn't a problem.

When Isiah and Deena arrived at Todd's law office, Isiah was a little surprised. Isiah expected a large law office with 10 or more employees on the 14th floor of a fancy high rise. The building wasn't rundown at all.

In fact, it was relatively new or renovated. It was just a two story office park on West Cypress Creek Road. There were 20 different business offices in the building. Todd was a sole practitioner. He did share his suite with a personal injury attorney. Between them Todd had three employees and the other lawyer had six employees. They just shared the space, receptionist, kitchen and conference room. Todd's employees consisted of a secretary and a paralegal. There were files everywhere. His filing system was not as organized as Isiah would have liked. But it wasn't Todd's administrative duties he was retaining. It looked as if Todd had a large practice. Kellie was in the small reception area and gave Deena a big hug when she saw her. Todd came out of his office and did the same and introductions were made all around. Todd was a little taken by the fact that Isiah was black. He actually knew that fact, but was surprised, for some reason, when he actually met him. Not that he hadn't represented his share of black defendants. But this man lived in Boca Raton. It just surprised him that he was black. After all, it was a beautiful rich white woman lawyer who was murdered. The daughter of Donovan Taylor. But Todd got over that initial feeling quickly. Once Deena and Kellie left, Todd and Isiah went into the conference room. Three of the walls had chestnut wood paneling. The other wall was painted beige. There was a large conference table that could sit a dozen. There were 12 very comfortable conference chairs around the table, all on wheels which swiveled easily. The receptionist had brought in waters, coffee and some pastries.

"Sit down Isiah. I need to get some basic information from you for my file before we get into the meat of your controversy," said Todd. "My sister told me about your police stop in Boca last night. Nearly scared her to death. She just wasn't used to something like that. I have made a few calls to see why that happened."

"And maybe you think I wasn't scared?" said Isiah. "A black man driving a Lexus in Boca Raton is not the norm and the local police tend to be very cautious, right?"

"I didn't mean any offense with that statement, I just indicated that my sister has always been very sheltered on the West Coast of Florida and in a University setting. I really didn't want to get off on a bad footing. I apologize if I offended you."

"You didn't offend me," said Isiah, "I'm used to it. Actually it happens more often than you think, unfortunately. There aren't many black CEO's of major Fortune 500 companies around and how are the police supposed to know that? Let me know if you hear anything about that stop. I appreciate your concern. And by the way, FGCU University is 18% black. I wouldn't even be surprised if your sister dated one or two of them. So let's just start over."

"I'm so sorry. I agree we'll start over."

"I didn't see, from your brochure, that you had any investigators on your staff," said Isiah. "I know you'll need a lot of investigation on my matter."

"Actually I have a contract with an investigation company here in town. They have 40 investigators. I work with one specific investigator on all my cases. He has a lot of contacts, both legitimate and non-legitimate. He tends to be very organized and prompt and has a good sense of what exactly I am looking for. I have found that it is a lot cheaper for me that way. It also works out better since some of his contacts are a little sketchy. You understand what I mean. It's also cheaper for my clients if I just utilize his services on an as needed basis," said Todd. "I hope that works for you?"

"No problem, just trying to cover my bases."

Isiah then poured himself a cup of coffee and took a French pastry and put it on one of the Lenox dishes provided and grabbed a napkin.

"Now what information do you need before we get started?"

Todd then started with background information. Isiah answered his questions by giving Todd most of his personal information, family information, job information, school background and contact information. Todd was adamant that Isiah be forthright and give him all the information he was asking for since Todd never knew when, and if, the smallest of details may make a big difference in finalizing a matter in his client's favor. Isiah understood and wanted to completely cooperate with him. Although Isiah still wasn't quite sure if he was going to retain Todd, so a few facts he kept to himself.

After the background information was complete, Todd indicated, very truthfully, that he was quite surprised that his father-in-law was actually the Speaker of the House for the State. Todd was impressed. Isiah told Todd to wait until he met him before Todd really could assess him. Todd thought that was a strange comment.

Todd indicated that he had seen Isiah play basketball a couple of times. When Miami was playing Duke and then again when they played North Carolina. He was impressed with Isiah's athletic abilities. Todd was somewhat surprised that Isiah wasn't looked at by some NBA teams. Isiah told him right out, that he was never interested in that life. Isiah was surprised that Todd remembered him in those two games so many years ago. He wasn't sure that Todd was actually telling him the truth. Maybe he was just trying to cement him as a client. Isiah had a hard time remembering even playing in those games. But he continued to tell Todd about him and his wife.

Isiah indicated that he had met his wife while he was playing basketball. Donovan invited certain ball players to his home for dinner, from time to time. Isiah was lucky that the first time he went to Donovan's home Sophie was home on break. That's where they met. They even went out on a couple of dates during that time. Isiah had no idea that a beautiful white rich girl would even date a black man. He was more surprised that her father said nothing. Isiah admitted that he believed that a couple of dates would never amount to a serious relationship. Even though Donovan encouraged Isiah to call his daughter, Isiah was certain that Donovan either didn't know about the dates or probably just held his tongue.

Then Sophie, through her father's insistence and influence, as a Miami booster, attended law school at the University of Miami when Isiah was attending graduate school. Surprisingly, Sophie's father offered Isiah a job with his Company after Isiah received his MBA. Isiah much preferred business to basketball as a career. Even though several NBA teams did contact him, Isiah believed that a business vocation was much more lasting and stable.

All of the information that Isiah gave Todd made Todd even more interested in taking Isiah's case. He liked Isiah and his first impression was that Isiah was innocent. Todd understood police work. He knew that Isiah was just the token black that the authorities would be looking for in a high profile case like this. Also, Isiah was the spouse of the victim. Especially a beautiful white victim with a high profile job. The spouse was always the first person the police looked at. Todd had read a lot about the murder in all of the local newspapers before Isiah had come to his office. It was strange that none of the articles mentioned that Isiah was black. He never watched any of the news articles on the network news. To Todd it was just another murder. Now the circumstances have changed.

Todd asked Isiah to give him his version about his wife's murder, including his alibi, along with his version and proof of that alibi, his relationship with Mason 'Dusty' Francis, if any, and his relationship with Clayton Reed. Todd also wanted Isiah's version and proof of his alibi when Clayton Reed was murdered.

Isiah was a little taken back when Todd asked for his version of the events. Did Todd believe that he was probably guilty?

Isiah told Todd most everything he knew but left some facts out. If he told the whole truth Isiah thought that Todd may change his mind on representation. Also, the facts that were left out, at least in Isiah's mind, were not really relevant to his wife's murder. Isiah also didn't tell Todd much about Anya Taylor since he hadn't had much contact with her, even though she was his sister-in-law. He also said little about his older sister Dakala. Even though Isiah hired Dakala away from K-mart to work at Jetta. Even Donovan didn't know about that. It was a big Company. Isiah wanted to take care of his family. He mentioned he had a sister, Evy and a niece, Nicki, who Isiah was putting through Broward Junior College. He also wanted to hire her after she graduated. Isiah didn't think those facts were really important. Todd would have disagreed.

Isiah admitted there was still a lot to learn about the murders since Isiah hadn't yet seen any autopsy reports, toxicology reports, DNA reports, ballistic reports or any police reports. Todd told him that if Isiah wanted to retain him, he could find all of that out easily and he would stay by Isiah's side during the entire proceeding even if it had to go to trial. Todd never asked Isiah if he was the person who committed the murders. That was Todd's way of practicing criminal law. He didn't want to know. And he told Isiah that. It's easier for a defense attorney to defend someone when the attorney has no knowledge of whether his client is actually guilty or not. He would just take the position that the client was innocent. That way, as a criminal lawyer representing accused criminals, he could utilize more evidence, and enhance his witness list without putting himself in a compromising ethical position of having someone intentionally commit perjury. Or more important, leave someone off his witness list since he would then know that the witness would probably commit perjury.

Todd then asked Isiah if he owned any guns. Isiah indicated he owned two, a 9 millimeter Glock 19 and Glock 26. Isiah said he traveled a lot, and being black, he wanted protection, both on the road and at home. Isiah also volunteered that Sophie owned a 9 millimeter Glock 26 for her protection. Both had valid concealed carry permits. At that time neither of the two knew what type of weapon killed Clayton Reed.

Isiah then said, "I don't know how many contract murders you have been involved with or how many high profile people you have represented, but everything about this case will not be easy, trust me. The people involved are very important people and those kind of cases scare most lawyers. Those people look for scapegoats."

"Isiah, I am anxious to represent you and will give you my best representation, I promise you that. I have represented a State Senator, a Councilmen, an astronaut and a University President," replied Todd. "I am not afraid of anyone or a Courtroom. I have tried nearly 75 trials. When I get into a high profile case I am relentless."

"How's your record?"

"Well, due to the fact that most of my clients were guilty, that may tell you something?" said Todd. "But not all of them were guilty and you can ask any of them how my work was. I'll be happy to give you references. I believe you will get nothing but positive feedback. I can help you a lot. I can help you direct your responses, where you should be and when, antagonize the prosecutor and tongue tie any detective."

Isiah liked Todd. He felt comfortable around him. Also he was white and Isiah felt that was extremely important.

"No offense, but it's now time for the bad news. How much is this going to cost me?" asked Isiah. "Let's get that out of the way right off the bat?"

"I'm not cheap, Isiah. My hourly rate is $650.00 an hour. I require $100,000.00 up front as a down payment on the final bill. The first half of the down payment will be applied to the first monthly bills sent to you. The last half to be applied once the case is over. I also expect to get paid on time. I'm good so I expect to be paid. I'm sure you understand that concept."

"No problem," said Isiah as he took out his check book and wrote a $100,000.00 check. "Now, what do I do first?"

Just as Isiah said that, his cell phone rang. "I need to pick this up. It's one of the detectives on the case."

"Put it on speaker. I want to hear the conversation and now is as good a time to start to be involved in the conversation."

CHAPTER 14

Mason 'Dusty' Francis left the gas station after he washed his car, cleaned himself up and changed clothes. He had cuts all over his hands and arms and a small cut on his face. He had no idea that Sophie Daniels was that strong or such a fighter. Why didn't Clayton give him better information? He went into a drug store and purchased some gauze, tape and Band-Aids, He mended himself as best he could. All of this for only $1,500.00. Dusty, who was only a mediocre panhandler in Overtown, was not too bright. $1,500.00 was a lot of money in his world. However, had he known what he was getting into, he would have asked for at least double that amount. Maybe he should have even asked Clayton why he wanted her dead. She lived in a very expensive home in a very expensive neighborhood. What did she do to Clayton? An old semi-famous basketball player who no one wanted, especially the NBA.

All those stories about the trips he took, the girls he met, the wine and food he got for free, but no team drafted him. He was a walk-on for three NBA teams. Again no one wanted him. This woman must have been one of the women he met who probably jilted him at some time in his life. But those days were 15 years ago! Clayton still thought he could play basketball. He walked and talked like he had a chip on his shoulder. What a looser. Dusty wondered where Clayton got the money to pay him. Probably selling dope. Or maybe in a pick-up basketball game. That he was good at. Maybe he should ask Clayton for more money so he would keep quiet in case he was ever caught. But Dusty knew that wouldn't happen. Dusty also wondered, how Clayton knew the code to get into the development and what Sophie's house code was. But most of all, how did he know about the key? Was Clayton having an affair with her? What would a white woman like her want with a black man like Clayton? Something wasn't right. Dusty was just starting to figure that out. There had to be more to it for Clayton to want her dead. But, those thoughts weren't important now. Dusty needed to get away to some place where he couldn't be found.

Due to the difficulty it took to kill Sophie, Dusty was sure someone heard or saw something. Maybe even saw his car. It finally occurred to him that he needed a different car. Luckily one of the skills Dusty learned as a young man was how to hot wire cars. So Dusty thought that the best place to go ditch his car and get another one was at a shopping mall.

Dusty drove south about 20 miles from Boca Raton to Plantation and found the Fashion Mall on Broward Boulevard. The parking lot was full. He drove to the back of one of the lots in front of the Bonefish Grill. He left his car there and went looking for a car with an open door. There were plenty of them. All those stupid people. Dusty needed a car at least 8 years old since the new ones were too difficult for Dusty to hot wire. Too many electronics. He finally found a 2012 Malibu SS. It was beautiful. It was easy to hot wire. Once he started to drive out of the parking lot he noticed the fuel tank was on empty. More money he had to pay. Again he thought that he should have asked for more money from Clayton. Dusty was so sure Clayton must have had more. He always did. He stopped at the Mobil station to gas up just before the turn to I-75, better known as Alligator Alley. A full tank would take him to Naples and beyond. No one would find him there.

He quickly filled the tank and left the station. He made a right turn onto I-75 West and was on his way to Naples, Florida. He had no clue what he would do there or where he would stay until the cops gave up on trying to find his old car. Dusty had no idea how important Sophie Daniels family was. He had no idea that heaven and earth would be moved to find Dusty. But the most important person to find was the person who set up the chain of events ending with the murder of Sophie. Dusty knew that was Clayton, but he was not a snitch.

He just hoped he had enough money for food and motels. He would change motels every two days. That was his plan. If money ran out, Dusty was an expert on holding up small hardware stores, 7-11 stores and liquor stores. His last resort was always panhandling. He was really good at that. Dusty finally felt comfortable. In a few days, his cuts would heal. However, he thought someday, in the not too far future, he would confront Clayton Reed and give him a piece of his mind. Clayton should have told him about the victim and to better prepare him before he entered her home. At least he was told about the spare key. That saved him a lot of time and outside exposure attempting to break in the home. Dusty spent his first night in an inexpensive flea bag hotel with a small bar in Immokalee, Florida, just a few miles from Naples. He was splurging on a few expensive drinks. He was finally in a self-congratulating state of mind.

⟫●⟪

It was 7 days since Sophie Daniels was brutally murdered in her home in broad day light. There had been dozens of interviews by the authorities with neighbors, security guards at the Boca development, two autopsies of Sophie and one of Clayton. There were two sets of autopsy reports, two sets of toxicology reports, two sets of DNA reports both of which were very similar on the manner of death and the DNA on the victim and under Sophie's finger nails. The home where the homicide occurred was completely searched and analyzed. In addition, both of the Daniels' automobiles were searched. No warrants were needed for any crime scene. Also no warrant was needed for the automobiles since Isiah, with the approval of his attorney, agreed to the searches before Isiah was arrested.

The authorities found, in addition to the broken piece of the wooden handle of the gun used to bludgeon Sophie, dozens of finger prints, blood samples and the DNA of the intruder. It didn't take long for the authorities to determine that Mason 'Dusty' Francis was the person who murdered Sophie. His DNA information had been in the police computers for years. With several eye witness accounts of a mysterious old car in their neighborhood a block or so from the crime scene, it didn't take long to find the gas station where Dusty went to clean himself, change clothes and wash the inside and outside of his car. Even the drug store where Dusty purchased gauze, tape and bandages was only a few blocks from there. The entire transaction was on surveillance tape at the drug store. Mason Francis was the person who murdered Sophie Daniels.

The authorities also found one weapon in the home. A 9 millimeter Glock 19 in the master bedroom night stand. The State of Florida had a record of a concealed carry permit for both Sophie and Isiah. A review of background checks by the State found that the couple had purchased three weapons. They were all traced back to a gun shop near the Florida Turnpike on Southern Boulevard in West Palm Beach. Darby Lynch went to the gun store to interrogate the owner, Drew Austin. After Darby showed Mr. Austin her credentials she asked him if he knew Isiah or Sophie Daniels.

"I do, and I heard that Sophie was viciously murdered a few days ago. But what does that have to do with me and the police?"

"I would like to know what kind of weapons the Daniels purchased from your establishment and which one of them purchased each weapon?"

"We know that three weapons were purchased at this establishment. Were others purchased off the books?"

"Do you know," said Austin, "the Daniels are friends of mine and haven't you heard that there is a second amendment to our Constitution? I run a legitimate business. Nothing is sold off the books."

"I'm well aware of the Constitution sir," replied Darby, "but if the Daniels were your friends I would think you would like us to find out who committed this terrible crime."

"All my records are confidential. I don't have to tell you anything about who purchased what weapons."

"That may be true sir, but I'm sure that you don't want me to get a subpoena and come back here to go through all your records. Who knows what type of violations I may find. Just a little help here would be much appreciated."

"I don't like these Gestapo tactics. After all this is America. But if letting you see my sales to the Daniels will help find the animal that murdered Sophie, maybe I can oblige the police just one time," said Austin with a frown on his face. He felt like he was betraying all of his God given rights.

Darby determined that Sophie Daniels purchased a 9 millimeter Glock 26 with four boxes of ammunition. Isiah purchased two weapons, both 9 millimeter. One was a Glock 19 and the other a Glock 26. Darby also was given the serial numbers for all three guns. Darby thanked Mr. Austin for his patriotism. She wondered what the serial numbers were of the two Glocks that were found in the Daniels' home. All three weapons purchased by the Daniels used the same ammunition. After all, it was a 9 millimeter weapon that murdered Clayton Reed. The County lab was still attempting to determine if they could enhance the partial fingerprint on the 9 millimeter casing left at the scene of Clayton Reed's murder. They were also checking the serial number and possible finger prints on the gun found in a sewer a block away from Clayton's home.

<hr />

On day 8 after Sophie's murder, the funeral was held at the Gardens of Boca Raton Memorial Park. The press was everywhere. Both television news from local and cable companies were present attempting to get interviews. Several local newspapers were also there taking pictures and even speaking with security guards. Private security guards as well as the Boca police only allowed certain persons into the service. Those persons were set forth on the list compiled by the Taylor and Daniels' families. All others, including all media, were politely turned away. The service was small with only family and a few friends allowed to attend. It was a closed casket. Isiah made sure of that even though he was sitting in a holding cell at the Boca Police Department. He wasn't allowed to attend his own wife's funeral. Todd Hawkins and Deena Hawkins were on the list. Donovan Taylor asked his wife Sylvia, who Todd Hawkins was. She had no idea. Isiah had not yet told his in-laws that he had retained counsel. Also, both Douglass Fischer and

James Logan, Sophie's closest law partners were included. The firm was too big to have any more lawyers or administrate staff present. Sophie's secretary and several paralegals were not happy about that, but understood. Dustina Washington and her husband Jayden Robinson were on the list. They were Sophie and Isiah's best friends. Donovan was not happy. Along with Isiah's family there were too many blacks for his liking at his daughter's funeral.

Darby Lynch and Morgan Blackburn were not included on the list, however, they were able to convince the Boca police to let them through. Many times the perpetrator of a crime will show up at the victim's funeral. Both detectives were there with their phone cameras.

The burial of Sophia was a very curious event. Apparently due to the sand soil and high water table, an in-ground burial was problematic. Donovan refused to have his family buried in the shallow wet ground. So Sophie's final resting place was a spotless version of a Spanish burial vault, as they have in New Orleans. The funeral home had both outdoor and indoor vaults. The outdoor vaults were relatively modest. The cost of an outdoor vault was more in the price line of a new Honda. The advantage of the indoor vault was air conditioned comfort for visitors. Donovan insisted, when he purchased the vaults, that his entire family be buried within a special indoor vault. That made the cost more in line with a new Mercedes. Donovan didn't care about money. However, Isiah was paying the rest of the price for his wife's funeral even though Donovan had made that jester to the funeral director. There were certain disagreements that had to be ignored. This was one that Donovan decided not to pick. Donovan had already prepaid for his families vaults, so the rest of the cost was negligible in Donovan's mind.

The funeral director, Darrin Cole, said a few words about Sophie. He also told a few stories that Anya had told him to recount. However, the Taylor minister, Reverend Schofield, knew the family well and relayed many nice intimate tales of Sophie when she was growing up and a few nice words about the family and its philanthropy. It was strange to all present that Isiah's name was not mentioned by the Reverend or the fact that he wasn't in attendance. That was Donovan's doing. Isiah was furious. That fact also didn't get past the detectives. The detectives took pictures of everyone present, but kept their distance. Donovan knew the detectives were there and was not happy. Isiah was in jail for this horrible crime. Why were the detectives even at the funeral?

The funeral lasted only 45 minutes. No one from the family said anything. Isiah was unable to take the Dias and say a word. Isiah was furious with the detectives who would not let him attend. And that fact didn't get past the detectives. What kind of persons would not let a husband say something, even if was just his good byes to his wife? The evidence surrounding Isiah's arrest was very questionable. Very strange he was not allowed to attend Sophie's funeral. Donovan was delighted!

The family then got into their limos and the others walked back to their cars. The press practically attacked all of the people walking to their cars, but no comments were made. Sophie had been put to rest.

Both detectives drove back to the Boca police station. All of the autopsy reports from both pathologists on Sophie's death were waiting their review. The CSI report and autopsy report on Clayton Reed's death was also there. During the service the detectives had turned off their phones and radios. So they were unaware if Dusty Francis had been apprehended. All of that would be waiting for them after the 10 minute drive to the police station. Both detectives already had their theory of what had actually happened and who were involved. They knew any high profile case needed to be resolved quickly. They were just doing their job.

However, the mystery was not who committed the crimes, but what was their motive? Also a lot of evidence had to be put together in a nice, straightforward chronological manner, so that the Assistant States Attorney who would be handling the case would give their blessing to the detectives for their arrest of the perpetrators. Their real work was just about to begin. Would they find their theories plausible? Or was there something completely different going on?

Both detectives remembered Douglass Fischer telling them that Sophie was going to disclose to the firm's management committee why she was in the process of firing Jetta International as a client. However she needed to speak to her husband first. Did she speak to him? Also there was the fact that James Logan wouldn't say a word at their meeting. Only Fischer did the talking. That was also strange. And Logan didn't seem very surprised when Fischer told the detectives about the firing. What was that all about? They also needed to check the Daniels' other two guns. That may be able to put some finality to their theories. Police officers had been canvassing the area around Clayton Reed's apartment for almost two days. Both detectives were hopeful that soon they would find some answers to their questions. Or would they only find more questions?

CHAPTER 15

As Isiah's phone rang in Todd Hawkins' office, Isiah put the phone on speaker and pushed the on button.

"This is Isiah Daniels what can I do for you?"

"Isiah this is Darby Lynch. Would you be available to meet with detective Blackburn and me today at 3:30 at the Boca Police office?"

"Have you recovered some new evidence since the last time I was in your interrogation room that will tell me who murdered my wife?" asked Isiah.

"We do have some interesting evidence that I think you would like to know about," said Darby.

"Okay, I believe I can meet you, so long as my attorney, Todd Hawkins, has his time free for that time. He is on speaker. I am in his office now."

"Well Todd Hawkins, it's been a while since we worked together. No problem bringing your counsel with you. Todd and I have some history."

"How have you been Detective Lynch?" said Todd, "It's been a few years. I remember the Buller case very well. I enjoyed working with you."

"If I remember that case correctly, you drove our States Attorney crazy with your multiple motions to exclude every piece of evidence we gathered until there was no case left," irritably said Darby. "Someday Mr. Buller will get caught doing something and he will be put away for a long time. Men like that just don't change."

"Maybe your right detective, but let's concentrate on the current case. Let me assure you that my client has agreed to completely cooperate with you. He wants to find his wife's murderer as badly as you do," replied Todd completely ignoring the detective's last comment. "3:30 today will not be fine for me. I would like to review the evidence you have before we meet. It will make the meeting more productive."

"I can give you most of what I have, but not all. Some we are still working on. Why don't you send your courier to my office and I'll have copies at the Sergeant's desk. If you can do that today, maybe we can meet tomorrow at 3:30?" said Darby.

Make it in two days at 10:00 in the morning. I want to make sure the meeting is truly productive. I have matters to handle for other cases also," answered Todd.

"Fine, see you both then," and Isiah hung up.

"Are we ready to talk to the detectives so soon? Shouldn't you have more time to read all the reports including DNA reports? Don't you need your investigator to look into this Dusty Mason character? Black men start off with two strikes against them. I want you to be prepared," requested Isiah.

"Isiah, you need to trust me. I know what I'm doing. We will be able to get all of that information and we can review it together. That information may jog your memory about some other fact and maybe even determine who the real perpetrator was. I'll talk to my investigator and get him started on this case right away. This meeting will only just be a listening meeting. You need to say nothing unless I give you a nod. Remember, the burden is on them to prove who committed these crimes."

"Todd, I have no idea who Dusty Francis is. I never saw him in high school or at the Ritz, if he was ever at the Ritz. I know the police like to exaggerate or even lie to get someone to confess," said Isiah. "And as for Clayton Reed, it's been a long time since I have seen him. He and I got along okay as roommates in college, however, I believe he was a little jealous as to the amount of playing time I would get each game. But we still did things together with other team mates. We certainly ate most meals together and practiced together. He was decent to me. Coach Conrad told him to be my 'big brother' and keep an eye on me. He was a junior when I was a first year player."

"Did he ever call you, or did you meet with him, after the two of you stopped playing basketball?" asked Todd.

"Maybe a few times. After I was hired by Donovan at Jetta Clayton called several times about a job. Clayton never got any degree. He was certain he would play in the NBA. After he wasn't drafted he was a walk-on for three teams. He was cut by all three," said Isiah.

"Was he upset with you about basketball or not getting hired at Jetta?" asked Todd.

"I don't think so. He spent a lot of time with Martell Dixon, the point guard that would come into a game for me when coach took me out. I think they stayed friends for some time. I lost track of Martell. However, Clayton and I did get together for a few one on one basketball games and socialized a little. But that was some time ago." lied Isiah.

"When you say a little," asked Todd, "what does that mean? Did you give him any money?"

"Not much. And I stopped totally a long time ago," again lied Isiah, not really knowing when he exactly stopped giving Clayton money.

"Okay. Let me ask you one more question before you go," said Todd, "it may sound a little strange. How well do you know Deena?"

"I just met her a day or two ago. I believe she is a good friend of Anya's, why?"

"You know she is my sister. However I haven't really spent much time with her over the last several years. In fact, I haven't seen her since she went to FGCU. However, over the last year or so I have received several telephone calls from Anya asking me if I knew where Deena was. They saw each other often when they were in school and even after receiving their degrees. They remained good friends ever since. Deena seemed to disappear for several days, or even a week sometimes. At least that was what your sister-in-law told me over the phone. Why she called me I have no idea. But Anya must have known we weren't that close. I haven't ever brought it up with her, but I thought maybe you knew something about it."

"I don't, Todd," said Isiah, "why are you asking? Do you think this has something to do with my case?"

"Probably not, just curious. Let's meet tomorrow and go over the evidence I receive from the detectives. Then I'll meet you at the Boca police station at 3:30 in two days. If I tell you not to answer at any time, please don't say anything. Let me do the talking, okay?"

"Okay, see you then.

———————

Deena, Kellie and Donna got along very well. They talked for hours and caught up on everything that was going on in their lives. They each apologized about not keeping in touch, but Deena took the brunt of that and made it clear it was her fault. She was just too much into her job every time she thought about calling. So, it just didn't happen. The longer it went on, the harder it was to make that call.

Todd had called Kellie to tell her that he was going to work on his case and he wouldn't be home for dinner. Kellie said that she would take care of everything. It was just nice to have both girls home with her. Deena asked Kelly if she could use their telephone. Her cell phone battery was dead. She said she wouldn't be long. Kellie told her to use it as long as she needed and not to worry about it. The call was to Martell Dixon, the point guard at the University of Miami when Isiah was playing. Deena had a secret that no one knew. Martell Dixon had been invited to FGCU, by their athletic director, for an interview, a long time ago, to be an assistant coach for the school's basketball team.

While Martell was in Estero for the interview he met Deena at a café just off the campus grounds. They started to talk and found out that they had several mutual friends. That night Martell and Deena ended up back in Martell's room at the Drury Hotel. Since then the two have had an on and off thing whenever they could get together. It ended up that Martell did not get the job at FGCU. He thought about staying in the area, but he had many friends back on the east coast. Deena would be only 2 hours away in Estero. So they could get together from time to time. Deena never told Anya about the affair. Even though Deena didn't know how bigoted Anya was. She just didn't want to tell her about Martell since he was black. Deena was somewhat embarrassed.

Martell asked Deena if she could get away one night from the Taylor's so they could meet. She told him that it couldn't be that evening since it was too late, however, she could probably free up some time the next afternoon. They weren't going back to Estero until after Sophie's funeral. Martell told Deena that he was very upset about his friend, Clayton Reed, who had been murdered. They had played and coached basketball for extra money together for years. Martell believed, in his heart, it was Isiah that killed Clayton. He was also certain that he asked Clayton to murder his wife. Martell was sure Clayton wouldn't murder anyone, no matter how much money Isiah offered.

Martell said that it had been hard not to go see or call Isiah and confront him. However, Isiah would probably end up denying everything. He told Deena that Isiah had been sending Clayton money periodically, through an intermediary, to help him out. Martell thought that it was some lawyer who actually gave Clayton the money, but he had no idea who that was. Clayton wouldn't reveal the name. He was scared that Isiah would then stop sending money.

Isiah probably thought that Clayton owed him a favor since he had been giving him a lot of money. So Isiah probably tried to hire Clayton to murder his wife. Deena was shocked with all she heard. She found Isiah a good person. It was hard for her to believe that Isiah would murder anyone, especially his wife.

She told Martell to let the State handle the matter and to stay out of it. Her brother was handling his case, but Deena felt that Isiah didn't do it, even though she had just met him. Whoever did kill Sophie would probably get the death penalty. Deena felt bad for the Taylor's, especially Anya, but Anya had become even more racist since this incident. Deena guessed that some events bring out the truth about people. That had made Deena and Anya a little less friendly to each other. After that conversation, Deena said she would call Martell the next morning.

At about 7:00 that evening, Dijon Jackson, the manager of the Durham plant called Darius Williams, the manager of the Baltimore plant. Both were black managers for their respective plants. Isiah had promoting both of them to their current positions as well as many other qualified blacks to high level positions at Jetta. Donovan was upset but the Board of Jetta felt that they didn't want to say anything unless the Company's financials started to make a downward swing. Donovan was furious, even though he no longer worked for the Company. But he was a minority stockholder. After Donovan left the Company, most of his friends also resigned from its Board. Isiah, as set forth under the Company's By-Laws, appointed new Board Members to replace them. They were friends of Isiah that would rubber stamp anything Isiah requested.

Both managers had worked hard for their positions. Isiah was with Dijon when he received the call about Sophie. Dijon told Darius, on that phone call, that he was told by Isiah to look into several accounts at the Durham plant to determine if there was anything unusual about them. Darius was a little alarmed. Isiah had taken a quick look at the questionable accounts and said he knew very little about them. Isiah always prided himself in knowing everything about the Company's clients and the status of their accounts. Dijon assured Isiah that he was putting together a report on those accounts and would get it to him soon. That report would be fake. However, Dijon knew that Isiah would take Dijon's word about the report at face value. That calmed Darius.

"Darius, Isiah is getting too close to our scheme. You need to alter or forge some of the invoices sent to you by Jayden and do whatever else is necessary to make Isiah believe that those accounts are on the up and up. There is a lot of money involved in this scheme and we can't let Isiah know anything is out of whack. I'm still not sure how Sophie may have found out about those accounts. Someone from her firm may have indicated that those accounts were unusual. Maybe some CPA Sophie's law firm has on retainer. Isiah thought that those accounts were a little large to not be reviewed by him. Our necks are on the line here. Please make sure you cover our collective asses. James Logan can help you if you have any problems. He is a wiz at financial matters. Just call him. And I am sure Logan never would have said anything to Sophie that would jeopardize the scheme. There is too much money involved."

"I understand. Do you know when Isiah will be coming back to the plants?" asked Darius.

"I know he'll be tied up for some time with Sophie's death. The police may even believe he was the one who set up her murder. I hear he has a good criminal attorney, but I'm not sure that will help if we do our parts properly with this scheme. I'll make sure I keep on top of everything that's happening," answered Dijon.

"Don't call me under any circumstances. Again, call Logan if you need something, but it better be important. Logan is already a little nervous," demanded Dijon. Then he hung up.

About an hour later, Jayden Robinson, the husband of Sophie's best friend, called Darius Williams. "Have you spoken with Dijon lately?"

"Yes, we spoke just a while ago. I want to make sure we get our fake clients' accounts correct and all of the invoices are in the right order. I know how Isiah likes to look at the invoices and the checks for their payments," answered Darius.

"Good, just be careful. Isiah is asking about those accounts. You two need to get your act together," said Jayden as he hung up.

Jayden was somewhat worried, however, he believed that Isiah was going to have a tough time getting out of his current mess. He may even be charged with his wife's murder. His father-in-law was furious with him. Even naïve Anya was mad at him. All that will help. His attorney is good, but these plans have been in place for some time. There is a lot of money at stake. Too bad Sophie found out something about the accounts. At least that's what Jayden thought. He wasn't sure how, but he needed to speak with James Logan soon to find out what he and the firm knows about the accounts. Something concerning Jetta International got Sophie murdered. I hope Logan didn't screw up. It was supposed to have been the perfect crime.

Isiah and Todd arrived, in separate cars, at the Boca police station around the same time several days later. Blackburn and Darby were waiting for them in one of the interrogation room. Both Todd and Isiah were directed to that room by the desk Sergeant.

"Gentleman, come in and have a seat," said Darby. "Nice to see you again Todd. I hope your family is all well."

"Everything is fine, my practice is doing well and life is good."

Isiah wasn't very happy that Todd and Darby were so chummy. He hoped that wasn't going to prejudice his case. But over the few hours Isiah spent with his attorney, he was sure that he was still the right person to handle his case and have it taken care of quickly.

"Does anyone want any water or coffee?" asked Blackburn.

Both Isiah and Todd said yes. Blackburn called the desk to have the Sergeant bring them in.

While they were waiting for the drinks, both detectives and Todd made some small talk about past cases and their jobs. Isiah wasn't used to handling meetings that way. He liked to get to the point. However, this was Todd's meeting and he would follow his lead. Once the drinks came, Isiah took a bottle of water and Todd poured himself some coffee. Neither detective took anything. Then the interrogation began.

"You understand that this meeting will be recorded," said Darby.

Everyone nodded and understood the procedure.

"Mr. Daniels when your wife was murdered you indicated you were in Durham North Carolina, is that correct?" asked Darby who took the lead on the interrogation.

"Yes."

"How long were you in Durham and what were you there for?"

"The trip was for work. I meet with my plant managers at least every other month and went over the plants financials and any other administrative or personnel issues that may have been relevant to the Company."

"How long had that trip been planned in advance? And who was the person or persons you were meeting with?"

"All of those trips are planned at the beginning of each fiscal year which begins on October 1. The person I met with in Durham was Dijon Jackson, my plant manager."

Darby then asked several questions about the different plants and a little about Jetta International. That questioning went on for about 10 minutes. Finally, Todd Hawkins interrupted Darby and asked her why she needed to know about Isiah's work. Todd wanted to get to the main issues. Darby reluctantly agreed to move on. In the back of her mind was the fact that Sophie was going to be firing Jetta International as one of her law firm's clients. No one, at that time, seemed to know why. Sophie was murdered before she told anyone, as far as the detectives knew yet. Darby asked Isiah about how he found out about his wife's death. Todd again told Darby that everyone knew the issues and that she should get to the point of the meeting. Darby finally agreed.

"How long did you live in Overtown, Florida, Mr. Daniels."

"Come on Darby, get more specific and to the point. You are starting to strain my patience," said Todd.

"Okay, Mr. Daniels do you or your wife own any guns?"

"Darby, my client does not need to answer any more questions. Why don't you just tell him what you have and we can all go home," said Todd.

"I thought that you told me that your client wanted to help us find his wife's murderer? These are the type of questions that can do that. So either he wants to cooperate or both of you can leave now. We'll just do what we have to in order to make the necessary arrests with or without your client's help," said Darby, a little unhappy.

Both Todd and Isiah went into a corner and spoke for a few minutes. Both detectives could see that Isiah was a little upset with his attorney. When they came back to the table Todd said, "Against my advice, my client will continue to answer your questions."

"Thank you. Now, Mr. Daniels, tell me about your guns."

"Yes, we both have valid concealed weapons carry permits. I owned a 9 millimeter Glock 19 that I kept in my bedroom and 9 millimeter Glock 26 that I carry in my car and in my brief case when I am driving.

Sophie had a 9 millimeter Glock 26 that she carried in her purse or in her desk drawer while she was at work."

"Do you know where those weapons are today?"

"The police took both my Glocks when they searched my home and my car,"

"Where is your wife's gun?"

"I have no idea. I can assume the police found it in her purse when they searched my home or her office, but otherwise, I have no idea."

"Okay," said Todd, "this is where the interrogation stops. We came here to find out who you had determined had placed a hit on Sophie Daniels. We wanted to find out about Clayton Reed and Mason Frances. This is now an interrogation of my client. If you have not eliminated him as a suspect in this matter, we are demanding evidence to include all police reports, pictures of the crime scenes, at both Daniels' home and Reed's apartment, all toxicology and DNA reports and any other evidence as well as statements from witnesses or others concerning the death of my client's wife that you have not yet supplied us. You really sent us very little the other day. My client will not answer any more questions until we have had sufficient time to review those documents. So if there is nothing else, unless my client is under arrest, we are leaving."

Isiah was not happy that Todd made that statement. Isiah was really interested to know everything the detectives had concerning his wife's murder. He thought that's what he and Todd spoke of a few minutes before. He gave a look at Todd and Todd just put his hand up to Isiah as to say no more questions.

"I have a copy of all of those documents at the Sergeant's desk, said Darby, "you can pick them up on your way out. Since you client has refused to answer any more questions, we have no other choice but to put your client under arrest."

"What are you talking about?" said Isiah. "How can you do that? You don't have any evidence to arrest me."

"This is very strange, Darby," said Todd. "You invited us here to have a discussion about my client's wife's death and now you're arresting him?"

Darby asked Isiah to stand up and she cuffed him and opened the interrogation room door and asked the officer outside to take Mr. Daniels to processing. Darby told Todd that his arraignment would be at 9:00 AM the next morning. He could pick up all the evidence on his way out.

"At least tell me his motive, Darby," requested Todd. "You really are pushing this matter much too far and much too fast. You're making a big mistake. You're putting your department in line for a malicious prosecution law suit."

"We'll know more about that after the arraignment. We'll have a sit down after you have read the evidence and spoken with your client. We can talk about a deal at that time."

A shocked Isiah was taken to processing where he was fingerprinted, photographed, given a prison jumpsuit and put in a holding cell. He would be transported to Circuit Court first thing in the morning.

"Darby, what is going on here?" asked Todd.

"Exactly what you saw," said Darby. "We have probable cause to arrest your client for setting up his wife's murder."

"I heard nothing of the kind. You have no evidence that my client did anything wrong."

Todd attempted to talk to his client for a few minutes, but Isiah was already being processed into the system. Now what, thought Todd. How did this happen? What didn't Isiah tell Todd? He knew he would have a long night to read all of the evidence that the detectives left for him. But Todd really felt that the manner the detectives used him to get his client to their interrogation room was despicable. He heard no evidence of probable cause to arrest Isiah. Todd just wasn't going to just let this go. He was really mad.

CHAPTER 16

The next morning all of the detainees, including Isiah Daniels, were awakened at 6:00 AM. They were all given a small box of cereal, a pint of milk and an apple. They were given 15 minutes to eat their breakfast before they were told to get in a large police van to be driven to the County Circuit Court for their arraignments.

This whole episode brought back memories of Isiah's home life when he was a child. It scared him. Each detainee would go before a Judge for the opportunity to declare if they were innocent or guilty of the charges against them. The Judge would then decide the immediate fate for each detainee as to whether they would be allowed bail or would be remanded back to the County jail until their trial. Most arraignments had only a handful of spectators in the Courtroom. Just family members and close friends. This day was different. The press, both local and national, took up every seat. There were even press standing against the walls. This case was a national obsession.

The arraignment judge that morning was Judge Tanner Andrews. Judge Andrews and Donovan Taylor knew each other well. Both had contributed political cash to each of their political campaigns. Todd had found out about that by making some phone calls the night before. Todd also went through all of the information and pictures several times that he received from the detectives before he left the police station. He was surprised by some of the information, but he had concluded that there probably may have been sufficient circumstantial evidence for an arrest. However, Todd could not understand what Isiah's motive could have been. Motive is not one of the elements of the charges that is required to be proved against his client. However, Todd was a good enough attorney to understand that juries like motive. Without a viable motive, reasonable doubt can be put in any jurors mind. All Todd needed was one juror to find reasonable doubt in order to get a mistrial.

When Isiah's name was called by the Clerk for his arraignment, Isiah came to the podium. Todd joined him there after the Clerk read the charges against Isiah. They consisted of two counts of conspiracy to commit murder, two counts of murder in the first degree and first degree murder by hire. Any one of those counts was a capital felony in Florida or any one of those counts could give Isiah life in prison without parole. That was a question to be decided by a jury.

"Counselor, how does your client plea?" asked Judge Andrews.

"Before my client pleads, your Honor," Todd began to articulated, "I make a motion for Your Honor to recuse yourself from these proceedings due to the fact that you are friends with the defendants father-in-law and he and yourself have contributed funds to each other's political campaigns."

Todd also made a second motion for a change of venue due to the excessive publicity that had been going on in Palm Beach County concerning these murders.

"Mr. Hawkins you have been practicing criminal law for some time now. You have been before me dozens of times. You know that I can't rule on any change of venue. That's for the trial Judge to consider."

"I understand that Judge, however, I wanted to put it on the record at this hearing," said Todd.

"Good for you counselor, but I'm sure you wanted all of the press in the Courtroom to hear your beginning arguments on behalf of your client. However, if you accomplished anything at all, it was wasting my time. Now can I have a plea by your client concerning the charges pending?"

"My motion for recusal still stands Your Honor," replied Todd.

"Counselor, I admit I know Donovan Taylor and I admit we're friends. Half the people in this room either know Donovan or voted for him or for me as a Circuit Court Judge. All I want today is a plea of guilty or not guilty. I'm not going to harm your client by anything that may go on today in this proceedings. Shame on you. Do you not understand the procedure here today?"

"However, you are going to make a determination on bail for my client, your honor."

"I assume that statement means a not guilty plea, counselor?"

"Yes your honor, but...." as the Judge interrupted Todd. "This is a double murder case. Your client is accused of hiring someone to murder his wife and then he is accused of murdering the person he hired. There isn't a Judge in any County in this State that wouldn't remand your client." as the Judge hammered his gavel and said, "The defendant is remanded without bail. Next case."

Todd knew that Judge Andrews would not consider any of his motions, but he wanted to make sure the Court and press were aware of his client's future intentions in the case. Isiah was immediately taken back to the prison van to be transported back to the County jail.

The prosecutor for the case, Sidney White didn't have to say a word. Todd approached Sidney and said, "Sidney, you and I have worked on many cases together over the years. You have always been up front with me on nearly all matters. I have reviewed everything your detectives have given me on this case and I cannot believe they arrested him. There are so many holes in this case that no reasonable jury could find him guilty. I even believe I can get this case dismissed before it even goes to Court."

"Good for you," said Sidney. "If you believe that then send me the paper work and set a date for a hearing. Don't try to con me the way you always do. I don't have time for your amusements. I have a trial to prepare for. Your client is going down for this. The States Attorney is strongly considering the death penalty in this matter. He nor I care who your client's father-in-law may be." And she walked out of the court room.

That afternoon, Todd went to the County jail to speak with Isiah and go over all of the evidence he had been given by the detectives. There were some issues Todd wanted to clear up with Isiah that Isiah didn't reveal to Todd. Those facts were included in everything that the detectives had uncovered to date. When Todd arrived to speak with his client, the clerk at the sign in desk, whose job it was to handle security whenever anyone would come to visit with an inmate, told Todd that Isiah currently had a visitor. Todd would have to wait until that visitor left. It was extremely unusual for anyone to see an inmate unless it was a spouse or adult child, who all had to be prescreened first. Mostly attorneys came to see the inmates. Todd couldn't imagine who could be able to see Isiah so quickly. It usually takes a day or two to prescreen anyone, except attorneys.

Todd waited close to a half hour and then Donovan Taylor walked over to the gate to sign out. Donovan had a chat with Isiah. Todd then understood. No one was going to deny the Florida Speaker of the House from seeing his son-in-law. Donovan signed out and walked right past Todd without saying a word.

"Mr. Taylor, how is Isiah doing?" asked Todd.

Donovan just gave Todd a look that nearly made Todd shiver. He said nothing to Todd.

"Mr. Hawkins," said the security guard, "you can see Mr. Daniels now. Just sign in and go through the metal detector."

Todd, after being somewhat shook up from the look Donovan gave him, signed his name and entered the facility and walked through the metal detector. He was given a badge signifying he was a visitor in the facility. A guard then took him to an interview room where Isiah was still sitting handcuffed to a steel ring in the middle of the conference table. Todd asked the guard to uncuff Isiah, but the guard told him it wasn't part of the protocol. Todd knew that but thought he could convince the guard who he had seen and spoken with dozens of time.

"How are you Isiah?" asked Todd.

"How do you think? I am locked in a cage with a bunch of low lives for something I didn't do," angrily said Isiah. "Can't you get me out of here?"

"Isiah, we need to talk, and I mean seriously," said Todd. "I reviewed the detective's investigation reports and all other evidence I received yesterday. It seems there were a few facts that you didn't tell me in our initial meeting."

"I don't think so.

"Not true. Are you now ready to tell me everything? You know I can't properly represent you if you're not honest with me. Whether you were involved with your wife's murder or not, I don't want to know. I just want the truth to certain questions."

"You'll have to refresh my memory so just ask me what's on your mind."

"What's on my mind?" angrily said Todd. "You missed a lot of facts when we first spoke. Was there a reason for that?"

"The truth is that I didn't think every fact would be relevant for you to defend me."

"Isiah, I have been doing this for a long time. I know when people are hiding something and it usually turns out to be very important," said Todd." And don't tell me some crazy answer that if you would have told me those facts that I would have thought that you were actually involved. You must understand, that to defend you properly I don't want to know if you were involved in these murders or not. Actually, it will help if I don't know. However, if you want me to be your lawyer, you need to be completely honest and tell me everything. Otherwise find yourself another lawyer."

"Okay, you made your point. What did you find out?"

"Why didn't you tell me that Sophie was going to fire Jetta International as a client from her firm?"

"That's not true. Who did she tell that to?" asked Isiah in bewilderment.

"Both Fisher and Logan told that to the detectives."

"I don't believe it. Jetta is one of their firm's largest clients and a huge part of Sophie's income," said Isiah. "Did she tell them why?"

"No, she said she needed to speak with you about it first. Did she?"

"This is all preposterous. There is no way she would do that," insisted Isiah. "And no, she never mentioned anything like that to me."

"So we're at an impasse," said Todd. "You tell me why she would threaten to fire your company as a client from her firm. Lawyers don't usually fire clients. It has to be something really bad. Jetta was a very large client of her firm for years. A lawyer just doesn't fire a client like that."

"My God! You're really telling me the truth. Did she say anything about her reasons?"

Douglass Fischer said something about certain accounts at several of Jetta's plants," said Todd. "Does that ring a bell?"

"This better not have something to do with Sophie's father being a huge bigot. He has been throwing the 'N' word around lately especially to the Company's Board. He was not thrilled about my promotions of Dijon Jackson and Darius Williams as plant managers at two of the Company's plants. Both of them are black, but they are capable people who I hired and I trust them. And the people I appointed to the new Board are all competent business people."

"Explain further," said Todd.

"Dijon Jackson, Darius Williams and I played basketball for Broward Junior College together. We were really good friends. We won the conference title. Donovan and the University of Miami offered me a scholarship to play for Miami. I expected both of them to also play for Miami, but Donovan and coach Conrad wouldn't offer them anything. Not even a chance to walk on without a scholarship. I didn't think much of it then. I was just disappointed. Both of them were, however, offered scholarships at Florida Atlantic University in Boca Raton. We lost to them all three times we played them. Donovan was furious about those losses. I had no idea why. We lost a lot during the years I played. Donovan just took other losses in stride. I know he wanted a chance at getting the 'U' to March Madness, but it just wasn't in the cards while I was a player."

"So what does that have to do with Sophie's murder?" questioned Todd.

Isiah went on to explain to Todd that both Dijon and Darius received their MBA's from FAU. The three of them remained friends for a long time. Isiah even hired both of them to work for Jetta. Donovan didn't say anything about that. However, when Isiah promoted them to plant managers, Donovan had a long talk with Isiah about how there may be an appearance by some of the other employees of some form of favoritism going on in the Company? Isiah thought Donovan was speaking about their close friendship. Isiah immediately dismissed that thought since Isiah knew they were the right people for those jobs. Isiah never thought in the terms of racism. After all, Isiah was black and married to Donavan's white daughter.

However, Isiah went on to mention that after the promotions, both men seemed to distance themselves from Isiah. He didn't think much of it, but several times Isiah had to discipline both of them for certain expensive mistakes they had made on several of the Company's client's accounts. Isiah then thought for a minute. The accounts all dealt with one client who had multiple accounts. It was Xavier Corporation accounts. That company had several subsidiaries each with a separate account. Both Dijon and Darius had made mistakes by either crediting or debiting the wrong accounts on various orders. Isiah never spoke with anyone from Xavier about the mistakes. He didn't want any customer to know about internal mistakes made by employees of his Company.

After talking to the two plant managers, the three of them spoke much less after that and the three of them never really socialized thereafter. Only when it dealt with Company business. Even when there were manager meetings, both Dijon and Darius seemed to avoid Isiah. It was strange. But since Isiah was the boss he just dismissed it.

"But what would that have to do with Sophie wanting to fire Jetta as a client?" again questioned Todd.

"I have no idea," said Isiah, "but I guess I'll have to think about it. Maybe Donovan had a talk with his daughter about the promotions? But give me some time. This is all very strange. I promoted a lot of people while I was CEO. Some were black and some were white."

There was a slight pause while Isiah was deep in thought. Then he said, "So what else is out there that I don't know about? It can't be just the loss of two old friends and the promotion of some black employees."

"No, there's more," said Todd. "Why didn't you tell me everything about your relationship with Clayton Reed?"

"What relationship?" said Isiah. "I felt sorry for him. He was my roommate for two years. He never graduated, he never was drafted by any NBA team and he never made it as a professional basketball player. He even tried to walk on to at least three NBA teams, but they all cut him. He didn't have the skills and ended up in Overtown taking on low level jobs. He was fired by most of his employers when they found out he was using drugs. He called me, from time to time, for help. I would go see him, but not very often. I even gave him some money, from time to time. I tried to help him kick his habit, but he refused. He made most of his drug money playing pickup basketball games, for a few bucks, at different neighborhoods until the word got around that he played in college. I even tried to use some influence to get him a few jobs."

"But the truth be told," said Isiah, "I did continue to send him money. But only for a short period of time. I couldn't waste a lot of money on someone who wouldn't do anything for himself. The funds were sent anonymously through James Logan, one of the senior partners at Sophie's firm. I never told Sophie that I was helping Clayton a little. I felt I owed him a little something. He did help me some in college. I am fairly certain that Clayton didn't have a clue who was sending him the money unless Logan told him. He was the only one who knew about it.

But Clayton probably didn't care who sent him the money. If he thought it was me, Clayton wouldn't think I would send it through a lawyer anonymously. And why would Clayton believe that James Logan, who he didn't really know, help a drug addict? Clayton just took the money. It could have been anyone. He had lots of people he knew through his basketball contacts. He probably thought someone felt sorry for him."

"I was devastated when I heard Clayton was murdered," Isiah went on. "But I don't know anything about who would kill him or why. He was a man with a chip on his shoulder and tough to get along with. Maybe he was mad that I didn't hire him at my Company. But that would never have happened. That was my decision, not Donovan's or anyone else's. I know Clayton was mad about that. But kill him? Give me some credit."

"Then why did you call him the day he was murdered? Did you see him that day?" asked Todd.

"He called me," said Isiah, "I just returned his call. He wanted to talk to me about something. I have no idea what. I told him that I didn't want to talk to him or see him. He just got mad at me and hung up. That's the last time I spoke with him."

"Are you sure you didn't see him that day? It's important. Think about your answer," said Todd with complete clarity.

"No. Why."

"Because Clayton was shot execution style with a 9 millimeter Glock 26 that day. That was several days after Sophie was murdered. It was Sophie's gun that was used to murder Clayton Reed. When the police found his body, in his apartment he had nearly $25,000.00 in cash, mostly in $50 bills."

"Okay, stop right there. I'm not stupid Todd. I see where you're trying to take this," said Isiah angrily.

"Where am I taking this Isiah? You tell me. It was your fingerprints they found on the bullets and also on the clip in the gun that murdered Clayton."

"Were my fingerprints found on the gun?" asked Isiah again angrily.

"No."

"So what would my motive be?"

"He was murdered sometime late the night after Sophie was murdered. Where were you then?" asked Todd.

"At the Ritz in West Palm Beach in a room I rented while my house was still a murder scene. I also rented a room that night for a friend of Anya's. Your sister. How's that for an alibi? I'll take it even further. While on my way to the Ritz with your sister, I was stopped in Boca Raton by the police who thought I had committed several burglaries in the neighborhood. I was stopped for just less than an hour. Check that out," said Isiah.

"I did, Isiah. And I couldn't find anyone who set up that stop. I know you think it was your father-in-law. But the police don't have an exact time of Clayton Reed's murder. That may be a problem."

"What's my motive for the murders? If you find one I'll plead guilty. But they have the wrong person," said Isiah firmly enough for Todd to maybe start to believe that he didn't commit any crimes.

"Don't tell me whether you committed these murders or not, Isiah," said Todd. "I told you I don't want to know. I am just asking you the same questions the prosecutor will ask."

But Isiah wondered, who did kill Clayton? What was their motive? Todd would have to have his investigator get Isiah's time line straight for all movements during the time before he went to the Durham plant until after Clayton Reed's murder. Also, the comment that Isiah made about some accounts being entered wrong seemed to stick with Todd. Something was missing? But what?

CHAPTER 17

After Isiah was arrested and arraigned, Jayden Robinson called Dijon Jackson. "Did you hear about Isiah? He was arrested for the murder of his wife and Clayton Reed. I can't believe that happen. There is no way he would kill Sophie. I know them too well. And it wasn't me who arranged for Sophie's or Clayton's murder. Did you or Darius have something to do with it?"

"Not either of us," admitted Dijon.

"When my wife, Dustina, was asked by Sophie to help her confront Isiah about several of my Company's accounts associated with Jetta, I thought our scheme would be uncovered. But when Dustina told me about that, she told me that Sophie wouldn't reveal what the issues were until she had confronted Isiah. Sophie must have thought that Isiah was instituting some type of scheme."

"So Dustina doesn't know anything about our scheme?" asked Dijon.

"No, Sophie didn't tell her anything," said Jayden, "Now Sophie's dead. Maybe Logan was involved with Sophie's murder in order for our scheme not to be revealed. That was his obligation. To keep the scheme away from Sophie. However, I don't think anyone thought the answer to the problem was murder. That only ups the stakes on this scheme. I am not even going to ask him about Sophie's murder. And I have no idea why Clayton Reed was killed."

"Sophie may have told her firm that something was going on with certain Jetta accounts," said Dijon. "But how would she know the real facts? She had a lot of other enemies. She represented a lot of large corporations. There were a lot of environmental groups picketing her firm and trying to picket her home. I know she mentioned that to Dustina. But kill her? That is even going a little too far for protestors. But maybe not the crazies who set up the protests?"

"Makes sense," said Jayden. "That must be why she and Dustina told me that she and Sophie needed to speak to Isiah. Sophie didn't want to get Jetta involved in her firm's client's business. Although Logan mentioned to me that he didn't want Sophie speaking with Isiah or Dustina about her thoughts on what was happening with Jetta. So he may have misinterpreted what Sophie was going to tell Isiah. I hope he didn't make arrangements to have Sophie murdered. That would be way over the top without consulting us first, don't you think?"

"I'm sure Logan wanted the big payoff as much as we do. Sometimes that man is not too smart and much too greedy. He may had even made arrangements to have Clayton murder Sophie. I hope not. I'll talk to him. I don't understand how Sophie would have found out about the accounts between Xavier and Jetta," replied Dijon. "Isiah may have said something to Sophie while he was at the Durham plant. But he never finished his audit. Sophie is smart. She could have interpreted Isiah's remarks as someone was skimming from Jetta. She probably mentioned it to Logan, but couldn't go into details until she spoke with Isiah when he returned from Durham. I'm sure she wanted to make sure that Isiah wasn't involved."

"I don't know how and why Sophie was murdered, but the only good news concerning Sophie's death is that this will allow us to ramp up the scheme," said Jayden.

"You are a cold man Jayden, I wasn't even sure you knew about Darius and me starting the scheme. After all you were the one who thought it up," said Dijon.

⟫●⟪

Several months before Sophie and Clayton's were murdered, both Dijon and Darius had started the scheme by forging small invoices for the purchase of gold and other precious metals from some of Xavier's phony subsidiaries. Jayden had set them up with a flawless scheme, in mind, but hadn't done anything with them. The money was sent to those subsidiaries and Jayden said nothing to anyone in his company. Then he called Dijon.

"I received some money and invoices," said Jayden. "Did you decide to actually start that pretend scheme I spoke to you about?"

"Darius and I felt it was a great way to make a lot of money with little risk," replied Dijon. "We were so upset that Isiah wouldn't allow us to purchase some Jetta stock before it went public. This was our way of getting back at Isiah. We both love him, but he was a true jerk about the stock purchase. Maybe it was Donovan's doing, but in our mind Isiah could have helped us."

"Don't worry," replied Jayden. "I have complete discretion for all sales and distributions of income for all divisions and subsidiaries for Xavier dealing with Columbia and Latin America gold and other precious metals. I even have some communications, from time to time, with European companies that purchase precious metal, that are controlled by the European mob. Since I have been working with Jetta for so long, I know almost as much as the employees of Jetta who manufacture your electronics. For example, I know that Jetta needs, in order to produce one million computers, about 75 pounds of gold, 35,274 pounds of copper, 772 pounds of silver and 33 pounds of palladium. In several months, you and Darius, should start to triple the amount you purchase on each invoice, divided between all the fake subsidiaries of Xavier, for each of your two plants."

"Shit! You do know your stuff," said Dijon. "Besides those four metals, for the manufacturing of other types of electronics, Jetta needs aluminum, whetstone, nickel bismuth, iron, antimony and a few other miscellaneous metals. Darius and I will start doing the same on those invoices," said Dijon.

"Are you certain that no one else will be auditing the Jetta corporate accounts, especially the Durham and Baltimore plants?" asked Jayden, who just determined he was in the middle of a scheme started by two plant managers of Jetta.

"I'm certain," said Dijon. "Donovan has already resigned all of his positions and left Jetta to start his fund raising for his run for Governor. A large portion of his interest in Jetta will be up for sale once Jetta finalizes going public. And maybe we can even speed up that process. Many of the other Board members can easily be controlled by me since I just received word from Isiah, right out of the Palm Beach County jail, that he has resigned his positions as President and CEO as well as his position on the Board. Jetta was finalizing going public. He knew that was the right thing to do, at least until his criminal matters have been resolved.

Isiah has promoted me to the temporary CEO as well as keeping my manager job at the Durham plant," said Dijon. "I'm sure the new Board that Isiah put in place, will go along with my recommendations, now that Donovan and Isiah are no longer on the Board. The old Board were all good friends of Donovan and were put on the Board to rubber stamp whatever Donovan approved. They know little about the company workings and less about auditing accounts. With the enormous amounts of minerals Jetta orders each year, they wouldn't have a clue of any of the excesses from Xavier, especially with different invoices for different amounts from each subsidiary."

Jayden had told Dijon one afternoon, several months before, at a seminar, about an idea on how a perfect crime could be committed between the two companies. But Jayden never believed that Dijon would take it seriously. It was just a stupid remark made over a drink. But now it had been started and Jayden was in the middle. However, with Sophie dead, Jayden was somewhat shocked Dijon and Darius took him seriously. Now there was no reason not to continue the scheme. It would net them each millions.

Jayden then told Dijon to keep the invoices amounts on a small scale and gradually increase them over the next three months. Make sure each invoice is for different amounts for each mineral. He could even leave the invoices for several subsidiaries the same for a couple of minerals, so as not to bring too much attention to anyone in the plants. Jayden believed that between him, Dijon, Darius and now James Logan doing Jetta's legal matters, they could steal at least $300 million in just several years. Jetta's gross income was over $400 billion a year. No one would miss a few hundred million dollars.

Jayden who worked exclusively managing the importing of precious metals for Xavier Corporation for years knew that no one in his company would find out about the scheme. He also knew that no one would find out about how he could launder the excess funds through the European companies controlled by the European mob. He knew people involved with that mob and was introduced to some of them at a company seminar. He never thought he would ever be involved with any of them. But this opportunity came up startlingly. The United States depended on Latin America and Columbia gold and other precious metals to feed the ravenous demand of the jewelry, bullion and electronic industries. The amount of gold going through Miami every year was equal to roughly two percent of the market value of the vast United States stockpile in Fort Knox.

Xavier Corporation's Board were aware that much of the gold and other precious metals came from outlaw mines deep in the jungle where dangerous chemicals were poisoning rainforests and hundreds of poor laborers toiled for scraps of the precious metals for a livelihood. Also European mob companies, running mines, were also involved due to the large sums of money. This was according to human rights watchdogs and industry executives, like those at Xavier. The human misery mirrors the scale of Africa's 'blood diamonds'. Xavier Corporation wanted to distance themselves from any of that controversy. As long as Xavier was making a good profit, the Board of Xavier had left Jayden mostly alone to fend for the Company. They trusted him implicitly. No one on the Board wanted to be associated with the ravages of those minerals.

Several years ago, Federal prosecutors in Miami charged several gold and other mineral traders with money laundering, saying the men purchased $3.6 billion of illegal gold from criminals groups in Latin America and Europe. The Government claimed the gold traders, who eventually pleaded guilty, fueled illegal gold mining, foreign bribery and narcotics trafficking. Another reason the owners of Xavier Corporation trusted Jayden. He had never been accused of any illegal purchasing of precious metals. And all of his audits were perfect.

Among the now four conspirators of this dangerous scheme, Jayden, who immediately became enthusiastic, was the most confident that the scheme would work well. He was certain that the only people who could be able to detect the scheme were Donovan, Isiah or Sophie. With Donovan gone from the company and running for Governor, Isiah in jail and Sophie dead, the scheme would work until each of the four conspirators became very rich. Then the scheme could be slowly halted in the same fashion as it started with no one any the wiser. Each of the conspirators could then quit their jobs, all at different times, and live the life of luxury.

Dijon and Darius were somewhat nervous, but as long as Jayden was running the operation and handling the funds, they would continue the scheme. After all, he was the one who thought up the scheme. The rewards far outweighed the risks. Lastly, with Dijon, Darius and Jayden being black, it was even more difficult for anyone at Jetta, or Xavier, to contemplate what was really occurring without being labeled a racist. Sad, but true.

However, James Logan was the wild card. He was easy to convince to come into the scheme. He was greedy. He was very jealous of Sophie's salary. She made most of it due to her father and husband. In his mind that was just unfair. James Logan had tried different ways to increase his salary. He made a very good living, but not like Sophie. Logan's part in the scheme was to be able to keep the Jetta International account at his law firm with him as the attorney making all final decisions on the account, no matter which lawyer worked on it. Dijon and Logan spoke about that issue when Logan agreed to be part of the scheme. He was also the person who was forced to arrange a way to get Sophie Daniels off the Jetta account. He tried to think of any possible way to accomplish that. However, it came down to attempting to discredit her so badly that Jetta would not have her do any more of their business. But, he came to the conclusion that Isiah wouldn't ever let that happen.

There was one more event that James Logan had uncovered about Jetta, but he never said a word about it. Not even to Dijon or Darius. He thought that he may, some day, be able to use the information to make money, either legally or illegally.

Some time ago, both Dijon and Darius had put together an idea, unbeknownst to Donovan, Isiah or the Board of Jetta. This idea occurred before either of the two of them were promoted to plant managers, and before Jetta went public. They thought they could conspire to embezzle funds form certain accounts, all different, but mostly Xavier accounts, through the Durham and Baltimore plants. At the time they were in charge, subject to the plant manager's overview, of all the accounting for those plants. Amazingly, Jayden had also mentioned this possible action at the same time that he told Dijon about his perfect crime scheme while having drinks at a seminar.

Dijon and Darius discussed Jayden's, off the cuff remarks, liked the plan and thought that through actually doing what Jayden laughed about they could actually get promoted to plant managers. So they started the event to make some real money when, and if, the Company went public. Both of the plant managers of those two plants who were Dijon's and Darius' bosses were Donovan appointees. They relied exclusively on their assistants for the audits of the accounts for their plants. That was when Dijon and Darius decided to bring Jayden into this plan. It would be the catalyst that would eventually allow Jetta to go public and make all of them rich.

Jayden, who was a very greedy man, went along with the plan since, it was really a great way to make some real money. In the long run it wouldn't really hurt anyone except just some already rich shareholders of Jetta. Jayden, thought that through the help of Dijon and Darius he would be able to obtain some Jetta stock, which he could have Dijon's and Darius' hold his stock in their names. That would make a lot of money for them to help finance the real scheme after Jetta went public.

Dijon and Darius decided to reroute funds from their plant's accounts to off shore accounts in several banks in the Bahamas. The off shore companies were all set up legally by James Logan. Logan was greedy and looking for ways to increase his income. Setting up off shore businesses was a profitable way of making legal fees. Logan was unaware of the plan Dijon and Darius had at the time. He was just doing legal work for Jetta. Both Dijon and Darius then 'cooked the books' concerning Xavier's and a few other fake subsidiary accounts. That occurrence made Jetta look unprofitable during the time this event was occurring. Jetta's income at those two plants had decreased substantially.

When Donovan and Isiah noticed the fall in income from those plants they discussed the income loss with Dijon and Darius, who were in charge of auditing all of their plants accounts. Both of whom played dumb and unable to give any business reason for the loss of the income. Isiah then took action to cut costs and lay off employees to compensate for those losses. Donovan, who knew he was about to leave the Company let Isiah handle the crises. Then a year later, Dijon and Darius rerouted the off shore funds that were rerouted, randomly back into the Companies Durham and Baltimore plants under many different accounts, but mostly Xavier's. That then made the Company turn around and become extremely profitable. That was the event that made Isiah promote Dijon and Darius to plant managers. Both of them thought that Isiah, due to their long friendship back to their Community College basketball days, would allow both of them to obtain some of Jetta's stock before the finalization of going public. That never happened and it infuriated both of them, as well as Jayden.

That was the discussion that left a very bitter taste with both Dijon and Darius. With the company so profitable, the owners of the stock and the Board, with the legal help of James Logan's law firm, finalized the Company becoming a publically held company. All stockholder's made a fortune, but Dijon and Darius only got their promotions. Jayden also got nothing. They were all furious and this event brought on the start of the big scheme with Jayden to recoup the money that they felt they were entitled to when the company went public. At least, in their minds, they thought they were owed that money.

All three co-conspirators were contacted by Logan who informed them that he determined what they had done and threatened to turn them in to the authorities unless they paid him money. Logan was blackmailing them. All three decided to take a big risk. They informed Logan about their other scheme they were about to begin. They felt they had nothing to lose. They were starting to steal millions of dollars from the Company. Logan was intrigued. He would make a lot more money that way than by blackmail. The three co-conspirators recruited Logan in order to stop the blackmail. And with the lawyer who handled Jetta's accounts, it would make the scheme work even better.

When the scheme started, Logan wrote a memo to himself and put it in his lower desk drawer outlining their scheme in order to cover himself. He intentionally left himself out of the scheme, in the memo, and inserted Isiah's name. After all, Logan didn't want to have anyone know his part of the scheme. If anything went wrong, Logan would have an out with the authorities. Logan was a smart lawyer, but was very stupid when it came to criminal law. One day, years later, when Logan was out of the office, Sophie went to retrieve a file she needed from Logan's desk. She accidently came upon Logan's old hidden memo and read it in disgust. She couldn't believe that Isiah would do such a thing. She had to speak to Isiah. And why did Logan have this memo. Why didn't he discuss it with her? What was going on? Somewhere there had to be some kind of conspiracy and Jetta International had to know about it. Logan could have been involved which would have involved her firm. Sophie said nothing to Logan. However, when Logan heard that Sophie wanted to fire Jetta, he concluded that Sophie must have found out something about the scheme. He couldn't let her speak with Isiah. That was the beginning of the end for Sophie.

So Logan, regretfully, knew there was only one certain way to take care of the Sophie problem and keep the scheme on track. After all, there was a lot of money involved. Logan needed to get rid of Sophie permanently. The difficult part was to find the right way so no one would get caught.

Logan had befriended Clayton Reed when the scheme was in its planning stage. He used Isiah's name as his entrée into Clayton's life.

Logan told Clayton that Isiah was giving money to Logan to put into Isiah's Trust Account at Logan's firm. Logan would then, in turn, put the money in an account Logan set up for Clayton. Logan said it was from Isiah so he could live a better life. He told Clayton that Isiah felt bad that he couldn't hire Clayton at Jetta. That was Isiah's father-in-law's decision. Isiah knew Clayton well and had no reason to doubt Logan would make sure Isiah's money went to Clayton. However, Clayton was given one requirement in order for the money to keep coming. He could not mention that fact to anyone or tell anyone the truth as to where he got the money. He especially couldn't thank Isiah or even say anything to him when they would meet, from time to time. Logan told Clayton that if Donovan Taylor, or Isiah's wife Sophie found out about the money, it would immediately cease. Clayton gladly agreed. Every time Clayton spoke to, or saw Isiah, nothing was ever mentioned about the money.

There was one fact that Logan lied to Clayton about. The money was not from Isiah. Logan was funding it himself in case he needed Clayton as a fall guy or for some act that needed to be done. He would use the money as his club to get Clayton to do what was needed or say what was needed to help Logan if the time came to that.

Logan then grew to know Clayton well. He was sure that Clayton would do anything he was asked if the money was right. Isiah's money was the only way Clayton could afford an apartment, food and clothes. But Clayton played the 'poor boy' to everyone he knew, since he never wanted anyone to know where he got his money. Most of all, he didn't want the money to stop. Isiah's money was the catalyst that held back Clayton from keeping a job for a long time. This was due to a drug habit that Clayton had started using the money. However, when Clayton started to use drugs more heavily, Isiah cut back on the money he gave.

The day Sophie mentioned the possibility of firing Jetta as a client and turn the client over to Dustina Washington's firm, Logan knew what he had to do. Logan liked Sophie a lot, but was jealous of her. He also admired Isiah, but the money involved with the scheme was just too good. Logan was greedy. He could never make enough money. Logan decided to contact Clayton. He called him and asked to meet him at the McDonalds restaurant on Moapa Boulevard in Overtown. Logan didn't want to be seen at Clayton's apartment.

Clayton and Logan went into the far corner booth of the restaurant and Logan asked Clayton, "Are you in the mood to make some big bucks?"

"How big and what do I have to do for it?"

"I'm talking $50,000.00."

"Shit, for that amount I would probably kill someone," laughed Clayton to Logan's surprise.

"Good, since that is what I want you to do."

"What?" said Clayton slurring some of his words.

"Sophie Daniels needs to be eliminated. You need to be completely sober and make it look like a burglary gone bad."

"I can't kill Isiah's wife. I like Isiah. And I don't want to go to jail," replied Clayton firmly.

"Do you want the money to continue to keep coming each month? I have it all planned out for you. I will give you all the instructions you will need along with $25,000.00 cash up front. You will have the Home Owner Association's gate code along with Sophie's security code for her home. Also, Sophie told me she keeps a spare key for her side door under a flower pot at that door. I have some medical gloves for you to wear and a knife you'll need to do the job. The cash, gloves and knife are in this manila envelope with all of the security codes. You can sneak in and out without making any noise at 7:30 AM. Sophie doesn't come into the office until 9:30. Isiah is in Durham, North Carolina for work for a few days. Be sure to steal some jewelry and other valuables to make it look like a burglary gone bad. After you're done, come back to your apartment. We'll set a time and place to meet so I can give you the other $25,000.00. That should be enough for you to get out of town, get rid of your car and buy a good used one. I know you have saved a lot of the money that Isiah has been sending you so you should have sufficient funds to go to some nice beach in the Caribbean for a while. Just lay low for several months," said Logan very apprehensively. "You can do this Clayton. No one will be around that early. Everyone in that neighborhood is still sleeping, eating breakfast or at work."

"Shit, I ain't ever killed no one before," said Clayton. "And why Isiah's wife?"

"That is none of your business. You're getting paid well for the job. Do you want it or do I find someone else?"

"You got the money with you?" asked Clayton.

"It's in the envelope. All $50.00 bills. All the instructions are written down and in the envelope."

Clayton looked bewildered. Logan was as scared as he had ever been. What did he just ask a low class junkie to do?

After Logan left the restaurant, he wondered if Clayton would actually go through with it or would he just take the money and run? Maybe this was just a stupid move? His co-conspirators would probably kill him if they knew that he had just given a junkie the job of murdering the daughter of one of the most powerful men in the State. So Logan decided he wasn't going to tell his co-conspirators about who he hired for the job. He would just tell them he made sure that the Sophie problem was solved. He then went home, instead of the office, poured himself three fingers of scotch and commenced to get drunk.

———◆———

Clayton wasn't the brightest bulb in the chandelier, nor was he usually completely sober. However, as he thought about what just happened, he knew he couldn't kill anyone, especially Isiah's wife. But he had the $25,000.00. That was a lot of money. He could give it back, but after some thought he decided that wasn't a good idea. He had to do the deed the next day. How was he going to do it? Or was he going to do it? He thought about leaving town with the money right then. Logan would never find him. But how far could he go on just $25,000.00? He did have several thousand additional funds put away in a safe place in his apartment. But again, not enough to run. Plus he would no longer get his monthly stipend from Logan. He thought about it for another hour. Then it popped into his head.

He remembered his good friend Justin Francis from Isiah's old neighborhood. He played basketball against him when he played for

Overtown High School. He really liked Justin. And Clayton remembered that Justin had a younger brother, Mason, who everyone called Dusty. Dusty was a little off. He would steal one of the school teacher's cars for just $5.00. He was really good at hot wiring cars.

Clayton thought why not call Dusty. He'll do the deed for peanuts. Clayton can explain the instructions to him. How bad can Dusty screw up a fake burglary? But hopefully he could actually murder someone. Dusty had done dozens of robberies and only got caught a few times. He did some time and then he went right back to his old ways. Clayton was sure that Dusty would even kill someone if he gave him enough money.

So Clayton called Justin that afternoon and asked him if his little brother would do him a favor. Clayton would even pay him a lot of money to do it. It only took an hour for Dusty to knock on Clayton's door. Clayton explained everything to Dusty and gave him the paper with the address, name and time to be at the Daniels' home. Dusty had always thought that for the right amount of money he would even kill someone. But to be faced with actually doing it was a different animal. He had never done anything even close to that before. Then Clayton pulled out $1,500.00 in $50.00 bills and told Dusty that was all for him if he would do the deed. Clayton even gave him an old Smith & Weston 617 with a wooden grip and told him to keep it after he had finished. He knew Dusty couldn't use a knife to kill anyone. He said the gun was a classic worth a fortune. That was the frosting on the cake for Dusty. He felt like he had never felt before. He had a sense of entitlement. He was now rich and he could do this.

There was one more very important matter that Dusty had to agree to before Clayton would give him the money and the gun.

"What's that?

"If you were to get caught you must agree to say that you were attempting a robbery. You thought that the Daniels would have lots of expensive items that you could sell or pawn for a lot of money. You never expected Mrs. Daniels to be home. You thought she would be at work. Do you understand that? My name can never come up if you're caught by the police. I know you're not a snitch. You never were. However, if you can't agree to those terms, I'll find someone else. I'm sure I can find a lot of guys who could use $1,500.00 and a classic gun worth several thousand dollars," said Clayton with authority.

"You can trust me. I never go back on a promise, especially on a good guy like you. My brother said you're the best."

"Great, then the deal is done. You must do this thing tomorrow morning."

Then Dusty walked out of Clayton's apartment with a smile on his face and $1,500.00 in his pockets. Clayton was relieved. He just hoped that he would still get the other $25,000.00 from Logan once the deed was done.

CHAPTER 18

The morning after James Logan and Clayton Reed met in the Overtown McDonalds restaurant consummating their agreement dealing with Sophie Daniels, Dusty Francis was in the middle of an episode in which he never contemplated. He had successfully conned the security woman guard, as he had done at other gated communities, to let him in. He knew the Development's entry code. He also had a magnetic sign he put on his car indicating he was working for a security company. Dusty was good at conning security guards. They got paid poorly and basically just open the gate for anyone they believed belonged. Dusty had access to the key to enter the Daniels home. It was exactly where Clayton told him it would be. He had a loaded revolver to finish the job quickly. However, what was supposed to occur, in these types of matters, usually never happens the way it was supposed to. This job was no exception.

This event took almost 40 minutes to complete the one task for which Dusty had been contracted to do. Unfortunately for both Sophie and Dusty the event didn't end well for either of them. By the end of that day, Sophie was brutally murdered and the entire Florida police establishments were looking for Mason 'Dusty' Francis. His picture was being televised all over the State. The owner of the 2012 Malibu SS had immediately reported it stolen. Dusty's old car was found abandoned, with fresh blood in it. With an all point bulletin out for the Malibu and Dusty it wouldn't take long for someone to spot one or the other or both.

That evening, all four co-conspirators were at home watching the evening news. Three of those conspirators, Dijon, Darius and Jayden were in shock. They all believed that James Logan had probably taken this action before consulting with any of the other three. If he would have consulted with any of the other three and tell him what was happening at Logan's law firm with Sophie, they would have discussed all of the alternatives to keep Sophie quiet. Killing her would have been last on their list. However, whatever they would have decided, money would determine the results. There was just too much of it at stake. Murder would have been one of the options.

But for Logan to decide this himself, why in the name of God would he hire such an incompetent hit man to handle such an important job like that? It should have been done by a professional who would do it in a clean fashion, leaving no evidence as to who murdered Sophie. They would have all agreed on any amount for the fee, so long as the deed was done properly. This could all have been done in a manner that would never lead back to any of them. They all wondered what in the world Logan had done.

Jayden's wife, Dustina Washington, was hysterical when she heard about Sophie. She had just spoken with Sophie the day before concerning working with her as co-counsel on some issues at one of her client's corporations. Dustina didn't even know anything about which corporation or who may be involved. She attempted to contact Isiah, but was unable to reach him. She did speak with Shelia Taylor and Anya Taylor. They only spoke for a few minutes since they were deeply grieving. However, Anya made it very clear to Dustina that Isiah had to have something to do with Sophie's murder. She still believed that her father never should have let her marry a black man. Dustina was shocked that she would make that statement, especially to another black woman. Jayden tried to comfort his wife after that call, but it was difficult.

James Logan was literally in shock when he heard the news. All he could think about was who in the Hell is Mason Francis? He had just paid Clayton Reed $25,000.00. He was watching NBC national news' entire segment on Sophie's murder and the hunt for Mason Francis.

Logan was incensed. He immediately called Clayton Reed. As usual, Reed was high when he answered his phone.

"What in the Hell did you do you stupid ass?" angrily said Logan.

"I just couldn't murder Isiah's wife. He bailed me out. He gave me money. He watched out for me. His wife helped me when I was in trouble. But don't worry, Mr. Logan, the man I contracted to complete the deed will never talk. He would kill himself before he would snitch. We're both in the clear," said Clayton as he was slurring his words. "I hope that doesn't mean I won't be getting my other $25,000.00. The deed is done, just as you wanted."

"No, you'll get your money," said Logan. "In fact I would like to come over to your apartment tomorrow at 11:00 PM to pay you and get this whole transaction over. You're sure this Francis character is that trustworthy? It sure doesn't sound like it according to the national news. He sounds like he is an exceedingly bungling life time criminal."

"Well, to tell you the truth this was his first murder, and, I guess, it wasn't the cleanest one I've seen, but he did kill her. Although, he has committed dozens of robberies and other miscellaneous crimes, he has never snitched on anyone involved with him. He took jail time rather than snitch. That's why I called him."

"That was a stupid move on your part. You should have been honest with me at the beginning. I could have found a real hit man. How much did you pay this bungling Francis character?"

"I split the $25,000.00 with him," lied Clayton.

"You Stupid ass! I'll see you at 11:00," and Logan hung up.

Logan had to think quickly about what he was going to do to remedy the mess he had just created. He knew his partners would be really pissed. Luckily they had agreed not to call each other unless it was for business. Logan thought for a minute and remembered that Sophie would always either carry her Glock 26 in her purse or keep the gun in her bottom drawer in her office. She liked changing its location, from time to time. After Logan spoke with Clayton, Logan went into Sophie's office and found her gun in her bottom desk drawer. Many times she left it at work or just forgot about it. She was always thinking of two or three different matters at one time, especially when she left the office. Luckily, this time she left it at the office. Logan, with a sigh, took her gun with him when he went to see Clayton. He also brought $25,000.00 in a bag of $50.00 bills for the second installment payment.

———————⟫●⟪———————

There were at least 100 sightings of the 2012 Malibu called into police authorities from Key West to Tallahassee. But the one sighting that interested the authorities the most was from a waitress at a Cracker Barrel restaurant located on I-75 just West of Gainesville. In a booth, in the corner of the restaurant, was Mason 'Dusty' Francis. He ordered two scrambled eggs, a short stack of pancakes, cottage fries and two pieces of toasted rye bread. A television set was playing just above Dusty's head with his picture plastered on the screen. The 2012 Malibu was in the restaurant parking lot. The waitress who was waiting on him saw his picture as she took his order. She was scared to death. She told her manager about what she saw. The manager told her to immediately call the local police. He also told the cook to take his time on cooking Dusty's meal. Dusty was always oblivious. He just wasn't smart enough to be a good criminal.

In less than 20 minutes, just as Dusty was being served, the local police called the manager and asked him to evacuate everyone in the restaurant in a calm and slow manner. Dusty didn't even notice all the people leaving. He was too interested in his home made breakfast. Once the restaurant was mostly empty, six deputy sheriffs entered the restaurant, guns drawn, and went to the back corner booth where Dusty was sitting.

The most senior of the deputies pointed his weapon at Dusty and said, "Mason 'Dusty' Francis put your hands, palm down, on the table top. Don't make any moves or I'll shoot."

Dusty looked up and was surprised at what he saw. Dusty couldn't believe the authorities even found him, let alone so soon. He immediately complied with the deputy's demands. Another deputy walked over to the booth and told Dusty to stand up and put his hands in the air. Again Dusty complied. The deputy took Dusty's hands and put them behind his back and handcuffed him. The deputy patted him down and found that he had no weapons, drugs or needles on him. But he had nearly $1000.00 in $50 bills. Dusty was then escorted to the back of a Sheriff's patrol car and put in the back seat. The deputy emptied Dusty's pockets and checked his identification. He had an expired Florida driver's license along with several other state driver's licenses, all with his picture and name on them. All of the patrons of the restaurant were shocked that they were eating in the same restaurant as this cold blooded murderer that was being hunted throughout the State. The Daniels murder was publicized on television news nearly on an hourly basis.

The most senior deputy made a call to the Boca Raton police station and told the desk Sergeant that he had Dusty Francis in custody about 250 miles north of them. The Sergeant transferred the call to Darby Lynch.

"Hello, this is detective Darby Lynch of the Boca Raton police. Too whom are I speaking?"

"This is Deputy Sheriff Hunter Mcglone of the Alachua County Sheriff's department. I have Mason 'Dusty' Francis in the back seat of my cruiser. I plan to take him to the Alachua Sheriff's Department and put him in a holding cell. Do you want me to do anything else until someone from your department comes and picks him up?"

"Yes deputy sheriff," said Darby, "please arrest him for the murder of Sophie Daniels, car theft and other crimes unknown at this time. Then read him his rights. No need to question him. Leave that to us. If he asks for a lawyer let him make that call but have him tell his lawyer to meet him at the Palm Beach Court house at 9:30 tomorrow morning in arraignment court. Do not contact the press. If you get any calls from them please just answer 'no comment'. Let me handle them tomorrow. I appreciate all you have done deputy. I'll have all the transfer papers for signature with me when I pick him up. Was it a difficult arrest?" asked Darby.

"No, I think that Dusty was more upset we interrupted his breakfast meal than getting arrested. I got the impression he has gone through this process a lot of times," answered Deputy Mcglone.

Then Darby said he would like the names and addresses of the people who were involved in finding Francis. The Assistant States Attorney handling the case may want to speak with them.

Dusty was arrested and read his rights while in the back of the Sheriff's cruiser. He said nothing and didn't resist at all. The only thing Dusty wanted to know was what time dinner was served at the Sheriff's holding cell. Deputy Mcglone was surprised that the arrest was so easy. He couldn't tell if Dusty was really smart or if he was just a moron.

The only problem were the local press. They were everywhere. They were questioning patrons of the restaurant. They attempted to speak with every Sheriff's deputy, but got nowhere. They were photographing the police cruiser Dusty was in and wanted to get their stories ready for the next news broadcast or newspaper deadline. Sherriff Deputy Mcglone just drove off without saying a word to the press. When he arrived at the Sherriff's station, he and Dusty were mobbed by more press. Dusty was yelling that he hadn't done anything and had no idea what was going on. Deputy Mcglone just hurried Dusty inside as quickly as he could.

<hr/>

James Logan got to Clayton Reed's apartment at exactly 11:00 PM the next evening. He had the bag of $50.00 bills with him. He also had on a pair of medical gloves. Clayton didn't even ask him why he was wearing gloves. Clayton was a little high, but he didn't want to take any more drugs until he had concluded his business with Logan. Then he could celebrate.

"Hello Mr. Logan. I'm glad we are getting this done sooner than we had planned. I'm thinking of taking a short trip for a few days."

"Oh, really, where are you thinking of going?

"Just over Alligator Alley to Naples. I thought I would get a Gulf front hotel room and sit in the sun for a few days."

"Well that sounds like fun. Are you going alone or have you made plans with anyone to join you?" asked Logan to find out if anyone else may know about this transaction.

"No, just myself," said Clayton. "I like to sit at the pool bar and talk to people. I like to brag a little that I played some professional basketball. It brings a lot of different women around. They think I'm rich."

"I guess you'll need your money to help you fund that trip. I brought the $25,000.00 with me. Here is a bag of $50's. Why don't you count it to make sure I have the right amount? I put it together fairly quickly," requested Logan.

Clayton took the bag and turned it upside down and let all of the bills fall on the dining room table. Then he started to put them in $500.00 piles. While Clayton was in the midst of counting the money, Logan grabbed a throw pillow from the chair and quickly put the pillow against the back of Clayton's head. Before Clayton realized what was happening, Logan pulled the trigger of Sophie's Glock. It made a reduced noise, not quite loud enough for anyone to hear it over the noise going on outside in the parking lot. Usually a Glock is very loud, but Logan got off lucky.

Logan's hands were shaking. He was almost going to vomit, but he did his best to hold that off. It wasn't easy. There was blood everywhere. Logan was a high priced business lawyer practicing out of a downtown silk stocking Miami law firm. He had never even hit anyone with his fists, let alone shoot a man in the back of his head. He froze for a few seconds as he saw Clayton fall over the table. He was waiting for sirens, or people coming to the apartment. But after a few minutes he heard no sirens and no one was knocking on Clayton's door. He grabbed all of the money, put it back in the bag and slowly opened the outside door. He looked both ways to make sure that no one was around. Life was just getting started in that part of town. The people in the parking lot were all standing around their cars talking and drinking. So Logan walked quickly to his car that was parked a couple blocks away. He dropped the gun by a sewer drain before he got to his car so the police would find it.

Logan then drove off. When he got to the entrance of the Florida Turnpike he pulled off to the side of the road. His heart was throbbing. He needed some time to cool down. He opened the driver's door and vomited. He just couldn't hold it back any longer. He had purchased a burner cell phone in Kendall, Florida, a southern suburb, some time ago in case he needed to communicate with his co-conspirators. He told his co-conspirators to do the same just in case a call was necessary. He was glad he did that. He texted all three of his partners to tell them that Clayton Reed was taken care of. There was no way the Daniels murder could now get back to them. The Francis character knew nothing about who hired Clayton. He also told them to continue the scheme and they should not talk to each other for a while, except for normal business discussions.

Arrangements had been made by the four conspirators that all excess money collected by Jetta International from Xavier's accounts would be sent, all in cash, by Federal Express, to Logan's office. Logan's administrative assistants all knew never to open his Federal Express shipments that he received. It was a rule he had for years. Logan had, months before, incorporated several Off Shore business corporations, based in Coast Rica and the Cayman Islands, all for nonexistent clients of his firm. Then he had the corporations opened an Off Shore business account at a Costa Rica and Cayman Island bank with private account numbers. Costa Rica and the Caymans took private banking business very seriously. This was not unusual for Logan to do this for actual clients. He had done it dozens of times. Many of their clients wanted privacy, each for different reasons. He was sure no one at the firm would even take notice. Logan was the person who was to keep an accounting of all the funds and expenses for the scheme.

That text did not give any of Logan's co-conspirators a warm and fuzzy feeling. It was on their phones. Luckily they listened to Logan and purchased burner phones. Another good idea the other three couldn't understand. Now it became clear.

They were all not really sure what Logan meant by 'the problem had been solved'. But all of the co-conspirators knew that they had to continue working as usual and to help the Daniels family in any way they could. The funeral arrangements were probably being made and, if invited, they would all show up. However, only Logan, Jayden and his wife were invited to the funeral. Logan's next few days at work were nerve racking. He stayed away from employees as much as possible.

But he knew he had to show up for work as normal. Douglass Fischer, the other senior partner, noticed his demeanor and even commented to him about it. He asked his partner if there was something wrong or something going on that he should know about. All Logan would say is that he was taking Sophie's death very hard. Douglass Fischer understood that answer. He felt the same way.

⸻ ❖ ⸻

After Sophie's funeral and after Isiah was arrested for her murder, Donovan started traveling the State in order to attain a better name exposure and, most important, to raise money for his Governor's run. The fact that his son-in-law was going to be tried for his daughter's murder was not a political benefit. Even though Donovan was no longer part of Jetta, he still owned a small minority ownership of the stock. After the sale of some of his stock, all approved by the appropriate governmental agency, he owned 4% of the Company. Those shares of the Company were still up for sale. They were worth a lot of money.

There were several companies that were interested in purchasing his interest. However, negotiating the price was a problem. Isiah's legal issues came into play concerning the purchase price. A sale of a Donovan's minority interest of a company would also mean an audit of each plant including each account. Isiah still owned 10% and Sophie owned another 10% of the Company. Due to Sophie's death, her ownership interest would go to her husband, unless he was convicted of her murder. If he was convicted, his interest would go to his family. Half to his parents and the other half to his two remaining siblings. So ownership interest in the Company was an issue Donovan had to deal with in attempting to sell his stock interests.

One of the other concerns of the Company was the fact that Isiah had transferred the company's temporary management to Dijon Jackson, another black man. Donovan was furious and had contacted every Board member about overturning that decision. Several of the Board Members who were good friends of Donovan had resigned when Donovan left the Company. Isiah or Dijon had appointed other people who had no allegiance to Donovan on the Board. All of that was set forth in the By-Laws of the Corporation. All of the rest of the original Board members owned collectively only 5% of the stock. Other than Donovan's interest, Isiah's interest and Sophie's interest, all the remaining interests were owned by the thousands of individuals and investment banks and funds. However, the S & P stock exchange was contemplating eliminating the stock from trading on their exchange. Under the Stock Exchange's rules, both Isiah and Sophie's ownership interest were considered large stock holders. Also a large minority interest stockholder was running for Governor of Florida and attempting to sell a large, if not all, of his holdings. Lastly the past CEO of the company was under arrest for the murder of his wife, who was the attorney that represented the company. For those reasons, the S & P 500 was at least considering stopping the trading of the stock until all of these issues were resolved. Those issues were causing big fluctuation on Jetta's stock price and many people were short selling the stock. That made it difficult for Donovan to negotiate any realistic price for his shares.

The Board of Directors of Jetta were split on Dijon Jackson's temporary promotion. Therefore, the decision by the Board to overturn Isiah's decision to turn temporary management over to Dijon had been tabled when the Board first met after hearing about the promotion. It would come up again at the next meeting as all eyes of the Board were on Isiah's legal issues and Donovan's possible sale of his interest in the company. After all, it was Isiah's performance that increased the number of plants, increased the number of customers and had increased the stock price, which increased each owners net worth considerably. However, all of that was now in jeopardy until all of the issues involved with the Company officials was resolved.

What would happen with Isiah was a big question? Will the S & P Stock Exchange remove Jetta from its standing on the exchange? Many questions needed to be answered before the Board was willing to act. Also, the Board was aware of the talk among many of the white executives concerning the promotion of black executives with much less seniority. All of those issues were making Donovan's run for Governor even more difficult. The Board had placed its confidence in making some important decisions that needed to be made with the help of the Company's lawyer, James Logan. He had replaced Sophie after her death. They thought of changing law firms, but Dijon convinced them to stay with the Fischer firm until all of the current issues were resolved. Logan's advice to the Board was to stay the course until there was a determination on Isiah's innocent or guilt. Donovan had asked for a meeting with Logan to discuss the Company, however, Logan would not agree to such a meeting since Logan represented the 'Board' and not Donovan. Donovan was no longer a member of the Board. Donovan was contemplating hiring his own counsel to set up a shareholder meeting to have an election for a new Board. Logan was doing everything legal to delay that request. How long Logan could delay Donovan's request and whether the Republican Party was ready to nominate Donovan for Governor were two issues that would affect many people. Little did Isiah know about Logan's part, with three of his good friends, in the laundering scheme dealing with hundreds of millions of dollars. Isiah had his own personal problems which would be coming to a head very soon.

CHAPTER 19

Morgan Blackburn and Darby Lynch took a ride to the Alachua County Sherriff's department to pick up Mason Francis. It was a three hour drive from West Palm Beach to Gainesville. It took less than an hour to complete all of the necessary paper work to transfer Dusty Francis from the custody of one County to the custody of another. Dusty was in a holding cell while all of the paper work was completed. Morgan and Darby thanked all of the Sheriff deputies involved in apprehending Dusty. They all agreed it was one of the easiest apprehensions they had ever had. Dusty never argued, complained or attempted to get away. All he wanted was to get a full meal. Morgan and Darby didn't seem too surprised considering the way he handled himself in his abilities to commit crimes. The Deputy Sheriff of Alachua County gave Darby all of the names and addresses and statements of everyone at the Cracker Barrel restaurant that was involved with the apprehension. The 2012 Malibu SS was being towed to the Palm Beach motor pool for the local CSI crew to examine the car. Also, Dusty's old car that he abandoned was on its way to the same place. Those results would be available in about a week. With that completed, Dusty was handcuffed, leg shackled and put in the Palm Beach County police cruiser and taken back to a West Palm Beach holding cell. There he would be interrogated and arraigned.

When the detectives and their suspect arrived in Palm Beach, Dusty was put in the main detention center of the Palm Beach County jail after he was processed through their system. He was 12 jail cells away

from Isiah. When Isiah heard about Dusty being incarcerated so close
to him, he yelled out profanities at Dusty for an hour. Dusty just fell
asleep. The two inmates had never met and the guards were told to make
sure that they never were together as long as they were in detention.

The next morning Dusty was arraigned on the charges of conspiracy
to commit murder, first degree murder, theft of a vehicle and several
other minor crimes. He was then assigned a public defender lawyer.
He didn't have enough money to retain a private criminal lawyer. The
remains of his $1,500.00 fee was confiscated as evidence. His lawyer
got Dusty's case when the clerk called Dusty up to the podium where
his new lawyer pleaded not guilty on his behalf. They had never met
before that time. Sidney White the local prosecutor asked for remand
and there was no argument by Dusty's lawyer. Instead of transferring
him back to detention, he was taken to an interrogation room, with
his attorney, where Blackburn and Lynch interrogated him concerning
Sophie Daniels' murder.

"Mr. Francis, my name is Darby Lynch and this is my partner
Morgan Blackburn. We are detectives for Palm Beach County. Are you
aware of why you here today?"

"My client was just charged with first degree murder," said Hunter
Carr, the public defender representing Dusty. "I understand that Mr.
Francis is being accused of murdering Sophia Daniels, the daughter
of Donovan Taylor, the Speaker of the House and a candidate for the
Republican Party's nominee for Governor of the State. I have read the
County's file that I received this morning. There is all this abstract
evidence that may look like my client was at the scene of a crime and
didn't report it to the authorities. Also it alleges that he stole a car. I see
no proof that the gun the County found was my client's or he actually
murdered anyone. Especially with nothing showing that the gun was
ever fired and no evidence of motive."

Dusty sat at the interrogation table with no handcuffs on and said
nothing. He just listened to his lawyer talk gibberish. He had not even
been given time to speak with his lawyer privately yet.

"Dusty," said Darby, "who hired you to kill Sophie Daniels? How
much money did you get to kill her?"

"Talk to me Darby," said Hunter, "my client is saying nothing until we have an opportunity to speak privately."

"Hunter, you have been in the public defender's office for at least five years now," said Morgan. "We have worked with you dozens of times. Have you ever read a more comprehensive file with sufficient evidence to convict your client for first degree murder, by hire, with a compelling case for the death penalty? Now we want to know who hired him and why. Then, maybe, the States Attorney will think about taking the death penalty off the table."

Hunter thought for a while and finally said, "Why don't you give us some time to talk? Let me see what Mr. Francis has to say. I'll knock on the two way window when we're ready. And bring my client a sandwich and a soda. He looks like he's starving," as Dusty nodded his head agreeing with his attorney.

"Okay," said Darby, "but remember, this is an open and shut case for the death penalty. So be quick. I'll make sure your client gets something to eat."

"Make it a ham and cheese sandwich and coke. The real one, not that no caffeine and sugar shit," finally said Dusty.

Then the detectives left. A few minutes later an officer brought Dusty a ham and cheese sandwich from the vending machine with a can of Real Coke.

Hunter had defended dozens of murder cases including murder for hire. He knew that the evidence he read that had been compiled by the County was overwhelming. There was no doubt in Hunter's mind that Dusty did the murder, stole the car and tried to run away. It was one of the sloppiest murder scene pictures he had ever seen. The pictures were graphic, especially the pictures of the victim. Dusty still had evidence of cuts and bruises on his body and face. The officers took pictures of them as possible evidence if there was ever a trial. Hunter, even though just a public defender, knew that he would probably be able to negotiate a favorable plea which could take the death penalty off the table and even some amount of years instead of life in prison without parole. Dusty was 39 years old. Maybe he would even be able to get a parole? At least Hunter could tell Dusty that. But Hunter knew he would never be paroled for this crime. The number of years negotiated would be what Dusty would serve. Hunter's best bet was to start negotiations for 15 years.

So Hunter formally introduced himself to Dusty and showed him the evidence the State had against him and the pictures of the crime scene and the victim. He also showed him pictures of his old car in the Fashion Mall's parking lot and the Malibu in the Cracker Barrel's lot.

Dusty looked at the pictures as he ate his sandwich and read some of the statements and saw the evidence against him. Hunter then said, "Dusty, maybe you should think about telling the authorities who hired you to do this crime and why he hired you."

"I'm no snitch. Never have been and never will be. I want my day in Court. Let them prove I did this. I don't snitch."

"I understand, and you've been through the system enough to know that the State has the burden of proof to try to prove to a jury that you did this crime beyond a reasonable doubt," said Hunter. "But they have your DNA from the scene and from your skin under the victim's fingernails. The murder gun has your prints on the clip and rounds in it, and on and on and on. Do you really believe that a jury will believe a lifelong criminal with all that evidence? Such a brutal murder of a beautiful young lawyer practicing in a big time silk stocking law firm. The daughter of the Speaker of House for the State and a husband who is the CEO of a publically held Fortune 500 company?"

"I don't snitch, period," emphatically said Dusty.

"Dusty, you can tell me who hired you. I am your lawyer. Everything you tell me is confidential I can't tell the police anything you say to me. Plus the person who I believe hired you is currently dead. So that really wouldn't technically be snitching," quickly said Hunter to get Dusty's real attention and to open up.

"Are you trying to tell me that Clayton is dead?"

"Yes Clayton Reed is dead. He was shot, execution style, with a bullet to the back of his head," said Hunter. "Is he the man that hired you to commit this murder?

"Do the police know that Clayton hired me? Do they know he is dead?" asked a curious and confused Dusty.

"They know he is dead. They know he knew Isiah and Sophie Daniels. They found about $25,000.00 in his apartment. I believe they think that he may be involved with this murder, but they need to hear how he was involved from you."

Dusty then became furious that Clayton had all that money and only gave him $1,500.00 to kill Sophie Daniels. So Dusty admitted to Hunter that Clayton hired him. Dusty explained the relationship between Clayton and his brother Justin and the fact that they all knew Clayton. Dusty's parents even knew Isiah's parents. But Dusty didn't know any motive. Clayton just told him it had to be done. Dusty had no idea whether someone hired Clayton to do the murder or not. $1,500.00 was a lot of money for Dusty. That's why he agreed to do it. Dusty told Hunter what Clayton told him to say if he got caught. But now Clayton was dead. Dusty told him the whole story about how he got in the Daniel's home and the entire story of how he murdered her, cleaning himself up and stealing a car to try to get away. Dusty couldn't grasp the need to try to tell the police a motive. He didn't know it. However, that would go a long way to negotiate a reduction of his sentence. But Dusty had no idea about that.

Hunter asked if Dusty would tell the detectives everything he just told Hunter. Dusty agreed as long as Hunter got copies of the crime pictures that showed Clayton dead. Dusty never believed the authorities. He had never met his lawyer before. So he wanted proof before he told the truth. Then he wanted a reasonable sentence. Hunter promised him he would try to get those pictures. That's all he could do. He would get proof of Clayton's death and then attempt to negotiate the sentence before Dusty told his story. In that way, if he couldn't get a reasonable sentence, Hunter would make the State try Dusty. That, Hunter knew they didn't want to do. They wanted the person who paid Clayton Reed to have Sophie Daniels murdered. Hunter knew that Dusty would not be sentenced to the agreed amount of time until after he testified in Isiah's, or any other trial, that may come up for persons unknown at that time who may have hired Clayton. Dusty, after much discussion, finally understood that.

With Dusty's consent, Hunter knocked on the two way window for the detectives to come in. After 20 minutes of discussion, including the detectives showing Dusty pictures of Clayton Reed shot in the back of his head, the detectives agreed to recommend 15 to 20 years if Dusty told the detectives everything he knew, including a motive.

Hunter insisted on the Assistant States Attorney putting that in writing. Within 15 minutes Sidney White signed the agreement on the 15 to 20 year sentence if Dusty told the entire story that he knew and 20 years even if he didn't tell the motive. A recording machine was brought into the interrogation room and Dusty started telling his story from the beginning. Hunter was guiding him, and the detectives were interrupting asking questions. After an hour of confessing, the detectives were not very happy about the deal that Dusty received. The detectives after multiple forms of interrogation believed that Dusty had told them everything he knew. Nothing Dusty said incriminated Isiah Daniels or anyone else in the case. Now where did Morgan and Darby go from there? Isiah knew Clayton Reed but not Justin Francis. But what did that mean. Was that a coincidence. Morgan and Darby didn't believe in coincidences. At least that was a starting point.

Dusty would allocute to the crime of murder for hire in about a week. He would be sentenced to a minimum of 15 to 20 years, with the possibility of parole, even though he didn't say he knew the motive. Dusty's agreement required him to testify to the facts he outlined in his statement if the State may need him to collaborate those facts at any time. Dusty had no problem with that. After all, Clayton was dead. He didn't snitch.

⸺►●◄⸺

While Dusty was admitting his part in the conspiracy of the murder of Sophie Daniels, Todd Hawkins was in Court before the honorable Judge Tanner Andrews who was assigned the Isiah Daniels' case, by the luck of the draw. Todd had filed a motion to have the trial of Isiah moved to a location where there was not as much publicity as there had been in Palm Beach County.

"Your Honor I have to admit that I was surprised that you were assigned this case," said Todd Hawkins, "since your relationship with the defendant's family is well known in the County. In fact, I have heard that Donovan Taylor may have even asked you to be his campaign manager for the South Eastern part of the State for fund raising in his run for Governor."

"Well counselor, you seem to know more than I do about the defendant's father-in-law's run for Governor. I have not been approached to hold such a position and, if asked, I would have respectfully declined."

"I apologize if I may have gone beyond the parameters of this hearing. But I am glad to hear that you are not part of Donovan Taylor's campaign," said Todd. "So maybe we can move forward on my motion to change the venue of this case."

"Please do," said the Judge, "but I hope this motion to move this trial has nothing to do with the fact that it was a coincidence that I was picked randomly to handle this case."

"To be honest your honor, if you rule against my motion, I do plan on making an oral motion today to have you recused. You are aware of my concerns since I had indicated those concerns at my client's arraignment. But I'll move forward with my current motion," said Todd.

"Do you have anything to say at this point Ms. White?" asked the Judge.

"Nothing so far your Honor."

Todd then spoke for about 12 minutes outlining the reasons for a necessary change of venue. It included mostly press coverage of both the murder of the defendant's wife but also news shows on Fox, CNN, MSNBC television and talk radio about the defendant personally and as well as matters dealing with his Company, his relationship with the Taylor family and issues of race. Todd's principal concern was that all of those media comments and opinion editorials spoke mostly in a defamatory manner of the black/white issue of the defendant's marriage and his prejudices towards white people. There have been a large number of opinion editorials in local newspapers, and even the New York Times, alleging systemic racism in the defendant's Company including how the defendant handled personnel promotions and wage increases. Todd concluded that all of the negative press surrounding the defendant would make it impossible to find a sufficient number of impartial jurors in Palm Beach County.

"Ms. White," said Judge Andrews, "any rebuttal?"

"None your Honor," answered Sidney who knew that if the trial was not transferred to a more impartial venue, the defendant would have a very good argument, on appeal, if he was convicted and especially if he was given the death penalty. Last thing the Palm Beach States Attorney wanted was a new trial if the County were too loose on appeal.

Judge Andrews had listened closely to Todd's arguments and was somewhat surprised that the States Attorney didn't oppose any of the defendant's arguments. More surprising was that all of the defendant's arguments made sense. Todd was astonished by the Judge's response.

"Where do you think this trial should take place counselor?" asked Judge Andrews to Todd.

"I believe that the west coast of Florida would be the best location. It is near enough to where the murders took place, but yet only segments on the national news had been broadcast to that location. As far as I have been able to determine, there has been no local articles written about the defendant, little on the murders themselves, and no opinion editorials from any of the local press there."

"So how would you feel about Lee County Circuit Court in Fort Myers?" asked the Judge to both defendant's counsel and Sidney White.

"No objection Your Honor," Said Todd.

Immediately thereafter Sidney White also said, No objection Your Honor."

"Well pack your bags counselors, my clerk will contact the Chief Judge of the Lee County Circuit Court to let them know what is coming their way. I always wanted a vacation on Fort Myers Beach. And may God be with us all."

With that Todd filled in his prepared Order that he brought to the hearing, just in case the Judge ruled his way, by inserting Lee County

Circuit Court. Judge Andrews signed the Order right then on the bench. Todd was flabbergasted. Sidney was happy she didn't have to try the case in front of the east coast press. But everyone in that Court room knew that the east coast press was also packing their bags.

CHAPTER 20

The local press and television stations were heavily criticizing Judge Andrews for allowing a change of venue for the Isiah Daniels murder trial. They inferred that Judge Andrews was in Donovan Taylor's pocket and did whatever he was asked. Nothing could be less true. Donovan made it quite clear that he wanted the trial to remain in his back yard. The press never believed him and the overwhelming negative press had an effect on Donovan's poll numbers as he was dropping weekly. Just before his son-in-law's trial was to begin he was polling at 29% against two other Republicans running for the nomination of Governor.

All things seemed to be going badly for Donovan. His new attorney, Clifford Townsend, one of the best known corporate lawyers in Florida, was working on attempting to set a shareholder meeting for all Jetta International shareholders in order to vote in a new Board of Directors. Donovan had a handpicked group of five of his loyal friends and business people to serve on a new Board along with Donovan, who would be the sixth Board Member. Townsend's firm, was also located in downtown Miami on Brickell Street. Fischer and Logan, Jetta's counsel, had litigated many cases with Townsend's firm. This was just another large contested law suit involving the two firms. James Logan represented the current Board of Jetta. He continually filed as many motions and attorney meetings as possible to attempt to delay any final court proceeding which may allow Donovan to call his shareholder meeting. Logan knew Donovan wanted to control the Board with his cronies and to get rid of the current Board. One of the biggest issues

Donovan had was the fact that a large portion of the shareholder votes were in the hands of Sophie and Isiah. Everyone knew that usually only a handful of the public who owned stock in public companies comes to shareholder meetings or even sends in proxies for electing Board Members. They usually have no idea who are running. The vote would come down to only a handful of shareholders. Sophie and Isiah had 20% of the votes. The issue as to who could vote that 20% was a difficult issue that had to be decided before any shareholder meeting could be set. Judges were hesitant to rule on motions brought in favor of Donovan to hold a meeting until that issue was resolved. Donovan and his attorney were frustrated. Donovan's attorney even made a motion to have an uninterested third party be appointed by the Court to vote Sophie's and Isiah's shares. The Court denied that motion.

However, the controversy between Donovan and the Company's Board was working well for Dijon Jackson, Jayden Robinson and Darius Williams. James Logan was doing a good job keeping the current Board in power. That Board voting almost unanimously the way Dijon wanted. The Company had good sales and profits. Their scheme was in their middle stages and moving fast. Dijon and Darius were sending out multiple purchase orders to Jayden's fake subsidiaries. The largest purchase orders sent to Xavier Corporation was for the required purchases for precious metals needed by Jetta. Other purchase orders, which were bogus, were sent for smaller quantities of the most expensive precious metals. Those purchase orders went directly to Jayden Robinson and identified as orders to the fake companies that James Logan set up at his law firm. The bogus purchase orders to those fake companies were also put on the books of Jetta so as to make them legitimate.

When Jayden received the bogus purchase orders, he filled them and sent the precious metals to either Dijon or Darius. They, in turn sold the precious metals to middle men, in European nations, who handled the sale of those metals to various underground illegal organizations. The money that Jetta received from the middlemen was then sent directly to James Logan who deposited the money in the offshore accounts of the fake companies. Then Logan made up bogus invoices, on behalf of his law firm, from those fake companies to his law firm for work performed as if they were real clients. Logan's bogus clients actually got billed for any of the bogus work that was not really performed on their behalf. Logan actually paid his firm their fees. Under those circumstances no one in Logan's firm questioned him on his billing procedures. He was a senior partner in the firm. Everyone assumed he was honest concerning his billings.

The bogus funds in the offshore accounts started to increase quickly. It was in the multi-millions of dollars the first few months of the scheme and increasing quickly thereafter. The scheme seemed to be working as planned. With Isiah in jail he couldn't audit any of the Jetta's accounts. Sophie was dead so she couldn't help Jetta. Lastly, Donovan was not a part of the company. He was not a Board Member or employee, so he was unable to see the books set up in the Company. Only the public documents filed with the stock exchange could be reviewed by Donovan or his lawyer. They didn't reveal anything about fake or bogus invoices. The scheme was working perfectly.

━━━━►●◄━━━━

Judge Andrew's clerk called the Chief Judge for the Lee County Circuit Courts in downtown Fort Myers concerning the change of venue for Isiah Daniels trial to the Lee County Court. The clerk had emailed the Change of Venue Oder signed by Judge Andrews to the Lee County Chief Judge's clerk. After the Chief Judge reviewed the Order, he agreed to have Isiah's trial in Lee County. The case was assigned to Judge Benjamin Walsh, a senior Judge in that Circuit. Judge Walsh put Isiah's case on the criminal docket. However, Judge Walsh agreed to allow Judge Andrews to be the trial judge to handle the case. Judge Walsh indicated he would be available for consultation on any issues dealing with the local rules for the Lee County Court.

The criminal cases were set for trial as soon as possible under the Constitutional requirement for a speedy trial. A hearing was set for a case management meeting one week after the assignment to the Lee County Court. It was on a Monday morning at 10:30 with Judge Walsh and Judge Andrews. The purpose of the meeting was to have the Palm

Beach prosecutor, Sidney White, who would be trying the case, the Lee County prosecutor, Kaye Narin, who would assist, if needed, and Isiah's counsel meet to determine when the trial would commence, narrow the issues and determine about how long the trial would take. Any motions that any of those attorneys may have concerning the case would be set on the Judges calendar prior to the trial date.

Isiah was transferred from the Detention Area in Palm Beach County to the Lee County jail in Fort Myers pending his trial. Isiah's family was very upset with the change of venue. It would be difficult for Isiah's parents and his sisters and nephew to come to Fort Myers. All of them had jobs and it would be very expensive to drive 2 hours each way and to stay in hotels during the trial. Otis Daniels asked Isiah's friends, Dijon Jackson and Darius Williams if they could possibly be able to fund some of their expenses to be able to go to some sessions of the trial. After all, Isiah had promoted both of them to high paying positions at Jetta International. Both of them refused and gave sham excuses. Money was much more important to both of them than Isiah's fate. Both Otis and Clover were extremely disappointed with them. Neither Otis nor Clover would dare ask anyone from the Taylor family for funds.

The only other person they could think of who may be able to help them was Isiah's attorney. Todd was happy to hear from them. Todd told them that he would be getting several suites in a downtown hotel near the Court House at the Hotel Indigo. He, his paralegal and investigator would each have use of one of the bedrooms and each have a bathroom. The living area of the suite would be their work area during the trial. He told Otis and Clover that he would pay for a hotel room for them to use at any time they were able to come to the trial. It would be booked for them during the entire trial. He told Isiah's parents that it would be good for them to be in the Courtroom as often as they could. Also room service to the hotel room for meals would be included.

"Oh thank you Mr. Hawkins that is more than generous," said Clover.

"Don't thank me. The truth is your son will be paying for all of yours and my expenses. Thank Isiah. I'm sure he would want you and his sisters by his side during this time," said Todd. "I'll keep you informed when the trial will begin and when you are able to check in to the hotel room."

"How long do you think the trial will last, Mr. Hawkins?" asked Clover.

"I believe it should last about two to three weeks. Hopefully, Isiah will be found not guilty and this whole nasty mess will be over with, at least for Isiah," said Todd. "However, the States Attorney has finally announced that the death penalty would be proper in this case. If Isiah is found guilty of any of the charges, there will be a second trial to determine if Isiah will get either the death penalty or life in prison without parole. I will need both of you, Evy and Dakala in the Courtroom. I will also be calling some, or maybe all of you as witnesses to give your testimony as to Isiah's character and significance so to try to sway the Jury to spare his life, if it even comes to that."

"Mr. Hawkins I don't even want to talk about that. I can't comprehend that my baby did such a horrible thing. He cannot be put to death. Please make sure of that, please," pleaded Clover.

"I promise we will do our best. I have learned over the past few weeks that Isiah is a gentle person and not the type I usually represent in these types of matters. I believe we have many facts that are on our side. You need to trust me."

"If Isiah picked you to represent him, I am sure you are the best person to handle his case," said Clover as she hung up and cried.

Mason 'Dusty' Francis had his allocution hearing one week after he had confessed to detectives Blackburn and Lynch that he murdered Sophie Daniels. The allocution was before Judge Andrews. He was the Judge assigned to all aspects of the Sophie Daniels murder case. Both the Judge and Sidney White were not pleased about driving back and forth between Palm Beach and Fort Myers, but they knew it was necessary.

The Court clerk called the case of State of Florida vs. Mason Frances along with the case number. All the attorneys and Dusty went to their assigned table before the Judge's bench. Sidney White was the Assistant States Attorney representing the people of Palm Beach County and Hunter Carr, Dusty's public defender attorney, was representing Dusty. Both of the attorneys introduced themselves and who they represented to the Court. Even though the Judge knew everyone, it was required for everything to be put on the record.

"Your Honor," started Sidney, "this hearing is for the purpose of having the defendant in this case allocute to his participation, per the settlement agreement reached between the People and Mr. Francis, on the charge of murder in the first degree."

"Mr. Carr, is your client prepared to allocute to his participation in the murder of Sophie Taylor Daniels?"

"He is your Honor," answered Hunter.

In the Courtroom were Donovan and Shelia Taylor, Anya Taylor, Deena Hawkins, Martell Dixon, Justin Francis, Mickey Conrad, James Logan, Douglass Fischer, Dustina Washington and Detectives Blackburn and Lynch. Also present were over a dozen press people from local television news, and national reporters for Fox News, CNN and MSNBC. Usually no one shows up for an allocution hearings, but the Courtroom was packed. This murder was big news.

"Mr. Francis would you please tell this Court, in your own words, what exactly was your participation in Sophie Danials' murder?" asked the Judge.

Dusty turned to his lawyer and whispered to him, "What am I supposed to say?"

"We went over what you were going to say a half of a dozen times. Tell the Judge just as you rehearsed it in my office," said Hunter.

"Mr. Francis, we're waiting," said Judge Andrew.

Dusty then started from the beginning when Clayton Reed called Dusty's brother, Justin, to ask Dusty to do a favor for him. Justin didn't know what that favor was and Dusty never told him. He completed the favor Clayton wanted him to do for which he received $1,500.00 plus an antique gun that he was supposed to use to shoot the victim.

He was told that he could keep the gun after he shot the victim and he could sell it for as much as he could after the murder was over. Dusty then said some lawyer gave Clayton the gun to give to Dusty to use to shoot the victim.

"Wait a minute Mr. Francis," said Judge Andrews, "you said some lawyer gave the gun to Mr. Reed. Is that correct?"

"Yes sir," answered Dusty.

"Who was this lawyer?" asked the Judge.

"I don't know. Clayton just mentioned that a lawyer had given him the gun to kill the woman."

"Ms. White," said the Judge, "Did you know about a lawyer involved with this matter?"

"No Your Honor. This is the first I heard about any lawyer being involved. I was never told who hired Clayton Reed and what the terms of that agreement were. All I have been told, by the defendant, is that he was hired by Mr. Reed to murder Sophie Daniels. He never mentioned any lawyer or any motive and my office believed him," said Sidney.

"Mr. Hunter," said the Judge, "did you know about a lawyer giving your client a gun?"

"No your Honor and I spoke with my client many times and asked for every detail. This is the first I heard about this lawyer," answered Hunter.

Everyone in the Court Room was in shock. The press were frantically writing in their note books. James Logan wanted to get up and leave, but he didn't give Clayton a gun. He gave him a knife. Logan was confused and shocked.

"Well Mr. Francis, go on and finish your allocution," requested the Judge. Both attorneys looked at each other and Hunter shrugged his shoulders.

Dusty finished his allocution just the way he had rehearsed and finished when he stole the Malibu car.

"Ms. White, are the People satisfied with Mr. Francis' allocution?"

"We are Your Honor. We have agreed on a sentence of 15 to 20 years for Mr. Francis. However we request that the Court hold off on sentencing until Mr. Francis testifies in the trial of Isiah Daniels. That was one of the stipulations for this agreement. As you are aware, that trial will be happening soon in Lee County."

Judge Andrews then asked both counsel to come to the bench. Sidney and Hunter walked around their respective tables and up to the bench. The Judge was about two feet above them. He looked down on them and said, "I am not inclined to accept Mr. Francis' allocution until there is some investigation about this attorney that gave Mr. Reed this gun. I think it would be important to know who this attorney was and what he had to do with the murder of Ms. Daniels, don't the two of you agree?"

"I believe we can separate our Agreement with Mr. Francis from this illusionary attorney who popped up today. My detectives, who are in the Courtroom today can still investigate some of the facts of this murder. However, they and I are certain that the person who hired Mr. Reed was Isiah Daniels. Maybe Mr. Francis misunderstood Clayton Reed and thought that Daniels was an attorney. After all, Mr. Francis had no idea that someone actually hired Mr. Reed to murder Sophie Daniels. So he may be confused today. However, if you accept Mr. Francis' allocution, I will have my detectives look into this mystery lawyer issue," said Sidney with hopes that the Judge would accept the allocution so the matter could be finished.

"Mr. Carr," said the Judge, "do you have any thoughts on this issue?"

Hunter Carr was a public defender with 45 cases to try to resolve with more coming in each day. He didn't have the time nor did he want to keep this as an open case so he said to Judge Andrews, "I am in agreement with Sidney Your Honor. This mystery lawyer never came up at any time I was questioning or discussing Mr. Francis' allocution with him. I too think that Your Honor should accept my client's allocution. Mr. Francis had been confused often when I spoke with him."

"Okay, please step back," said the Judge.

Both attorneys returned to their respective tables.

"Reluctantly, I will accept Mr. Francis' allocution and defer sentencing until after he has testified in the Daniels matter. However, I am disturbed about the fact that a lawyer may be involved somehow in the Daniels murder. I am directing the detectives, who I understand are in the Court Room today, as I can see Mr. Blackburn and Ms. Lynch here, to do some additional investigating on that matter. At sentencing I would like an answer to the issue of this unknown lawyer and if any of it is true. With that, this matter is concluded subject to the detective's final investigation."

Everyone in the Courtroom was astonished. Both attorneys knew what that evening news headline would be. Dusty didn't understand all the fuss. He thought he did just fine.

Darby and Morgan were pissed about Dusty not ever mentioning a lawyer being involved. They could not think of any lawyer suspects, but they agreed to follow up. What were they going to find? They had no clue where to start. Donovan Taylor was thinking to himself about who that lawyer could be. If there was one, he wanted to know who it was. Maybe he would hire a private investigator? The Dusty Francis case was not over yet.

CHAPTER 21

The headlines in almost all news publications in Southeast Florida, and the headlines in the local Fort Myers and national news was who was this 'mysterious lawyer'. Dusty just mentioned the fact that Clayton Reed was visited by a lawyer just before he was murdered. At least that is how the press phrased it. Detectives Blackburn and Lynch were taken by surprise. Why had that fact not surfaced anywhere in the investigations? Sidney White was furious with Hunter that Dusty mentioned this fact in his allocution. At no time did Dusty say anything about any lawyer being involved. Sidney immediately met with Blackburn and Lynch and instructed them to further interview Dusty again and again and again to come to some definitive conclusion as to this new controversy. That fact may critically affect Isiah's trial.

The next morning Dusty was in an interrogation room with Sidney White, Morgan Blackburn and Darby Lynch. Hunter Carr, to his dismay, still represented Dusty, and was also present.

"Hunter when did you first hear about this mysterious lawyer?" asked Sidney. "I really hope you didn't know about this and not reveal that fact to the States Attorney or me. Withholding exculpatory evidence is an ethical violation. One I would have to report to the Bar Association's Ethical Committee."

"Just hold on. That fact was as much as a surprise to me as it was to you, Sidney," said Hunter as he turned his head toward Dusty and shrugged his shoulders and said, "Dusty, where in the Hell did you come up with the idea that some lawyer met with Clayton Reed and gave him a gun to give to you?"

"I thought I told you that when we first met. My brother, Justin told me that some lawyer was giving something to Clayton. That's what Clayton told him. They were good friends."

"No, I never heard that Dusty. Didn't you think it may have been important to mention the fact that a lawyer came to visit Clayton before he was murdered?" said Hunter in an annoyed voice.

"Do you know the name of this lawyer or who he worked for or even what he looked like?" asked Sidney.

"All I know is what I told you. That's it. I thought I was done being interrogated. Why don't you go talk to my brother?" replied Dusty.

"I think that's a good idea," said Hunter to the detectives.

Neither of the two detectives believed Dusty. He had been confused often on several of the issues in this matter. He never mentioned a lawyer before. That fact was all a big waste of time in the minds of the detectives, but they knew that they needed to speak with Justin Francis. The prosecutor would insist. Hopefully that would put this new issue to bed.

"Sidney, we're on our way to Justin Francis' home to speak with him," said Darby. "We'll be back to you as soon as possible so we can clear this mess up."

"I hope so," said Sidney, "The press is continually asking my office about this mysterious lawyer."

During Dusty's interrogation, Isiah was in the Lee County jail. Todd Hawkins was setting up his Suite at the Hotel Indigo. Neither Todd nor Isiah were at Dusty's allocution. Todd heard about this 'mysterious lawyer' while listening to the NBC nightly news. That was a significant fact that could change everything. It could be the 'smoking gun' that may put reasonable doubt in the minds of the jury concerning the hiring or murdering of Clayton Reed. It may be that game changer they were looking for.

Todd immediately called his investigator who also heard about this lawyer issue on the news. Todd asked him to look into it. He asked him to look into the whereabouts of every lawyer Dusty or Isiah ever dealt with. Todd was sure Sidney White was doing the same. Isiah's trial was going to begin in a week. Todd had brought several motions before the trial Judge, the week before the trial, to try to get all charges dismissed. Todd argued that there was no actual forensic evidence linking Isiah to anything. There was no eye witnesses that saw or heard Isiah hire Clayton Reed to murder his wife nor to murder Clayton Reed. But most important of all of Todd's arguments was the fact that there was not any motive ever mentioned by the prosecutor or even Dusty during his allocution. The Judge denied all of Todd's motions. The Judge indicated that most murder cases, including murder by hire, are proven on only circumstantial evidence. Motive was not a necessary element to sustain a guilty plea from the jury. Even though it would help to have a motive, it wasn't necessary. Hence the Judge's rulings. Thereafter the trial date was set.

⎯⎯⎯⎯➤●⧫⎯⎯⎯⎯

Donovan's fight to acquire his control of Jetta International back was going badly. Logan brought 4 different motions on behalf of the current Jetta Board of Directors to have the case dismissed. Those motions were based on the fact that there were issues still unresolved concerning Isiah's ownership interest and Sophie's ownership interest for voting purposes. In addition, Donovan's attorney, Clifford Townsend, could not convince the Judge that the company was being mismanaged by either the company's current Board or its officers. Jetta was still operating soundly, making a profit with no real significant impediments in its operations. There was, however, a lawsuit recently filed by several white management employees alleging discrimination by Jetta management concerning the promotions of black employees. The Judge in Donovan's law suit didn't look at that issue as mismanagement. Those type of lawsuits were filed frequently in many large companies. So, the Judge in the matter, after the fourth motion brought by James Logan, finally dismissed Donovan's law suit. The Judge indicated it was the current Board's obligation to set shareholder meetings when they were required by the By-Laws of the Company or if extraordinary issues required such a meeting. The Judge did not believe that Donovan met his burden to prove otherwise. Donovan's bid to take over Jetta was a setback. Dijon Jackson, Darius Williams were elated when they heard the ruling by the Judge. The scheme would be able to continue as planned. James Logan did a great job delaying and extending the time in which Donovan could cause the scheme to be shut down. Logan's anxiety concerning the scheme, and the death of Clayton, was slowly disappearing.

It just wasn't a good week for Donovan. He lost his bid to retake control of Jetta International and his bid for the Republican nomination for Governor was fading quickly. His polling numbers were plummeting due to the issues in his personal and business life. He became a public figure with the local and national news pundits pounding him about his problems almost on a nightly basis. A meeting with the State wide Republican Party committee and Donovan's people went badly. The State Republican Party was in the process of endorsing their candidate. There were four possible candidates. Donovan was their first rejection. His race for Governor was over. That decision was a big part of Donovan's bad week. All of this was happening while he was still mourning the loss of his daughter.

At the end of the brutal week, Donavan was at home with his wife, having a drink before dinner, discussing with her his harsh week. He talked about the number of people who he had helped over the years who turned on him due to circumstances Donovan believed he never instigated. How could that be, he questioned. Even though he didn't say it out loud to his wife, Donovan believed that his love of the basketball program at the University of Miami may have been a part of his down fall. Too many blacks. He recruited most of them. That was his own fault. They were the best players, but as it turned out the school's basketball team never even made it to the National Title Tournament. All those blacks and all the time and money he spent on them with no real results. One black even married and murdered his daughter. Blacks were running the company he started. Blacks, in Donovan's mind, were the lowest form of human beings, and the cause of all his problems.

Finally after a long pause in their conversation, Shelia asked Donovan what was really bothering him. Donovan didn't want to talk about all of the blacks who were tearing down his world. He just told his wife that he wanted the trial of his beautiful daughter to be over. Both Donovan and Sheila would be testifying. They were nervous and upset about that fact. But Donovan was confused as to where his life would take him in the future. He was still the Speaker of the House for the State Legislature. Although he had not been very involved in many of the committee meetings he should have been attending. People were aware of that and were wondering whether he could handle his current position any more. He wondered if all of his current issues would cause him to lose most of the Republicans confidence of his constituents who lived in his district. Then he even wondered whether he could even win his seat back in his own district. What did his constituents think about him after hearing all of his issues on the local and national news? All those damn blacks.

Donovan was at the low point of his very successful life. Money was not a problem. He had lots of it. But he was still depressed. Shelia could see that. She tried to help him, but he was just finding it hard to move forward. He just couldn't get off the notion that the blacks in his life were his scapegoats causing him to plummet into failure. How could he change that? Isiah Daniels was the number one issue. Why did he let his daughter marry him? He should have spoken up at the time and stopped the relationship. But his standing in the community and his ego just wouldn't let him do that. A big mistake. Maybe the biggest of his life. Those damn dinners with the players. Why did he even do that? He knew Anya felt the same way as he did. Shelia just went along. She thought it was a kind act on the part of her husband. She never even thought Isiah was a bad husband. She still didn't believe he was the one who murdered her daughter. But she said nothing. Where does life take the Taylors next? They would soon find out.

Detectives Blackburn and Lynch, as ordered by the Assistant States Attorney, drove to Overtown to meet with Justin Francis. On the way to Overtown, the two detectives discussed how this was such a waste of time. They already knew who murdered Clayton Reed. Isiah Daniels had a plausible motive, had the opportunity and had the means to murder Clayton Reed. Isiah hired Clayton Reed to kill his wife. As to motive, Isiah knew that Sophie was upset with something to do with the law suit being filed for discrimination against black management of Jetta and believed that, in some fashion, it would hurt her law firm if they defended that law suit. But they were still trying to figure that out. They knew they would have to answer questions, under oath, concerning the motives.

Sophie's father, one of the largest minority shareholder of the company, was running for Governor. Her husband was black. Would the press damage her law firm due to some blatant conflict of interest, or some racist matter? Would the press damage Sophie and the firm if they defended a black man promoting more black men over more qualified white men with longer seniority? Only Sophie's legal mind understood those issues and what that would have done to the firm. Also, there may even be criminal actions by the Federal government against Jetta and Isiah, as its CEO, for intentionally violating Federal Discrimination laws. Was it necessary, in Sophie's mind, that her firm no longer be associated with Jetta International until all of these issues were resolved? Isiah wouldn't let that happen. He knew he would never be able to change Sophie's mind. The company was too important and her firm knew everything, bad and good, about Jetta. Would some other firm be able to represent Jetta without other possible incriminating confidential matters being disclosed which would then come out at Isiah's trial? Would some of that confidential information place blame directly on Isiah? Or maybe on Sophie? But Sophie was dead. Who else could answer those questions?

Also there were rumors of infidelity by some of the black managers, including even Isiah. True or not, Sophie must have believed it was bad for the firm to be further involved with Jetta. It wasn't the best motive to murder someone. Everyone in the Palm Beach States Attorney office knew that. But that's the only motive that had been found against anyone by the States Attorney's investigators. It was strange that no one in the States Attorney's office remembered Sophie mentioning certain accounts that were somehow incorrect at the Durham plant. After all, that was the reason that Isiah was at the Durham plant the night Sophie was murdered. Or maybe Sidney White didn't even know about that fact. Todd knew why Isiah was in Durham that night, but even Isiah's own attorney never connected that fact with a possible motive for Sophie's murder. The law suit for discrimination had to be a part of the motive to murder Sophie Daniels. It had to do since it was all they had. It was the prosecutor's job to prove it in Court, not the detectives. They were thankful for that. Since all other evidence pointed to Isiah.

As to opportunity, Isiah said he was in a hotel room at the Ritz, by himself, the night that Clayton Reed was murdered. The police believed that he had time to drive to Overtown and kill Clayton and get back to the hotel room without being seen. Deena had her own room and didn't communicate with Isiah until the next morning at breakfast. Plus, and most important, Isiah had access to his wife's gun and his fingerprints were on the gun's clip and bullets.

So why were the detectives going to interrogate Justin Francis? Only because they were ordered to do it. Darby had contacted Justin to let him know they were coming to talk to him about Clayton Reed's murder. They just had a few more questions before Isiah's trial was to start. Justin was somewhat hesitant to cooperate since his brother had just admitted to murdering Sophie Daniels.

When the detectives arrived at Justin's home, both of his parents were sitting on the front porch with Justin. They were upset about their son, Francis, going to prison for murder. They were even more upset with the fact that Justin allowed Francis to get involved with Clayton Reed. Justin's parents never liked or trusted Clayton. They also never liked the fact that Justin and Clayton were friends.

When Blackburn and Lynch approached the front porch of the Francis home, Justin's father wanted to know why they were there. Hadn't their family gone through enough trauma? Darby said that they just had a few more questions for Justin. It was only matters dealing with the Isiah Daniel's trial. Mr. and Mrs. Francis were not thrilled with the police at their front porch, but they knew that they couldn't do anything about it. Justin knew he didn't do anything wrong so he was willing to cooperate. Justin never really looked out for Dusty and was never close with him. His parents were also upset with Justin for that. They wanted to make sure their son didn't do anything more harm to Dusty.

"Mr. Francis," said Darby looking at Justin, "when Dusty and Clayton met to agree on a contract on Mrs. Daniels life, were you aware of any lawyer involved with that agreement?"

"No mam."

"Do you know how Clayton Reed came into the possession of a Smith & Wesson 617 revolver?"

"When Clayton called me to ask Dusty to do a favor for him, he told me that he had everything Dusty needed. Clayton said that it was really more than a favor. It was sort of a job. He told me Dusty would like the job, especially the money. He never told me what the favor was or what he wanted from Dusty. If I would have known that it was for a murder contract I never would have said yes to Clayton," said Justin.

"But did Clayton mention that some lawyer gave him anything?"

"I think so, but I'm not sure," said Justin.

"You know you are going to have to testify at Isiah Danial's trial," said Morgan. "Isiah's attorney will be asking you these questions. So are you sure or not sure."

"I think that he may have mentioned a lawyer about something, but I really can't remember. I'm really not sure," said Justin.

"This is really important," said Darby, "you will get grilled on the stand unless you know all the answers to these questions. Maybe's will not work. So try again to remember."

"Did Dusty ever tell you that Clayton said something about a lawyer to him?" asked Justin.

"That's not what we're asking you Justin," said Darby, "Did Clayton tell you, not Dusty, there was a lawyer involved?"

"Now it's coming back to me. To tell you the truth, Clayton did tell me several times about a lawyer paying him some money to Clayton.

So I think I may have been confused. Clayton never said that a lawyer was involved with the job Clayton was giving Dusty," finally admitted Justin.

"What do you mean that a lawyer payed Clayton some money? Was it for his living expenses or to murder Sophie Daniels?" asked Morgan.

"Just what I said. A lawyer paid Clayton, from time to time, some money for him to live on. It was like a gift or something," said Justin. "Clayton mentioned that to me once some time before Ms. Daniels murder. He told me not to say anything to anyone or he would get in trouble.

"Okay, you got what you came here for," said Justin's father, "now get off my property."

"Just a few more questions, please," said Morgan.

"No. I said that's enough. Now please leave. You all have caused us enough grief. Justin told you what you wanted to know, now get out of here."

Darby looked at Morgan and they both thought that they didn't want to antagonize anyone on this notion that came up at Dusty's allocution. So they said thank you to the Francis family and left.

Both detectives knew that they had to tell Sidney White that Justin told them that he didn't say anything about a lawyer being involved in the murder contract between Clayton and Dusty. Also, Justin had no idea Clayton wanted Dusty to kill someone. Then the detectives agreed that they had to mention the fact that Clayton may, or may not have, been getting payments for living expenses from some lawyer. It probably wasn't true. So why complicate what is already done. But they agreed to mention it to Sidney. What a mistake. That mistake could change many people's lives.

CHAPTER 22

A week after the allocution of Mason 'Dusty' Francis, Isiah Daniels trial was set before Judge Tanner Andrews. Isiah was charged with two counts of first degree murder and conspiracy to commit first degree murder. The States Attorney for West Palm Beach County had formulated his statutory decision that the crimes, and the way they were achieved, warranted the death penalty under Florida law. Sidney White agreed with him. This was not Judge Andrew's first death penalty case, however it had been some time since he presided over one. He knew that the case would be longer than usual and it would take some time to pick a jury. Each potential jury had to go through the normal Voir Dire but also be questioned and analyzed by the attorneys trying the case as to their beliefs on the death penalty. That was the most important and difficult part of a death penalty trial. Sidney White had tried several death penalty cases before, with success in each trial. Todd Hawkins, however, had tried one death case, but his client was acquitted so he never got to the penalty stage. Both attorneys were excellent trial attorneys and both were well acquainted with picking the right jury.

However, before the candidates for the jury were brought into the Courtroom, the Judge asked both attorneys to step up to the bench to finalize the issue brought up during Mason Francis' allocution.

"Counselors," started Judge Andrew, "has the issue of whether or not there was an attorney involved during, or at any time, in the meeting between Mr. Francis and Clayton Reed resolved?"

"My detectives extensively questioned everyone who may have had any knowledge of the facts of that meeting, Your Honor," answered Sidney. "There is no evidence that any attorney was involved in any way concerning the negotiations to murder Mrs. Daniels. My detectives indicate that Mr. Francis was confused when he brought up the attorney in his allocution. There is some evidence, whether creditable or not, that Mr. Reed may have been receiving money from an attorney for some time before their meeting, but for a completely unrelated matter."

"Really?" stated the Judge. "How about you Mr. Hawkins?"

"My investigator also did not find any evidence concerning an attorney involved with the meeting between Clayton Reed and Mr. Francis. However, Mr. Reed's financials did reveal that he was receiving funds for a long period of time before the meeting with Dusty Francis. The money came from an off shore Lawyers Trust Account at least six to eight times a year. My investigator attempted to determine the owner of that trust account, however, it does not appear, on its face, that there is any relationship between those funds and the meeting establishing the murder of Sophie Daniels. However, that does not mean that more investigation could be warranted."

"Ms. White, did your detectives also find this string of funds to Mr. Reed from some off shore Lawyers Trust Account? Was it really an attorney's Trust account?"

"No Your Honor," replied Sidney. "I don't believe they looked that far into the finances of Mr. Reed. The funds that were in Mr. Reed's apartment were sufficient for my detectives to conclude that no other funds were involved."

"I am not happy with either of your conclusions," said the Judge. "I want to make it very clear from the beginning of this trial that if either side brings up any facts about some attorney involved in Francis' and Reed's meeting, or anything to do with a string of funds coming to Mr. Reed from any off shore account, there may be sanctions imposed on that attorney. Is that clear?"

Sidney White wanted to consult with her detectives, and Mr. Hawkins wanted to speak to his investigator and Isiah Daniels for several minutes. Sidney White came back after a few minutes and agreed to the Judges wishes. Todd Hawkins' investigator wanted to do more investigation concerning the money from the off shore Trust account, but Isiah totally refused to let that happen. Todd was confused with Isiah's insistence about leaving it be. He asked Isiah several times if he knew about the money Reed was receiving. Isiah answered in the negative, but insisted, if he was receiving money, it had nothing to do with the case. Isiah indicated that he didn't send any money to Clayton from any off shore account. Isiah said that he never created any off shore account. Todd wanted to know what was going on. Isiah admitted he gave some money to Clayton on a few occasions, but he stopped years before Sophie's murder. Isiah insisted that there was sufficient evidence to prove him innocent without this off shore money coming into the trial. It was probably not true anyway.

"I think we need some time to discuss this and do some more investigating," said Todd to Isiah. Todd's investigator insisted he could attempt to find out the owner of that account, if there was one, given sufficient time.

"No, leave it be. I swear on my parent's lives that I have no off shore account and don't know of anyone who does. What does this have to do with my wife's murder anyway?" answered Isiah.

Todd was upset that Isiah didn't seem to get it. The person who was sending the money may have been involved with who hired Clayton to murder Sophie. Isiah may be lying and had not told Todd everything. He thought about asking the Judge to have him replaced as Isiah's counsel, but he finally looked at the Judge and Isiah, then he agreed to the Judges request. Todd knew that there was a problem. For the first time, since he met Isiah, Todd questioned his belief that maybe Isiah did have something to do with his wife's murder. If Todd thought that, what would a jury think? Todd was not pleased. But he was a professional and would try his client's case to the best of his ability. So Todd told the Judge he agreed with the Judge's request. Then the Judge asked the jury pool to come into the courtroom.

With Donovan's suit to attempt to take over Jetta International was over, leaving the current Board in place, Jayden Robinson, Dijon Jackson and Darius Williams started to escalate their scheme to a higher level. They were skimming money and laundering it in the sum of hundreds of thousands of dollars a month. Isiah's trial was beginning and James Logan was certain no one in his firm knew about his fictitious clients and their off shore companies or bank accounts. Their scheme was in full force with all participants thinking of nothing else but becoming extremely rich.

Even James Logan, who was the one person that was apprehensive at first, felt more comfortable. With Isiah now being tried for a double murder, Clayton Reed dead, Dusty Francis going to jail, and the only person who actually found out about their scheme, Sophie Daniels, was also dead. James and his co-conspirators felt free to implement the scheme intensly according to the plan.

Even though all four conspirators had agreed to wait to take any of the fruits of their crime for several years, Jayden Robinson seemed to become somewhat greedy a little more abruptly than the others. This change did not escape his wife or his other participants. Dustina even saw a change in her husband's greediness. However, she thought that may be part of the fact that her husband never really mourned the death of their best friend Sophie. She was a very intelligent person. Sophie had mentioned that the case she wanted to collaborate on with Dustina may have dealt with Sophie's law firm and Isiah's company. Why was her husband's basic personality and compassionate manner changing? Isiah was a good friend of his. But yet he had not even mentioned that he wanted to go to the trial to support Isiah. He had mentioned just after Isiah was arrested that he was sure that Isiah had nothing to do with Sophie's death, but he wasn't doing anything to support their good friend. It was all very strange to Dustina. She needed to have a long talk with her husband. Something was different. Or worse, something else was going on. Was he having an affair? Or was it something to do with Sophie's death? Their relationship had changed very abruptly.

Jayden would usually drag Dustina to many dinners with several of his co-workers or clients. But he hadn't done that for a while. Yet he was spending more time at work than usual. Where does Dustina begin to confront her husband? Does she need to help Isiah's attorney to investigate Sophie's law firm or Jayden's work? She wasn't sure. She could speak with James Logan. He and Sophie were friends. He worked on both Jayden's company's legal matters as well as legal matters for Jetta. Maybe a call or visit to James would be worthwhile. Or, maybe it could be just her imagination. Maybe James could confirm that. But she had to find out. No matter the results. She would give James a call in a day or two.

The jury pool consisted of nearly 150 local residence. Most came in and sat in the spectators seats in the Courtroom until all seats were taken. So some of the remaining jury pool were standing at the back of the Courtroom. The clerk then opened the Courtroom door and requested 14 more potential jurors to come in and sit in the jury box. There were still more than 25 locals waiting outside the Courtroom in case they may be needed. Both attorneys and their staff knew that picking this jury would be difficult. Selecting a jury is among the most critical aspects of any trial, especially a death case. The death penalty was the aspect that would always be in the back of the mind of both attorneys trying this case. Picking a jury requires a great deal of insight, intuition and the understanding of people. Most people called for jury duty didn't want to be there, especially for a death penalty case. That element would make it even harder for the attorneys to choose the right people to serve.

Each of the potential jury members had already filled out an extensive form with all of their essential information for the attorneys to review. The one missing question on that form was each person's beliefs concerning the death penalty. That issue would have to be determined when the attorneys questioned each potential juror. Both of the attorneys in this case had substantial trial experience. They know that when they interview a potential jury they need to keep the jurors talking. If either of the attorneys does too much talking, the wrong juror may be picked. Both attorneys had to check their egos at the door.

Sidney knew that when she picks a juror, she will be looking for someone who is sympathetic to the victims, Sophie and Clayton. Todd, on the other hand, must make an effort to find jurors who can make an effort to look sympathetic to what happened to Sophie and Clayton, but still seek to explain why Isiah wasn't responsible for what happened. For Todd it's a case of proper storytelling, humanizing Isiah, and not spending a great deal of time over educating the jury. Since Todd would go second in questioning each juror, he needed to adapt and adjust to the tactics being established by Sidney. He needed to listen carefully to what was being asked and the answers given.

Selecting the jury is the only time the attorneys have the opportunity to discover the life experiences, biases, beliefs and attitudes of the people who will decide the case, especially their belief and ability to decide on the death penalty. To be good at picking the right 12 jurors and 2 alternates, each of the attorneys must find people who seem to like them. Most people don't like attorneys. If one of the attorneys is really good at picking a jury, they will find the 14 people who like them enough to want to spend a week or two in trial with them. But more important, that attorney must know that each juror is comfortable knowing that the attorney will be returning that same feeling. If one of the attorneys is really lucky, their adversary will have demonstrated how important they are as a lawyer to the prospective jurors. Then those jurors won't feel the same way about their adversary. It was a cat and mouse game with the life of a real person at stake.

After two days of questioning each of nearly 75 of the more than 150 potential jurors, the final 12 person jury, and 2 alternates, were seated. Every one of the 14 jurors had heard something about the case since it had been on the national news for weeks. Also, each of the jurors had heard of Donovan Taylor since he had been in the State Legislature for several years and was one of the major contenders for the Republican Party to run for Governor of the State. But the 14 jurors picked had never had Donovan Taylor on any of their voting ballots. He was from the east coast of Florida. That was a positive for Todd since the east coast was a different world. Each juror saw that the defendant was a black man and each knew that he was accused of hiring a black man to murder his white wife, the daughter of Donovan Taylor. All of the seated jurors expressed that the color of the defendants skin and Donovan Taylor's influence on the laws of the State would not influence their decision. More important, each seated juror voiced an opinion that if the defendant was found guilty they could seriously consider the penalty of death. It was difficult for Todd Hawkins and his investigator to determine the veracity of each of those juror's statements. Not every potential juror would enlighten a room full of people as to their true prejudices. But every person has some sort of prejudice. Todd and his investigator had to make some very difficult decisions. Todd knew he was the underdog in this trial, even though the location of the jurors were over 200 miles away from where the events took place.

As it turned out the final jury consisted of 6 men and 6 women. Three of the men were black and one was Latino. Their ages ranged from 33 to 59 years old. One of the men had just been laid off from his job. Five of the six woman were white and ranged from 28 to 66 years old. The other woman was black and 41 years old. The jury was a mix of white collar and blue collar workers, retired persons and home makers. Some were married, some single and some had been divorced. Both attorneys believed the final chosen 12 were as favorable as possible for a cross segment of the community. Each attorney believed that they would all be sympathetic to their side. However, Todd knew that it would only take one juror to believe his clients story, or determine the lack of a motive, to get a mistrial which would be a win for his client. This was not only true for Isiah's guilt or innocence, but would then take the death penalty off the table. Sidney needed all twelve to not only believe her side but also be strong enough to vote for the death penalty.

The trial was now ready to commence. The Judge had the Clerk swear in the jury and indicated that the trial would begin first thing the next morning and instructed the jurors to be in their seats at 8:30 AM. The Judge also instructed the jury to refrain from listening to anything on the news and not to read any news articles about the trial. Everyone knew that was an impossible task, but the Judge was not inclined to sequester the jury. Todd argued for sequestering the jury, but he knew the Judge would not do that. The Judge had already changed the venue of the trial at the request of Todd. He only made the argument, on the record, for a possible element for an appeal. There were no objections from Sidney on not sequestering the jury.

Isiah's parents and sisters were in the Courtroom the entire trial. Otis and his children took off work to support Isiah. Donovan and Sheila made an appearance every few days. Friends of Sophie and Isiah would also make appearances, from time to time. That included Dustina Washington and even, reluctantly, her husband Jayden. Dijon Jackson and Darius Williams, as well as several other managers of plants for Jetta International even attended. They would take the long ride to Lee County for a day or two of testimony. Anya Taylor refused to attend, but Deena Hawkins and Martell Dixon attended almost every day. That gave them some extended time together. A lucky break for them. Their relationship was still unknown to anyone who knew them. Except for Donovan and Anya Taylor, none of the friends attending could believe that Isiah had committed the horrible things for which he was accused. Dustina was still on the fence. She had attempted to speak with James Logan several times, however, he avoided her. Why was Dustina still questioning the facts? Should she continue to do some investigating on her own? Todd had asked her to not get involved since she may be a witness. If she did investigate, would she find anything? Her best friend was murdered. Should she speak with Todd again? She was torn. But her instincts were usually correct. That was one of the reasons Sophie liked to work with her. Jayden would dismiss her ideas and willingness to do something. That only made Dustina more adamant to try to find out the truth about why Sophie wanted her to work with her on the Jetta matter. That had to be the key to her murder. And Dustina and Jayden grew further apart. She knew the trial would only take a couple of weeks or so. But where should she start? No one from Sophie's law firm would speak to her. But Dustina was determined. She owed it to her good friend. Jayden was furious with her thoughts and adamant that she stay out of it. Dustina just couldn't understand why.

CHAPTER 23

The third day after jury selection, Sidney White began delivering her opening statement. It was nearly three hours long. She enumerated all of the elements necessary to prove first degree murder against the defendant for both murders. She emphasized that there would be testimony that Isiah Daniels had the means, the opportunity and a motive to hire a man to murder his wife. She also indicated that she would have witnesses testify as to the same elements for the circumstances concerning the murder of Clayton Reed. She referenced the allocution of Mason 'Dusty' Francis and indicated that the jury would hear from him directly as to how he was contracted by Clayton Reed to murder Sophie Daniels. She admitted to the jury that Dusty was not the person that the defendant, Isiah Daniels, actually hired to kill his wife. She expressed to the jury that they would hear testimony that Isiah wanted Clayton Reed to handle the murder. However, Clayton took it upon himself to outsource the murder of Sophie Daniels. Facts would be shown how Isiah had the means, the opportunity and the motive to then murder Mr. Reed. Those facts would be clear to the jury after all of the testimony was completed.

The most difficult aspect of Sidney's opening statement was articulating Isiah's motive to have his wife murdered. Sidney struggled her way through a difficult conspiracy web between Isiah and other black employees of Jetta International in order to make the company a mostly black run company. That was the first time that Sidney mentioned a racial motive. It shocked most of the jury. Sidney went on to explain that

Isiah's father-in-law, Donovan Taylor, was the person who started Jetta International. He hired Isiah Daniels who then expanded the Company so as to eventually be able to take the Company public. Once the company went public, Donovan, who then made a fortune, retired from the Company to run for public office. At that time, Jetta International had only one black manager out of thousands of workers and dozens of managers. That black man was Isiah Daniels. Isiah took over the Company, with the consent of Mr. Taylor, and grew it substantially to a Company worth nearly $10 billion. There were a dozen plants in eight states with over a thousand black employees. Some of those black employees were currently plant managers, officers of the company, and several even on the Board of Directors. All of those blacks had their MBA degree or higher. Isiah promoted those blacks over dozens of white employees who had the same, or better, credentials, with much more seniority.

There was a revolt by those white employees who were passed over by blacks for management positions. Sidney alleged it was Isiah's intention that the Company would become mostly managed by blacks. A racial discrimination suit was even filed by the Government, at the behest of the disgruntled white employees. The suit was in the Florida Federal Court in Broward County. It named the Company and Isiah Daniels as defendants. The same disgruntled employees also filed claims with the National Labor Relations Board for civil actions enforcing ramifications of the discrimination of the Company against white employees. The Federal law suit was initiated by the Federal Government for possible criminal action under the Racketeer Influenced and Corrupt Organization (RICO) Act against the Company, its officers and directors, including Isiah. This suit was initiated by the Federal Government after extensive interviews with dozens of white employees of the Company. Isiah wanted Fischer & Logan, the law firm that had always represented Jetta since Donovan Taylor started the Company, to represent the Company in those matters.

Sophie, then a senior partner in that law firm, abruptly wanted her law firm to immediately fire Jetta International, as their client, after the actions were filed. Her reasoning, argued Sidney, was to exclusively protect her firm from having to reveal certain confidential matters that had occurred in the past when Sophie's law firm gave advice to Isiah and the Board. Those matters occurred while Isiah was promoting blacks. Those facts then could be interpreted, by the jury, as her firm being part of the conspiracy with Isiah through her firm's advice as their Company's counsel. That advice allowed Isiah to accomplish his goal into making the Company black managed.

Most of Sophie's other partners were not aware of everything that Sophie was involved in with Isiah and Jetta. Her staff of attorneys usually did most of the representation for Jetta on behalf of Sophie's father and Isiah. Sophie was a very ethical attorney, however, as to her husband's intentions Sophie may have crossed a line, from time to time. Isiah didn't want Sophie to have to be a witness in any of the current litigation so he insisted that Sophie's law firm continue to represent Jetta so that they could claim privilege for any indiscrete matters initiated by Jetta and approved by their legal counsel.

There was a long discussion about this issue between Sophie and her partners. Most of Sophie's partners were unaware of some of the matters in which she represented Jetta. Large fees were earned by the firm on Sophie's representation of Jetta. These pending law matters would also encompass large fees for the firm. Isiah wanted Sophie to prove that Isiah's solutions to the issues of the Company were to make sure that the subtle legal matters that Sophie worked on while representing the Company were not revealed. The issues were so subtle, and possibly illegal, that eliminating his wife was his only solution. That was better than Isiah, and other Jetta employees, possibly going to jail, and paying large fines for acts that Isiah never wanted any outsider to find out about. What Sophie must have legally accomplished for Jetta, and for her husband, must have scared Isiah enough to murder his own wife. This, Sidney alleged, was Isiah's motive. The Jury was a little confused since no particulars were stated in Sidney's opening statement, but both attorneys felt that the jury may have understood that some type of motive may have actually existed.

Todd Hawkins opening statement attempted to persuade the jury that he could produce facts that would disprove that Isiah had neither the means nor the opportunity to have his beautiful, smart wife murdered. Those facts would include evidence that Isiah couldn't have murdered Clayton Reed. However, Todd took most of his opening statement to discredit the very flimsy, and implausible motive that Sidney had articulated. What husband would go so far as to have his wife murdered for corporate deeds, even if they might have been unethical or even illegal? Todd went so far as to indicate that, even if it were true that there were illegal or unethical events between Sophie and Isiah concerning the Company, murdering his wife was a preposterous solution. Even if there was some disagreement as between Sophie and her law partners about the representation of Jetta International, how could that be a motive sufficient enough to have his wife murdered? In fact he suggested it was even ludacris to believe that any slant that the prosecution could articulate on what Sidney stated could never be a motive to murder one's wife. Sophie and Isiah had been married for almost 15 years. There is no evidence that either cheated on the other or that their marriage was nothing but thriving. Even if Isiah were to go to jail for something he may have done, why would he murder the woman he loved?

After listening to the opening statement of the two attorneys, the jury still seemed somewhat confused about Isiah's motive even before any witnesses took the stand. However, before the jury would deliberate, the Judge would make it clear that motive was not an essential element needed to be proved, beyond a reasonable doubt, in order to convict Isiah of the pending charges. However, since this was a death penalty case, everyone in the Courtroom, especially the jury, knew that in order to convict Isiah, some reasonable motive needed to be proved. If there was a conviction on both counts of the murders, the jurors would more than likely inflict the death penalty. In everyone's minds, including Sidney and Todd, it was a motive that was needed to convict the defendant. Could Sidney convince the jury? It would be a difficult task, but one she was ready to pull off.

After both opening statements, the Judge dismissed the jury for the day and indicated that the prosecution would begin calling their witnesses the next morning. He again cautioned the jury to not watch any news or read any periodicals that may mention the trial. The Judge knew that was almost an impossible task, however, the less each juror heard or read about the trial, the higher the probability that the jury would come in with the correct verdict. The Judge, with some concern, had previously allowed television cameras in the Courtroom during the trial. That decision was made on the condition that the cameras never showed the faces of the jury or mentioned any jury's names to the public. Any news publication or any person revealing the names of any juror or showed a picture of any juror, to the public, would be held in contempt. That would include jail time plus a large fine. Many people in Southeast Florida, and especially Boca Raton, watched the trial daily on the television. This trial was to Palm Beach County as the O.J. Simpson trial was to the Country in the 1990's.

⟹⟸

The next morning at 9:30 AM, Courtroom 607 of the Lee County Court House was completely full. There were 15 rows for spectators. The first row was for family members of the deceased victims and the defendant's family members. The Taylor family occupied most of that row. Isiah's family felt more comfortable in the back of the Court. The next two rows were for the press. Those rows were filled as tightly as possible every day of the trial. There was one camera situated on the right side of the Courtroom, just next to the jury box. In that manner the operator of the camera could not position the camera on any of the jurors. That camera was open for viewing by any news agency in the Country interested in showing the trial. The remainder of the rows were for the public on a first come basis. It was full every day.

"Ms. White," asked Judge Andrews, "are you ready to call your first witness?"

"Yes Your Honor, I call Mason Francis," replied Sidney.

Out of a door just behind and to the far left of the Judge, two prison guards brought in Mason Francis. He was in an orange jumpsuit with the initials PBCDF on his back. Those initials signified the Palm Beach

County Detention Facility. He then swore, on a bible, the required oath to tell the truth.

After Sidney asked the witness several preliminary questions, she then asked him, "Mr. Francis are you the person who murdered Sophie Taylor Daniels?"

"Yes mam," answered the witness who was well prepared by the County Attorney's office.

"Did you make a deal with the Palm Beach County Attorney's office concerning that murder?"

"Yes mam."

"Would you please tell the Court and jury what that deal consisted of."

"So long as I testified to the whole truth about how I killed that woman, I would get a maximum of 15 to 20 years in a State correctional facility."

Sidney then walked Dusty through his criminal history and the entire scenario of the murder. She started when Clayton Reed called Dusty's brother to ask him to have Dusty do a job for a large fee. Then she asked about the meeting with Clayton and how much money Clayton gave him to kill Ms. Daniels. The witness then answered questions about how the murder was accomplished. What type of gun he brought with him to shoot her. Where he obtained the gun. Why he didn't shoot the gun to kill her. How he was wounded attempting to murder Ms. Daniels. How he finally thought he had killed Ms. Daniels. How he attempted to get away. The questioning went all the way through how he appropriated a car in a Plantation, Florida mall and was finally apprehended at a Cracker Barrel restaurant just outside Gainesville.

Sidney also showed the jury photos of the crime scene. Todd objected since they were so prejudicial to his client, but he was overruled by the Judge. When Sidney had completed her questioning, Dusty was relieved. The jury was shocked that such an inexperienced criminal could have murdered the deceased in the manner he did. Those facts and photos stayed in the back of most of the jury's mind.

"Any cross examination, Mr. Hawkins?" asked the Judge.

"Yes Your Honor."

Todd interrogated Dusty as to the reasons Clayton Reed wanted Sophie Daniels dead. Dusty had no idea. Todd wanted to know why Dusty didn't make any inquiries into why he was murdering this beautiful, smart and successful attorney who lived in one of the most expensive areas of the State. Dusty may not have been the perfect citizen, but he had never come close to killing anyone in the past. Didn't it seem strange to Dusty that he was chosen to murder someone who lived in one of the riches cities in the State? Dusty just answered that he needed the money and didn't know, at the time, that she was an attorney from such a well-known family. Todd badgered Dusty about not knowing the motive to kill Ms. Daniels until Sidney finally objected and the Judge stopped Todd from continuing to badger him.

Todd went on to ask Dusty about how he managed to get into the gated development in Boca Raton. Why he didn't investigate the background of the victim. Why Clayton didn't give him any information on the victim except where she lived and when she would be there alone. Dusty got very flustered. Sidney objected but the Judge let Todd continue.

Then Todd asked Dusty, "Did you know the name of the attorney that met with Clayton Reed and asked him to kill Sophie Taylor?"

"Objection," yelled Sidney as she rose from her chair.

"Did you indicate in your allocution of this crime that an attorney came to meet with Clayton Reed at his apartment to ask Clayton to kill Sophie Daniels? asked Todd.

"Objection," said Sidney as she was still standing, "may we approach Your Honor?"

"What's this all about Sidney," asked Judge Andrews as he covered his microphone.

"Defendant's counsel is attempting to assert some alternative motive to this murder that has no basis in fact," said Sidney. "We spoke about this before the trial began, Your Honor. Neither side was to mention this unclaimed fact."

"Did the witness refer to an attorney in his allocution asking Clayton Reed to murder the victim?" Sidney was asked by the Judge.

"He did Your Honor," inserted Todd.

"Not really. That was a fact that was never revealed by the witness during his extensive interrogation by the Boca Raton detectives as well as in his written statement as to all the events concerning the murder of Ms. Daniels." Answered Sidney. "He mentioned this fact after being asked by Your Honor, when it was brought up inadvertently during his allocution. The witness indicated that he didn't know why he said it and couldn't even remember an attorney was involved. It may have been that his brother had mentioned an attorney at some time but there is no correlation or evidence as to when this illusionary attorney may or may not have visited Clayton Reed. It's prejudicial with no basis in fact and against your instructions," angrily argued Sidney.

"But he did mention it in his allocution Your Honor," answered Todd, "I should have a right to pursue it."

"I agree with Ms. White on this issue," said Judge Andrews, "and there was an agreement that sanctions would be brought if either party mention it. Mr. Hawkins you owe this Court $5,000.00 for bringing this issue up. I expect a payment to the Clerk by the end of day. There shall be no more mention of this illusionary attorney. Is that clear?"

"Yes Your Honor," answered a distraught defense attorney. The jury didn't hear that conversation, but they did hear about some attorney who may have been involved. That was worth the $5,000.00 contempt amount.

Todd Hawkins went on to cross examine Dusty for another hour. He asked him if he knew Isiah Daniels or if he had any contact with Isiah ever. He even asked the witness again if he knew any possible motive that Isiah Daniels may have had to murder his wife. Dusty was clueless and answered no to all of Todd's questions. After his testimony the only facts that Dusty established were that he killed Sophie and that Clayton Reed paid him $1,500.00 to murder her. There was no reference to Isiah Daniels and no motive established. The witness was then excused and immediately sent to the Lake Correctional Institution just north of Clermont, Florida to serve out his 20 year sentence.

Dusty's testimony took up the entire morning session. After Dusty was excused, the Judge adjourned the trial for lunch. At 2:00 PM the trial resumed. For the rest of the afternoon and for the next few days, Sidney called a few additional witnesses concerning the death of Sophie. Diane Saunders, Sophie's neighbor across the street from her home was called to testify as to the condition Sophie was in when the neighbor called 911.

Dr. Dominick Hamilton, the surgeon who operated on Sophie was then questioned as to her condition when she arrived at the hospital and when she died.

Detectives Blackburn and Lynch testified as to their investigation into Sophie's death and the manner in which they determined who killed Sophie and who hired him. The detectives testified that they interrogated several of Sophie's law partners but were unable to conclusively determine any plausible motive for the crime. Sophie delved into the questioning of Mr. Fischer and Mr. Logan. Both detectives indicated that Mr. Fischer was very cooperative, however, Mr. Logan said very little and wouldn't answer most questions. Sidney kept delving into Sophie's relationship with her senior partners, but Todd finally objected. She was getting nowhere and the Judge told Sidney that she had made her point. The detectives did confirm Isiah's alibi when Dusty was at Clayton Reed's apartment getting his instructions for the murder as well as the time his wife was murdered. However, the detectives did indicate that there may have been a gap of time when Isiah could have been at Clayton Reed's apartment when he was murdered. However, that was mostly discounted on cross examination by Todd. No one from the Ritz had seen Isiah leave his room after he had dinner with Deena Hawkins. The next time he was seen was when he met Deena for breakfast the next day. No one saw Isiah, or his car near Clayton Reed's apartment when he was murdered. There was no one to indicate Isiah was anywhere near Clayton Reed's apartment the day of his murder.

Todd cross examined all of the officers that canvassed the area around Clayton's apartment the day of the murder and when the murder weapon was found. None of those officers found any evidence of Isiah Daniels near Reed's apartment that day.

Both pathologists, the Palm Beach County Coroner and the private pathologist, Dr. Benedict Hawker, testified as to the cause of Sophie's death. Both doctors came to the same conclusion. Her death was caused by blunt force trauma to the head and body. The weapon was the butt of a gun and several kitchen pans and several other unknown objects. The testimony of the two pathologists confirmed Dusty's account of the murder.

Also, the Miami-Dade County assistant coroner was called as a witness to confirm the death of Clayton Reed. One 9 millimeter bullet from a Glock 26 to the back of his head. The gun was recovered by the Overtown police and introduced into evidence by Morton Edwards and Abby Schmidt, the two police officers who were first on the scene at Clayton Reed's apartment after his murder. They recovered the weapon from a sewer drain several blocks from Reed's apartment. They also introduced just over $20,000 in cash that was in Clayton Reed's apartment when he was killed.

Drew Austin, the owner of Shoot Straight gun shop then testified that Sophie Daniels had purchased the 9 millimeter gun from him. He testified she told him she was purchasing it for protection. He confirmed that the gun found by the officers in the sewer was the gun Sophie bought.

All in all, the first few days were boilerplate testimony concerning the murder of Sophie Daniels. No damaging evidence was introduced concerning the motive, or the opportunity of Isiah to murder his wife. Todd was excellent on cross examination of all of Sidney's witnesses through those first few days of trial.

The only element of the crime that Sidney produced dealt with Isiah having the means to kill Sophie. Isiah knew about Sophie's gun and where she kept it. However, Sidney had more witnesses and the meat of her case was still to be argued.

CHAPTER 24

As Isiah's trial was continuing in Fort Myers, Dijon Jackson was still the temporary CEO and President of Jetta International as well as manager of the Durham, North Carolina plant. Darius Williams was still the manager of the Baltimore, Maryland plant. They both had several assistant managers for those plants, all of whom were black. As President, Dijon set a date for the annual shareholder meeting as per the By-Laws of the corporation. The meeting was to take place while Isiah's trial was still in progress. Most of the Board Members were relatively new members and some of whom were black. Each of the directors on the Jetta board had either been elected by a majority of the shareholders at the last annual meeting or appointed by the President of the Company, per its By-Laws. Each of the black Directors had three year terms. The white directors had either a one year or two year term. Dijon also set the agenda for the meeting, which was approved by the Board.

Donovan Taylor didn't want to miss many days of Isiah's trial so he appointed his attorney, Clifford Townsend as his proxy for his current remaining 4% ownership of the stock. Donovan's interest in the company had been diluted through a stock offering of additional corporation stock to the public by the Board during the last annual shareholder meeting. The agenda had a line item for an election of two Board members whose seats were up for election. Both of those Board members were white. They were re-elected. It would be another two years before any Board seat held by a black would be up for election.

Donovan's proxy attended the shareholder meeting and attempted to change the agenda so no Board member's seat could be longer than one years. That request was quickly objected to and a Board of Director's vote to change the agenda was not called for by the Board chairman, Dijon Jackson. Donovan, after he was notified by his attorney, was furious. He had started the Company, was originally the only shareholder and was not going to let a mostly black Board keep him from taking back his business. His attorney told the Board, as he got up and left the meeting that the Company would be hearing from him as to their illegal methods in not following the Company's By-Laws or Florida corporate law. He told the Board that Mr. Taylor would eventually get his Company back and all the "black bullies" on the Board would be looking for work somewhere else.

Except for Donovan attorney's uproar, the shareholder meeting went as usual. When the meeting was over, all of the current Board members were re-elected to the Board. The Company was doing well and the dividend that the Company was giving its shareholders was approved for another year. Since the Company was public and many owners were located all over the Country, there were just a handful of shareholders who actually attended the meeting. Most of the shareholders mailed in their proxies before the meeting appointing the President of the Company as their proxy. Dijon Jackson had over 60% of the votes. Dijon and Darius were pleased with the outcome of the meeting and after it was over they both returned to their respective plants. The first thing both plant managers did was to prepare purchase orders for the Company's illusionary clients and forwarded them to Jayden Robinson at Xavier Corporation. The scheme was moving forward more quickly as the embezzled funds were growing rapidly in their Off Shore banking accounts in the Caribbean, courtesy of James Logan.

The trial was now in the middle of the second week. Sidney was still calling witnesses. She had established, through the testimony of James Logan, the fact that Isiah knew where his wife's Glock was located and that he had access to that weapon. She still needed to conclusively prove that Isiah had ample opportunity to hire Clayton Reed and give him funds for the purpose of killing his wife. She also had to prove that Isiah had the opportunity to be at Clayton Reed's apartment when he was murdered. Sidney needed to positively prove a motive for having his wife murdered. She believed she was prepared to do that, but neither she nor Todd had any idea of the coming events that would considerably assist her in that element of the crime.

Sidney's next witness was the manager of the West Palm Beach Ritz Carlton. He testified that Isiah would frequently stay at the hotel, however, the witness never questioned Isiah as to why he was there. It was really none of his business. He also testified that in some cases Sophie would join Isiah for their stay. When she was with Isiah they usually were there to de-stress from their jobs. They would use all the facilities such as the spa, pool and fitness center. Most of their meals were in one of the three restaurants on site. Sidney asked about the day that Sophie was killed. The manager remembers hearing about the murder that afternoon. He also remembered that Isiah did not check in to the hotel until very late or maybe even very early in the morning the next day. He had a woman with him, for which he paid for her separate room. Isiah was very distraught and stayed at the hotel until he indicated to the staff of the hotel that his house was no longer considered a crime scene. That took about four days. The woman checked out after breakfast the next day. The manager believed her name was Deena Hawkins. The manager remembered having a discussion with Isiah that he was in North Carolina at one of his plants when the murder occurred. It took him more than half a day to fly back to Palm Beach in the Company's private plane. Isiah told the manager that he had gone home from the coroner's office, but he wasn't able to stay there since it was a crime scene. The manager testified that he was unaware of any persons who visited him while he was staying at the hotel. The records concerning Isiah's calls were all to his parents home, his in-laws home, the coroner's office, his work offices and the funeral home. No calls were made to Clayton Reed. The manager had no knowledge of the calls from his cell phone. Sidney had those records but didn't ask about that phone. Since no phone calls were made that evening from his cell phone.

Sidney's next two witnesses shed a little more light on her case. But before she called them to testify, her assistant notified Sidney that neither Dijon Jackson, Darius Williams nor Jayden Robinson had responded to being available to testify. She told her assistant to immediately have subpoenas served on them to show the next day to testify.

Then Sidney called Mickey Conrad to the stand. After the usual swearing in and some preliminary questions, Sidney asked the witness, "You were the defendant's basketball coach when he played for the University of Miami, weren't you?"

"Yes."

"Did you get along with the defendant while he played for you?"

"Isiah was a fine person as well as a very good basketball player. Many schools had offered him a scholarship. He was disciplined, smart and a leader of the team for several years. He helped out the other players both academically and emotionally. I couldn't have recruited a better person. Yes we got along well," answered Conrad.

"But you weren't the person who actually recruited Isiah were you?"

"Well, actually Mr. Taylor did a lot of the recruiting back in those days. But I had the final say on whether to put Isiah on the team and give him a scholarship."

"Were you aware of Mr. Taylor's thoughts about black people sir?"

"Mr. Taylor recruited some black boys for the team. He treated them well. He had them to his house for dinner. He bought them clothing. He housed some of their parents in one of his apartment buildings on campus. He even hired Isiah to work for his company," replied the Coach. "When he asked me to give Isiah a scholarship, there were two other players on Isiah's Community College team who played with him that I wanted to give a try out for the team, however Mr. Taylor refused to allow me to do that."

"Did you find that unusual?" asked Sidney. "And what were their names?"

"Dijon Jackson and Darius Williams," replied the Coach. "Mr. Taylor didn't want them to play for Miami."

"Where they both black?" asked Sidney.

"I had no idea why Mr. Taylor didn't want them to play for Miami. I found them to be above average prospects."

"You didn't answer my question Mr. Conrad," said Sidney.

"Objection, Your Honor. Where is Ms. White going with this line of questioning?" asked Todd.

"Over ruled. But get to your point counselor," stated the Judge.

"Was Isiah upset when the two other black players on his Community College team were not invited to try out for your team Mr. Conrad?"

"I have no idea. I know Isiah and Mr. Taylor discussed that issue, but I have no idea what their discussions were about. I tried to stay out of Donovan Taylor's issues." answered the coach. "However, both did get scholarships and played for Florida Atlantic University."

Sidney went on to inquire if Coach Conrad was still coaching. He indicated that he had retired from coaching and was currently a sales representative for Dick's Sporting Goods Stores. She then inquired if he still kept in touch with any of his past players from the University. For which he replied that he did. In fact he kept in touch with three of his players from the team Isiah played on. Isiah, Clayton Reed and Martell Dixon. The three of them were fairly good friends for several years after they all left school. The Coach had no idea how long their friendship lasted thereafter. Sidney continued to inquire how all three of them were doing in the real world. Coach Conrad told her that Isiah had done very well and became CEO of Mr. Taylor's Company when Donovan ran for public office. Martell got an advanced degree from FGCU here in Fort Myers and became a business consultant on the East Coast of Florida. Clayton, however, had a hard time and never really accomplished much. He never finished college. He tried desperately to find and NBA team to play on. Although, he never accomplished that dream either. In fact he got in trouble several times for various crimes including drugs.

"Do you know if Martell or Isiah ever helped out Clayton at all when he became down on his luck?" asked Sidney.

"I heard that both Isiah and Martell had giving Clayton some money, from time to time. I don't know how much or for how long. That's all I know," answered the Coach.

"Do you know what happened to Dijon Jackson and Darius Williams? asked Sidney.

"I believe they were hired by Jetta International."

"Do you know who hired them and what their current positions are?" asked Sidney.

"Objection," yelled Todd. "Again, where is the prosecutor going with this line of questioning?"

"Over ruled," stated the Judge.

"I heard that it was the defendant that hired them. I also believe they are currently in high management positions with the Company." replied the Coach.

"Did you know that Isiah married Donovan Taylor's daughter?"

"I did."

"Have you kept a relationship with Mr. Taylor since your coaching days?"

"Again, Your Honor, I object to this line of questioning. There is no relevancy here concerning my client's charges," demanded Todd.

"Sidney get to your point now or I'll let this witness go," harshly said the Judge.

"Coach were you aware of Mr. Taylor's feeling about the defendant promoting black employees to high managerial positions at Jetta International?" finally asked Sidney.

"He wasn't happy," replied the Coach.

"Can you explain your answer Mr. Conrad?

Mickey Conrad went on to say that he and Donovan Taylor remained good friends for many years. Donovan had agreed to Isiah marrying his daughter strictly for political reasons. He hated the fact that his beautiful, smart good natured daughter fell in love with a black man. However, he said nothing. The minority vote in Florida is imperative for someone who is running for a State office, like Governor. Donovan thought that having a black man in his family was good for his political ambitions. Isiah made it his business to do whatever he could to take all of Donovan's influence out of Jetta. He diluted his father-in-law's ownership interest in the Company. He led the fight to keep Donovan out of Jetta forever. Donovan was extremely upset every time another black man was promoted at Jetta. Donovan had told Conrad that many times. Donovan knew that Isiah and Clayton remained friendly. Donovan even wondered if Isiah was buying drugs from Clayton for himself and Sophie. He was always upset when the subject came up between them. Donovan even spoke with his daughter about dropping Isiah and Jetta as her firm's clients. He was sure Isiah would do something illegal while in charge of Jetta. Donovan didn't want to get his daughter, as the Company's attorney, in trouble. Donovan, disliked blacks. Donovan knew, and told Conrad that he would encourage some of the white managers who were passed over by Isiah's promotion of blacks to sue the Company and Isiah.

Todd objected to Coach Conrad's entire testimony as irrelevant and hearsay. Todd indicated that Donovan Taylor was in the Courtroom and could speak for himself. The Judge over ruled Todd's objection and Todd could see that the jury was starting to understand the complicated relationship between Sophie, Isiah and her father.

In order to destroy confidence in Coach Conrad's testimony for the jury, Todd, on cross examination, asked Coach Conrad if he knew any facts that would implicate Isiah in his wife's murder. He asked if he knew if Isiah had given Clayton money to murder his wife. He asked if he knew whether Sophie Daniels was ever disciplined by the Florida Board of Ethics for anything that involved representing Isiah or Jetta International. He asked if Donovan Taylor ever treated any of his black players any different than his white players while Isiah was playing for him. The answer to all of those questions was no. Todd sat down.

With little time left in the day to continue the trial, Sidney convinced the Judge that her next witness would only take a few minutes. She called Martell Dixon. After a few questions as to his relationship with Isiah and their time playing basketball together, and keeping in touch from time to time, Sidney got to the heart of her questions.

"Do you know for a fact that the defendant gave Clayton Reed money on more than one occasion?" asked Sidney.

"Yes."

"Did the defendant meet with Clayton Reed when he gave him money?"

"No, it is my understanding that the money was wire transferred from some account into Clayton's account. I don't know if Isiah's money came directly from Isiah or whether it came through a third party," answered Martell.

"Was any of that money in consideration for Clayton to murder Sophie Daniels?"

"Objection, Your Honor, speculation," Said Todd.

"Not if he knows, Your Honor," said Sidney.

"Do you know Mr. Dixon?" asked Judge Andrews.

"Yes sir. Isiah paid Clayton to murder his wife," answered Martell.

Sidney sat down and looked at Todd and said "Your witness counselor."

The jury was in shock. So was everyone else in the Courtroom. Clover Daniels started to cry. Donovan Taylor got up and left the Courtroom with his family who were still sitting in the front row. The press started to talk to each other and several of them got up and quickly left the room to make a call to their editors. The Judge hit his gavel several times to calm the room. He told everyone that if anyone else said anything they would be removed from the Courtroom. Todd and Isiah couldn't believe what they had just heard. They both knew there must be some other explanation. But the jury heard what Martell had said.

Todd got up to cross examine Martell. He knew he had to take a gamble in his questioning. "Mr. Martell when was the last time you were with Mr. Daniels?"

"A couple months ago. I was in Fort Lauderdale for a seminar and I called Isiah to get together with him for dinner."

"Was Sophie Daniels alive when you and Isiah had dinner?"

"Yes."

"Yet you knew that Isiah was going to hire Clayton Reed, your mutual friend, to murder his wife?"

"Objection, Your Honor, asked and answered," said Sidney.

"I want to hear this answer. Your objection is over ruled," said the Judge.

"Well, I wasn't completely sure at that time that Isiah was really going to murder his wife," answered Martell.

"So when exactly did you find that out. Did you ask Isiah?" asked Todd.

"No, when I got back to Miami and went to my home, I told a friend of mine that I had dinner with Isiah. She was appalled. She told me that she was aware that Isiah and Sophie were having problems with the way Sophie was representing Jetta International. She said that Isiah was going to do something to Sophie to stop her from hurting his Company. She was certain that Isiah would hire Clayton to murder Sophie. Clayton needed money"

"So you have no direct knowledge that Isiah paid Clayton to murder his wife? You just heard that from your friend?"

"Well my friend is Anya Taylor. That's Sophie's younger sister. She knew all of this from her discussions with her father."

"So, again, you have no direct knowledge that Isiah paid Clayton to murder his wife, correct?" asked Todd

"Not exactly, but Anya told me that her father and Coach Conrad talked all the time and Coach knew that Isiah was giving money to Clayton. Anya's father knew that there was some type of trouble between Isiah and Sophie about Sophie representing Isiah's Company as her client. So I just put two and two together," replied Martell.

"Your honor, I move that Mr. Dixon's testimony be completely thrown out. Everything he testified to is hearsay or double hearsay. Everyone he spoke with is available to testify themselves. In fact, Coach Conrad specifically testified, in this Courtroom, that he had no knowledge of Isiah paying any money to Clayton Reed to murder his wife. Sidney White should be sanctioned for subordinating perjury," exclaimed Todd.

With that statement the Judge called both counsel to the bench. The Judge asked Sidney if she knew about this and if she had prepared Mr. Dixon for this testimony. Sidney denied knowing he would say what he did including basing his testimony on other people's remarks. The Judge was annoyed and told both counsel that he would have to deal with this in the morning. He asked Sidney to be ready to explain herself to the

Judge and maybe even the jury. Sidney looked and sounded exhausted. Isiah was furious and Todd wanted a mistrial. Judge Andrews got up and told the jury to go home for the night and they would deal with this witness's testimony in the morning.

CHAPTER 25

Dustina Washington came home from work and found a subpoena laying on the dining room table addressed to her husband, Jayden. She wondered why in the world her husband would be subpoenaed, by the prosecution, to testify at Isiah's trial. Dustina had discussed the possibility of her testifying at some point in the trial. Dustina told Sidney she couldn't imagine what facts she may know about Sophie's murder, however, she agreed to testify if Sidney felt she may need her. However, what facts would her husband know about the murder? Why did Sidney serve a subpoena on him? When Dustina walked into her kitchen there was a note on the center island. It was addressed to Dustina from her husband:

> Honey,
> I attempted to call you, but you were out of the office and you're cell phone must have been turned off. I assumed you were in a deposition. I left a copy of a subpoena I received from a process server this afternoon at work. I'll be in Fort Myers at the Hotel Indigo. I have to testify at Isiah's trial. I have no idea what they want me to testify about, but I guess I'll find out tomorrow or the next day. I'll call you tonight.
>
> Love you,
> Jay

Jayden's note indicated that he called Dustina on her cell phone? Why didn't he leave her a voice message? Dustina tried to think about what was going on with Jayden. They had been moving further and further apart. She thought she had to get to the bottom of this when he called that evening. It was very strange. Dustina then remembered Sophie asking her to help her on a matter that her law firm may have been involved in with Jetta and Xavier Corporation. But why Jayden? He wasn't an owner of the company, just an employee. Even stranger, Jayden didn't call that evening.

━━━►●◄━━━

The next morning Judge Andrews asked both attorneys, their staffs, and the defendant Isiah, to meet in his chambers before the trial continued. Todd's motions for excluding Martell's testimony at the end of the previous day, or in the alternative, declaring a mistrial needed to be resolved.

"Okay counsel we have a problem," said the Judge. "This trial has been going on for almost two weeks and I do not want to declare a mistrial and lose all that time and start over. I have been living in a hotel to long already. So tell me Sidney, what do you propose?"

"I called Anya Taylor last night and she has agreed to testify today as to her conversations with Martell Dixon. That should clarify where and how she may, or may not, have direct knowledge of Isiah hiring Clayton Reed to murder his wife," suggested Sidney.

"Your Honor, we all know that no matter how Anya testifies, she has no knowledge about my client hiring anyone to murder his wife," replied Todd. "If she did, she would have been the first witness on Sidney's list to testifying about those facts. Anya never even contacted the Boca police. All of her testimony will be hearsay, at best, or perjury at worst. I believe a mistrial is the only solution."

"I'm sorry Todd," answered Judge Andrews, "I am not declaring a mistrial. Let Anya Taylor testify and let the jury hear what she has to say. If you object to any, or all, of her testimony for some legitimate legal reason, I will instruct the jury to disregard both Ms. Taylor's and Mr. Dixon's testimony."

"Your Honor, with all due respect," pleaded Todd, "You can't un-ring a bell. The damage will already have been done."

"I'm sorry Todd but that's what's going to happen," replied the Judge. "Appeal my decision if you want to. Now let's get on with this trial."

Todd was certain that this was all Anya's doing. He and Isiah had spoken about Anya. Isiah told Todd how much Anya hated blacks and how upset she has always been about Sophie's marriage. She only agreed to be friends with Martell since her friend, Deena was close with Martell. Anya disliked blacks. But, she knew Isiah and Martell were friends. She was just waiting for the right time to do whatever she could to hurt Isiah. Todd felt he could use that in his cross examination on Anya. Then they all went into the Courtroom to continue the trial.

"Call your next witness Ms. White," was the first thing that was said in front of the jury after the meeting in the Judge's chambers. This seemed confusing to the jury considering the way the trial ended the day before. The jury believed that they would get some explanation concerning the issue with Martell Dixon's testimony. After all he had testified that Isiah hired Clayton Reed to murder his wife. Most of the jurors, at that point in the trial, now believed Isiah was probably guilty.

"I call Anya Taylor," stated Sidney. That seemed to startle several of the jurors. Other jurors thought that this may be the 'smoking gun' that would convict Isiah. However, Sidney actually did not want Anya to testify. She believed she was forced into calling Anya due to Martell Dixon's surprising testimony. Sidney didn't like to be surprised, especially by her own witnesses. Martell had done exactly that. Sidney believed Anya was also an unknown witness. Something all lawyers fear. Sidney had tried many criminal trials and always attempted to stay away from unknown witnesses. They are the type of witnesses that can change a jury's mind and turn a trial around.

Anya was sworn in and asked the usual preliminary questions. She also was not happy being on the witness stand. Her family was also not ecstatic that she was testifying. They had not spoken to her in some time. They were afraid at what she may say. She was not trustworthy when it came to Isiah.

"Ms. Taylor are you related to Sophie Daniels?"

Yes. I'm her younger sister."

"Where are you currently residing?"

"I am living in a rented home in the Reserve at Estero."

"Is anyone currently living with you?"

"No."

"Have you and Martell Dixon ever been romantically involved or are you currently involved romantically?" asked Sidney with some trepidation.

"Are you kidding," answered Anya, "he and I could never be involved. He is just a distant friend. He's black for God's sake."

Sidney was appalled by that response. But she was where she was and had to continue.

"Do you and Mr. Dixon communicate often since you do have common friends?"

"As little as possible," replied Anya, "he and I are as different as can be.

"Prior to your sister's murder, when was the last time you spoke to her?"

"My sister and I spoke very little. Ever since she and Isiah married I have had little to do with her. I just don't understand how she ended up marrying him. That's the reason I moved to the west coast of Florida. My family and I had sort of a falling out. I can't remember the last time I spoke to her," answered Anya.

"When was the last time you spoke to Isiah?"

"Years and years ago. He isn't a friend and never will be. He and I come from different worlds," answered Anya.

"How about you and your friend Martell? Do you speak to him about your life or your family? Or have you had a conversation about your sister's death with him?" asked Sidney dreading Anya's answer.

"We don't communicate often but I believe I told him that Isiah probably murdered my sister," answered Anya.

"Any objection Mr. Hawkins?" asked Judge Andrews.

"No Your Honor."

"Ms. White I am going to finish questioning this witness," said the Judge. That was extremely unusual during a trial, but Sidney was somewhat relieved.

"What facts do you have Ms. Taylor that the defendant hired Clayton Reed to murder your sister?" asked the Judge.

"He's black. All black men beat their woman and some actually bludgeoned them to death. Isiah probably didn't have the guts to do it himself so he must have hired Clayton Reed to do it for him."

"That is your testimony, under oath, as to you accusing the defendant of murder?" asked the Judge.

"Yes sir, I truly believe it."

"You are excused as a witness in this case Ms. Taylor. And consider yourself very lucky.

Anya's family, Isiah's family, the press, Sidney and especially the Judge were outraged. The Judge looked at Anya and told her that she was as close as she could get to have the Judge lock her up for perjury and also hold her in contempt. Sidney sat down waiting for some ruling that would come from the Judge. Putting Anya on the stand was a big mistake, but maybe something good could come out of it in order for Sidney to actually prove the true motive for Sophie's murder.

"Mr. Hawkins, do you have anything to say?" asked Judge Andrews.

"I renew my motion for a mistrial Your Honor. The testimony of Martell Dixon and now Anya Taylor was so prejudicial, and obviously perjury, that a fair verdict cannot be obtained in this trial."

"Ladies and gentleman of the jury," started Judge Andrews, "I am not going to rule on Mr. Hawkins motion for a mistrial until all of the evidence in this matter is complete. I do not want to waste all of your time that you spent here the last two weeks. However, I am instructing you to completely disregard all of the testimony of Martell Dixon and Anya Taylor when you are discussing your verdict in this case. This is very important."

"I object Your Honor," said Todd as he got up from his chair.

"Sit down Mr. Hawkins," said the Judge, "Ms. White call your next witness.

While Anya Taylor was testifying, Dijon Jackson, Darius Williams and Jaden Robinson were having breakfast at the café at the Indigo Hotel. They spoke for a few minutes about how their scheme was progressing well, but didn't want to talk about it in public so they went on to another subject. All of the men had no idea why they were subpoenaed to testify for the prosecution concerning Isiah's murder. Did Sidney White know about their scheme? James Logan had already testified. Nothing was asked to him about Clayton's murder or the scheme. He was the one who actually met with Clayton and arranged for Sophie's murder. Sophie may have just found out about the illusionary corporations Logan had created at their law firm. She probably thought that more partners in the firm should have been signatures on those accounts, not just Sophie's partner Logan. Sophie was hiring Dustina Washington, Jayden's wife, for the purpose of retaining a private investigator to find out what exactly was happening. All four men knew that something had to be done. They were actually surprised to hear about Sophie's murder. All four men knew that something needed to be done with Sophie, but eliminating her was their very last choice. That was completely Logan's call. Maybe Dustina had sufficient time to discuss the issues with Sophie prior to her death? Why didn't Dustina say something to her husband? So many questions. They knew that they needed legal advice before they testified. The only attorney they could trust was James Logan.

After breakfast they went back to Jayden's room and called Logan. To their surprise Logan told them that he was just served a subpoena by Todd Hawkins to come back and testify some more. Logan said that Sidney White and Todd Hawkins were both excellent attorneys. Sidney believed that if all three of them testified, one or more of them would contradict the others on some facts, at some point, in their testimony. That may start the unraveling of the scheme.

Todd believed that James Logan would be able to best contradict the other three men. He knew everything about Jetta. The only answer Logan could come up with, short of not showing up to testify and to be held in contempt. was to take the Fifth Amendment on every question. That would shorten their testimony and at least give them time to determine their next move. Logan was fairly certain that Sidney White could probably prove to the jury sufficient circumstantial evidence to convict Isiah. That evidence would deal with the discrimination law suits. That was the conspirator's goal for this trial. That would take the pressure off any further investigation into the scheme.

They all agreed. James Logan didn't realize how bad his impact of his advice was that he had just given his co-conspirators. That advice may be the beginning of an event that may start an investigation that could not be stopped until whatever the four men were hiding became public. But Logan really didn't know what questions Sidney would ask them. He was scared. So he asked the first person who would be called to testify to start to answer Sidney's questions. Maybe she would get nowhere. If she did, Logan would jester, from the public seats in the Courtroom, to the first witness to start to take the Fifth Amendment. All agreed to follow Logan's advice. They had no other choice.

⟫●⟪

"Call your next witness Ms. White," said Judge Andrews.

Sidney called several more witnesses that day. First was the owner of the gas station where Mason Francis cleaned up and change his clothes after Sophie's murder.

Then she called the owner of the Malibu automobile that was stolen from the parking lot outside the Bonefish restaurant in Plantation, Florida.

The waitress that recognized Dusty at the Cracker Barrel restaurant outside Gainesville was called next.

Then the sheriff's deputies who apprehended Dusty testified.

Her next witnesses that day were Amy Sutherland, who was Clayton Reed's neighbor who called the police after she smelled something strange coming from his apartment. Then Morton Edwards and Abby Schmidt, were the first two police officers who answered Ms. Sutherland's call. They then testified as to the scene of the murder. They also testified as to how the murder weapon was found in the sewer close to Reed's apartment and how they determined who the owner of the murder weapon was.

Lastly, the Miami-Dade coroner testified as to the cause of the death of Clayton Reed as well as the day and approximate time of his death. Sidney had finally felt she had proven means and opportunity for both murders.

The next day Sidney would call witnesses that could show motive on the part of Isiah to have his wife murdered. It would be a difficult task to prove that Isiah was a racist with an agenda to make Jetta a black run company. It would also be necessary to prove that Isiah's agenda, was more important not becoming public, than having his wife reveal decisions that may be considered criminal on his part. Sidney believed that, under oath, some of Jetta's black managers and customers, such as Xavier, would prove that premise. She may have been somewhat naïve and maybe even moving into a dangerous testimony. But being a death penalty case, she had no choice. Motive was going to determine the verdict in this case.

CHAPTER 26

The next morning, Sidney called Darius Williams to testify. Darius was sworn in, asked the usual preliminary questions and then was questioned about his background. That included where he grew up, which schools he attended, what degrees he had obtained, his basketball background and his current position with Jetta International. Darius had received a Bachelor degree from Florida Atlantic University where he played basketball. He received his MBA from Howard University, a black university in Washington D.C. He was 96th out of a class of 125 students.

"How long have you been working for Jetta?"

"I have been working for Jetta International for over 12 years now," answered Darius as he saw no signal from James Logan.

"Who was the person who hired you when you started with Jetta and for what position?"

"Isiah Daniels hired me as the assistant line manager for the plant in Baltimore, Maryland."

"Can you tell this Court what position Isiah Daniels held at the time you were hired?"

"I believe he was the assistant personnel manager for the Company at that time," answered Darius.

"Do you know how long Mr. Daniels had been working for Jetta at the time you were hired and if he was an officer of the Company at the time?

"I'm not certain, but he had been working there for maybe a year or two. I don't believe he was an officer yet."

"Did you interview with any officers of the company such as one of the vice presidents or the then manager of the Baltimore plant?"

"No Mam."

"Were there any officers of the Company working at the Baltimore plant when you were hired?"

"There was the Vice President of operations for the plant. The manager of the plant was an Executive Vice President."

Sidney continued to ask Darius about how long those officers had been working for Jetta and where those officers went to school, what degrees they had obtained and what their class rankings were. Darius knew some of those answers. One graduated from Yale Business School and the other from The University of Pennsylvania Warton School of Business. Both had graduated with high honors, but Darius had no idea about their class ranking.

"I understand that you are currently an Executive Vice President and manager of the Baltimore plant. Is that correct?"

"Yes."

"Can you tell us how long after you were hired by Mr. Daniels as the assistant line manager, it took you to be promoted to your current position?"

"It was just over a year after I was hired when I was promoted to Executive Vice President and manager of the Baltimore plant."

"At the time you were hired by Jetta, who was the CEO of the company?"

"I believe it was Donovan Taylor. He was also Chairman of the Board."

"Was Mr. Taylor still in those positions at the company when you were promoted to your current position?"

"No Mam, he had resigned all of his positions to run for public office," answered Darius.

"So who promoted you to your current position?"

"Isiah Daniels, Mam. He took over as CEO of the Company when Mr. Taylor resigned."

Sidney went on to ask the witness about the two officers who were at the plant when he was hired. Darius told her he had no idea, they just left the Company. She continued to ask him how many other people in the plant had more seniority than Darius when he was promoted. Darius wasn't sure, but he told her there were quite a few. She then asked Darius how many of the employees at the Baltimore plant, who had more seniority than him, were black. Darius then received a jester from James Logan. Darius then said, "I respectfully invoke, on advice of counsel, my Fifth Amendment right not to answer that question due to the fact that my answer may intend to incriminate me."

Todd objected several times during those questions as to relevancy. The Judge over ruled his objections when Sidney indicated that the answer to those questions went to motive. She again went on to ask Darius how many of the new employees hired at the Baltimore plant after he became manager were black. Again an objection and again over ruled. Darius then asserted his Fifth Amendment rights again. Sidney wanted to know who hired the employees for the Baltimore plant after Darius was manager. Darius again asserted his Fifth Amendment rights.

"Did Isiah Daniels instruct you to hire black employees at any time? demanded Sidney.

"On advice of counsel I assert my Fifth Amendment rights," answered Darius.

Sidney then produced a file with the applications and resumes of all of the employees Darius hired. Nearly every one of the white applicants for any certain job had more experience and a better education than the black applicants that were hired. Sidney asked Darius to confirm that fact. Darius again asserted his Fifth Amendment rights. Sidney looked directly at the jury when Darius asserted his Fifth Amendment rights. Sidney then asked Darius if he knew what had happened to the two officers of the Company who 'just left' when Darius was promoted. Darius again asserted his Fifth Amendment rights. Sidney asked the witness if there were any complaints by any applicants who were not hired. She also asked if any current employees expressed concern about the people who were hired. Also, if there were complaints by current white employees who were passed over for promotion by less qualified black employees, promoted by him or Isiah. Darius again asserted his Fifth Amendment rights to all those questions.

"Did the Company hire an attorney to represent them concerning any complaints? asked Sidney.

Darius again asserted his Fifth Amendment rights.

Again, Sidney turned and stared at the jury as to make sure they understood what may have been going on at the Baltimore plant after Donovan Taylor left the Company and Isiah took over.

Lastly, Sidney asked Darius if the Baltimore plant had any business relationship with the Xavier Corporation and who Darius dealt with at that company. Darius for the last time asserted his Fifth Amendment rights and indicated to the Judge that he no longer wanted to continue to testify. He said he would not answer any more questions. Judge Andrews asked Darius if it was his intention to continue to assert his Fifth Amendment rights. Darius affirmed that to the Judge. The Judge then excused the witness.

Todd indicated that he had no opportunity to cross examine the witness. Judge Andrews said that Darius Williams was excused. Todd then requested the Judge to explain the ramifications of this witness asserting his Fifth Amendment rights to the jury. Todd knew that most jurors believed only criminals used that tactic. The Judge did explain that even though a witness asserts their right not to answer a question under the Fifth Amendment, it did not necessarily mean that the answer would incriminate the witness in any way. The assumption the jury must use in evaluating the witness' testimony is that the witness did nothing wrong. The Judge did what Todd asked him to do, but he could see in the jury's faces that they didn't believe what the Judge told them. Darius' testimony took most of the morning and the Judge dismissed the jury and called for them to return at 2:00 PM after the lunch break. He again advised them not to discuss anything about the trial.

After the lunch break, Sidney called her next witness, Dijon Jackson. After he was sworn in, Sidney began to ask him the usual preliminary questions.

"Please tell the Court your full name and your current position at Jetta International."

"On advice of counsel I assert my Fifth Amendment right not to incriminate myself," answered Dijon.

"Mr. Jackson, all I am asking is for you to state your name," angrily said Sidney.

Judge Andrew intervened and asked the witness if it was his intention to assert his Fifth Amendment right for all question that the prosecutor may ask him. Dijon answered in the affirmative. The Judge immediately dismissed the witness. Sidney became enraged and argued to the Judge that the witness was required to answer some questions that could not incriminate him such as his name. Judge Andrews indicated that the witness was not a defendant in the pending matter and had the right to exercise his constitutional rights. Todd was ecstatic as to the Judge's ruling. Sidney was worried that she would be unable to produce evidence of motive. But Todd felt exactly the opposite. These Black employees, by invoking their Fifth Amendment rights, were giving the jury a possible motive of wrong doing at Jetta. Isiah was in charge of that company while this was happening. This was bad for Isiah. Why didn't Isiah mention this to Todd? Todd needed to speak with Isiah.

Sidney, who thought she was not doing enough to prove motive, spoke with her staff. They then decided to use their 'Plan B'. She called one of the named plaintiffs in the law suit filed by over a dozen white employees alleging race discrimination against white employees as well as dirty tricks to have some of the white employees discharged on fake incidents that occurred at some of Jetta plants. Sidney went through each of the alleged allegations in the complaint, for which the witness was a plaintiff, and asked the witness to explain each allegation.

Todd objected on the grounds that the prosecution was attempting to prove allegations pending in another Court for the purpose of connecting his client to some motive to murder his wife. Todd asked the Judge to ask the jury to disregard the witness' testimony. That law suit needed to be litigated in another Court at another time. Judge Andrews agreed. However, Sidney got her point across to the jury that something was happening at Jetta International concerning white and black employees and Isiah was the CEO. More important, Sophie his wife, was representing Isiah and Jetta on those law suits. Since the Judge stopped the testimony the jury had to determine, in their minds, if Isiah and Sophie were conspiring to do something illegal.

Sidney wasn't done. Her next witness was a Federal United States Attorney for the Southern District of Florida. It was Sidney's intent to have this witness testify as to allegations under the RICO act for matters occurring at Jetta International that could be considered civil and criminal acts by the management of Jetta International which may have been aided by the Company's attorney. Todd again objected to calling this witness on the same basis as he argued as to the last witness. The Judge agreed with Todd, but the damage was done and the jury heard Sidney's argument for calling the witness. It would stick in their minds even though Judge Andrews instructed the jury to disregard what they had heard about the last several witnesses.

Sidney had two more witnesses to call that afternoon. The first witness was Jayden Robinson. After he was sworn in, and Sidney asked him his name, Jayden immediately asserted his Fifth Amendment rights. Judge Andrews dismissed the witness. Sidney was getting somewhat discouraged as to her full ability to put forward a reasonable motive in the case. Todd was concerned what the jury must be thinking about what Isiah's black employees and major customers were trying to accomplish. In addition, what kind of advice had Sophie Daniels been giving her client about some unknown possible criminal enterprise? Todd had to make sure that the Judge would instruct the jury, before they deliberated, to disregard all of these witnesses. But again the 'bell had been rung'.

Sidney called her last witness for the day. It was the manager of the McDonalds restaurant on Moapa Boulevard in Overtown, Florida. Sidney asked the manager if he recognized a picture of Clayton Reed. The manager told the Court that Clayton was a frequent patron of his restaurant. She attempted to get the witness to remember the day before

Sophie Daniels was murdered and if Clayton Reed was in the restaurant that day. The manager answered that he may have been there since he frequented the establishment regularly. Sidney asked the witness if he may have met a man that day. The witness said that Clayton may have met a man that day. Since Clayton usually came alone he remembered Clayton meeting another man. Sidney asked him if the man he met was white or black. The manager told her that he if he met anyone it was usually another black man.

Todd objected on the grounds that the witness couldn't testify as to what day he was referring to. The Judge over ruled the objection.

Sidney then asked whether the black man may have given Clayton some envelope. The manager wanted to please Sidney, after all he had just spent the night before in the Indigo Hotel and had a very expensive meal paid for by the prosecution. So he answered that he may have seen some exchange. Sidney asked the manager if that person who gave Clayton the envelope was in the Courtroom. The manager pointed to Isiah. He indicated that he believed it was the defendant.

Todd was licking his chops. What a bad witness. Sidney must have been desperate. Todd cross examined the manager.

"Are you certain, beyond a reasonable doubt, that Clayton Reed met a black man who looked like the defendant on the day before Sophie Daniels was murdered? asked Todd.

"I believe so," answered the manager.

"You believe so. Can you tell this Court the day Sophie Daniels was murdered?"

"I can't quite remember the exact date, but Clayton was in the restaurant a lot," answered the manager.

"Did Clayton ever come to your restaurant and never order something to eat or drink?"

"No, he always had something to eat. Actually he ate a lot."

"So you don't remember if he ever was at your restaurant with someone and didn't order anything?"

The manager thought for a while and then said, "Come to think about it, I do remember him and some man in the back corner one day and neither of them ordered anything to eat or drink."

"Do you remember the date that occurred?

"Not really. Clayton was there a lot, but I did find it unusual he didn't order anything," said the manager.

"Was the man with him white or black?

"I do believe the man was white and he was wearing a fancy suit. No one comes in the restaurant wearing a suit," stated the manager.

"Did the white man in a suit give Clayton an envelope?"

"I don't remember," answered the manager. "I really don't know. I guess he could have. Someone gave him an envelope but now I'm confused," stated the manager.

"So am I. Thank you sir, I have no more questions," Said Todd.

The witness was excused. As he walked past Sidney, he turned to her and said he was sorry he may have screwed up his memory, but he thanked her for the hotel room and dinner. Sidney gave him a dirty look. The Judge called the trial off for the day and asked Sidney if she had anymore witnesses. She said she had one more witness to call the next morning. The Judge wanted the trial to move on a little faster. He asked her how long the witness would take. She said less than an hour. The Judge then told Todd to be ready to present his client's defense the next morning. Todd was ready.

CHAPTER 27

After Anya's testimony was ruled by the Judge to be completely disregarded by the jury, she left the Courtroom disgusted and demeaned. She had always been considered, by her father, as the difficult daughter. Her grades were above average but not excellent. She needed her family's influence to get her into the schools she attended. She never married or had any children. Her family even suspected that she was gay. So Sophie was the favorite daughter Anya's whole life. Anya could never live up to her father's standards. Sophie always made high grades. She got accepted to the best schools. Got the best job offers. Dated the right men. She made her family proud in every endeavor she attempted. Her only fault was marrying a black man. If it weren't for her father's political ambitions that marriage would never have happened. Now Anya had a chance to please her family by making sure that Sophie's black husband was convicted of her sister's murder and pay the ultimate consequence. That pleasure was erased by the Judge. Anya was certain that her father was embarrassed and offended that his only remaining daughter couldn't help his crusade to have Isiah convicted.

Over the next few days, Anya believed that her family may never speak with her again. She felt that she needed to take matters into her own hands to make sure Isiah was erased from her father's life. Maybe that would change her father's opinion of her. She had been attempting to achieve her father's favoritism. She discussed what she could do to accomplish that with her 'off and on friend', Martell. It was ironic that a sophisticated woman, who disliked blacks, discussed those ambitions with a black friend. Anya actually thought about killing Isiah herself, as he left the Courtroom. Martell quickly brought her back to reality. He convinced her that she had done her best on the stand, as he did, but their testimony, as fabricated as it was, just wasn't enough. He attempted to convince Anya that just by testifying as she did probably made her father have a much higher acceptance of her. At least she attempted to do what she could to convict Isiah. Anya didn't believe him, but let the subject go, at least as Martell was concerned. But it still bothered her. She needed to do something. But what and how?

⸻⸻⸻◈⸻⸻⸻

The next day at the trial, Judge Andrews asked Sidney to call her last Witness. She called Dustina Washington. Dustina was Sophie's best friend and was very confused as to why her husband was called as a witness. She was even more disturbed that he refused to answer any question and invoked the Fifth Amendment. Dustina was shocked on both accounts. She had not spoken to her husband concerning the subpoena. She couldn't imagine what facts he may have known concerning the issues in Isiah's trial. She had no idea that Jayden would invoke his Fifth Amendment rights. She was not in the Courtroom when her husband testified. She also hadn't spoken to anyone, except Sidney, before she testified. Sidney said nothing about her husband's testimony. She had driven over Alligator Alley to Fort Myers early that morning to be Sidney's witness. What could her husband be involved in that would cause him to invoke his Fifth Amendment rights? Dustina was embarrassed.

Dustina was a seasoned trial attorney and spent some time, over the phone, with the prosecutor about her testimony. Neither was certain it would shed a lot of light on the issue of motive, however, Sidney was certain it would give the jury some facts to think about while deliberating in the jury room.

Sidney attempted to get Dustina to reveal some reason for Jayden to take the Fifth Amendment when he testified. Todd objected strenuously. The Judge agreed with Todd.

However, Dustina thought that there probably was something going on between Jayden's company and Jetta International that was questionable or even unlawful. However, Dustina could not believe that her husband would be involved in any unlawful acts. They had been married for a long time and his loyalty to Isiah and Jetta International were obvious to Dustina and was reflected that way in her testimony.

Sidney asked Dustina if Jayden had voiced any racial discontent with the way Jetta's management seemed to be changing. Dustina, being black herself, never saw any inkling of anything like that. The only changes in Jayden over the last few months was the fact that he had purchased more expensive gifts than normal for Dustina's birthday and anniversary. He even bought her gifts just to be nice. He had purchased himself a gold Rolex watch and a gold necklace. But Dustina believed that was due to salary increases he had received from his Company. At least that's what she thought provoked that spending spree. However, she was aware of the fact that Jayden had opened a new bank account under just his name. She never really questioned it since she felt he probably wanted some money of his own and not comingled with their joint account. She had thought about doing the same thing several times before, but after some thought, didn't see any reason to do that. Sidney listened and attempted to determine if Jayden's new wealth may have had something to do with Jetta International's internal management changes, but just couldn't connect them.

Dustina's testimony had some probative interest in a possible motive for Isiah to have to deal with Sophie as his lawyer. However there was no 'smoking gun' when Dustina had finished her testimony. There was testimony that Sophie and Dustina had spoken several times concerning the fact that Sophie was ethically required to either leave her firm or fire Jetta International as a client of her firm. Dustina attempted to get specifics as to why she felt that way. However, Sophie insisted that before she made any allegations, she needed to speak with Isiah first. She was to speak with her husband the evening after Sophie's and Dustina's last communication. Sophie was murdered the next morning. Dustina couldn't give any further information about any motive.

Sidney had no more witnesses. Everything that Sidney had brought up during the trial was all circumstantial evidence. There was no direct evidence by any of her witnesses except for the fact that Mason 'Dusty' Francis was hired by Clayton Reed to murder Sophie. It was not unusual that most murder cases are usually based on circumstantial evidence. As a prosecutor, Sidney believed that she had put sufficient circumstantial evidence on the record for a jury to find Isiah guilty, beyond a reasonable doubt, for both murders.

Todd and Isiah had many discussions, before and during the trial, as to the worthiness of the evidence to be presented by the prosecution. Both concluded, after the prosecution rested, that all of the evidence, other than Dusty's, was insufficient circumstantial evidence needed to obtain a criminal conviction. Also a lot of the testimony was disregarded so that the jury could not use it in determining a verdict. So with Isiah's hesitant permission, Todd decided on two ways to proceed.

"Mr. Hawkins, are you prepared to present your client's defense?" asked the Judge.

"Prior to presenting a defense, Your Honor, I move that this Court order a directed verdict, as a matter of law, in favor of my client and declare him not guilty on all charges based on the fact that the prosecution has not presented sufficient probative evidence to prove, beyond a reasonable doubt, that my client committed any crimes at all, let alone these ghastly crimes he is currently charged with."

Without blinking an eye or asking Sidney to reply to Todd's motion, the Judge denied the motion. Todd was somewhat surprised that no discussion was allowed by the Court for his motion. Usually that type of motion is routinely denied by judges, however, Todd believed that, in this case, some arguments should have been allowed. "Move on Mr. Hawkins," stated the Judge, "call your first witness."

"Judge it is my client's contention that some time should be given to argue my directed verdict motion,' argued Todd. "Most of the prosecutions witness have had their testimony thrown out. There is little or no probative evidence to convict my client, beyond a reasonable doubt, for the crimes in which he is charged."

"Mr. Hawkins, I have already made a ruling on your motion. Now move on," said the Judge angrily.

The next few moments shocked the entire Courtroom. That shock included both Sophie's and Isiah's family, but especially the press. No one saw what was to come next.

"Your Honor, the defense rests," stated Todd Hawkins.

The Judge was stunned and turned to the defendant. "Mr. Daniels," said Judge Andrews, "do you understand the ramifications of what your attorney has just said?"

"I do Your Honor."

"You are aware that you have the right to call witnesses in your defense?" again Judge Andrews questioned Isiah.

"I do Your Honor," again replied Isiah. "I have discussed calling witnesses for my defense with my attorney many times before and during the trial. I have also been advised by Mr. Hawkins that I have the right to decide whether or not I may choose to testify on my own behalf. My attorney has fully explained to me all of my rights. He and I have concluded that no further testimony is necessary for my defense of these crimes. After the prosecution's presentation, I'm sure the jury will do the right thing."

"Mr. Hawkins," replied the Judge, "If your client has decided not to testify, please refrain him from attempting to sway the jury."

"I'm certain that is not what he meant to do," replied Todd.

"Maybe Mr. Hawkins. But you understand that this case is a capital case. Your client's life is in jeopardy here," advised the Judge.

Before Todd could reply, the Judge insisted on a short 15 minute adjournment and requested Isiah and his attorney have a private discussion in his chambers. Sidney objected on the grounds that she had the right to be present in any meeting between the Judge and the defense. The Judge, in this case, didn't see it that way. The Judge assured Sidney that what he had to say to Isiah and Todd would not prejudice her case. Sidney feverishly disagreed and insisted on attending the meeting. The Judge told her to sit down and relax. Then the Judge told everyone in the Courtroom to stay seated where they were. He then told everyone he would be back in 15 minutes or less. With that statement, the three men met in the Judge's chambers.

That meeting only lasted 5 minutes and all three of them returned to their places in the Courtroom. The Judge then said that the trial would be adjourned for the day and both counsel should be ready for their final arguments first thing the next morning. The press rushed out of the Courtroom to call their bosses to relay what had just happened. The pundits on Court Television were all speculating as to the events that had just occurred and delivered their thoughts and opinions on the fact that the defense was not calling any witnesses. This was unheard of in a capital case. Everyone following the case were all flabbergasted. Yet many in the press and the television world speculated that the prosecution may have not proven, beyond a reasonable doubt, that Isiah was guilty of either murder. Everyone was speculating as to what the jurors might be thinking. However, more than that, what was Todd Hawkins thinking?

⟫●⟪

The next morning both attorneys were prepared to give their final arguments to the jury. Todd based his argument on the fact that, other than Mason 'Dusty' Francis murdered Sophie Daniels, the prosecution failed to show, beyond a reasonable doubt, that Isiah Daniels had anything to do with either his wife's murder or the murder of Clayton Reed. He went as far to argue that Dusty Francis may have actually wanted to just rob the Daniels home and had no idea that Sophie would be in the house at that time. Dusty was a two time felon and had committed a numerous number of crimes, even though some were fairly insignificant. The sloppy manner in which Sophie Daniels was murdered showed that Dusty had no intent, let alone the experience for anyone to trust him to kill another person for money. Dusty was a persistent liar and could not be trusted to even tell the truth when he testified for the prosecution. He did that for a deal to keep himself from being imprisoned for life, or worse, tried for a capital offense.

As to Isiah having the opportunity to hire Clayton Reed to murder his wife, Todd argued that there was no credible testimony indicating that the defendant had ever been in Clayton Reed's apartment or that he ever met Mr. Reed in the Overtown McDonalds or anywhere else. It was true that Isiah and Clayton Reed played basketball together while in college. However, there was no credible evidence that they stayed friends thereafter or that Isiah ever helped Reed out for anything other than offering him a job. And that offer came nearly 13 years before his murder occurred.

Todd argued further. The prosecution attempted to prove that the defendant had access to his wife's gun. Therefore, he had the means to murder Clayton Reed. However, other than the fact that Isiah knew his wife had the weapon, there was no evidence that Isiah took her weapon out of her purse or her desk at her office. That testimony was pure speculation that didn't even come close to believable circumstantial evidence. Dozens of people had access to Sophie Daniels desk. No one testified that Isiah was even in his wife's office prior to Clayton Reed's murder.

Todd left his most persuasive argument for last. He asked the jury if they could determine if the prosecutor's case showed any evidence of a scintilla of motive for Isiah to kill his wife with whom he was faithfully married for so many good years. Todd reminded the jury that they could not consider or even infer anything concerning Dijon Jackson, Darius Washington or Jayden Robinson taking the Fifth Amendment when they were asked questions by the prosecutor. However, even with that being the case, and even it were true that Isiah was promoting less qualified black employees over white employees at his Company, why would Sophie Daniels, as the Company's attorney be murdered over that issue? It wasn't unusual for people to be promoted over more senior employees. There could be a dozen reasons for that. Todd told the jury that he had attempted, during the trial, to try to understand where any motive for murder would fit into that scenario? There was no evidence presented that the employees who were promoted didn't deserve those promotions. It was only implied that race was the issue. But where was the motive for murder? Todd looked the jurors directly in their eyes and conceded that he knew that motive was not a necessary element in order to prove murder, beyond a reasonable doubt. However, he emphasized that any person who was accused of compensating a hitman to kill his wife and then take his wife's gun and murder the hired hitman had to have some kind of a motive. That motive had to make sense. However, the prosecutor didn't even come close to providing any evidence that any motive, on the part of Isiah, existed to murder Sophie Daniels or Clayton Reed. No means, no opportunity and no motive made his client an innocent man. He pleaded for the jury to find his client not guilty of either crime.

With that, Todd took his seat. His arguments had passion, logic and a lot of the truth. The jurors listened intensively and everyone in the Courtroom saw some of the jurors shake their heads in a manner that made them feel that his arguments also made a lot of sense to them.

CHAPTER 28

After Judge Andrew concluded the trial for that day, Anya was upset after listening to Todd Hawkins give his closing argument. She felt that Isiah may actually be found not guilty. She couldn't fathom that the black man who arranged for her sister to be so brashly murdered would walk a free man. She immediately called her father and vented her frustration as to how the trial was proceeding. He also felt the same way. Anya was certain that her father had connections to make sure that Isiah was either found guilty or never became a free man, whatever that meant.

"I already have people looking into the background of some of the jurors," said Donovan. "There are several jurors whose financial situations or employment situations may be in a difficult situation."

"Can your people get to them before they start deliberations?" asked Anya.

"Maybe, but things like that have to be done skillfully and in such a manner as to make sure anyone of the jurors, who may be approached, would accept some sort of arrangement. But most important I would have to approach all of the jurors. Only getting to a few jurors to vote to convict would only cause the jury not to come to a unanimous verdict. That would just cause a mistrial. Neither of us want that."

"I'm not quite sure what that means, but if that doesn't work, there must be other avenues?" queried Anya.

"Just leave it up to me, Anya," said her father," "I'll make sure Isiah gets what he deserves. Just remember, this conversation never happened."

Anya hung up and felt relieved but scared. She knew her father was an important man, with many different types of acquaintances, but could he really do what she thought he could do? In her heart she hoped so.

———————

The next morning at 9:30 sharp, Judge Andrews called his Court to Order. First on the agenda was Sidney White's opportunity to present her closing arguments. She got up from her seat and walked to the jury box and began her argument. Shockingly she began by asserting that some of Todd Hawkins' final arguments were basically correct. First, Dusty Francis was just a two-bit criminal that didn't have the intelligence to pull off a professional burglary. He didn't possess the know how to commit the murder of one of the highest profile attorneys in Miami, whose father may have become the next Governor of the State. He didn't know the first thing about how to gain entrance into one of the most secure neighborhoods in Boca Raton. But he conned his way in just like a two bit criminal would do. Sidney agreed with Todd that Dusty did terribly botch the murder. She told the jury it was one of the sloppiest and most gruesome murders she had ever seen or tried in her professional career. But she questioned Todd's assertion that Dusty was only in the Daniels home just to burglarize it and he was surprised by Sophie Daniels during that burglary. She reminded the jury that nothing was taken from the home. Even an inept burglar would have taken something of value after he thought he had killed Ms. Daniels. There were many expensive items in plain sight at the scene of the crime. Yet nothing was missing.

"There is nothing in evidence to substantiate that Dusty Francis was in the Daniels home that morning to burglarize their home," said Sidney. "Everything points to Clayton Reed subcontracting out Ms. Daniels murder. There was nearly $25,000.00 in $50.00 bills at Reed's apartment when the police found Reed dead. There is no evidence of any other connection between Dusty Francis and Sophie Daniels other than Clayton Reed. The only conclusion is that Reed was not the type of a person to murder someone, especially the wife of a man he thought was supporting him. There is no doubt that Reed was getting money, on a periodic basis, from someone. Reed didn't work. He had a nice car, an apartment, clothes and other necessities. Who would be funding him the money he lived on?" as she looked at the jury. "Who had sufficient wealth to subsidies Clayton Reed? Who knew him for almost 20 years? Who offered Clayton Reed a job at his business? Who spent several years with him in college as his roommate and who played basketball with him? There is only one person that fits that bill. The defendant," as Sidney turned and pointed to Isiah.

The defense gave the jury no evidence of any other person who could have done those things. In fact they didn't have one witness dispute those facts. She agreed that most of her evidence was circumstantial. However, the jury heard evidence directly from Dusty Francis that Clayton Reed paid him $1,500.00 to kill Sophie Daniels. Who else would have been able to give Clayton Reed the Daniels security code to get into the Daniels neighborhood and the whereabouts of a key to their side door? She again pointed at the defendant.

Sidney's argument took much of the Court's morning session. She went over and over the damaging circumstantial evidence of how Isiah had the opportunity to leave the Ritz, on multiple occasions, without being noticed by anyone. After all he had stayed at that hotel dozens of times. He had ample opportunity to meet Clayton Reed to arrange for the murder of his wife, and later to murder Mr. Reed when he found out about Reed's subcontract to Dusty Francis.

Sidney made it clear to the jury that Isiah knew everything about his wife's weapon and where it would be at any given time. Why were Isiah's fingerprints on the clip and bullets of his wife Glock 26? She argued who else had those capabilities? There was no question that Sophie Daniels' weapon was used to murder Clayton Reed. The jury heard where the weapon was found and forensic evidence about the fact that it was the murder weapon. She was convincing. Even Anya and Donovan felt more assured that Isiah may actually be found guilty.

Up to that point, Sidney felt that her arguments were persuasive. But to make sure there would be a conviction she knew she needed to make sure that the jury was convinced of a solid motive. Why else would someone commit two murders, one of whom was his wife of nearly 15 years? So Sidney used the testimony of Dustina Washington, Sophie's best friend to put together a scenario whereby Sophie wanted her best friend to handle a case dealing with Isiah and his company concerning issues that may have been illegal and unethical. She brought in the fact of the Federal agents that filed a RICO case against Isiah and others as well as the civil discrimination law suit.

"Objection Your Honor," claimed Todd. "Facts not in evidence. No Federal agent testified in this case."

"Ms. White," demanded the Judge, "be careful. Stick to the facts." But Sidney got her point across.

Sidney went back to Dustina. Sophie died before her best friend was able to take the lead on those cases because the deceased wanted to speak with her husband about those matters first. Sophie Daniels was murdered the next morning. Coincidence? Sophie argued to the jury that it wasn't just a coincidence. Sophie was even willing to leave her firm and a lucrative partnership because of these unknown events.

Then to further emphasize the dangerous matters that Sophie's husband may have been involved, she brought up the responses to her questions dealing with Isiah's company of certain witnesses who pled the Fifth Amendment.

"Objection, Your Honor. Can we talk?" exclaimed Todd.

Judge Andrews motioned both counsel to come to the bench. "Your Honor instructed the jury about Ms. White's witnesses taking the Fifth," angrily stated Todd. "I again reiterate my motion for a mistrial. She is ringing that bell another time."

"There will be no mistrial here counselor," stated the Judge as he looked directly at Sidney White. "You mention that one more time Ms. White and you will take out your checkbook and write this Court a large check for contempt and spend some time behind bars. Do you understand?"

"I'm sorry Your Honor, said Sidney. "It won't happen again." But she had done that intentionally just to remind the jury about her witnesses who wouldn't answer any questions about what was happening at Jetta

International. A typical ploy when an attorney knows the Judge would not declare a mistrial that far along in any trial. Sidney was a seasoned prosecutor.

Both counsel than returned to their places at their tables. Sidney continued for over an hour making a circumstantial argument, including some facts that had not even been brought up during the trial to give the jury the idea that, beyond a reasonable doubt, something illegal was occurring at Jetta International and Sophie Daniels may have been involved, in some unknown fashion, in those matters. Todd objected several times but was overruled every time. When Sophie's husband heard about his wife quitting her job and passing the Company's defense of those lawsuits to Dustina Washington, he knew something had to be done. In order for him not to get charged with a crime, he made arrangements with Clayton Reed, his old friend who owed him, to murder his wife.

The jury listened intently to Sidney's arguments. She gave the jury something to hang their hat on as a motive for murder. Todd was extremely upset with her arguments, and the manner in which she argued her case. However, he didn't want to object and ask for a mistrial another time. The Judge wanted this trial finished. Todd knew that Judge Andrews did not want to retry this case. An appeal would be Isiah's only remedy. But Todd still felt that the prosecution did not meet the necessary standard to convict Isiah. So he hoped for the best from the jury.

Late that afternoon Sidney concluded her final argument. It was time for the Judge to instruct the jury on the legal issues involved. He explained and defined what reasonable doubt was and that it was the prosecution's requirement to prove all charges against the defendant. He instructed the jury to fully disregard the testimony of Anya Taylor and Martell Dixon as well as any witness that took the Fifth Amendment on the witness stand. He fully explained the intent of the Fifth Amendment to the jury again. Then he told them to go home and be prepared to decide a verdict in this matter. He also reminded them not to watch any news programs or read any news articles about the case. Then the

Judge concluded the day and indicated that the jury meet in the jury room at 9:00 AM the next day.

Todd met with Isiah in the holding cell at the Lee County Courthouse and went over Sidney's arguments. Todd just couldn't understand why Sidney had the right to argue that he had some criminal action being held over him. He again pleaded to Todd that he had done nothing wrong. Todd consoled him and told him to be optimistic that the jury would be able to see that. But Todd was worried. Little did Todd know that Sidney felt the same way.

———————→➤●◄←———————

That evening, Donovan Taylor received a call from one of his acquaintances concerning the results of delving into the pasts of the jurors. Donovan was very disappointed when he hung up the phone. He knew that he should have begun an investigation on the jurors several weeks ago. One day was just not sufficient for what he wanted. Now he also could only just wait. Others who had to just wait included not only the family and friends of Isiah, Sophie and Clayton Reed, but the press. The news all over the Country waited for the jury's verdict. Every news cast on CNN, MSNBC, Fox News and many local stations in Florida had stories to begin their broadcasts on each of the four days that it took the jury to deliberate.

On the morning of the fourth day of deliberations, the jury had contacted the Judge that they had reached a verdict. The clerk contacted both Sidney and Todd that the jury had a verdict. It only took 20 minutes to fill the Courtroom with both families involved, spectators and as many press commentators and newspaper correspondents that the room could hold. All of the major networks stopped their regular presentations in Florida to broadcast the jury's verdict.

It took nearly an hour for the Judge's clerk to get everyone situated and the single news camera crew in place. Then Judge Andrews entered the Courtroom. He immediately called in the jury. Each of the jurors walked into the jury box and took the seat that they had been in for nearly three weeks. None of the jurors gave anyone in the Courtroom any eye contact or made any unusual jesters. It was all business. With the news monitor set on Judge Andrews, he said, "Madam Foreperson, have you reached a unanimous verdict on both counts of first degree murder?"

The Foreperson was the 41 year old black woman. "We have Your Honor," replied the Foreperson. "We find the defendant, Isiah Daniels, guilty of first degree murder on both counts."

There was a lot of groans, clapping, crying and clatter by everyone in the Courtroom. "Quiet," yelled Judge Andrews, "or I'll clear the Courtroom." After a little over a minute, and some cries from the back of the Courtroom, the Judge looked at the jury and, without any request of either counsel, he asked each of the jurors, individually, if that was their verdict. Each of the jurors answered the Judge in the affirmative.

"This trial is adjourned for three days," stated the Judge. "At which time the penalty phase of this trial will resume."

Isiah turned to his mother who was attempting to get through all of the news people to her son so she could hold him. She finally got to him and hugged him as she sobbed, "I love you son, and don't give up."

"I didn't do any of this mother," said Isiah as the Court clerk took Isiah's hands and cuffed them to take him back to his holding cell. Sidney looked at Todd with a blank face. Todd was in as much shock as Isiah. Donovan and Anya Taylor had grins on their face. Sheila Taylor was crying. All of them knew that the worst was yet to come.

CHAPTER 29

It only took a jury of Isiah Daniels' peers two hours to sentence him to death, even after 8 witnesses pleaded for him to live. Those witnesses included Isiah's family, and several employee managers from Jetta International. Isiah was immediately transferred to a Death Row cell at Florida State Prison in Raiford, Florida. That cell was 6 feet by 9 feet wide and 9.5 feet high. It had a bed, sink and toilet. Isiah wore an orange t-shirt, which designated him as a prisoner on death row. His pants were the same blue cotton pants worn by all prisoners at that prison. He was served his meals, prepared by the prison staff, and transported in insulated carts, three times a day, at 5:30 AM, 11:00 AM and 4:30 PM. He was allowed to shower, by himself, every other day. Death row inmates were counted, by the guards, at least one time every hour of the day. They were escorted in handcuffs and wore them everywhere except in their cells, the exercise yard for 30 minutes a day, and while showering. Occasionally, if Isiah was on his best behavior, he was allowed some snacks. Also, from time to time, a radio or a 13 inch black and white television, without cable TV, was positioned outside his cell. There was no comingling with other prisoners at any time. Isiah was not prepared for this type of a life and its isolation. He hated it and knowing he was innocent made it even worse. It was an extremely hard transition. His execution was set, by lethal injection, on no less than the 30th day after all of his required appeals had been exhausted. That may take as long as 6 years or more.

Todd Hawkins was required, under Florida law, to remain Isiah's attorney while he was a death-sentenced inmate. Todd was not allowed to withdraw from that representation, even if it was at the wish of his client. However, Isiah wanted to have Todd remain his attorney during the appeals. Todd had tried other death cases, but this was the first client he had represented that had been sentenced to death. Todd, unfortunately didn't have the time, resources or expertise to competently handle all of the required death case appeals. They would take years to investigate and complete. Isiah was aware of that fact, but still needed Todd. He was there from the beginning of Isiah's nightmare.

Several weeks after the trial ended, Todd received a telephone call from Dalton Leitch, an attorney who had handled over a dozen death cases in his career. He had followed the Daniels trial on television. Dalton was a senior partner, practicing out of the Orlando office of Wilkerson & Campbell, a large national law firm consisting of over 600 attorneys in 14 states with 32 offices. Dalton discussed the Daniels case with Todd for over an hour giving Todd some worthwhile advice concerning death case appeals. Finally after Todd had patiently listened to Dalton's advice, he asked Dalton if he would consider becoming co-counsel for the appeal. Todd told Dalton that Isiah still had about $50,000.00 left in several bank accounts that could be used as a retainer. He was also still the record holder of a 10% interest in the publically held company of Jetta International. That was a large interest for one person to hold in a publically held company and it was worth a large sum of money. Dalton graciously agreed to Todd's request, even though that was his real intent before he called Todd. The fact that Isiah could pay for his appeals was not Dalton's incentive. Dalton thrived on handling death cases. He would have done it for nothing.

The next week, Todd met with Dalton in his Orlando office and they both traveled to Raiford, Florida to meet with Isiah. They wanted to go over all the procedures, costs and time frame for his appeals. Dalton was optimistic about a favorable outcome and voiced that to Isiah without criticizing Todd's competency. Dalton believed that the prosecution had a poor circumstantial case. Not enough evidence to warrant a guilty verdict, let alone a death sentence. Todd believed the same thing, however, he felt that he had done a poor job selecting the jury. But his biggest regret was that he probably should have put on several witnesses in Isiah's defense. The only witnesses Todd called, during the trial, were family and friends of Isiah's during the penalty phase to try to convince the jury that Isiah's life was worth saving. It was as if someone had gotten to one or more of the jurors. It only took 2 hours for the jury to unanimously impose the death penalty. Dalton exonerated Todd as to those thoughts and told him that he did a very good job. There was just a bad outcome.

Both attorneys agreed that there needed to be much more investigation into all of the evidence presented, not presented or even missed at trial. Todd questioned Dalton as to evidence possibly being missed. Dalton graciously told Todd that he had to look at that possibility every time there is a death case. Dalton was not accusing Todd of mishandling the case. Dalton said he knew where to get good help for the investigative part of the appeal. New evidence was the major key to get a new trial or find the actual killers. That would be the only ways to stop Isiah's execution. Isiah also understood that this process and time frames to get in front of a Court may take at least five to six years. Isiah was depressed thinking about living that way for such a long time. But there were no other options.

Of the good news, Isiah liked Dalton. Dalton told Isiah that he had watched him play basketball, several times, when Miami came to Orlando to play Central Florida University. Dalton thought that he had a chance to go professional. However, at the time, he was unaware of Isiah's relationship with Donovan Taylor. Once he found out about that relationship and the fact that Isiah married Donovan's daughter, it gave Dalton a reason to follow Isiah's trial. Dalton and Donovan had several brushes, over the years, dealing with both political matters and several business law suits. Dalton was anxious to represent Isiah for those personal reasons. But, nothing was said about that to Isiah. Dalton never liked or trusted Donovan Taylor.

After their discussion, Isiah agreed to Todd and Dalton becoming his co-counsels. Arrangements were made to add Dalton in the court records and at the prison as Isiah's co-counsel. Isiah signed the necessary papers to close Isiah's bank accounts and divide the $50,000.00 between Todd and Dalton's firm as a retainer for the appeals. Isiah also signed a document securing the remainder of his fees and costs with his 10% interest in Jetta International. The SEC had to approve any possible transfer of publically held company stock over 5%. After waiting 6 weeks, the SEC approved. However, both Dalton and Todd knew that if a new trial could not be achieved, the 10% interest in Jetta stock would transfer to Isiah's family. Both were fine with that.

Thereafter, Dalton took control of Isiah's appeal, ordered all of the required transcripts, exhibits and investigation reports. Dalton also contacted the administrator for the Florida International University Law School Death Penalty Clinic, Carlos Webb. He had used him and his students in several of his other death case appeals. The clinic was well known all over Florida. A competent and well respected team of legal experts were about to embark on a highly visible appeal.

⸺⟫●⟨⸺

Just over two years after Isiah's trial, Donovan Taylor was found dead, at his home, by his wife when she returned from playing bridge at the home owner association's clubhouse. Apparently, Donovan died of natural causes, a massive heart attack. He was 79 years old. He was retired and only volunteered to help Republican candidates run for public office. He had retired from politics after his downfall in his quest to become the Republican candidate for Governor. He still attended University of Miami basketball games as often as he could. But he never had anything to do with Jetta International after Isiah appointed Dijon Jackson as CEO. Donovan had sold all of his stock in the company to various investors through his financial broker.

The majority of his large estate went to his wife Shelia. His estate was worth just under $100 million dollars. The vast majority of the estate consisted of the cash proceeds he received from selling his interest, over several years, in Jetta International. Even though his interest had been diluted over the years due to the company issuing additional stock offerings of the Company's stock he still received a fortune when the

Company went public and again when he sold his remaining stock. It was a very large sum of money. Most of it was reinvested in quality dividend yielding public companies such as AT&T, Proctor & Gamble, Verizon, Comcast and 3M. Donovan used some of his proceeds from the Jetta sale for gifting nearly $10 million to the University of Miami. An athletic dormitory was named after him just before he passed. He had attended the ceremony. Basketball was still one of his passions. No one in his family ever understood why. Anya, his only remaining child, received $5 million dollars. She never married and continued to work on environmental issues and continued to teach at FGCU. She spoke regularly to her parents and was devastated when her father passed. She never followed the track of any of Isiah's appeals. In her mind Isiah was dead.

Dalton's investigators looked deeply into all facets of Donovan's life, but could not find anything connecting him, or his family, to the death of Sophie or Clayton Reed. Even when Isiah was told about Donovan, he still felt nothing about his passing. Everything Donovan may have done for Isiah disappeared from his mind. He was just another bigot. He had done nothing to help his son-in-law after he was arrested for Sophie's death. Isiah felt betrayed. Neither Shelia nor Anya Taylor ever spoke to Isiah again. Isiah often wondered if that would have been true if he were white. But that was the last thing on his mind at the time.

⟫●⟪

The two major lawsuits brought against Jetta International that were used as part of the strategy for the prosecution in Isiah's trial to prove motive quickly disappeared about 10 months after Isiah was sentenced to death. They were settled quietly by the Company paying an undisclosed amount into a fund for white management personnel and white MBA's or its equivalent that were applicants but weren't hired by a black plant manager. Non-disclosure and Confidentiality Agreements were signed by all parties.

The Governments RICO case was settled by the Company by executing a Consent Order agreeing that the Company would not associate with any individuals or entities that may be involved in any collection of any false debt, or control any entity involved in any false enterprises that would be engaged in transactions to launder any funds in interstate or foreign commerce. Dijon agreed to the Consent Decree before the Government had the time to an opportunity to do a complete forensic audit of every customer of the Company. Dijon knew the assertions in the Settlement Agreement, which he signed were false. Dustina Washington, Sophie's best friend was Jetta's lead counsel for both law suits. She arranged, at the request of Jetta, to have both of the proceedings permanently sealed. The Securities and Exchange Commission signed off on both settlements. Dustina settled the RICO matter as quickly as possible for her client. She also didn't investigate any of Jetta's customer accounts or Off Shore banking accounts. She never believed there was ever a problem. She believed her client and was skeptical of the Government. Jetta's stock value increased substantially after the settlement. That increased the net worth of all four co-conspirators since they had a large chunk of Jetta stock. But it was small change compared to what was sitting in Off Shore Banks.

Dalton Leitch knew that he needed to unseal those law suits to have any opportunity to either get a new trial for Isiah or prove his innocence. Isiah vetoed that request. Isiah still naively believed that Dijon Jackson, Darius Williams and Dustina Washington were good people and would not do anything illegal to damage Isiah or Jetta. To Isiah it was a waste of time. Even if he lost his life, Isiah did not want to invade those people's lives for something, he believed, in his heart that his lawyers would never find.

Isiah never knew about the anger of Dijon, Darius and Jayden when they were not granted an opportunity to obtain some of Jetta's stock before it went public. That thought never passed Isiah's mind. Little did Isiah realize that if those three had received stock prior to the Company going public, Sophie and Clayton would still be alive and Isiah never would have been charged with a crime.

Isiah's reluctance to reopen the sealed lawsuit settlements caused Dalton's enthusiasm for the appeal to start to decompose. But Todd convinced Dalton that it was Isiah's life and he should respect Isiah's wishes. Dalton documented his disapproval of Todd's strategy but continued his quest to free Isiah.

With the lawsuits settled and the Government's Justice Department and the SEC gone, Dijon, Darius and Jayden continued their scheme. They continued diverting corporate funds by laundering the money from fake transactions through European fences and into fake off shore companies. This was still all conducted by James Logan through his law firm. Before Isiah's trial had even ended, Douglass Fischer, the most senior partner of the Fischer & Logan firm died from colon cancer. Fischer was aware of his cancer for almost 16 months, but kept it private from everyone except James Logan. Fischer's death elevated James Logan to the most senior partner as well as the new managing partner for the firm. This made it even easier for the scheme to be continued by Logan. Even each fake Off Shore Company paid legal fees to Logan's firm as well as commissions to the three other conspirators companies. It all looked legitimate. Within four years after Isiah had been sentenced to death the four co-conspirator had accumulated over $325 million in the Off Shore bank accounts.

Dalton brought a motion before the Lee County Circuit Court to have a forensic accounting of all of the customers in Jetta International's system. It was a long shot, thought up by Dalton and his investigator, to get around not being able to unseal the lawsuits. However Jetta's lawyer, James Logan, argued that the cost, the amount of time that it would take and the disruption that it would cause for the publically held Company and its customers would be enormous. Even the Judge took the side of the Company. Dalton's motion was denied. Even an appeal of that ruling, which took 6 months, was affirmed. Isiah's lawyers were not going to get to look at Jetta International's books. It was now almost three years that Isiah had been on death row. The appeals and investigations all had dead ends. Death appeals are expensive and time consuming.

With that final appeal concerning the Company's settlement of the audit of accounts being denied, the four conspirators decided to begin to taper off the stealing of funds, slowly got rid of the fake clients and, as agreed, slowly started to withdraw their ill-gotten funds. Jayden and

Dustina divorced several months after Isiah's trial. The stress between them during the time Dustina was representing Jetta while Jayden was secretly stealing from both Jetta and Xavier Corporation led to a marriage with little or no more intimate communications or passion. In addition, Dustina found out about an affair Jayden had with a coworker. Jayden had his divorce planned some time before Sophie's death. With the money he was going to be making through the scheme, Jayden would be able to start life over again as a free man. Without divorcing, Dustina he would be badgered by Dustina on every large purchase he would make. He needed to separate his life from Dustina to enjoy the fruits of his dishonesties. The scheme was beginning to guide all four participates way of doing their jobs and their personal lives. There was a lot of money involved and the consequences and the collateral fallout for each of their lives was small in comparison to the large amount of money.

⟿⟾

Dalton's investigators was one of the best in the business. Dalton used him often and was usually successful when he helped Dalton. He was famous for putting an orderly 'list' together for Dalton, on each case, in order for Dalton to keep track of the many complicated matters.

The investigator was instructed to look into every employee at the Ritz in West Palm Beach to see if any of them had any interest in lying about not knowing if Isiah had time to leave the hotel to meet with Clayton Reed. Even Todd's sister, Deena was investigated since she stayed at the Ritz for a night after the murder. Isiah had booked and paid for her room. Nothing was found. That item was checked off the list. Isiah's opportunity to leave unnoticed from the hotel could not be disputed.

The manager of the McDonalds restaurant in Overtown was investigated and interrogated extensively but nothing incriminating was found and he continued to stick to his testimony stated at trial.

Drew Austin, the owner of Shoot Straight gun shop in West Palm Beach was also a dead end. Those items were crossed off the list.

Dalton was starting to believe that Isiah may have actually murdered his wife or some unknown person or persons committed the perfect crime. Unfortunately, after over 4 years of investigations, 6 appeal hearings before the Florida Court of Appeals and one denial of the Florida Supreme Court to hear Isiah's appeal, there was only one more direction to go. Dalton didn't like his last hope. However, Dalton's investigator had come up with some ideas after investigating all the matters Dalton and Todd had requested. Dalton would let his investigator run at his imaginary target even if his last hope was futile. But it would probably be too late.

The current Governor of Florida, who had the constitutional right to pardon or commit sentences, was a longtime rival of Donovan Taylor. They both disliked each other. However, the Governor was a fair minded person. He attempted to make sure that personality issues were never a part of any decision that he made. He even instructed his aids to intervene if they ever thought that a decision was going to be made based on the Governor's biases. The current Governor and Dalton knew each other well. Each presented many arguments before the Florida Supreme Court. Several of those cases the two men were on opposite sides. But this would be the first time Dalton would be making an application to this Governor for either a pardon or clemency on behalf of a client. And not just any client, but an educated successful black client. A client who hired another black man who he had not seen in years to murder his wife. Then he turned around and murdered that same black man. So said a jury of his peers.

The Governor, under Florida law, had the unfettered discretion to deny a pardon or clemency at any time for any reason. However, in order for the Governor to grant a pardon or clemency, it also had to be approved by at least 2 members of his cabinet. The Governor along with 3 members of his cabinet together made up the Clemency Board in Florida. Dalton knew there wasn't a chance in Hell in getting a pardon or clemency for Isiah.

After close to 5 years of intense investigation, 6 appeal hearings and the denial of the Supreme Court to even hear Isiah's appeal, Dalton's investigator still had that unsettling feeling in his gut that Isiah was not letting his attorneys look at the real issues. Isiah's grasp that friends would not betray him held his attorneys back from some obvious matters. The investigator had no connection to Isiah. So Dalton let the investigator look at matters that Isiah would have disapprove of. The biggest issue the investigator couldn't get out of his mind was why would Sophie Daniels want to quit her job and stop representing Jetta International for just a couple of go nowhere law suits? Only a non-legal mind thought that way. There had to be more to it than that. However, Dalton, Todd and the FIU Death Penalty Clinic had felt that they had exhausted that avenue. And time was running out. So Dalton's investigator convinced Dalton to let him look under some rocks that he was originally told to leave alone. Dalton and Todd wouldn't disclose that fact to Isiah. Could it be accomplished in a very short period of time? All of Isiah's appeals had been legally exhausted. His execution date would be set at any time. Was the Governor the best use of his time left? Dalton was in one of the lowest points of his professional life. How could he let someone who he believed to be an innocent man die? He decided to call Todd and tell him about his investigator's speculations. He hoped that Isiah, after all the time he spent on death row, would go along with him and, most important, that there was still time to save Isiah.

CHAPTER 30

Dalton contacted Todd and they both drove to Florida State Prison to meet with Isiah. Dalton explained that applying to the Clemency Board would probably keep the appeal going, but most probably a waste of valuable needed time. The Governor and Isiah's father-in-law were never on good terms. Also when a double murder is involved, it would be very difficult to persuade the Governor and 2 of his cabinet members to agree to some sort of clemency.

"But I still don't understand why you both can't explain to some Court or the Governor how slim the circumstantial evidence that was presented at trial could justify my conviction, let alone a death sentence." said a very depressed and changed Isiah. He was no longer that optimistic hard aggressive businessman. He was broken and had made his peace with his death.

"Isiah," answered Dalton, "in a Clemency hearing, the case cannot be retried. There has to be other extenuating circumstances or new evidence. Also we would need some reference letters from individuals indicating to your moral character, and that you have a personal hardship, or have life threatening health issues, etc. Very similar to the penalty phase of your original trial. And you saw how that went."

"So what do you propose?" Isiah asked Dalton.

"My investigator had a long shot idea. Please don't get upset. We need to get into Sophie's law firm records and client lists. There has to be something there that would cause her to want to quit her job and not represent Jetta other than the discrimination matters. That had to be a very difficult choice to make for Sophie," answered Dalton. "Did any other partners work on Jetta's legal matters other than Sophie?"

"I only let James Logan supervise any matters dealing with Jetta," Said Isiah. "Many other younger attorneys did some work, but James supervised it all if Sophie wasn't handling the matter. But you already looked into that issue. I have come to grips with my future. I don't want to see you interrupt Sophie's old law firm and the good attorneys who work there. It could ruin them."

"I know. But you are our only issue. We need to dig much further into that issue. We may have to straddle the legal lines to accomplish that. But that's where we have to start," said Dalton. "Do you think Logan would cooperate or do you think he would require another set of subpoenas? He successfully opposed the first set of subpoenas we obtained. However, he was one of the few persons who no one really looked at during your trial or the appeals. I thought that he and Sophie got along so well. I can't believe Sidney didn't put him on the stand. He also refused to testify in the penalty stage. Why was that?"

"I told you I screwed up," said Todd.

"It's not your fault," said Dalton. "I just thought of it myself after, speaking with my investigator, more than five and a half years after working on this appeal. How could we all have missed the possible James Logan trail?"

Just then one of the death row guards knocked on the door of the attorney conference room. He was motioned to come in by Dalton.

"Two matters. Both bad." said the guard. "First your time is up for attorney visitation today."

"We only need another 15 minutes officer," said Dalton. "This man's life is at stake."

"I understand," said the guard with some compassion. He liked Isiah. "Just take whatever time you need. Isiah is a good man. If anyone may be innocent in here, it would be him. Just don't tell my supervisor I let you stay longer."

"Thanks," said Dalton. "There was a second matter?"

"Oh yes," said the guard as he put his head down. "Isiah's execution date is set for midnight October 31. That's 40 days from today." Then the guard quickly left.

If anything can make a room silent with two attorneys in it was that news. Isiah just put his head in his hands and told Dalton and Todd to do what they could to get Logan to cooperate. Time was really short now. Even though he knew that day was coming, that news hit Isiah hard.

"If I can get some cooperation from Logan it may be enough new evidence to get a short stay from the execution date," said Dalton. "We'll keep you informed. And keep your spirts up. We're here for you 24 hours a day."

Isiah called for the guard to take him back to his 6 X 9 cell. He thanked the guard for his consideration. Then both attorneys talked as they left death row to go to their cars. They discussed what each should do, and they hadn't pressed James Logan more over the last few years in order to try to get him to cooperate more in order to try to find some new evidence. Both attorneys were disgusted with themselves concerning that issue.

Dalton agreed to call his investigator to check the public records for anything Logan may have filed, with any agencies in Florida or other states, or even off shore, around the time or before Sophie's murder. Dalton needed him to add some more tasks to his list. Dalton requested Todd to see Logan and determine if he might cooperate with them to check out any clients of Sophie's, or any that had dealings with Jetta, without having to get a Court Order. Todd nodded.

Todd wanted to know what this list was that Dalton had just mentioned. Dalton said that it was a technique that his investigator would compile for Dalton when they were working on criminal cases. It was just something between the two of them that seemed to work well. He was excellent with his investigations. Todd couldn't understand why Dalton hadn't discussed with him this list before. Dalton, from the beginning of the appeal, didn't think that his investigator's list would help much in this case so he didn't feel the need to communicate it to Todd. But maybe Dalton had been wrong. So he just brought it up. Todd thought that strange with only 40 days to go. Dalton had previously been very successful with his investigator's lists he would use on Dalton's other appeals. Why not this one. Both attorneys knew time was short. If they wanted to accomplish something substantial during their careers of practicing law, now was that time. Todd insisted that Dalton's investigator get moving on one of those lucky lists. Todd also suggested to Dalton that he should call Carlos at the FIU clinic to get him and his students started on drafting the legal documents necessary for a petition to the Circuit Court for a short stay. They would only use the petition if they were able to find any new evidence from Logan's firm. They needed to be ready to file for an expedited hearing in front of Judge Andrews as soon as possible.

James Logan was married, had three grown children and four grandchildren. He and his late partner, Douglass Fischer, made a very good living after they started building a small law firm, on the first floor of an old office building in Plantation, Florida. They expanded it to a large multi-office firm with 25 partners and 6 offices in Florida. But lately, even his wife questioned him as to his new spending habits on luxury items. He was wealthy but not overly rich. Yet he had recently purchased four new suits, each costing him over $2,000.00 each. The ties separately were $350.00 each. His wife commented that he had never spent that type of money on clothes before. He also purchased a new Mercedes-Mayback GLS sports utility vehicle. That car's sticker price started at $160,500.00 and was fully loaded, when James purchased it. The cost was $196,995.00. His wife and colleagues were astonished. Logan had also hired a realtor to look for a second home in Aspen, Colorado as a vacation home. His wife knew that James, who was 74 years old, didn't have much skiing left in him. But James response was that it was for the kids. He said business had been very good lately. He had been married a long time. His wife was not naïve. Where did this money come from, she thought? Business couldn't have been that much better. They haven't hired a lot of new lawyers to handle the additional cases to generate that much in fees. The whole firm was whispering and Logan's friends couldn't believe it. They wondered if he had just settled some huge contingency case or something else happened for which the firm was unaware. This gossip didn't get past Dalton's investigator as he was working on investigating James Logan's work with Jetta's activities. It also didn't get past Dijon and Darius,

Todd had made an appointment to meet with James concerning the Sophie Daniels murder. James knew Todd was working on Isiah's appeal. However, he was certain that he had covered all the bases in guiding him and his co-conspirators in their very lucrative scheme. It's been over 6 and a half years since the scheme started and no one has been even close to finding the truth. But Logan and Robinson were starting to spend money like millionaires.

"This firm has nothing to hide," said Logan to Todd when asked about matters dealing with Jetta. "I will cooperate as far as I can ethically. Anything to help Isiah. No one believes he could have done those terrible things," arrogantly stated Logan. "But why did it take you so long to come and see me again? I thought all of Isiah's appeals had lapsed."

"Logan, you were never a person of interest to speak to in our investigation. But I hope you are now willing to cooperate." replied Todd. "Would you give me a list of all of the public filings for entities tied to Jetta International?"

"What kind of public filings?"

"Anything and everything that may be in anyway connected to subsidiaries or other companies that Jetta may have had some nexus to, like their customers or suppliers."

James started to sweat. He indicated that revealing the incorporating of customers or suppliers of Jetta may be an ethical issue if he revealed anything like that. Anyway, if they were public they could retrieve them in the public records. Todd disagreed. Unless there was a law suit between Jetta and one of their customers or suppliers then there might be a conflict on the part of your firm as to the representation of either party. Otherwise those documentations concerning the incorporation of those entities are just public records. But Todd didn't know which

State or County or Caribbean Island to look into. Time was short. That was why Todd's request was made to Logan. James agreed, but knew he wasn't going to supply those documents that may incriminate him. He was also sure they would never locate the Off Shore corporation documents. And if they did, they could never find out the owners of those accounts. Those banks prided themselves on privacy.

James indicated to Todd that he was certain that there were no public filings that could be associated with Jetta that his firm would handle other than security exchange documents required by the SEC, from time to time. Todd asked James to have someone copy those documents and call him when they would be ready to be sent by Federal express to Todd's office. Time was of the essence. James agreed reluctantly.

Todd could see that James was somewhat nervous. His posturing and the way he walked the room was a 'tell' for Todd that he was hiding something. The Boca detectives had told that to Todd. He would discuss that with Dalton later. Plus, Dalton's impeccable investigator should be able to check all State records and even all off shore filings in nearly all Caribbean Countries. But everyone knew that would take a lot of time. The two lawyers said goodbye as Todd thanked James for his help.

James became more relieved when Todd left. He contacted one of his associates and asked him to have copies made of all SEC filings for Jetta over the last 7 years. No copies of corporate documents or subsidiaries were requested to be copied by James. Why didn't Dalton or Todd think of this years ago? It just didn't seem to fit into the narrative of the crimes involved. That just couldn't be a reason for Sophie to fire Jetta.

Todd immediately called Dalton and told him about his meeting with Logan. Dalton agreed that the SEC filings probably wouldn't help, but it could be a start. However, Dalton mentioned to Todd that his investigator had started to put together his list by researching all 50 states and as many Caribbean Countries as possible who were secretive on their banking customers. He had already located over 50 incorporations created by the Fischer firm for the incorporation of companies dealing with their firms clients including Jetta and possible some of their customers. He is investigating all of them right now. Both attorneys weren't sure what that may uncover, but it was at least another new avenue to explore. They hoped that the investigator's list would encompass something that probably could be used, at least for a short stay of execution.

Dalton told Todd that they would meet in Todd's office first thing the next morning. Hopefully Dalton's investigator would have something interesting started on his list and maybe they would even get the SEC filing that day to review.

———————

Isiah had now been moved from his death row cell to a death watch cell. This was near the execution chamber where the three legged electric chair was housed. It was made of oak by the prisoners in the wood shop in the main prison. That meant that not only was Isiah's execution date and time set, but the Governor had also signed his death warrant. Isiah had not heard from either of his lawyers in several days, and he now started to face the reality of his situation. His new cell was a 12 by 7 cell with an 8.5 foot ceiling. He could see the execution room door from his cell. There was no more exercise time for Isiah. It was just wait in his cell and eat his meals. No reading literature was available and his clothes were changed to an orange jump suit. It was the most scared Isiah had ever been.

Isiah was asked if he wanted the warden to call anyone to attend to the execution. Such a stupid question Isiah thought. That question made him cry. Why would someone be 'invited' to an execution? It would kill his elderly parents, both of whom were in bad health. And his other family members couldn't watch him die. He told the guard that he would have to speak with his lawyers about that question. The guard told him that the Florida Press Association and the Florida Broadcasters Association will be selecting 12 press people to witness the event. Isiah still couldn't stop crying. He was also told to start thinking about his last meal. He could have anything reasonable from any restaurant close by up to $50.00. Why put an amount on what someone could order for their last meal? Again Isiah thought that was insulting. Then the guard gave him a pat on the back and left. Isiah couldn't believe that what was happening to him was real.

⋙●⋘

Todd, Dalton and the investigator met at Dalton's office late the next afternoon. The SEC filings for Jetta international, for the last 7 years, were delivered to Dalton's office by Federal Express that morning. The investigator reviewed the large stack of SEC documents before he was to meet with the attorneys. The one outstanding feature in the documents that he put on his list was the fact that there was a large amount of payments to European companies for precious metals. It was not unusual for a technology company to purchase precious metals but not from European companies, however, several other issues stuck out to the investigator.

First, the companies that Jetta paid for the metals provided in their manufacturing process were different every year during the 7 year period. Second, the largest provider of precious metals to Jetta was Xavier Corporation, who provided more metals to Jetta each of the preceding years, for each of those 7 years. Of course there may be many factors accounting for that event such as price, quality of the metals, etc.

However, Dustina Washington, was married to Xavier's Executive Vice President of sales, Jayden Robinson, during that time. They divorced not long after Isiah was found guilty. Dustina then began representing Jetta for the issues concerning the discrimination suit and the RICO suit by the government. Dijon Jackson would have had to approve that. Both of those matters were settled fairly quickly after Isiah's trial and the settlements were sealed by the Judge at the request all parties. Dustina didn't object.

Then, Judge Andrews ruled on two occasions, at separate hearings, that Isiah's appeal counsels didn't present sufficient new evidence in order to have those settlements unsealed for the purpose of Isiah's appeal. Dalton wasn't sure how both of those issues should be interpreted so he needed to see what his investigator uncovered.

When Todd and Dalton met the investigator, the investigator told both attorneys that he had uncovered through various people he worked with certain public records that indicated that James Logan had been the attorney of record for incorporating at least 500 companies in Florida, Delaware, Nevada and Alaska. Over 20 of those companies were for one of Jetta's main customers, Xavier Corporation. All of those companies then organized Off Shore companies in the Cayman Islands and Costa Rica and each opened an Off Shore bank account, in the name of those Off Shore Companies.

"That's not unusual. All of that could be legitimate. So long as those companies report all income to the IRS wherever it was earned. The incorporations could be for a dozen different business purposes. However, we don't have their tax returns." said Todd.

"I know that Todd," said Dalton, "but I think my investigator has some more information than just that. Am I correct?"

"You are" said the investigator, "I have several inside relationships in the Islands that found 18 off shore companies had no affiliation with any United States company. They were formed originally as Cayman Island or Costa Rica corporations. They each opened bank accounts in the Caymans and Costa Rica at 18 different banks. James Logan incorporated all 18 companies. All of those accounts received funds deposited from the same European companies that Jetta International ordered certain precious metal materials. However, I never saw any invoices from any European companies when I reviewed, for the third time, Jetta's books. So my list indicates that those precious metals may have never been delivered to Jetta."

"Gentleman," continued the investigator, "let me make this very clear. My Island relationships must always remain anonymous. None of them can testify for you. Even their names must be kept secret. They make their livings being anonymous. This information cost you a lot of money to find. You'll need to do some fancy lawyering to figure out how to present this to a Judge. My friends all want to keep breathing. All of this is itemized on my list, which I am still in the process of completing."

"James Logan?" said Todd, "could he have been involved with Sophie's death? He was Sophie's partner. But they were good friends.

However, I do believe this turn of events does require some explanation. We have James Logan and maybe Jayden Robinson, but I still don't know where or how they may fit in? And how does Jetta fit in?"

"Todd, think about what the list may be telling us," inserted Dalton. "What if James Logan incorporated those 18 Off Shore Companies for Xavier Corporation at the request of Jayden Robinson? What if Jayden and James were conspiring with someone from Jetta to launder the proceeds of certain orders through European mob run companies to the Off Shore accounts? Maybe Sophie found out about this diversion and may have thought Isiah was involved? Maybe that is why she wanted to speak with him before she said anything to anyone. That would be a huge scheme embracing hundreds of millions of dollars."

"That would be such a huge amount of money involved that someone had to find out about it," said Todd. "Jetta is a public company. The Board should have known. Unless they were involved. But that's a lot of people. It had to be more intimate. And money changes friendships. Sophie may have wanted to distance herself from this possible scheme if Isiah and her partner, Logan, were involved. But she was murdered before she could find out."

"Sophie had told Dustina about some matter, dealing with Jetta that she didn't want to handle, and she also wanted to distance herself from her firm for some reason," said Dalton. "Sophie wanted Dustina to represent Jetta but wouldn't tell her the details until she spoke with Isiah. Dustina probably mentioned that to her husband Jayden. Then he told James that Sophie may had found out about this scheme. The only questions are whether it was Jayden or James who hired Clayton Reed to murder Sophie? Also, was it Isiah who was the Jetta connection or did he even know about it?"

"That is a little too complicated for me," said the investigator. "I understand that my list has certain investigative facts in it, but how did you two come to that concocted conclusion?"

"It does make some sense," said Todd. "We need to talk to Jayden or someone at Xavier. Do you have the names of those Off Shore Companies?" looking at the investigator.

"Yes. They are all on the list with all pertinent information about the companies and people involved." As the investigator gave both attorneys a copy of his list which included the companies, the names of the banks, the European companies that transferred funds to those accounts and the amount of money in each account as of several weeks ago. The total was just under $300 million.

"Don't you think we should bring the police into this?" asked Todd.

"Not yet," replied Dalton. "Let's see if any of this is even remotely true. If it is, it could be enough 'new evidence' to bring a petition before Judge Andrews for a stay of Isiah's execution while we continue to investigate. Even Judge Andrews wouldn't want an innocent person put to death. But it would be better if we had some more hard evidence."

"What about Sophie?" said Todd. "Wouldn't she have files on this matter? She was the one who must have found out about all this. Her law firm must have her files in boxes in their storage. We need to look at all of her file boxes concerning Jetta. There has to be some connection in those files. Maybe, we can find something that made Sophie turn on Isiah and Jetta. We need to definitively determine if Isiah was the Jetta International go between of this scheme, or, if there was really any scheme at all. I would hate it if he lied to us about all this. I really believed he was innocent."

"I agree Todd," replied Dalton. "But remember Isiah's trial. Who was it that took the Fifth Amendment? Dijon Jackson, Darius Williams and Jayden Robinson."

"Yes, but Isiah insisted on not testifying either, said Todd. "What could that mean? Why didn't we think of this years ago? We need Sophie's boxes. I'll call Logan and ask for them. We can go through them in his conference room so he doesn't think we will destroy or steal anything."

"I hope we find something that exonerates Isiah," said Dalton. "But if it doesn't, we'll need to change course in some fashion."

"Don't put the cart before the horse Dalton. I still believe Isiah is innocent," said Todd.

CHAPTER 31

After the meeting with Isiah's defense team, Carlos at the FIU Law Clinic was updated by Dalton. He gave Carlos some of his thoughts on the petition for a stay of execution. He sent Carlos a copy of his investigator's list and explained most of the entries. Carlos indicated he would start his students on several forms of petitions as soon as possible. Once the final facts were known, they could then make any changes necessary to fit those facts very quickly. Dalton thanked him and told him he owes him.

Dalton told Todd that maybe they needed to confront Isiah and give him the list they received from Dalton's investigator and see if they get any kind of reaction. They had to get assurances that Isiah was not part of this complicated scheme, if in fact, there really was a scheme at all. Isiah's body language should tell them a lot. Both men silently hoped Isiah was not involved. Only a month before the execution and all of this work and money spent by a dozen people may not even prove a scheme existed. The pressure was on Isiah's defense team and each of them felt it.

James Logan reluctantly agreed to allow Todd, Dalton and the investigator to review all of Sophie's files and personal papers concerning her Jetta representation during the last 7 years. Logan was glad the files wouldn't leave his office for obvious reasons. He knew that nothing about the scheme would be found in those boxes.

When the defense team arrived at the firm, there were at least 50 boxes of files on the conference floor. Todd and Dalton didn't know where to start and actually wondered if it was even a good use of their time? However they decided, after some discussion about where to start, that if Sophie was telling the firm's Board about firing Jetta a day or two before her murder, something may have come up close to that time. So they decided to start on the boxes with the files from the closest date to her murder and work backwards. Each of the attorneys reached for a box, when the investigator saw a box that had the word "personal' written on it. Logan's clerk who gathered Sophie's files accidently grabbed the box that Sophie kept her personal documents. Dalton told his investigator to check out that box.

It wasn't 10 minutes after they opened their boxes that the investigator found a copy of a memo written by James Logan. It stated that it was for his personal use only. It was dated three days before Sophie was murdered and had the word 'CONFIDENTAL' stamped on the memo several times. It was only a copy and not the original. On the bottom of the memo someone had written in blue ink, 'Found in bottom drawer of James Logan's desk'. It had the initials in blue ink 'STD'.

"Gentleman," exclaimed the investigator, "you need to see this."

It was only 10 minutes after they started on the long project of reviewing hundreds of files when neither Todd nor Dalton could imagine what got the investigator so excited. After both attorneys read the memo and the hand writing at the bottom, they both knew that "STD" meant Sophie Taylor Daniels. The smoking gun may had been found.

It was a memo written by James Logan, over 6 years ago, outlining the entire scheme incriminating Dijon Jackson, Darius Williams, Jayden Robinson and Isiah Daniels. It was all there in black and white. How did Sophie get this memo? She must have come across it, by accident, somewhere. She must have immediately made a copy of it. Then she must have made her written note on the bottom of the copy of the memo to cover herself. Isiah's name was in the memo as part of the scheme. But why hadn't James Logan revealed this scheme to anyone long ago? After all these many years, Logan surely wouldn't have forgotten about it.

He probably should have destroyed the original after Isiah was convicted. And maybe he did. After all, the memo that was just found was only a copy. So the scheme must have been going on for some time before Isiah was convicted. That memo had to be the reason why Sophie had to speak with Isiah before she did anything about firing Jetta. She wanted to hear his explanation. However before she had a chance to speak with her husband she was murdered. And now Isiah has been in jail for nearly 6 years.

"Gentleman," said Dalton, "Logan must have written this memo to cover himself, at least 6 years ago. At least that is what the date on the memo states. It was his insurance policy in case the scheme was found out soon after it started. However, someone from the Fischer Law Firm had to be involved, or the scheme would never had worked. The memo only incriminates Jetta and Xavier employees. Logan must have inserted Isiah's name instead of his own to protect himself. Why else write the memo?"

"My God," exclaimed Dalton. "And it took us almost 6 years to find this one piece of paper. But who would have guessed that the smoking gun would have been in Sophie Daniels' possession all this time?"

"Dalton, we need to absolutely determine that Isiah's name was in this memo to mislead anyone who may have found out about the scheme when it started. We also need to prove that James Logan was the person who was, more than likely, the person from the Fischer firm who was involved. We need to prove those facts for the Judge," said Todd.

"Your right," replied Dalton. "Now is the time to get the police involved. I think we just uncovered that new evidence that may give Isiah, at least, a Stay of Execution. I just wish we had the original memo. Let's just hope the police see this the same way we do. After all, it was Sophie who found this memo and she is dead. We need to get enough evidence to make it impossible for Logan not to confess."

Meantime, Dalton's investigator was contacting his secret connections in the Costa Rica and the Cayman Islands to acquire as much information, and possibly documents, about the activity in all of the 18 Island bank accounts in which James Logan was involved with. The investigator asked his contacts to obtain as much information as possible concerning the amounts of money involved, the exact places where those funds may have originated, any names or companies associated with any transfers, where the funds were transferred and names on those transfer documents. A very tough, and very expensive, task for his contacts in a very limited amount of time

Dalton told his investigator that he would have access to as much bribery funds necessary that his contacts may need to be available to obtain that information. The investigator's contacts would be spending much of their local capital for this information, as well as possibly their livelihoods. However, even if the contacts could obtain all of the requested information, it would still be a difficult task to convince a prosecutor, and a Judge, to recognize, as a matter of law, several anonymous informants' uncorroborated information in order to obtain a Stay of Execution. It's been nearly 6 years after Isiah's conviction and less than 30 days before the execution. However, if James Logan's name can be found on any of those accounts, the task may be slightly easier. Both Dalton and Todd knew that the prosecutor would require that Dalton, and his investigator be required to reveal the contacts names as well as produce them, in Court, for cross examination. Or, in the alternative, produce specific and reliable information, with verified facts, for Dalton and Todd to positively confirm, to a Judge, that the information obtained was legitimate. Dalton and his investigator knew that, under no circumstances, would their contacts in the Islands let their identities be revealed. That would mean either a death sentence or banishment from the Islands forever. The lack of identity of the contacts may also prove to be very problematic for Isiah's legal team in obtaining that Stay of Execution, even if they find James Logan's name on any of the Off Shore accounts.

The investigator was also going to look into the financial activities of James Logan, Jayden Robinson, Dijon Jackson and Darius Williams. It would be interesting to see if they had gone on any sort of spending spree, or transferred large sums of money into their accounts. If so, where did those funds come from? Both lawyers knew that they could prove, without the benefit of their investigator's contacts, the source of the funds used for their spending spree. Time was ticking and there was less than 30 days left before the execution.

The next morning Todd and Dalton arrived at Florida State prison to meet with Isiah. Isiah was brought to the attorney conference room with chains on his feet and hands. When in the room, the hand chains were removed.

"Have you uncovered any new evidence?" asked Isiah before even greeting the attorneys.

"First thing first," said Dalton.

"Gentleman time is ticking," replied Isiah. "You can't understand what I am going through without walking in my shoes. However, I know you are doing everything possible to help me. I'm more than just curious."

"We understand, and no offense is taken," said Todd.

"We have a list compiled by my investigator that we would like you to look at concerning Jetta International transactions with some of their customers," said Dalton. "Let us know your knowledge concerning this information and if you had any connection, or even knew, about these transactions. If so when and how the Company transactions worked. In addition, there is a memo written by James Logan years ago that we believe Sophie may have found, probably by accident. We need an honest response from you concerning the list and the memo."

Dalton first handed a copy of the list to Isiah. He looked at it and read it through several times.

When Isiah was reading the list he looked confused and said, "What exactly is this list supposed to represent? You know it's been nearly 6 years since I was involved in any of the workings of the Company, and no one has asked me for any assistance with the operation of Jetta since before my trial." replied Isiah. Both Dalton and Todd thought that Isiah was sincere with that response. So they then gave Isiah the memo to read. He must have read it five times. He was more than astonished.

"It looks like James Logan, your wife's partner, incorporated 18 Off Shore companies for Xavier Corporation," said Dalton. "None of those companies are registered to do business in any State. We have double checked that fact. All 18 Off Shore companies set up Off Shore bank accounts in different banks in the Cayman Islands and Costa Rica. The 18 Off Shore companies all received funds from European companies for orders Jetta made with them for precious metals. The precious metals were sent to the European companies by Jetta. Then those European companies paid money, for the metals they received, less a big fat commission, to James Logan's Trust Account. This list also shows that all of the Xavier Corporation's subsidiaries were incorporated on the instructions of Jayden Robinson to his attorney, James Logan. All of the proceeds of those orders ended up in the Off Shore bank accounts and not in Jetta's or Xavier's' bank accounts. They came through the Trust account of the Fischer & Logan law firm. And the memo, Sophie found, incriminates you along with Robinson, Jackson and Williams concerning those transactions."

"That's sort of correct so far," said Todd. "But it is a little more complicated than that. Just understand that Jetta ordered precious metal from either Xavier Corporation or a non-US subsidiary company incorporated by Jayden Robinson. Then the money was supposed to be received by Xavier or their subsidiary for sending the precious metals that actually went to the European companies via Jetta. The European companies then sent the proceeds to the Off Shore banks for the goods ordered. And, for the biggest surprise yet, all of these transactions went through either the Durham plant or Baltimore plant. No other Jetta plants were involved with these orders. All attorney fees billed by James Logan were paid by one of the non-US subsidiary of Xavier so Logan's law firm's audit for their Trust Account always balanced. The precious metals ordered by whatever corporation were always received by Jetta, and paid out to the European companies. All of those European companies were controlled by the European mob."

"Isiah," continued Todd, "Do you remember your trial when Darius Williams, Dijon Jackson and Jayden Robinson all invoked their Fifth Amendments rights? At the time it was assumed that had something to do with Jetta's discrimination law suit or the Government's RICO action.

No one knew about this scheme at the time of your trial, unless you did. However, this scenario makes much more sense. At the time, I couldn't understand what crimes any of those three may have committed dealing with anything but discrimination or kickbacks on promotions. It was supposedly just your employees that were coming after you and Jetta for discrimination. The Government thought you were committing some type of racketeering crime dealing with discrimination and giving kickbacks to black employees. Most important, you also refused to testify. Is that why your name is in the memo? Were you involved or know something about this scheme?"

"Now I am really confused," replied Isiah. "What is it that you two concluded from this list and the memo. I was in jail most of the time some of this embezzlement was going on. And James Logan handled all the money. Why is my name in this memo and not his?"

Dalton looked at Isiah and said, "You tell us. What do you think it means?"

"I'm still not really sure. And if it shows what you may think it shows, it's not true. My name is in the memo, but I had nothing to do with this scheme, I knew nothing about it. I also believe you have the wrong people. These people have always been my friends. I took care of them. So where did this memo come from?"

"Isiah we have reviewed all of Jetta's SEC filings," said Dalton. "The gross income for the Baltimore and Durham plants showed modest losses several months before your arrest. There was only one year where there was only a slight increase in revenue for both plants before your arrest. Didn't you notice that when you executed the SEC documents? After your arrest, both plants gross income severely declined. Yet all of Jetta's other plants continued to do well. You had left the Company by then and Dijon was signing the SEC documents. Dijon Jackson became Jetta's CEO, by your appointment, after your arrest. He did nothing to correct any possible financial troubles at those two plants. No new personnel changes. No new salesman hired or fired. And no new work rules to offset the losses at either of those plants."

"Dijon, Darius and Jayden were all my very good friends," said Isiah in astonishment, "James Logan was Sophie's partner and her good friend. Explain to me this list your investigator compiled, and this memo, in one syllable words, not in legal mumbo jumbo."

Dalton explained his theory of what the list indicated and what was happening at Jetta, both, just before Isiah's arrest and especially after he left the Company. He reminded Isiah that Sophie was willing to quit her job at her firm and have another lawyer represent Jetta on this very delicate unknown issue. Dalton truly believed that the issue Sophie was concerned about was not a discrimination or RICO law suit. Nothing about that issue made any sense to kill Sophie. Plus, Dalton went on, Sophie wouldn't tell Dustina exactly what the true issue was until she spoke with Isiah. After Sophie found the memo, she may have thought that Isiah was involved. That is why Sophie wanted to speak to Isiah before she did anything.

"I believe Sophie found out about James Logan's incorporation of the Off Shore companies and bank accounts, after reading this memo" said Dalton. "She also must have concluded that someone, including her partner Logan, must have been stealing money from Jetta and having it laundered through some entities somewhere out of this Country. Sophie may have even thought that you may have been involved. That has to be the reason she insisted on speaking to you before giving Dustina the case. However, you were in Durham with Dijon Jackson when Sophie was murdered. She never got a chance to speak with you. Was that a coincidence? Or, were you involved?"

"Of course not. I had no idea about this or I would have told you, Todd. You were my lawyer. You couldn't have disclosed that to anyone," said Isiah. "Why my name is in this memo must have been to protect Logan if anyone got caught. I can't believe this. How much did they steal?"

"A lot. Maybe hundreds of millions of dollars," said Dalton. "My investigator is trying to find out that information."

"One of our other outstanding issues still deals with who hired Clayton Reed to murder your wife? We both thought that maybe you could enlighten us?" said Todd.

Isiah thought for a long while. Then he finally admitted, for the first time that he had been helping Clayton. He was transferring money to James Logan, on a bi-monthly basis, to be put in Isiah's personal trust account. Then Logan would transfer the funds to Clayton Reed for some of his living expenses. Clayton was good, most of the time, when Isiah and he were roommates in college. He helped Isiah on his basketball skills for big time college competition. Isiah wanted to return the favor since Clayton was in a low point in his life and Isiah was doing so well. Clayton must have thought Logan was giving him the money since Isiah made it very clear that the money was to go to Clayton anonymously. Isiah even offered Clayton a job with Jetta, but Clayton declined since he didn't want to move out of the Miami area. Also, Clayton made it clear that he hated the fact that Isiah had married a white woman. Not only a white woman, but the daughter of Donovan Taylor, a real two faced bigot.

"Isiah," said Dalton, "look at item #12 on my investigator's list. It states that Logan was not giving your money to Clayton. He was keeping it for himself. He never put it in his trust account. He put it in an Off Shore bank account in James Logan's name. He must have done that so his partners would not know about the money he was stealing from you. Even his co-conspirators didn't know about that. It was Jayden that was actually giving the money to Clayton. His money was actually put in Logan's trust account. Logan was actually telling Clayton it was you. It was Logan's and Jayden's insurance policy if someone found out about their scheme. They could blame you and Clayton. That's in the memo. Also if they ever needed a favor dealing with their scheme, such as having something physical done to someone, or even kill someone, Logan could go to Clayton and use you as his entree. He could then request Clayton to do whatever needed to be done for the scheme to keep going, even kill your wife."

"Didn't Logan know about Sophie's gun and the fact she kept it at work in her desk?" asked Todd.

"Your right," said Isiah. "He always told her to get rid of it. He didn't want a gun in the office."

"So it could have been Logan who may have hired Clayton to murder Sophie," said Todd. "Clayton thought he owed you a favor since he thought you were supporting him. And for some reason you may have wanted your wife to disappear. Maybe he thought you wanted out of the marriage and didn't want to divorce her due to the complications of a divorce."

"Well, Isiah?" said Dalton, "is this scenario possible?"

"I don't know," answered Isiah. "This is just too much at one time. All my friends' stealing from me and the company and even blaming me. Clayton killing my wife? James Logan then murdering Clayton? Who would think something like this type of betrayal would be done by good friends? And my Sophie? And then even let me die. It must be an enormous sum of money."

"We figure, through my investigators contacts, that hundreds of millions of dollars were stolen. We'll tell you later about your wife's partner's spending spree. We are currently investigating your so called 'friends' spending habits as we speak."

"It's still hard for me to believe. And if it is true, how do you prove all this in the next 29 days?" asked Isiah.

"We'll take care of that," said Dalton. We don't need to completely prove it in 29 days. All we need to do it provide this information to the Court as new evidence to try to stay your execution. We believe Judge Andrews does not want any chance of an innocent person to die. Thereafter we'll work on the necessary proof. We just need you to do one thing. Do you think your friendly guard will let you make one phone call?"

Maybe. Give me a hundred dollars and I think he'll let me do it. Who do you want me to call?"

Dalton had several phone calls to make and Todd was to make another. Time was still ticking. But they needed Isiah to make only one call. Isiah finally convinced his friendly guard, by slipping him a hundred dollar bill, to allow him to make that one phone call. He told the guard it was to his best friend concerning the execution. Without telling the warden and after taking the hundred dollar bill, the friendly guard appropriated a phone for Isiah with the caveat that the guard had to listen in on another line. If there was anything not appropriate said, the guard would immediately disconnect the call. Isiah didn't see a problem. Dalton had told Isiah exactly what to say. Isiah called Dijon

Jackson. When Dijon heard Isiah's voice, he almost passed out. It had been nearly 6 years since they saw, or spoken to each other.

"Dijon," Isiah said, "you have been my friend for a long time. I very much want to say my good-byes to some old friends. I really feel I need to do that. I can only do it at one time. I will only get one more phone call. Do you think you can arrange a meeting place for me to call just for old times sake?" That was hard for Isiah to say.

Dijon was more than shocked. If only Isiah knew what he and his friends had done to him, he thought. He wasn't really sure what to say. Finally he said, "Of course, Isiah. I feel so bad I haven't come to see you, but I just wouldn't have known what to say. What do I need to do?"

"I understand, no one wants to come to visit someone in a place like this, so please don't worry about that. Just call Darius and Dustina. Also call Jayden even though I heard Dustina and he had gotten a divorce. I think they can be in the same room for a short phone call from me. Also, please call James Logan from Sophie's old firm. I worked with him for years and Sophie was so fond of him. If it's not too difficult, please have all of them meet you at Jetta's Fort Lauderdale office, in the main conference room. Make it three days from today at 12:00 noon. I really want you all in one place at one time since I can make just the one call they will give me. Having you all together at once will make it so much easier. That would mean a lot to me to be able to say good-bye. You have all been such good friends for so many years," as Isiah could hardly hold back his contempt for Dijon.

Dijon, couldn't believe it. If Isiah only knew the truth, thought Dijon. How could Dijon say no? So he promised he would do whatever was necessary to make sure that all of them were there at that time. He thought that was the least they all could do for him. Isiah had now done his part in Dalton's plan, whatever that was. He just hoped it worked. The more Isiah thought about what he had been told about all those people the angrier he got.

Todd then called detective Darby Lynch. A person he had spoken with from time to time over the last few years on other matters. He asked her cordially if she would convene her and her partner, Morgan Blackburn, to join him at Jetta International's main office conference room at 10:00 AM in three days. Todd said he would meet them there and produce some substantially new evidence that had just surfaced concerning the Sophie Daniels and Clayton Reed murders. Darby didn't quite understand at first. In a few weeks Isiah was to be executed. However, she had worked with Todd several times before and he was upfront with her. So she thought, what the Hell, she might as well see this through. Todd sounded sincere on the phone. She couldn't conceive what new evidence could possibly have surfaced from a crime that occurred almost 6 years ago. But, as a detective, she was somewhat curious. What was an hour or two of her time to burst the balloon of Isiah's appeal attorneys? She basically disliked attorneys anyway.

Dalton then called Carlos at FIU and gave him the new facts for him and his students to draft the petition for Judge Andrews as quickly as possible. He wanted to review it and finalize it and file it with the Court as soon as possible after Isiah's call with his old friends. He told Carlos he would be e-mailing him an updated list compiled by his investigator and a memo which should better explain everything.

———➤●◄———

Judge Andrews went back on the bench in Palm Beach County after he sentenced Isiah to death. However the Judge did rent a condo on Fort Myers beach for a short vacation after the trial. It was exhausting. He needed a few days of rest and relaxation.

Dalton then called his investigator and arranged to meet several times in the next three days so he could be up to date on all additional evidence the investigator, or his informers may find on the spending spree of Isiah's good friends as well as the names of signers on the Off Shore bank accounts.

Lastly, Dalton called Judge Andrews clerk to arrange an expedited hearing date to present the Court with a petition for a Stay of Execution on behalf of Isiah Daniels based on substantially new evidence that had just surfaced. The clerk indicated she would call him back after she spoke with the Judge. Dalton told her to tell the Judge to trust him.

He needs to read the petition and schedule a hearing. He told the clerk that the police would be there for any questions, or testimony, the Judge may desire. He attempted to convey to the clerk his urgency and that this was more than just another off the wall attempt to get more time for their client. Dalton also asked the clerk to contact the prosecutor's office so someone from that office can attend the hearing. He suggested it be Sidney White, if at all possible. Dalton would just have to wait for a return call to see if the Judge would give him a hearing date.

Isiah had no idea that he wasn't really going to make any call to his old friends in three days. It was Dalton's plan to have all of the newly discovered evidence sufficiently documented along with the petition for a Stay of Execution for Isaiah while the new evidence was being investigated. Dalton's plan was to convince the detectives to either hold Darius, Dijon, Jayden and Logan in custody, or at least, convene a Grand Jury. Lastly and more probable, Dalton wanted the prosecutor to get an Order to require all four conspirators to stay in town until an arrangement could be set, before Judge Andrews for a hearing on Dalton's petition.

It was a very long shot, but time was precious. Dustina was asked to come to the meeting so the four co-conspirators would have an attorney present if any of them needed to ask any legal questions. Maybe she would oblige. Todd knew she would be furious when she heard about the scheme. But her presence would be helpful. Dalton was sure that the detectives wouldn't hold any of the four perpetrators unless he had some more definitive evidence that would convince Sidney White to get search warrants for Jetta's books, Logan's law firm files on the Off Shore companies and all the financials on the conspirators. A very long shot. The clerk tried to get Sidney White to come to the meeting, but she refused. She told the clerk to tell Dalton, that only if a Court proceedings were set before a judge would she attend.

Three days was not a long time. But at the meeting in Fort Lauderdale, Dalton's investigator had hard proof of a long list of

Jayden's, Darius' and Dijon's spending over the last several years. Just James Logan spending spree came to over $8 million in the last year. It included clothing, boats, cars, gambling sprees, woman and vacation homes. Logan didn't make that much money practicing law. Electronic transfer slips were provided, unknown to where they were obtained, from the European companies to the Off Shore banks. Then additional transfer documents, again from unknown persons, to the schemers from the Off Shore banks. That information was stolen from the records of those Off Shore banks by the informer's contacts.

On the third day after Isiah's call, all of the requested persons were at Jetta' conference room at exactly 12:00. The others had been meeting in another room during the several hours before 12:00. Dalton, Todd and the investigator gave, to the detectives, a full explanation of the investigator's list, Logan's memo with Sophie's notes, and the full scale scheme. Darby and Morgan were very skeptical, but a man's life was at stake. The evidence was somewhat compelling. However, they didn't understand how Isiah couldn't have been involved in some capacity. But even if Isiah may have been involved, the detectives still called Sidney White. They gave her a brief explanation of what they heard and saw from Isiah's legal team. They suggested that she obtain a search warrant for what Dalton had requested. The detectives also requested the subpoena to include any electronic transfers between the European companies, Off Shore bank accounts, all of the transactions concerning Jetta's transactions with Logan's firm including their trust records for Isiah Daniels and Jayden Robinson.

Most of those records may have been impossible to obtain, but Dalton wanted Darby to at least add them to the list so Judge Andrews could see what was requested. Dalton also mentioned to Sidney the relationship between James Logan and Clayton Reed. Sidney again was skeptical, but willing to listen. Even though a subpoena wouldn't result in obtaining all of the requested information, the investigator's contacts were in the process of doing their magic. They were bribing several people in the Caymans and Costa Rica to steal copies of some, or all, of those records. Sidney did not believe she could have missed this big of a scheme. She was somewhat difficult to persuade that any of this really happened. But since there was a man's life at stake, she finally agreed to at least see this through.

Sidney did demand that all of the investigator's contacts and all original information provided would have to be produced for review and for the informant's contacts to testify. Otherwise it was just hearsay or even double hearsay. Dalton and Todd knew that wasn't ever going to happen. However, Dalton and Todd were heavily counting on the fact that Judge Andrews would never want an innocent person to be put to death, especially after he reads Logan's memo. He would want every stone unturned before any execution. All they needed was a hearing.

Sidney reviewed as many of the records as she could in a few hours time that were obtained from the search warrant obtained from a friendly Judge of Dalton's. The friendly Judge executed the subpoena after Dalton, a longtime friend of the Judge, convinced him that a man's life was at stake. Reading the list showed Sidney a possible intent of a crime by the four conspirators, but it just wasn't quite enough for Sidney to call for a Grand Jury and try to obtain any indictments. After all, someone else had already been convicted of the crime of a double murder almost 6 years ago.

To the shock of both Todd and Dalton, Judge Andrews, after much scrutiny and deliberation, agreed to a hearing 10 days before the execution date. After listening to the arguments of Dalton and Todd, the Judge, knowing the significance of the matter, signed an Order for an indefinite Stay of the Execution during which time the police could investigate this possible scheme and the people involved. The Judge was not keen on capital punishment and decided some time was needed just to make sure that the original trial convicted the right man.

All four conspirators were in the Courtroom at the hearing for the stay. When Sidney asked them to testify, again they invoked their Fifth Amendment rights. The Stay Order, however, was still not enough to overturn Isiah's conviction. He was still required to remain on death row until the investigation was complete. An indictment was needed against the four men from a Grand Jury. If no indictments could be had, then Isiah's stay would be lifted. Dalton and Todd had done 90% of their job. Isiah was relieved but not yet feeling very free. But now it was the detective's job to start investigating the two murders all over again. They were not enthralled. But they had Dalton's investigator's list and the memo. That would be where they started.

⟹➤●◀⟸

After two months of investigation, Darby and Morgan knew it was going to be a hard uphill battle to get sufficient evidence to substantiate a majority of the items on the list in order to obtain an indictment against any of the four perpetrators. Even the memo mentioned Isiah with no reference to James Logan. So the detectives decided to find out if this was real by doing it another way.

Darby and Morgan brought all four men into the Boca police station and put them in separate rooms. By then Darius, Dijon and James had retained their own attorneys. Dustina was retained by Jayden. The other three attorneys argued Dustina had a conflict since she had represented Jetta on the discrimination and RICO cases. However, Judge Andrews ruled that no conflict existed since this matter was only about the individuals and had nothing to do with those two cases. Jayden also wanted his ex-wife to represent him. He still trusted her. He knew how good of an attorney she was. And he was the one who caused the divorce.

Sidney White listened to the detectives findings. Over the last months documentation from the Caymans and Costa Rica had emerged. With those documents and reviewing Dalton's investigator's list and lastly the finances of the four co-conspirators, she determined that sufficient evidence had been uncovered for a Grand Jury to be convened to hear the evidence.

It took the Grand Jury just 3 hours to indict the four men on embezzlement and murder charges dealing with both Clayton Reed and Sophie Daniels. Three of the four attorneys still took the stance that the evidence indicated on the list was obtained illegally and their clients should be released. The detectives then used one of the oldest interrogation methods and announced that the first to talk would have the death penalty taken off the table. Maybe even the prosecutor would give some consideration to the first to talk on their sentence. Maybe even 25 years to life with an opportunity for parole.

Dustina had seen all the evidence. She knew Jayden would be indicted for felony murder. She still loved him, but never told him that. She remained professional. She attempted, for his welfare, to try to get him to tell the truth. After all it was Dijon's who started the scheme, even if Jayden had mentioned it one night while they were drinking. Dijon was the one who threw his old friend, Isiah, to the wolves. It was Logan who arranged Sophie's murder and killed Clayton. Even Clayton's neighbor who found his body, Amy Sutherland, was interviewed again, along with other residents, who all gave statements that it was a white man that had come to Clayton Reed's apartment often, including just before Clayton's body was found. One resident even picked Logan out of a line up after 6 years! Where were the police back then? That made James Logan the prime suspect for Clayton's murder. Evidence showed that Logan was also the person who brought Isiah's money to Clayton each month. Even the McDonalds manager in Overtown and some of the old employees were interviewed again. They finally admitted it was a white man who gave Clayton, their frequent customer, an envelope before Sophie's death. How convenient thought Logan.

Dustina wanted her ex-husband to turn on the other three to get the deal. It took some convincing. But Jayden was not stupid. He knew he wasn't innocent and there was sufficient evidence to convict him of the crimes. So he finally agreed. Sidney White then took his written statement and used the indictments from the grand jury to arrest the men for the crimes that Isiah Daniels gave up over 6 years of his life. She would recommend 25 years to life with a possibility of parole for Jayden.

The next day Jayden was arraigned by himself. The other three men were arraigned together for a long list of crimes starting with the two murders, embezzlement, bank fraud and much more. All pleaded innocent. Jayden pleaded guilty under his plea agreement. Jayden allocuted, the next week, and told the Court Isiah had nothing to do with the scheme. Jayden was then sent to a local holding cell until he could testify against the other three. Darius, Dijon and Logan were all remanded until their trial. The trials were set for 6 weeks from their arraignment. Just prior to their trial, all three of the remaining conspirators pleaded guilty to all charges in order to avoid the death penalty. Isiah was thankful that he never needed to testify in any more trials. All four former good friends of Isiah, turned out to be greedy murderers. Their lives were now over. Isiah never spoke with any of them again.

⟶➤●◄⟵

Two days after Jayden's allocution and the arraignment of the other three perpetrators, Isiah was in front of Judge Andrews. Dalton and Todd were there as his counsel. A petition had been filed by Isiah's counsel to have Isiah's conviction vacated and removed of record. The Judge asked Sidney White if she had any objection to vacating Isiah's conviction. She had none. Judge Andrew's signed the Order without arguments. Only a handful of reporters were in the Courtroom. The original circus was just a crime from the past.

Judge Andrews looked at Isiah and said, "Mr. Daniels, on behalf of the people of the State of Florida, I deeply apologize for your wrongful conviction and for those many years of your life that you have lost. With my innermost pleasure, you are now free to go. Isiah looked at his attorneys and just gave them a hug. Now what was Isiah going to do. He had no house, no job, few friends and had missed what had been going on in the world for over 6 years.

So Isiah decided to go back to his roots. He moved in with his elderly parents in their home in Plantation, Florida. He frequently saw his sister and niece and they helped him get oriented back in his new world. He received calls congratulating him from his old college coach, Mickey Conrad, as well as Martell Dixon, and Dustina Washington. Isiah knew that the next few years would be difficult, but he was the type of person who always needed a challenge. He knew that with the help of his family he would always fall on his feet. Unfortunately, Isiah's father passed four months after Isiah moved in. He had heart issues for over a year. One evening his heart just stopped. That devastated Isiah, but he moved on. His mother, Clover tried to keep the family together after her husband passed, but old age was creeping up on her. She passed 10 months later. The home Isiah bought for his parents after he got his MBA now became his home. And the rest of the money that went to Isiah's parents from the sale of Jetta stock went back to Isiah. He then invested those funds well.

During the next several years Isiah became the assistant basketball coach for Overtown High School. If there were black kids on the team that needed help, or were trying to be recruited by gangs, Isiah took them into his home until times were better for those kids. Soon he was asked to be promoted to head coach, but Isiah decided to decline the offer and go back into the world of business again. With the funds from his parents left from the sale of his Jetta stock, Isiah purchased an old gymnasium in Overtown and remodeled it. He had a lot of help from many old acquaintances who gave him funds for the renovation. His goal was to help and counsel young black kids, mostly from his old neighborhood. He wanted as many of them as possible to become productive individuals later in life. He taught them about what greed and power can do to people, including black people. He told them the stories of his black friends who turned on him.

Isiah organized everything from basketball leagues, volleyball leagues, and gymnastics for black kids to learn the basics. His gym became the center of the community. Isiah began receiving grants and donations as small as a few dollars from Overtown residents, to several thousand dollar grants from many local businesses and businesses from all around the metropolitan Miami area, including the University of Miami. Todd and Kellie Hawkins both volunteered to help Isiah, at least once a month, for several years. Isiah and Todd became friends for life. Deena and Martell stopped seeing each other soon after Isiah's trial. She moved to the east coast to be closer to her brother. They became very close. She found a good job in Fort Lauderdale and also helped Isiah out by volunteering several times a year. Her and Anya never spoke again. Over all, Isiah felt as if he had finally found his true calling. He helped and saved many troubled black kids in order for them to find their way to better and productive lives. He set up a foundation in the name of Sophie Daniels and funded college for many black boys and girls. He followed most of them until they graduated from college. He even helped a few get good jobs with some of his corporate sponsors. Isiah turned out to become a blissful person, and well-liked and admired by almost everyone he encountered for the rest of his life.